Praise for
Holly Williams

'Holly's beautiful prose smoulders, crackles and roars'
Daisy Buchanan

'Delightful, insightful and immersive'
Kate Eberlen

'An unforgettable story with writing that sparkles'
Holly Miller

'Heartwarming'
Bella

'Stunning, skilful, deftly drawn. A cockle-warmer of a novel'
Lauren Bravo

'Wonderful, original and powerful novel. She is wild and brilliant'
Elaine Feeney

'An invigorating debut'
Observer

'Exquisitely conceived and with the most beautiful sense of place'
Abbie Greaves

'A clever concept that casts a light on the different social mores
of changing times'
Best

'A brilliant, witty, defiantly unsentimental examination of
privilege and class and sex and selfhood'
Marianne Levy

'Holly Williams is already being compared to David Nicholls'
One Day'
Evening Standard

'A fabulous love story and insightful social history in one…
a perfect summer read'
Metro

Holly Williams is a journalist and critic. She writes for publications including the *New York Times*, the *Financial Times*, the *Telegraph*, *Vogue*, and the BBC, as well working as an arts editor at the *Independent*. She reviews theatre for the *Telegraph* and *The Stage*, and books for the *Observer* and the *Times Literary Supplement*. She was born in Wales and lives in Sheffield. Her debut novel *What Time is Love?* was published in 2022 and sold in 12 languages. *The Start of Something* is her second novel.

THE START OF
SOMETHING

HOLLY WILLIAMS

ORION

First published in Great Britain in 2024 by Orion Fiction
an imprint of The Orion Publishing Group Ltd
Carmelite House, 50 Victoria Embankment
London EC4Y 0DZ

An Hachette UK Company

1 3 5 7 9 10 8 6 4 2

A CIP catalogue record for this book is
available from the British Library.

ISBN (Hardback) 978 1 3987 0634 7
ISBN (Trade Paperback) 978 1 3987 0635 4
ISBN (eBook) 978 1 3987 0637 8
ISBN (Audio) 978 1 3987 0638 5

Typeset at The Spartan Press Ltd,
Lymington, Hants

Printed and bound in Great Britain by Clays Ltd,
Elcograf S.p.A.

MIX
Paper | Supporting
responsible forestry
FSC
www.fsc.org   FSC® C104740

www.orionbooks.co.uk

Chapter 1

Will

What about right now?

Will puts his phone face down on the counter. Notices how many crumbs are all over it. Turns his phone back over. Types.

My Friday night plans just fell through, annoying.

This is a lie.

Up for a drink if you are!

In a preparatory act which is possibly absurdly optimistic, he wets a dishcloth and starts cleaning the surfaces of his kitchen. Just in case.

She had said she was only around for the weekend. So.

The early evening light is coming through the window, both illuminating the flat's dustiness and prettifying it somehow, making the cramped beige kitchen-dining-sitting-room space look more elegant. But it also reminds Will of what he's missing outside. Golden hour.

He wants to go out. Anywhere, with anyone.

Teodora always used to go on about *golden hour*. Always used to go on about the light being the only good thing about the flat.

Will still agrees with her on that, actually, and picks up his phone to once more scroll through SpareRoom and Gumtree for potential new houseshares to move out into. Potential new flatmates. (Potential new friends.) But it's proved hard to find shared houses that aren't even more tired than the mid-terrace flat he's currently in in Hillsborough; the places coming up are almost like student digs, really, with adults still living like students.

He's too old for this shit, is the problem. (One of the problems.) He wasn't meant to be back to roommates and labelling the milk at his age. Thought he was past all that.

But living by himself doesn't feel possible, really, either. It's not just that it's financially unsustainable – it's also that the quietness of the half-empty flat spooks him. Makes it impossible to ignore just how—

Just how alone he is, in this city he still barely knows.

A notification flicks up in the corner of the screen, and with it the small thrill, which Will always considers himself pathetic for even noticing.

Sounds good!

Where do u want to meet?

And Will feels that sudden shot of *success* – a brief surge of adrenaline, or some other chemical he doesn't know the name of, pushing round his chest, shooting up and down the back of his legs. It is a feeling that has become familiar over recent months, yet there is still giddy elation in the instant gratification of matching like this: the sweet synchronicity of being drawn to the square images of a stranger, and them somehow also being drawn to his – of matching – of responding – of being free *right now* – being keen, even.

He looks again at Manda's profile. Doesn't say too much, just that she lives in Manchester and manages a cocktail bar, enjoys late nights and lie-ins. He doesn't *love* the abbreviations she uses in her messages, but he's also not the type to be too picky about such things. And she's definitely attractive: strong features, lots of dark wavy hair, her pictures not too posed or pouted or pretentious. A gorgeous, if somewhat guarded, smile – like she doesn't quite trust a camera.

Will actually kind of likes it when profiles don't give that much away. Sure, it can lead to disappointment later on, but it means that this time – this humming anticipation – rings with potential. The imagined idea of some perfect stranger, or some perfect brief encounter, at least. Just glittering with possibility.

Apps hadn't been a thing the last time Will was properly single. 'Serial monogamist' was what Teodora called him, even though it was her that put the moves on almost the minute he broke up with his previous long-term girlfriend. And so it had all felt new to Will.

But fun – a safe digital way of trying out flirting again, of 'putting yourself out there' (something his sisters told him he needed to do). Of trying different approaches. Different identities. Different people.

And it was *validating*, after the months of colourless blankness that followed the shock of Teodora fucking off back to London. Back to living with her mates in their over-priced shared house in New Cross, back to her old studio that it drove her mad to have to time-share with two other artists, even crawling back to her old boss and begging for her former job back, the assistant work she'd claimed to be 'completely *over*'.

Will gives a tiny shake of his head, as if to dislodge the thoughts of Teodora and the fact that she would actually prefer all of that to living with him, here. In the place *she* had dragged them to. To being in a stable, comfortable relationship, with him. One he had thought was full of grown-up love, one that he had thought might even last the rest of their lives. That old sentimental image he'd had, of the two of them in matching chairs in front of a fire – like his nanna and grandad, still adoring each other in their eighties—

He pictures these thoughts as being little pieces of plastic snow in a snow globe, that can settle too thickly and cover him in a blanket of thick white if he lets them. He has to keep shaking the thoughts away. Shake them off. *Shake it off.*

Will plays Taylor Swift through Spotify and a cheap portable speaker, and thinks again that he must invest in a proper stereo. Once he moves house. Or maybe he can move somewhere where they have a great hi-fi, a record player, a big TV ... Binge watching series together, or nightly conversations about music, or cooking wholesome house meals—

He flicks back to Tinder.

Cool. What about Social Works, in Kelham?

Will is usually happiest just going to cosy old man pubs, but he's noticed that the women he's taken on dates seem to respond better to cocktail bars, somewhere with a bit of supposed 'buzz'. Seem to prefer the hip, post-industrial bit of town, exposed brick and steel beams bouncing the sound around till it distorts. Will prefers to be able to hear himself speak. To hear the other person speak. But given Manda's job, he doesn't think a pint of bitter will quite cut it.

Besides, he doesn't know how important great chats will be on this particular occasion. It seems fairly clear what they both might want from the evening.

Yet Will always holds out hope: for incredible instant connection and conversation that goes immediately and effortlessly deep. But that has proved rare. In fact, that's only happened with one person since Teodora . . .

Will is about to flick over to a different WhatsApp chat, his mind trailing away, when Manda replies.

See u there in an hour?

Stay focused.

Great. See you then.

Sometimes, the ease and simplicity of online dating still amazes Will. He knows a lot of people hate it. But a lot of people seem to like *him*. And it all seems so straightforward. Even if the connections he's made are mostly surface and fleeting, Will doesn't find it hard to make them. He knows how to ask the right questions, and seems to have the knack for making people feel seen, and heard. Feel *special*.

He likes making people feel good, and he also likes the fact that that often makes them want to sleep with him. There is power in it, and wielding that power momentarily takes away the sting, of Teodora leaving him like that. The absence of that *one-special-person*. The Teodora-shaped hole in his life.

Although sometimes relying on dating-app hook-ups to make yourself feel better does seem like trying to stop a bleeding wound with a blister plaster.

Will wonders as he begins to get ready (brushing his teeth, changing his polo shirt) if it was actually *her* life, and he's just the hole: he's the blank, the space where Teodora cut him out, discarded him. Because there isn't that much left in his life from before Teodora. She persuaded him to move to Sheffield, and it was through Teodora and her contacts that he had found a job here. But there hadn't really been enough time to make new friends, before she suddenly left – and Will is out of practice at that anyway. Even before they moved, their friends in London were *her* friends. It was true that they were more fun, more interesting than the lads he worked with or the guys he'd been to school with. But it was also that Teodora was strong-willed, and more organised; it quickly merely felt inevitable that they would go to the club nights her friends ran, and on holidays with them.

These friends have all been very decent about the break-up (abandonment). But fundamentally, they knew Teodora first. And have welcomed her back.

So he can't return to London. He is stuck here.

That's too negative, Will tells himself. He isn't *stuck* here – he's just beginning to find his feet. He's got to change the narrative: frame it as a new start, not a failed move. And it *is* all pretty promising, because Will has been surprised at how much he likes Sheffield, how much it just works as a home for him, despite the—

He won't even think that word.

Despite *being alone*.

He'd always assumed London was the centre of the world, and maybe it is, but it turns out Will prefers being off-centre. The ability to walk to most places, less rushing all the time, and the relative calm and friendliness of this city. And the country-side – the Peaks, right there, on the doorstep. All that green, and sky, and air. There is nothing like the burn of lungs on the ascent of hillside, then the space and scale and vastness of it. He tries to get out into the countryside every weekend: something he never knew he needed, and now can't imagine living without. It reliably makes Will feel like things might, one day, be OK. It is ... *transformative*.

For him. Teodora, however, hadn't been bothered by all that;.

had even left behind the (quite expensive) hiking boots he'd bought her.

He will walk, Will decides. Tonight. Even just to Kelham. Get out into that light.

He'd showered straight after work, as he always does, washing away the sweat and the generic grime and the specific tiny tiny tiny particles of metal that sometimes he thinks he can feel, like glitter, all over himself even after the shower. But Will spends a little time fiddling with his hair, attempting to make it less obvious how far his hairline is receding, although it's too short and springy to do much with (he really just needs to buy some clippers and take the plunge).

By the time he is outside, golden hour is almost over, the sun a wobbly-looking crimson ball on the horizon, glimpsed only occasionally between buildings, shooting the last intoxicating rays across the city. All the windows on a street of houses are illuminated, as if every one along the terrace has a fire raging inside it, simultaneously.

The temperature is nice though, thinks Will, after an oppressive day in the workshop. One of Stephen Schad's enormous steel pieces had, somehow, been damaged in the move from the Whitworth to the Yorkshire Sculpture Park, and Will had to oversee its return to the workshop for emergency repairs, the artist breathing down his neck about getting it done in time for the next opening.

Most of the time, the zen-like Stephen drifts around just staring at things and occasionally speaking with a profound slowness that Will both respects and can be infuriated by. So when Stephen gets rattled, everyone else in the workshop gets rattled too. He had been panicking, pacing; making snippy comments and literally tapping his watch. *Telling* them how to do

7

their job. And this is a breaking of the silent contract between him, as the artist, and them, as the fabricators. The workers.

Usually, there is trust there. Stephen has a quiet respect for their skills, with the welding irons and heavy machinery and hammers and the great globules of fiery liquid. The transformational process, turning brute metal into a work of art. But when he doesn't trust them, the balance of the whole enterprise goes out of whack, thinks Will. Resentments begin to glow.

They have a pretty good idea how much he sells his sculptures for. How much institutions buy them for.

And they certainly know how much they get paid per hour.

Will arrives at Social Works (terrible name) almost exactly on time; an advantage of walking, although the disadvantage is that he does feel slightly sweaty again. Just from the walk: he doesn't really get nerves, not anymore. Not after the first few dates, realising how it paid to be simply upfront about what you wanted. Will likes this: compared to the dance of working out if someone fancied you in the pub or at a club or at work, the parameters of a pre-arranged date are so *clear.*

It's just much more straightforward.

Not that he's met anyone yet through the apps where it's gone further than a couple of drinks, maybe some food, and some easy, enjoyable casual sex. But that's absolutely fine. For now, anyway. While he licks those still-fresh wounds. A healthy *distraction.* From the lone—

The tiniest shake of the head, as he reaches for the door handle.

And another thought intrudes, the increasingly persistent thought of the one person Will has met who he can't get out of his head. It's funny, that the only one who'd got under his skin (and Will can't help but see a flash of Teodora's wrinkled face, objecting to this English idiom: 'such a dis*gusting* phrase') was someone he had met in real life. The old-fashioned way. Who just came up to him and started talking at the opening of Stephen's installation, *The Equation of Time* (pretentious name), outside the Whitworth in Manchester. Seemed impressed that Will had helped actually make it.

But now is not the moment to think about that encounter, or the WhatsApps they'd shared that he's read and re-read, nor where it may all yet lead.

Now is the time to be in the present, for walking into this bar.

Will does the opposite of steeling himself: he tries to drop his shoulders, loosen his arms. To appear relaxed in his own body as he moves through the space.

Manda is there already. Sitting at one end of a long brushed-metal bar. She is half a drink down, by the looks of it.

Well, good. Will prefers to make the approach than to be approached.

But he still hates the moment – here it is, here it comes, the switch-flicking, lightbulb-clicking moment – when the other person realises you're there, for them. The eyes and smiles, gesturing across a room, before contact can quite be made. Just enough time for both parties to involuntarily tense up again. To plan, and forget, opening remarks.

To form a very quick, probably lasting judgement about whether you want to fuck each other or not.

Yeah, maybe? Probably. She looks a little older than her picture, he'd guess closer to forty than thirty. But Will suspects he looks older in the flesh too. That's just standard.

She's standing up to meet him – and it's slightly awkward, now she has to sort of wait and hover as he navigates round a table of noisy Prosecco blondes – and she has one of those frames of larger women, tall and fairly broad of shoulder and chest, excellent legs in tight jeans, but where you can somehow tell she's had a lifetime of feeling like she's towering over people. Of not quite knowing how to fill up the correct volume of space.

As he gets closer, he sees that she is in fact taller than him. Will wonders if she'll care about that, or if she's used to it. There seems to be a lot of importance placed on age and on height online, which Will finds bizarre. It doesn't bother him – someone doesn't need to be younger or smaller than him for him to find them attractive. Weird metric.

And then it's as if she finds her confidence, or an impersonation of it at least – Manda flicks her hair, using the gestures to straighten up, throwing her shoulders back. As if enjoying the status in her height, rather than shrinking from it.

'Hi,' Will says, as soon as he gets close enough. *Keep it simple* is another lesson he learned, quickly. There is power in holding on to your words. Only the nervous, the needy, say too much.

'Hi! Will? Hi.' They face off, eyes meeting, almost squaring up to each other. Taking each other in.

Nice, thinks Will. He likes that Manda isn't flappy, isn't going in for some awkward hug. Seems reassuringly grown-up.

'Shall we get a table? Or sit at the—' Nonetheless, her apparently casual gesture behind her almost knocks over a plastic holder full of long, narrow cocktail menus.

Will looks around. The bar is dim, barely lit by hanging filament bulbs, while a soundtrack of anonymous, personality-free beats stamps over every conversation.

'Let's go there,' he says, pointing to a table in the corner that a couple are just vacating. 'Can I get you – another? – drink, before we sit down?'

He thinks this might embarrass her, but instead she gives

a big, bright grin and, while holding his gaze, downs what's remaining in her glass. 'You absolutely can.'

Will inclines his head, as if in deference to her drinking prowess. 'What are you having then?'

'Uh, well what are you— I mean, they do cocktails, or if you wanted to get wine...'

Will could murder a pint, but instead picks up a cocktail list. It is slightly sticky, despite a chic matte black surface.

'These look good...'

First round, anyway. He wants to make the effort, knows it's worth making her feel comfortable ordering whatever it is she really wants. Besides, there's nothing less appealing than someone being tight on a first date.

They lapse into silence, perusing the menu, and then after debating the merits of various different flavours of artisan gin (none of which Will has any real feelings about), lapse again as they try to attract the attention of a busy, tattoo-covered bartender.

Will feels as if he has entered into a silent battle with the man waiting next to him: leonine, with a mane of blonde hair, lean-ing louchely on tanned forearms and waving an Amex around. Clearly trying to impress the chic brunette he's with by asking the barman questions about spirits Will has never heard of, and chummily calling him 'mate'. Somehow this approach works, and the barman serves the blonde man next, and with a good deal of performance: flicking the bottle and pouring liquids from a great height.

Will meets Manda's gaze, and rolls his eyes at the wait. But her smile is a little tight. And he realises she probably has soli-darity with bar staff, and feels bad.

'I suppose you're watching all this with a professional eye...' he offers.

'Oh, I don't know about that – it's good to take a night off now and then, in't it?' Her smile stretches, but remains taut.

Still, Will notices she is much more effective at getting the guy's attention, ensuring they are served next. She lays on a heightened, leaning-over charm as she places their order, too, tossing her thick hair again so her waves almost bounce. Yet although the bartender only looks at Manda as he makes their drinks, even giving her a wink as he sets them down with a flourish on tiny black napkins, he automatically proffers the card machine to Will.

Will hates having to be the man on a first date. Being forced into performing that stupid role.

They make their way over to the table. Some kind of cherry is floating in Manda's heavy cut-glass tumbler, and Will feels like it might be eyeballing him as they sit down.

'So, you're just in Sheffield for the weekend then?' Will wants to wrest back control of the situation, delivering a perfectly inviting, sunny smile as he sits back on the teal-velvet and brass chair. (Tries to ignore Teodora's voice in his head, commenting that this place 'looks like an explosion in an Oliver Bonas shop'.)

'That's right. Just visiting my – visiting my dad. It's been a while...'

'Ah, the parental duty. I get it.'

She gives a vague shrug.

'So, have the two of you got any fun plans for the weekend?'

'Um... not really. He's not much of— he's not really one for going out and about. That's why, you know, tonight – I mean...' Now she won't meet his eyes, and Will feels a sharp tug of sympathy for her, behind his ribs.

He knows better than to press, at this early stage anyway. He's obviously found a tender spot. After all, no one goes on random

Tinder dates when visiting their family unless they really don't want to be spending the evening with their family.

He smooths over the gap with details of his own weekend plans, such as they are, and Manda makes the effort to sound interested as he tells her about his Kinder Scout walking route – although when he turns the questions back onto her, a hasty dismissal makes it obvious that, really, she has about as much interest in hiking as Teodora did.

Still, there is something, just a little glint, between them. Will can feel that Manda is trying to reach out, to tune in to him, even if occasionally he thinks he sees a flash of panic somewhere behind the eyes: almost like she's learned how to socialise, to flirt, and is trying to remember the cues rather than feeling them instinctively.

'Now then, what brought you to Sheffield?' Manda says, after a natural lull in the conversation where they both slurp towards the end of their drinks. 'I mean – you're obviously not from here . . .'

Will feels himself automatically bristle, and then realises she just means his accent. Obviously.

'No – South London, all the way. In case you couldn't tell.'

'I could tell. Well, that you're from London. Not sure I could spot the difference between north and south to be honest.'

'Yeah, fair. Sheffield's cool, though,' Will says, hoping to endear himself to her.

But Manda just does a head movement, which could mean *yes it is* or could mean *if you say so*.

'So, I came here with my ex, actually.' Will knows he needs to move quickly to neutralise this honesty. 'But then she didn't like it! Moved back to London, a while ago.'

This is not even *really* a lie. Timing is just a matter of per-spective.

13

'But I'd got a job that I like here, and we had a while on the lease of the flat and that. So, I stayed.'

'Shit. That's brutal. What a cow.'

Women on dates always respond to this story one of two ways – pained, sympathetic, but clearly also slightly worried (*what had he done to drive her away?*), or acting exaggeratedly outraged on Will's behalf, as if eager to prove that they *would never*. Attempting to bond over her as a mutual enemy.

'So what's the job then?'

'I was working as a welder down in London, but my ex – honestly, I promise this is an important detail, I'm not gonna just go on about her all night' – Will uses this as an excuse to lean in, to smile that promise right over to Manda – 'well, she's an artist, but she mostly works as an artists' assistant. Like, helping them do their work . . . do you know about this?'

Manda looks sceptical, shakes her head.

'Well, most famous and successful ones, they don't actually do most of their own work – they just get young assistants to, like, do the making bit or the boring bit or whatever for them. Damien Hirst gets grad students to paint all his dots.'

He thinks he's lost her.

'They don't do their own . . . painting? But that's cheating, isn't it?'

'Well, you might think. Very standard though—'

'That's fucking bullshit.' Manda looks more angry than he'd have expected. 'What a con. It's not . . . really *theirs* then, is it? It's not *real*.'

'Tell that to the market,' Will shrugs. And then realises he's just parroting the world-weary way Teodora used to talk about it, and feels fraudulent himself. '*Anyway,* my ex wanted to move here because it's cheaper, you can get affordable studio spaces and all that, and focus on her own work. And she got a studio near the workshop of this Sheffield artist – Stephen Schad...?'

Will leaves a pause that people often flood with impressed coos, or at least hmms of faint (or fake) recognition. Manda does not fill the space. Will wonders if she doesn't know the name, or is just stubbornly trying not to show that she's not bothered.

'Anyway, he's really quite famous...' He regrets this the minute the words fall from his lips – so patronising! – and sees an involuntarily slight curl to Manda's mouth *Not arty then.* Fair enough. He won't attempt to explain about *The Equation of Time* and horology and sundials and the patterns Stephen Schad's sculptures and their shadows make at different times of the day. He has other angles.

As it were.

'Well, his work is sculpture – I mean, it's made of metal. Big fuck-off hunks of it. Steel—'

Manda rolls her eyes. 'Course it bloody is. What else would it be made of, from here.'

Will grins, and makes air quotes 'Right – "traditional craftmanship", innit. Except he doesn't actually *do* the crafting. Stephen might have the brains but he certainly doesn't have the...' *dare he put it like this?* 'The brawn, to make it all. So he works very closely with this metalwork company, fabricators, who make art and sculpture and structures and all this stuff.'

'And you're with them?'

'Yep. My ex heard via Stephen that they were taking people on, and it seemed more interesting than your average job. I help do the builds – the hands-on stuff – but also oversee installation wherever the sculptures end up...' He spreads his hands, as if to offer his skills – and his self – up to her.

And of course he notices her eyes flick to his flexing biceps, his forearms, which he knows this pose effortlessly displays.

Everyone is always either interested in the art, or in his man-handling of large chunks of metal (or often, both).

'Wow. So you're actually, you know, dealing with all the raw steel – like, banging it—'

Will indulges a slight eyebrow raise. Cheesy. *Obvious.* But effective – she's grinning her proper grin again, and flicking the back of a hand across the table at his shoulder (an excuse for contact, he notes).

'Oi! You know what I mean . . .'

Will laughs. 'Yeah. Yeah! And his sculptures are proper massive, so it's like . . . it's at scale. It's a challenge. Big machinery, a lot of close teamwork. Get pretty filthy and sweaty by the end of the day, not gonna lie! But I like it.'

'Yeah, that must be really . . . hard work?' She sounds impressed, but there's also just a hint of a suggestive smile, a mutual acknowledgement that they both know what is rippling beneath all this job talk.

'It is.'

He holds eye contact, just long enough to make her a little flustered again, although the edges of a smile are still dancing around her mouth.

'Another drink?' she asks as she reaches decisively for her handbag, a squarish black thing. Reasserting her own control.

'Sure. Just a pint for me this time though, please. Green Mountain, ta.'

Will feels secure enough, now, to know that this particular woman will probably prefer a pint-drinking kind of man anyway.

It is after the third drink that Will decides he needs to move things on, one way or another. He doesn't want to just keep chatting and wondering and spending money. He's probably heard enough about what it is like to manage a bar in central Manchester. Heard enough about what various Sheffield neighbourhoods were once like and exactly how they've changed over the years. Manda gives lively answers, but she isn't that great at asking interesting questions; he feels like he's making a lot of the effort.

The way he sees it, they have two options. They could each go home alone. But although Manda has carefully avoided really saying anything more about her dad, it is obvious that she is not very keen to get back to his company. There's a sad story there, Will feels sure, and he'd wondered – hoped – that they would maybe open up to each other after a couple of drinks. But he can practically see the walls she's built up around her personal life, the cold suit of armour she wears to protect herself. Her chat seems restricted to only the most surface topics, that can glance off that metal carapace.

The other option is that they go back to his. There's enough crackle between them that Will feels pretty sure she's equally keen, and is also pretty sure that they have the potential for a decent shag. And the intimacy, however flashing, that brings with it.

If he is honest with himself, the thing that Will often craves most is the lying in bed with someone, not talking, just feeling the reassuring weight of a head on his chest. Looking at Manda, Will decides, on balance, that he would like to hold her warm, solid body in his arms. Even if it is just for tonight.

'Do you want another one...?' Manda asks. And when Will doesn't reply immediately, adds, 'Or we could go somewhere else...?'

'What about my place.' There isn't really a question mark.

She blinks, and then grins, and there's something actually incredibly appealing about her face when she lets go like that – when she properly smiles that warmest, widest smile. It is unguarded, and real.

But then she closes it down, and it's like there's a shutter rattling over her expression. She tosses her hair a little haughtily, and stands up with the slightly drunk arrogance of someone who believes they are looking good.

She absolutely does look good. But she looked even better when she was being unselfconscious about it.

'Let's go then.'

Will pays for the Uber. *Of course.* That gendered assumption of who will pay for what when dating. Funny how much he prefers it when that simply isn't part of the equation.

Then he reminds himself they are going to his house – his address – and that sometimes, it is just a question of practicality. Nothing deeper than that.

It's a short journey, and they make it in near silence, the night still warm and the air cloying in the back of the cab. Radio 1 is blaring from the stereo, a pop song Will doesn't recognise. Then another one, that sounds almost exactly the same. *Getting old*, he thinks. Again.

'Do you want anything?' Will asks, switching on the light as they step inside. The slow, greenish energy-saving bulb does not cast the flat in the best light. A pale and sickly hue.

As he draws a glass of water for Manda, Will feels a small pulse of shame at his home's shabbiness. At least when Teodora had been there, she'd livened it up. Laying down the rugs she'd brought over from Bulgaria, and covering the walls in proper prints from Frank Bowling and Cy Twombly and Lee Krasner exhibitions, and pictures she'd been given by artist pals. She had a good eye.

When she'd left, Will hadn't bothered replacing all that, because he hadn't planned to stay, really. But here he still is, in post-Teodora limbo, in a flat that looks like a second-hand furniture showroom. A British Broken-heart Foundation charity shop.

This weekend, he's going to do something about that, Will decides with a rush of certainty, even if this flat is only temporary. He'll clean, properly, and get better bulbs and lampshades, and a rug, and a throw. Go down to the antique shops on Abbeydale Road, or look on eBay. Work out what his taste even is, when a space is all his own.

Stop thinking of it as an empty shithole, and start thinking of it as a blank canvas.

Because he would like to bring new people back to his place without this shame. And now – intruding once more – is the thought of *one person in particular*, with their impeccable, effortless taste, who he'd love to bring here but who would surely be just horrified by—

Will realises with a jolt that Manda is staring at him, expectantly. Definitely not thinking about the furniture.

She lifts the glass of water, and drains it, decisively.

As she swallows, she holds eye contact with him. And to Will's surprise, this causes an instant stirring in his boxers.

She puts the glass down, very deliberately, on the pale pine dining table, and steps towards him.

'That's better,' she says.

And Will feels a rise of heat as she steps closer again, relishing, as he always does, the first moment. The slow, stretching sensation of pure *happening* that is a first kiss. A new mouth. A fresh possibility.

She tastes of water, but there's a sugariness lingering beneath it. A hint of almonds, maybe.

Manda's tongue is soon insistent. Hands grabbing. Wasting no time.

Fast, then. Fine by him. Ideal in fact. This was a good decision. The excitement rises inside him—

But then – *here it comes* – Will begins to feel himself splitting in two. The dislocated duality he so often experiences, even in the supposed throes...

A part of him that is *body* responds to the pleasure of pressure against the zip of his jeans: hardening and heart-rate speeding, hands going where they're expected to on a kind of eager auto-pilot as he manoeuvres her back towards a kitchen counter...

Feeling it. Being in it.

But a part of him that is *mind* stays removed, just watching the whole thing unfold. Almost narrating the experience his body is having to himself:

> *She's digging her nails in your back; you gasp, a bit too loud*
> *(sounds fake although it's not).*
> *You kiss her neck.*
> *She seems eager. She's gasping too ... or is she just trying*
> *to mirror you?*

Observing it. Seeing it all play out.

This disconnect isn't always there. It wasn't there with Teodora, or his other girlfriends. It wasn't there, the recent night in Manchester, the shock of connection...

But usually it is there, up until the moment of eyes-squeezed-tight oblivion. Which is, Will reflects, perhaps partly why he seeks these encounters. For that brief escape, into pure bodily experience. (And then after, the warm body, the resting head, the emptied mind. The illusion of closeness.)

Manda draws away again, and Will's eyes flick open. She gives him a heavy-lidded look, then reaches down to finally unbutton his jeans with a flourish, and slowly unzips the fly. He assumes it is meant to be seductive, knowing. But there's something slightly off-putting about it, like it's a performance of sexiness rather than the real thing.

Will shuts his eyes again. As if in pleasure, but really to try to block out the critical thoughts, determined to enjoy the moment...

And when she takes him in a firm grip and also starts to kiss him again, it doesn't take long before the pleasure *is* real, and the urge to get close to her returns, the heat and resolve and the need—

'Are you going to take this to the bedroom, then?' she whispers in his ear.

Wordlessly (for what is there to say?), Will leads Manda up the very steep flight of stairs to an attic room with a sloping ceiling, where you can only stand up on one side. It is stifling, the air hot and dry, and he turns on a lamp and cracks the skylight open.

When he turns, Manda is sitting down on the bed, her hands behind her, head tilted up to him. It is a position that makes her breasts look good, something she is no doubt well aware of. And then together they're pulling off her top, her bra, wriggling out of their respective jeans, and Will thinks how much he loves this bit of a first encounter too – the newness, the urgency. The body revealed, and experienced in close-up. The surprise mole; the revelation that is the pink or brown of a nipple. The discovery of soft velvet at the most private patches of skin.

Not at all like the easy, practised movements and habits you get stuck in, sleeping next to the same person night after night, year after year. Ugly pyjamas and scrolling your phone in bed and hogging the duvet.

Will notices that he is, in fact, scrolling through and cataloguing other sexual encounters he's had, rather than really being in this one. Tries to shake himself free.

Manda begins giving him a blow job. Her lips feel incredibly good; her hair tickles a little at his thigh ... But he still has that distant sensation, of watching himself. In the interests of fairness, he switches things up, to return the favour, and wonders if he has the right rhythm for her. She is making positive noises. So he keeps going.

But Jesus it is hot up here. Sweat is running down his chest, his behind. A faint meaty, salty smell in the air. Really ought to buy a scented candle, thinks Will. And maybe get a fan in Aldi...

Suddenly Manda is unleashing a series of short, sharp cries, and he wonders if it is as real as it sounds, or if it is just a performance of pleasure, for his benefit. He attempts to continue, just in case it was fake – or in case there's more pleasure to be had, because he would actually like to make her feel good – but Manda reaches down to grip his wrist, pulling him up to her level, and decisively passes him a condom she's got from who-knows-where.

And *then*—

Then, as he enters her, Will finally drops into himself. And the whole world shrinks to the bed, the whole world existing just in that small circle of touch, all consciousness narrowing as the sensation grows and grows and grows—

His thoughts shut off, exploded by the single moment of *happening*.

Hearing himself grunting to the end of a sound he didn't even realise he was making, Will begins to come back to himself. Pulls out. Flops down next to Manda. Deals with the condom. Misses the bin. (Leaves it.)

Does steel himself, this time, when looking over at her.

Manda is lying on her back. She's also sweaty, a light film covering her forehead. As if she's been gloss-painted.

Then she flicks her head to the side to meet his gaze, and out breaks that smile. That bright, real one, suggesting it really had been *great* for her too.

And the relief rushes through Will, as he watches her chest rise and fall, gradually slowing to a more normal pace, matching the movement of his own. And affection rushes through him, for her, for this stranger who he has made such escaping bliss with.

Will reaches over and pops a kiss on her temple, and there's something soft in her smile. He's about to pull her in, to hold her tight and damp against him, when something else flicks across her face – the harsh, sudden return of self-consciousness.

Manda breaks the tender moment, reaching up to scoop and rearrange her hair, flapping a hand around her face, in a weirdly forced performance of disgruntlement. As if to cover up the abrupt awareness of finding yourself naked with a stranger, as the adrenaline of sex subsides. That protective wall, being thrown back up around her.

'Jesus Christ, it's hot up here,' she says, a little too loud, pretending to pant.

'I know.'

'You need to get a fan or something.'

'I know. Been meaning to.'

'Really though – why is it *so* hot? It's ridiculous. You need a fan!'

'I know I know I know, you're not the first to say so . . .'

This is true. It has been far too hot like this on at least two other occasions.

Still, Will doesn't know why he needed to spell this out like that. So pointed. And so unnecessary, to bring in mention of . . . *others*, in this immediately post-coital moment.

Manda stops moving about. She pulls a bit of the sheet that he's been sleeping under up over some more of her body.

'Having a busy summer then is it . . .' Her tone is newly ironic, detached, but somehow unconvincing.

23

Oh come on, thinks Will. They both knew what this was.

Surely she can't expect him to pretend that he's not seeing other people.

'Well, yeah. Something about a British heatwave. Makes everyone . . . you know. Go a bit mad. It's a free for all on the dating apps, innit?'

'Not really, to be honest. Not for me. I hate dating. Dating apps.'

Will can feel the sweat chilling on his body, cooling off even in the thick, risen heat of his attic room. So quick.

And his swollen heart begins to sink.

'Really?'

'Yep. Full of dickheads. People who don't reply, fucking . . . *time-wasters.*' Manda is still dead flat on her back, addressing her comments at the skylight, as if it is that exact rectangular patch of universe that has wronged her.

But given they'd *literally just met* through a dating app, Will finds it hard not to take this a little personally. And it's also just somehow weirdly embarrassing. For her to admit this. And he realises that he doesn't want to hear that things are hard for her – he just wanted this encounter to be fun, and free, and *easy* . . .

'Well, I dunno, *I'm* having a pretty good time – everyone's really up for it, if you know where to look—' Will breaks off, hearing how harsh he sounds. He hadn't meant for it come out like that.

'Are they.'

Will rolls more onto his side, towards Manda. Reaches out to stroke her shoulder. *They're meant to be silently holding one another in the dark now*, he thinks. Not doing this. Whatever this . . . competitive *iciness* is. These sudden sharp little barbs.

He wants to soothe her. To smooth this all over. To drift, and doze, in softness together.

'Yeah – sure. I mean . . . I bet you also have plenty of options.' But Will can hear that it simply doesn't sound convincing. And he can see Manda swallow heavily. *Oh no, please don't cry, please don't be upset, please be OK—*

Will is not sure how this conversation has so quickly slipped from his grasp.

'Not exactly,' she flashes another brighter, faker smile at him. 'So. Go on then. Who else are you seeing at the moment.'

He retracts his hand, keeps it curled by his own chest.

'Tell me all about all your other conquests, then!' she continues, but it's so clear she doesn't really want to know, that it's mere stupid bravado. As if she's holding the blade of a knife at her own flesh and asking him to press it down.

And suddenly, that annoys Will. Evaporates his sympathy for her, for whatever it is that she's going through. Because if you don't want to know, don't ask. If you sleep with someone within hours of meeting them, it makes no sense to enact some pretence of fidelity, or wounded pride. He feels a flare of impatience with Manda, at this pointless, unnecessary *drama* she's bringing into an encounter that was meant to be simply clean and brief.

Fine then. Let her have the answer that she definitely doesn't really want to hear.

'Oh, a few people. A woman from Hinge the other night. Might see her again this weekend,' – a lie; they'd had no contact since – 'and there's a guy, although he lives in Manchester too actually, so it's not very regular. At the moment. Early days.

'He's really great though, actually.

'Elijah.'

It instantly feels wrong to hold Elijah's name in his mouth, in this bed, with this woman. And the thoughts he's been trying to keep at bay now flood him, and Will is so utterly transported by the thought of – the thought of—

Elijah.
Elijah.
Will rarely gets approached by men. Almost never in public.
Doesn't give off the vibe.
Occasional signals, read and acted on in private. The silent language of desire between two men, who hold their lust close to their chests.
Men who might have girlfriends, wives. Men who fuck in the back room, in the back of a car in a lay-by, in a dim back street of a town they don't live in.
But since Teodora . . .
Since it became possible to have two profiles, two identities, gay and straight . . .
Since it became possible to just type in exactly what you want . . .
It can all be arranged so smoothly. There have been men in private. And women in private. And women who he meets at bars and restaurants and parks. And men who he meets on benches and in pubs and cinemas. And even men who see him, and approach him . . .
Well, just one man. Just one man who really sees him.
(With the most remarkable green-brown-gold eyes.)
Elijah
Elijah

—that he does not notice that Manda is clenching at the edge of the sheet hard enough that her knuckles have gone the yellow-white colour of an old piano key.

And then he does notice. Because she flicks her face back round towards him and he is shocked by what he sees there, by how completely transformed she looks: her features tightened, scrunched, reddened. Is it outrage he sees there? Or disgust, even?

'You're *gay*? Why – why didn't you tell me—' She shuts her eyes tight, as if she can't fathom something. Or as if she can't bear it.

And Will's body feels frozen. In place and time. His limbs heavy and immoveable, like one of Stephen's sculptures.

Not this reaction, he thinks. Please, not this.

Then her eyes flick back open, and there is something wary in them.

Will snaps to it. Then snaps at her.

'Jesus but I'm not fucking gay, am I? Obviously. I'm . . .'

She makes a frustrated *what are you then* gesture.

'I'm . . . bi! What's the big deal?'

He makes sure his voice sounds breezy. But Will knows very well what the big deal is.

Because he's seen it in the reaction of women during speculative 'what would you think *if*' gossiping sessions in the pub ('no, ew, no, I wouldn't *like* that . . . wouldn't *trust* it'). And because he's watched the men in every job he's ever had work so hard never to let a chink of desire be seen through their metal-bashing, mate-joshing, male male male armour.

Because he can't help but be overtaken by the memory of what a big deal it was to the first person he ever fell in love with. That fluttering, rushing memory, whirling in again, unstoppable—

Another tender night, when his first girlfriend, Briony, had
confessed in a tiny whisper in his ear I love you.
Seventeen, and he felt like he had no skin anymore. How
they'd stayed up talking, and Will had confessed to how his

27

parents had really reacted to his terrible grades, and how their
disappointment just made the words and the meaning slip
even further away from him. Ungraspable. And Briony confessed
to cutting herself – how the line of blood was less painful than
how much she hated her body, which made Will cry because he
loved every fucking too-thin inch of it.
And how she'd blushingly confessed that she fantasised about
the idea of them having sex in public – maybe a swimming
pool . . . And Will had felt so open, so seen, that when Briony
asked about his fantasies, he had felt safe to say he sometimes
thought about men as well as women – that he thought that
maybe he was—
And the disgust on her beautiful face
The revulsion
The recoiling—

Will shakes his head – *not these thoughts not these thoughts not these thoughts* – not now, not here, not again. He always tries so hard not to let these thoughts ever settle, to keep them moving, keep them out, because what comes with them is a

thick
white
heavy
snowy
downy
blanket of shame
smotheringhimsmotheringhimsmotheringhimsmotheringhim

Because for so long, those thoughts had meant that he'd refused to allow those desires in himself, in case women didn't want him anymore. In case no one wanted him.

Because even now, when both men and women *do* want him (he has the empirical proof!), he has still taken to using two separate dating app identities. Because they don't want him *that* much: his respondents halve immediately if he puts *bisexual*.

Will knows he ought to be completely honest, but sometimes it just seems to make things more complicated. Sometimes, it gets in the way of simply getting what wants. And he has wanted people in his bed more than he has wanted to be honest. (*To hold a warm, solid body in his arms.*)

The wrong approach, perhaps, Will now reflects.

Because clearly it is a *big deal* to Manda too. She's propelled herself half upright, yanking at the sheet, trying to cover her body.

'You should – you should have *said* something,' she says, her voice sounding small, and petty, and faintly wretched.

'Why?'

Manda busies herself trying to find her clothes, at once awkward in her nakedness. She locates her bra down the side of the bed, and as she slightly struggles to put it back on, he senses she's floundering, too, in trying to find the words to explain why she's drawing away from him so suddenly.

'It's just . . . it's *deception* . . .' she musters, eventually. But something is smouldering in her eyes as they dart towards his still-naked body, then quickly away.

This is really a ridiculous reaction to have, these days, Will tells himself. He is trying to keep his breathing steady. He sits up more fully and puts his hands round his knees, still below the sheet, and attempts to assemble his best, most charming, neutralising smile.

'Look, Manda. Calm down. It's no big deal. This was clearly

a casual hook-up, I didn't tell you lots of things – my second name, my birthday, where I was born . . .'

Then she rounds on him, as she pulls her jeans up forcefully, her eyes now fully blazing. Clearly, the charm has not worked, has in fact had the opposite effect – gasoline on the embers.

'Yeah but I'm not trying to fill out your passport application am I!' Manda explodes. 'I'm having *sex* with you! And don't you *dare* tell me to calm down.'

She yanks up the zip, almost with a flourish.

'But *why* does it matter who else I have sex with? Have had sex with—' Will keeps a perfectly light rationality to his voice that he isn't really feeling.

'Don't.' Manda holds her hand up. 'I don't want to know!'

'OK, OK! But you asked, who else I was sleeping with, and it was you who just told me off for *not* telling you I liked men?' Will can hear his voice speeding up, his faux calmness curdling into condescension. 'So maybe *you* need to work out what it is you *really* want – what *exactly* it is you want to know—'

'Oh, shut *up!*' she bursts out, and Will flinches. The room feels too small, airless, as she flings broken words at him. 'I wanted you to be *honest* – not playing me, for some kind of— but I mean – I don't want to actually *know* who else you're fucking – I don't want to *hear* about what a great time you're having, I don't want to *hear* about how good other women are, and I *definitely* don't want to hear about how good me— *God*, just *no*—

'I've got to—'

And she turns and is down the stairs and out of the door of the flat before Will can find the words to stop her.

He doesn't want to stop her.

(*Will she be— oh, whatever, she can get her own cab*)

He realises that his hands are trembling.

The disgust.

The revulsion.

Or was that just what he was expecting to see – what he chose to read into it—

Will shakes his head and tries to laugh it off: *just a stupid weird overreaction!* But his mouth is dry, and barely a croak comes out. It sounds pitiful.

He reaches for last night's glass of water, still by his side of the bed (he still thinks of it as *his side* and *Teodora's side*). The water tastes stale and does not refresh him.

Fuck.

He notices the knotted condom on the floor, coiled like some sad dead sea creature. Its clamminess makes Will shudder slightly, as he lifts it and drops it in the litter bin.

He picks up his phone, and looks at his email, as if very urgently needing to check for replies from potential house shares (there are none, obviously, since he last looked just a few hours ago, on a Friday night).

And he wonders who he is trying to save face in front of – the flat is *empty.*

His brain is not really processing anything he scrolls anyway; it is still turning over what exactly just happened. His thoughts grinding, clanking like the machinery at work, sparks of anxiety flashing, too fast and too sharp . . .

She has rattled him. Shaken him.

And all the memories of Briony's reaction, the years of fear and trying to hide it, guarding himself so carefully, denying it – all stirred back up—

The usually pacifying device – the phone, whip-out-able at the first sign of boredom or discomfort or awkwardness – is not, on this occasion, doing the job.

31

Will goes into WhatsApp and considers messaging Teodora. *Bad idea.* He considers texting the guy who lives down the road about buying some weed. He considers watching this ASMR channel that helps him sleep, a soothing simpering woman who pretends to brush your hair. He considers throwing the phone at the wall.

Instead, he opens his conversation with Elijah, looks at the last message from him.

Can't wait. See you soon!

But soon is not soon enough, is not simply *right now.*
Will types.

Fucking hell, I just had the worst date.

Too negative. He deletes.
He types.

Well bi-phobia is alive and well in Sheffield!

Too dramatic. Too . . . self-aggrandising. He deletes.

You're not going to BELIEVE my night . . .

Ugh. No.
For some minutes, Will doesn't type anything.
Just thinks about Elijah.
And why is it Elijah he wants to message, right now? This man – a beautiful man – but a man he barely knows, really. He doesn't know Elijah's last name, or his birthday, or where he was born. Doesn't know how he'll react to needy texts, to confessions of shame and loathing. To a hand held out, in fear.
In hope.
Elijah. Elijah, who he barely knows . . . *yet.*

Because something tells Will that he *is* going to know Elijah. Some tingling sense, that they're just at the very start of something. Something significant.

Trembling on the edge of a deep, delicious pool together.

And that's the reason it is Elijah who he wants to message: because he wants to get it right with him, from the very start. Not to play the efficient games, to use smooth seduction techniques. But to make something real. To let Elijah really see him. To tell him *everything*.

Will lets his thumb hover over the screen, then messages Elijah.

Can I tell you something?

Can I be honest with you?

The ticks do not immediately go to blue, and of course not, Elijah is probably on that holiday he was taking to Seville or at that wedding or the festival, or in a club or on stage, he always seems so busy – certainly doesn't have to worry about loneli—

No. Stop it. He won't even *think* it.

But Will feels very, very alone suddenly.

The empty, rumpled other half of the bed. One long dark hair, curled like a question mark that's missing its dot.

The weekend stretches ahead – walking Kinder Scout, alone, because his co-worker backed out this afternoon (a family 'do' they'd 'forgotten' they have to go to). A Zoom call with his parents, his father wandering in and out, his mother just talking about his sisters' achievements, their babies.

Will watches the ticks refusing to turn blue, and although his heart rate has returned to normal now, the space inside him feels hollow, and he doesn't know how to fill it up again.

He throws his head back, and groans.

When he opens his eyes, he can see one bright star, neatly framed in the rectangle of his skylight.

Will reaches over to the lamp and turns it off. As his eyes become accustomed to the total dark, the star seems to glow brighter.

He stands on the bed. He is still naked. He reaches up, and tilts the skylight as far as it can go. Then he finds a grip on the ledge of it, and pulls himself up – slowly – his head out in the air, legs kick kick kicking below, till they find the edge of the window and he is curling heaving pressing his body into the night air.

It is cooler now outside, but there is a radiant heat from the tiles that surprises him.

Will's body is taut, his mind flickering with the thought that *this is insane, you will slip off and die . . .*

But there is something about being outside. Above it all. On top of his house. And simply in his own skin, which now feels cool and dry and caressed by the thickness of the navy night. There are more stars visible up here, above and around him. And the city, spread away, twinkling and gloriously indifferent, and the knowledge of the dark, unbothered mountains beyond. This unspoiled air, drunk by so few other people – he can only see the odd moving car, a couple making their way home, streets away, and far below him. There is no one else up *here*.

He is alone.

Will lets a big, tremulous breath go, and tries to exhale the evening. The long day. The long week. The whole long fucking terrible last *year*.

And then he breathes in.

Breathes in the air of the streets. His city. His mountains. His home. This is *his place* – or if it isn't yet, he must make it so.

A new start.

Then below him, on the bed, his phone buzzes.

Will looks down.
And yes. Yes . . .
A new message.
Elijah.

Chapter 2

Manda

'Right. What are you having?'

Manda hits the lights, so that the glass windows that square around the front of the bar go dark, letting in only tangerine haze from the streetlights outside, and then slaps a palm on the counter. It's still smeary from being cleaned; the performative spritz and scrub she makes the staff do when there are customers in is automatically reduced to a perfunctory wipe when there's no one but her to witness it at the end of the shift.

It's 12.23 a.m., according to the slanting neon clock over the locked door, the numbers refracted in the still-lit mirrors that run behind the bar, chopped between glinting bottles of spirits. God, she's ready for a drink.

It's been a long night.

'I've gotta go, sorry mate,' says Femi, rubbing his hands on his jeans.

'Told to get home is it yeah?' teases Ben, adding without even glancing in Manda's direction that he'll have a double vodka 'to get things going'.

She begins to line the shot glasses up, treats them to the premium spirit. They deserve it, don't they, these boys. It had been a particularly hectic shift. And she deserves it, too. The liquid looks almost silver in the half-light.

'You wouldn't turn that down now would you, Femi,' Manda asks, as she slides the shot glass containing a splash more than a double, really, towards him.

'Oh ho, Manda, the good shit. What, are we getting *on* one?' Mikey strolls out of the back room, all wide swaggering hips. But there's a jumpiness to how he's holding up those knackered shoulders, his palms – an expectation, an excitement, picking up on her own hunger, perhaps. A deliberate telegraphing to Manda, to the whole staff, that it could be *one of those nights*.

Then it's as if she can track the relief coursing through the veins of her arms. *The night bus, trundling down Stockport Road – her cold empty bed – the stretching Sunday morning* – all get pushed out of her mind, the prospect of an active, immediate *present* filling it up instead.

Mikey holds her gaze as they down the shots.

It is on.

Mikey hits Femi on the arm, and literally pulls his jacket off him, as Femi rolls his eyes extravagantly and holds up his arms, OK OK one drink. But the one drink is gone in a single head tilt, and Manda is reaching for the glasses, scooping them in towards her, for silent, authoritative refills.

And the vodka begins its work. Smudging her edges, like a charcoal line drawing being fuzzed. *It is on.*

Ben starts fiddling with Spotify, till Mikey tells him to just put on the usual after-hours playlist and Ben does what he's told, rather more willingly than when Manda tells him off for putting his music on during service. Ben's penchant for obscure techno tracks doesn't go down well with their city centre, pornstar Martinis and over-priced burgers customer base.

Mikey helps himself to another shot, grinding up behind Manda briefly. The flare inside her is instant. Fucking hell, she

37

thinks, it doesn't take much to get the imagination going at the moment.

Outwardly, however, she ignores him, giving just an indulgent smirk. Won't grind back – not yet, anyway. She's the boss, after all. But maybe – *maybe* – her brain allows herself to think just that. Maybe later. Maybe this will make up for last night.

Last night. The obscure shame she can't quite look at yet burns in her skin, and she refills a glass and brings it round with her out from behind the bar, thinking she'll perch on a stool next to Femi, so that Mikey – now strutting around to the music, chest puffed, one hand doing gun fingers – can be reminded that she does have very good legs for a woman her age. Long legs. Hips not as slim as she'd like, but still good. The day-off Pilates classes in the grim community hall down the road from her flat. Long days on her feet. At least she's tall enough not to have to bother with heels. Can meet most men at eye level above the pumps.

But as she's casually crossing her skinny-jean-clad legs, while still hoping they register in the dim spill of light, the reason for Mikey's particular excitement is revealed.

'I tell you, she was fit. And just fucking... *up* for it, if you know what I'm saying?'

Manda sticks what remains of her cool unbothered smirk to her face. She does know exactly what he's saying.

So there it is. Another man, who isn't actually interested in her.

Never mind.

She remembers as a child, making a mask out of plaster of Paris strips, like a mummy, and the tight feeling as it set rock hard over her features.

Never mind then.

Fuck him.

'Now then, where the bloody hell is Si?' Mikey practically shouts. 'He could do with the tips on how to get—'

'Finally crapping himself, I expect, after dealing with those wankers earlier,' says Ben.

They'd all watched as Si managed to get an order wrong, twice, for a table of couples, angry men with red necks and women bulging out of bodycon dresses. She'd teased him about it, but when he looked like he was about to cry, Manda had found herself squeezing his arm, involuntarily.

It was only once she'd taken her hand away that she realised that she had never actually touched Si before. *Hardly touched any of them, did she – not appropriate. And anyway, she hardly ever touched anyone—*

Touch-starved. Wasn't that official term for it? Something like that, anyway. And how long had it been before Will? Ages. Almost a *year*.

This isn't what she thought her life would look like, Manda reflects, glancing around the bar. And the young men in it, who only see her as a boss. She had assumed there'd be someone to go home to by now. Someone to share her life with. A house, and kids. The normal assumption of what a normal life would be. But it hadn't happened – and the possibility of starting a family seemed to have simply slipped through her fingers too, as the years went by. Looking back, her life was like a long corridor of locked doors, that she had never had the right key for.

Manda has always kept herself deliberately busy, so as not to be confronted by her loneliness. Only now she wonders if that's also what's caused it. She's not had much time for dating or for nights out, because evenings and nights are for working. And working nights handily ate up plenty of the day, too – sleeping, recovering.

That was the reason why she'd started working in bars in

the first place, at nineteen: to avoid those silent evenings on the sofa with her dad. Working five nights a week at the Brothers Arms gave her a valid reason for getting out of the house, in the bleak years when she moved back in with him. Manda even made herself fleetingly popular by always agreeing to cover anyone's shifts when they had a birthday or a wedding to go to, always saying yes to the after-work drink, not quite realising that making proper friends – or getting a proper boyfriend – took more than just being... *there*. Kept quietly, patiently waiting for it to simply happen to her.

Manda had thought that the place where life would start was at uni. She'd always felt like she'd got off on the wrong foot at school, and never managed to regain sure standing. Her mum had given her a terrible haircut in year seven, the classic blunt pudding basin chop, to save money. And although after that Manda took control, growing out her unruly brown curls (a perpetual battle with conditioners and diffusers and horrid slidey serums), the initial brutishly short bowl-cut led to a persistent identity and strand of bullying: called a *lesbian, lesbo,* and other, nastier terms. Later, she wasn't sure if she embraced hanging out with the lads and being up for the hand jobs and fingering because boys were keener to have you around if you were indiscriminately willing, or because being called a slag was at least better than lezza.

But uni was meant to be a *fresh start* – everyone said, it was where you really found yourself, and Manda had known the need for that. Felt it in her chest, like the need was gnawing at her rib bones. She'd only gone to Nottingham Trent – not that far from Sheffield, but far enough to feel new. Economics and business management. She'd liked the idea of running her own business, the independence of that. Liked the idea of being her own boss.

She'd been in a lecture in Freshers' week — Freshers' week, not even one whole week in! — and not really absorbing it because she was so busy looking around at everyone, separating the boring boys in chinos from the cooler-looking girls she should try to talk to, with their low-slung jeans and belly piercings, when the door opened and a woman with old-fashioned glasses on a little gold chain interrupted.

'Amanda Rogers? I've got your father on the line — I'm afraid it's urgent.'

All the blood in her body seemed to rise into her head as she squeezed along the row, fumbling her notebook and biro, and down the stairs to the waiting door. *Brilliant — what did he want, could he not even manage one week without both her and her mum there, looking after him—*

The words 'turning right' and 'lorry' and 'all this rain' came down the line. And it was as if a torrent of rain was crashing down inside Manda's skull too — actually inside the ear canal maybe, roaring and overwhelming. A white-water rapid, swirling life as she knew it away, lifting it right up and smashing it down on some rocks.

And then something cut through, her dad, saying over and over again 'I'm sorry, I'm so sorry'.

It was the only time she ever heard him say those words, as if he got them all out in that one rush, used them all up. Had no words left, for the rest of their lives, to discuss what had happened.

The secretary's hand on her arm, a chair there under her and a sweet cup of tea with a bit of cold water put into it so she didn't burn herself, which just made it undrinkable.

But then, everything was undrinkable — unthinkable, impossible, incomprehensible — after her mum died.

'Oi, Minty, get out here you dickhead!'

Mikey's bellowing across the bar brings Manda back to herself. He is constantly trying to give everyone nicknames, none of which are clever, or even usually funny. Minty had somehow stuck for Si, who is Polish – his full name, which she has in her phone for staffing emergencies, is Szymon (a beautiful collection of letters, she thinks, that angled z sharply reinforcing that s). But when Mikey was casting about for variations on 'Pole' for a nickname – despite her telling him to shut it, *not appropriate,* leave the poor boy alone – Si had made the mistake of revealing he didn't actually know what a 'Polo' was. The performative display of disbelief that followed from Mikey – 'not know what a Polo is? A *POLO*? A classic English sweet of the mint family, my friend, the one with the gagging *hole* in it' – had dragged on for half a quiet Wednesday night shift.

Si emerges out of the doorway that leads to the staff room and loo, in a faded hoodie. Manda can momentarily feel his arm in a phantom grip – the surprising solidity of it, given how skinny and lanky he is. And something twinges, just at the edge of her vision.

'All right our kid. Shots.' Mikey's tone is affectionate but demanding. 'You've got to catch up.'

Si opens his mouth as if to protest, then clearly picks up on the atmosphere – Manda's commanding drinks pouring, Mikey's arms stretched in welcome at his arrival, the sense that even though none of them particularly like each other, tonight they will be going down together. Kendrick is playing at a volume Manda knows she'll have to turn down soon, but not yet, not till they are all too far into it to want to leave.

As Si lifts his first shot, the liquid trembling in a glass full to the brim that he struggles to get to his mouth without spilling, he flicks a look to Manda that she doesn't know how to read.

Could be anticipation.

And she has the strange vertiginous feeling you get when your focus pulls differently on a person, and they suddenly appear new to you.

Then Mikey is cutting fat lines, and she slips him a twenty because that's what a good boss does. This wasting of wages. But she earns more than them, and it is the best way, she's discovered, to silently keep your staff happy, these unacknowledged acts of generosity. Especially as a woman, at the head of a team of mostly men.

People always assume it must be a handful, managing these lads, but Manda has long been on top of it. She intimately knows the rhythms of the shift, and the wider cycles of employment. Can tell immediately whether a newbie will fit in or sink. And as long as you make clear to them who is the boss, she finds men either accept the situation or leave sharpish.

Mikey had to be broken. She saved the ice-cold bollocking, delivered more loudly than remotely necessary – 'can you not do simple mental arithmetic Mike? Do I need to go back to your CV and check Maths was actually one of your three GCSEs?' – for a moment when he was serving, and clearly making headway with, a very hot blonde at the bar. It was of course all an exaggeration, Mikey was no fool, was blatantly overqualified for this job and just struggled to concentrate a bit because of his ADHD. He'd ignored Manda the rest of that shift. But he never tried to undermine her in front of anyone again.

If anything, Manda actually prefers having an all-male staff team on. Less time lost in flirting, for one thing. She hates having to order people back to work when they're slacking off to flirt. Makes her feel like a teacher, or a mum. Makes her feel *old*. Besides, blokes are simpler to control. No endlessly multiplying rivalries or petty complaints; no one taking against her, as a person, taking it all personally when she tells them off. The boys grumble, but they don't hold grudges.

It's just much more straightforward.

But then she's always found men more straightforward. Manda has never had a gang of girl mates, and doesn't quite understand the way they flutter and flock, the endless wittering positive reassurances she hears tossed out like handfuls of confetti during nights out, 'babe you're too good for him', all that. The way those women seem to pull their guts out, spread them over the tables in the bar, and expect each other to rearrange them correctly, to squeeze them back in so that everything is better. Tears and hugs and doing each other's make-up in the loos, as if *in solidarity* at their shared state of *being a woman*.

Manda prefers the blokes' way of just getting on with it. Not *dissecting* everything that's ever happened to you, raking over it and over it—

Like last night . . .

Will's face comes to her as she bends over the mirrored surface of the chrome tray, and she closes her eyes tight, briefly.

When she opens them, all she sees is her own face, reflected far too close. Features smeared and blurred.

She lets the anticipation tingle, for a few seconds, before inhaling sharply. The anticipation is partly for the coke: the strong, certain desire that she didn't know she had for it roaring into life the minute it was revealed it was, in fact, an option. But it's also the confirmation that they are truly *in it* now. It'll be hours and hours now, of banter and viciousness and affection, and although they'll all groan about how bad they felt afterwards on their next shift – maybe they'll even WhatsApp each other in real time about how shit it is in the morning and what takeaway they've ordered in the evening – it means that stretch of time till she's working again won't quite register as real. A

44

grim but completely understandable self-inflicted comedown to be waded through, rather than the cold neutral reality of a blank Sunday morning.

The chlorine taste floods her skull, and numbs the back of her soft palate. She tries not to wince, to show her flinching.

'Nice one, sound,' mutters Mikey, taking back the twenty off her, and beckoning Si over.

Si shrugs as if not bothered, but Mikey gestures more strongly, and he joins them. Si looks sheepish, his dark eyebrows drawing down, before his whole head bends over the tray. It's weird that those eyebrows are so much darker than his very fine, almost sandy-coloured hair, Manda thinks.

She finds her eyes keep being drawn to him after that. A fine crust of white around one nostril, which – as if sensing her gaze on it – he brushes away, his whole slight body dipping in the action. The way he twiddles his bony-knuckled fingers and thumbs. Si is watching, with what looks like polite reluctance, a hyperactive routine of Mikey's – supposedly enacted for his education – about how to pull. It owes a fair amount to some tired old pick-up-artist videos on YouTube which Mikey has clearly forgotten he told Manda about, in great detail, the last time they had coke, and is now attempting to pass off as his own innovation.

'Yes, women just *love* being insulted,' she says with a drawl, moving back towards the fridges to deliver them all some beers. They bud with beads of condensation immediately; it's a warm night. Warm enough for customers to sit on the decking outside till closing, adding to the boys' journeys in and out, with precarious trays of lurid cocktails or the pink and purple gins served in balloon-sized glasses that the bar is currently really pushing. Manda had done a good bulk deal with a local distillery, and the ridiculous pageantry of it – the sprays of

45

rosemary, scatterings of juniper berries – means they can still seriously hike up the price.

Then a pulse of memory: the sugar-tang of the cocktails she'd drunk the previous night, how the Amaretto almond flavour seemed still on her tongue as she first kissed Will. A good first kiss. And then the slick of savoury sweat between their naked bodies, in the thick, risen heat of his attic room.

A peculiar and hasty intimacy, she thinks now, sharing bodily liquids with a stranger like that. When you have no idea who they really are. Who they might turn out to be.

And yet that intimacy is what she's been chasing. Isn't it? What she yearns for.

A teenager in a strappy sundress was sitting opposite her on the train to Sheffield had been reading a magazine, which declared on its shrieking pink-and-red cover that this summer was set to 'sizzle' and to 'scorch': 'The summer of love we've all been waiting for is here – and it's going to be hot, hot, HOT!' But so far, Manda's has been a damp squib.

After a cold, seemingly endless winter stuck in her box-sized studio flat, Manda decided she had truly had enough of the solitude. Had been ready – properly eager, even, for once – to get out, to get back into dating. *Meeting people.* Trying to find that elusive significant other. Signed up for the lot of them, all the apps, Hinge and Tinder and Bumble and OK Cupid. But actually getting anyone on a date seems just as hard as Manda remembered from the last time. Maybe worse.

It is all just empty chat – half a dozen lacklustre messages, that fizzle out, or a few extremely flirtatious ones that go suddenly silent (presumably when they match with someone younger and hotter, or who sends younger, hotter nudes). People who can't even spell her name correctly despite it being *right there* on the screen (*hey mandy, I like mandy If u now what I mean lol you up for*

46

a good time then? Tongue emoji, pill emoji, inexplicable broom emoji). A man who admitted, when she tried to pin him down to meet up, that he had a girlfriend, was just 'enjoying the chat'.

The few dates Manda has managed, she'd somehow known weren't likely to work out, although she still dragged herself across Manchester for them on her day off anyway. Recognising, on some level, that it was just blind hope. There was the man whose flattering profile picture was at *least* five years out of date, yet who lectured her about how fast she drank ('I'm just really not into women who don't look after themselves'). The one who didn't show and merely texted 'sorry' – nothing else! – four whole hours later.

It wasn't even blind hope. It was desperation.

And then there was Will, she thinks, picking at the label of the beer bottle, realising she's totally lost the thread of the story Ben is telling (something about something that happened last time he was DJ-ing, something about a doorman?) Ben's stories are always labyrinthine, a quality coke only makes worse.

Will was only really meant to be a distraction: an excuse to go out, not to have to stay in for a second night at her dad's. For years, when going back to visit her dad, Manda planned escapes to meet her one enduring friend from school, Gav, in the same pub they'd gone to during sixth form. But Gav had got married and had two kids and recently moved to some village beyond Barnsley, and she never saw him. Had the strong sense that she literally wasn't worth navigating the time and the cost of the train fare for, let alone a babysitter. A brutal, mathematical assessment of a friendship's worth.

So when Tinder scoured the local area and threw up Will, and when he'd actually replied immediately – his Friday night plans cancelled, her only up for a couple of days, why not seize the moment and meet *right now* – Manda had been relieved, even if he did pick a try-hard trendy bar in Kelham Island. Of course she never seriously thought that Will – living in Sheffield, obviously not somewhere she wanted to have to spend *more* time – was going to be a long-term thing. Their drink was just a legitimate way out of the house.

But then Will arrived, and compared to the other men she'd dated recently, he might have been Ryan fucking Gosling. He was on time, not without charm, and remarkably attractive (she didn't care that he was shorter than her, although she did think that, like many men in their thirties, he really should've just given in and shaved his head already). He made it clear that he was flirting with her, a clarity Manda appreciated.

And those forearms. Practically *sculpted*.

Even when it also became clear, as the conversation wore on, that they didn't have all that much in common, she liked that he continued to be courteous, still making the effort to really listen to what she had to say. That he was interested in who she was. What she might want.

Manda had felt – for once – *special*. Chosen.

Perhaps that was why it stung so much when it turned out he *wasn't* really interested in her, as herself. As a person. As a *woman*. When it turned out she was just another conquest in a busy summer. Manda feels again the prickle over her skin, at the icy thought that she could have been anyone – utterly interchangeable, not even just any woman, but any *man* – really, just anybody, *any old hole*—

The label on the beer bottle refuses to come away in the middle, leaving scrappy streamers of white. They look exactly like the torn thin clouds that stretched across the moon, as she'd fled his flat at whatever-o'clock that morning.

She sees Will's smirking face again.

'*I'm* having a pretty good time – everyone's really up for it, if you know where to look—'

Well lucky you, you greedy—

The sudden feeling she'd had – the instinctive flicker of revulsion, at the thought of the mouth she'd been kissing wrapping itself around another's man's dick – briefly rises up in Manda once more, all mixed with the cokey chemical taste and the vodka and the lack of sleep. And with it, an accompanying twinge of guilt, for having what she distantly recognises is an old-fashioned and un-cool response.

But worst is the return of the surge of despair that had overtaken her as she lay on Will's slightly damp sheets as he told her. How even in a moment that was supposed to be soft and yielded and *intimate*, she had instead felt newly aware of her own hard outline, her solid separateness from him – from everyone . . .

How she had felt so *alone,* even there. Realising how very little she mattered to him. How little he cared about her one and only female body. Wouldn't even remember her in a month. In a week.

Well, actually he might remember her now, reflects Manda, draining the last dregs of the beer, noticing she's drunk it much faster than the others. After running off like that, she'd probably become one of Will's own 'terrible dates I have known' narratives.

She stands up in a hurry, heading to the staff loo, as if needing to move away from her own self. Fuck's sake, she hates turning inwards like this on coke, she's meant to be having a good time, not doing this, not *wallowing*.

But the thoughts keep coming, as she pisses in the toilet that she also makes a mental note to tell Si to clean on his next shift.

The main thought being: Why did she have to ruin the only vaguely pleasant interaction she'd had in months?

Manda eyeballs herself in the small mirror above the sink, its surface rust-spotted in a way that reminds her of the new, dark patches of sun damage on her own skin, that she has to cover up with foundation now. And she mostly just feels annoyed with herself for messing it up. After all, it wasn't Will's fault he could have his pick of men and women, while she had her pick of absolutely sweet fuck all.

'You all right?'

It is Si.

He's come to find her.

Wait, no, he just needs the loo.

'Yeah, fine – sorry, just having a . . . moment.' Manda laughs a too-loud laugh that, even to her own ears, doesn't sound remotely reassuring, as she fluffs up the curls on one side of her head, hoping it looks like she was just grooming herself in there. *Not staring into her own eyes in the mirror and hating everything about herself.*

There's something swelling in his eyes, too. What is it – pity? No, not that bad, she thinks, it's just some kind of . . . soulfulness. An understanding.

'You all right Si?'

'Yeah, sound, like.' His accent is a strange mish-mash, a hint of Manchester but cut with the clipping pronunciation of his mother tongue. There is something about the way he picks through every syllable that's charming, to Manda, in this moment.

Although she suspects there's a more articulate boy lurking behind his reticence somewhere. She remembers when a few of his school friends – trendier looking, in their pastel-coloured baggy trousers and eighties-print shirts – came into the bar once, smirking at it (*so basic*, she could practically hear them say), and Si seemed to come to life, with a laugh she'd never heard before, chattering away over the bar till she had to give him a look.

It is rare to have to give Si a look. He works hard, and even if he often messes stuff up, he's always full of agonised apologies. She can see it genuinely pains him to get things wrong for her, to have to call her over to the till — unlike the blasé, cynical attitude of most who work there. She doesn't blame them: why should they care about this minimum wage, going-nowhere work? But it's touching that Si *does* care.

Sensitive — that's what he is.

And he needs the money. Really needs it, in a way that not all of the others do.

'Really, though, are you OK? Are things OK . . . at home?'

Manda wants to look after this boy, this thin boy, this — actually, in the half light — this quite beautiful boy. The presence of his collarbones, the nub at the outer corner of his wrists, which he doesn't seem to quite know how to hold, is peculiarly moving.

Or is it just that she wants to make sure he doesn't think she's the one who needs looking after. To reassert her power.

She is the boss after all. His boss. She tells them — them *all* — what to do.

And they actually do it.

'Yeah, things are . . . you know. Things are good. Bit better now, actually, yeah. My mum — she's doing OK.'

'Good. *Good.*'

Had Si been able to tell, somehow, that she would understand, when he first asked her for help? Had he sensed somehow that she knew what it was like to have one parent gone, the one left behind always struggling?

He'd come to her, after a shift, his head ducked, his hands knotting into each other, all elbows and angles. Had choked out the words, that he didn't know how they would manage – it was just him and his mum, his dad was gone, she just worked in people's houses – but she'd been ill, been in hospital, and he'd looked up benefits on his phone but they couldn't get them because she didn't have settled status yet, and he just really needed extra hours while she couldn't work . . . It was a hot, fast stream that Manda hadn't even been able to totally follow, but she knew exactly the flickering flame of fear lit inside Si's chest. Recognised the way he tried to hide it with that slouched, don't-notice-me posture, as if his own shoulders might be able to protect his heart from the indignity of having to ask for help.

Not that she had reacted well then, either. She somehow couldn't bear seeing that vulnerability, and she deflected, swiftly, offering breezy, professional reassurance – 'I'll do what I can, yeah. Don't worry about it.'

But Manda had rejigged the rota, giving a load of extra shifts to Si. And one Friday evening, when he was the last one there, diligently mopping the floors, she'd slipped him a 'bonus' in an envelope that no one else had got.

'I'm so glad things are working out OK. Happy to help.' And Manda reaches out again, the arm again, squeezing it. Warm, underneath the hoodie, its rough cotton pilled and bobbly from over-washing. That surprising solidity. Quite masculine, actually.

She flicks her hand back to her side. She doesn't want to touch him in a motherly way, a comforting way. A boss-looking-out-for-you way.

'Get back out there and let's get fucked then, hey?'

Si ducks into the toilet, and Manda breathes out through her teeth. That wasn't the right tone to strike with him either. Sounding so desperate to be cool. Young.

Back around behind the bar, and she turns the music down and Ben reaches over cheekily and turns it back up and she turns it back down, but a bit less, as he continues the conversation he was deep in with Femi.

'How the fuck do you have time to watch it though? It's on *every night*. You're here most nights?'

'My girlfriend doesn't watch without me. Saves it up, catch up next day, you get me?'

'You watch *Love Island together*?'

'Bet you're well distracting mate.' Mikey mimes wanking, extravagantly.

'Nah though, it's good. Couples bonding like, you get me. I admire the girls, she admires the mans . . .'

Ben looks sceptical, swivelling on a bar stool, back and forth, back and forth, too fast. You can practically see the energy hissing up and down his Adidas-clad limbs, thinks Manda. They're all like that, now, electric. The usual dumb chat of the shift given a charge, so it seems like it's urgent. The illusion that it might actually matter between them.

'Dunno about how you stand up next to that competition,' Ben says warningly, and Femi shows off his guns in comically exaggerated postures.

Not a patch on Will's—

'It's healthy, bruv – it's only fuckin', like, toxic relationships an' that where you can't be just *admiring* another person. No harm in it. We all human innit, what else you gonna do? Better to be chattin' 'bout it than hidin' it.'

And Manda feels another little shiver. Another little intrusion of Will, and last night. Not wanting to hear the person she'd just slept with admit he fancied other people.

Not other people. *Men.*

She doubts Femi's girlfriend would be into Femi eyeing up

53

a Brad or a Tyler night after night, next to her as they watch in bed.

'Oi, Minty, who do you rate on *Love Island*?'

Si shrugs as he gets back on a stool, and sips at his beer bottle.

'Not watching it,' he mutters.

Mikey performs a comic display of outrage, even though he hadn't bothered when Ben declared his own lack of interest.

'Mate. What *are* you watching?'

'Nothing.'

'What? You've fucking . . . *completed* Netflix is it?'

Si shrugs, and Manda feels a pang in her heart. *What if they can't afford Netflix – what if they don't have a telly – don't have a laptop—*

'Nah just busy, like.'

'Too busy for television? Doing *what* my man?'

'No, just too busy for *Love Island*, it's . . . shite. Got other stuff to watch, yeah.'

Expressions of outraged faux amusement at this unlikely strong opinion from the usually noncommittal Si.

'Like what then?'

'You wouldn't've heard of it.'

And now Manda feels a little flush of irritation. At his presumptuousness, the suggestion of superiority. At her own misplaced sympathy for him. She can see Si regrets this comment instantly, as everyone else feels it too, it's like a red flag to the bulls of piss-taking.

The others go on and on at him about it, till it's getting boring.

'Oh just spit it out, Si,' she says, in her best boss voice, and then feels instantly weird for using it in this *nothing* conversation about telly.

'All right! Whatever. It's a documentary from, like, the

seventies, *Ways of Seeing*. It's for my art A level, and it's sound actually—' Now Si is talking double-speed. 'About how, right, the way we look at stuff, at like art and adverts and films and *everything*, is always as men, looking at – perving on – women...'

Si briefly runs out of puff, then grimaces, and runs a hand through his silky hair. Nonplussed expressions meet him.

'Oh I knew I wouldn't be able to explain it right!' Si shakes his head, annoyed at himself. 'It's like the male gaze – everything is looked at like you're a man looking at a woman. And when you've seen it, you just see what they're on about, everywhere, like on billboards and definitely in *Love Island,* and it's, oh, I dunno—'

'Fuck-in' *hell* Si.'

'Documentaries from the seventies? Yeah, sounds bare good, fam, can't wait.'

'It's on YouTube,' Si says, a little desperately, as if that helps.

'What if women like being looked at by men though?' Manda's voice is surprisingly assured, meaty in its confidence.

Somehow, she feels the urge to counter Si's clever art A level theories. Which is daft, given they're probably on some syllabus, proved and accepted.

But Mikey and Femi 'wahey' loudly, and she seems to grow taller. Mikey begins to get out more coke.

She could do with a bit more being looked at, Manda thinks. The problem is *not* being seen.

Si shrugs and fiddles with the beer bottle, but she continues to look at him, can feel her own gaze acquiring more weight.

And when he finally looks up, she thinks he feels it too.

A split second between them, something charged.

As if he *does* see her.

Sees her differently. In a new light, perhaps.

And when she has another line, her appetite for it only grows. She should be looked at. She *does* look good.

Manda gets out a bottle of red wine, thinking her arms probably look attractive wielding the corkscrew so seamlessly, the smooth, single-motion twist-pull-pop, and then she starts lining up the glasses. (She'll have to pay for this one, will leave the bottle somewhere so she can ring it through next time she's in).

There's some grumbling about red wine as a choice, and she is vaguely aware that maybe they are right, maybe it is a bad idea, as the liquid gathers warm in her low belly and the evening slides briefly out of her control.

Manda checks her phone, wants to see if there are any messages on all the apps now. Saturday nights can bring a sudden desperate flurry of new matches or half-arsed replies. And there are some but not as many as she thinks are her due. Sitting in one of the banquettes, bending over the phone's lit surface and sucking almost at her glass of red, she speedily replies to three men, the confidence of the coke making her sure they'd be lucky to hear back from her even if, at the same time, she knows it's not really a good idea to message in this state. Funny how opposite thoughts can be held, so lightly, in equal suspension in her mind, when she's had enough.

Hi. Cuuuute picture.

You look hot. Why haven't we met up yet?

So why didn't u replied to my last message last week then?

And she's scrolling in WhatsApp and trying to remember if there's anyone else lurking in there she's been talking to when there's her chat with her dad, and she's into it before thinking and it's so one-sided, it's just a ladder of green.

How are you dad?

How are things dad?

Dad, can you call me back?

Did you get my voicemail?

*Looking forward to seeing you – my train gets in at 17.02,
and then I'll get a bus. See u soon.*

*I'm home now. So nice to see you!
Make sure u find that form!!*

Well, she's done her duty. For a little while at least.

She'd left it way too long this time. The thoughts – that she must be a better daughter, must visit more often, that it isn't that far, that he's the only family she's got for God's sake – have been circling Manda's head insistently all day and all the previous evening too, even when she should've been focusing on what Will was saying.

Bad daughter bad daughter bad daughter – be better be better be better . . .

And leaving it so long had just meant that this trip was even worse than usual. The house had been – for the first time? Or had she just been in denial about it previously? – not just messy but outright disgusting. Even the photographs of her mum (wearing glasses with huge, goofy, objectively ugly frames, and that warmest, widest smile), which were the one thing her dad usually always kept devotedly clean, were now covered in a layer of dust you could write your name in.

And when she'd gone to hug him, a sickly sour-milk smell emanated from his ancient blue-and-white Sheffield Wednesday shirt, its stripes globbed with food, and Manda felt overwhelmed with so desperately wanting to help, and with failing to. Then

57

he just shuffled back to the sofa, staring ahead as if he saw her every day rather than not-nearly-enough. Just like he'd done, night after silent night, in those immediate years after her mum died.

Visits home always somehow both stretched thin, and pressed heavily on her. From the moment she stepped back inside the terraced house – the same peach carpet everywhere that her mum had chosen (now bruised a greyish colour by decades of dirt), the same awful sunken sofa – Manda felt like a weight was pushing down on her chest. A chest which already felt over-full, with both love and sadness. It was hard to breathe there.

Sometimes, her dad would be OK. Would answer her overly bright, falsely chirpy questions about if he was getting out, dad? Been to the pub quiz lately, or to a match? What about that men's walking group? One time she was back, Manda had bumped into Bill, a very old friend of her dad's, from his days at the factory, who'd told her about the minibus he organised, taking a group out for Sunday rambles on Kinder Scout or up Mam Tor. She always mentions it; her dad always seems to have some excuse for why he hasn't gone.

If he was doing OK – and OK is the absolute best that can ever be hoped for – he would even manage to ask *her* some questions while they ate the defrosted cod and parsley sauce on their laps, the telly burbling away in the background. She'd struggle to fill even the ad breaks with stories from her life, about the intricacies of managing the bar or buying a new sofa (not telling him it was just second-hand off Gumtree). If he was doing OK, he might tell her not to worry about running the Hoover round, and she'd be able to say brightly 'oh it's no bother Dad, I've got it out now', and she would still feel the sorrow and guilt pressing on her sternum all the way home but wouldn't have to actually go into the train toilet to cry.

Other times – and certainly *this time* – there were no questions at all. Not so much as a pilot light in his eyes. No way in for her; no way to reach him.

But there were way, way too many dishes not done, caked with indeterminate brown matter that she'd had to scrape at before they could even be soaked before they could be scrubbed. And all the unopened letters, the chivvying from social workers or the stern reprimands for missed appointments, the bill payments missed. Letters that she would now have to deal with, weeks of phone calls and deliberately maddening hold music and obscure reference numbers that he'd claim never to have been given, and underneath it all the silent blaming that was a crucial tactic of this system. Cold, dehumanising; almost viciously punitive.

Even so, Manda couldn't get her head around how could it come to this – how could he not notice that the money wasn't coming in? It was hard, then, to keep the annoyance out of her voice, its encrusted ridge of irritation. 'Dad, just *tell* me about this stuff, I can help before it gets to this point, to bloody . . . *sanctions.*'

The one thing she still drew the line at was changing the bedclothes for him, glimpsing the same ancient floral-patterned duvet cover through the bedroom door, left ajar. That had to be at least twenty-five years old. In her most uncharitable moments, she wondered if her mum had ever felt like this too. He hadn't been as bad then, though, had he – or was it just that her mum had protected her from the dulled depths of it, from how much she had to run so that he could just sit still. On the sofa. Refusing to talk to anyone about it. Refusing to go to the doctor.

It must have got worse after she died, though. Everything got worse after she died.

Manda hadn't felt able to leave her dad, then. Had more of

a sense of familial duty, then. For as long as it lasted. Five years, was it, before she moved to Manchester. Telling herself, trying to convince herself: maybe he would even do better without her, maybe he'd have to stand on his own two feet.

Maybe her own life would start there.

Really, it had all just repeated itself. A new job in a new pub, long nights, camaraderie, transient staff teams, the half-friendships of a shared house where everyone is on wildly different schedules. The odd fun hook-up, or relationships that somehow always started fading after a few months, rather than deepening. Eventually a promotion. Eventually another one. Eventually her own studio flat (rented, of course, and far enough out that it was technically in Stockport).

It was like Manda missed the bit of life where you learned how to ... *connect,* with other people. To let them in. And the great transformations – the great revelations – that films and TV shows promised would happen, never quite came; the best friend, the lover, the co-parent. The one special person who really saw you, who knew your depths. She remained merely her own self. Unknown. Alone.

'Oi, Manda!' It is Mikey bending over her table. 'Phones away during shifts' – he imitates her work voice, a mardy, high-pitched take on a Yorkshire accent (*is that really anything like how she sounds?*) – 'Put. It. A. Fuck. Ing. Way. You gotta live in the moment! Mates before dates!'

He waves her own twenty at her in reprimand, and she pastes the smile back on her face and squashes her thoughts about her dad back into a small closed chamber of her heart.

'I know what'll get you in the mood.' Mikey scoots over to the laptop, and puts on his playlist of old-school garage – which reads nostalgic or nineties revival cool, for different members of the team, equally expressed in ecstatic whoops – and Mikey raises his hands with like he's just discovered a cure for cancer.

The dancing begins in earnest. Femi gets up on one of the banquettes and begins to move his hips; Mikey's gun fingers are going again. Ben has a ghostly blue mouth from the red wine.

Manda's limbs feel faintly distant, as if her head and her body have become untethered. But it still feels good, letting herself sway, her arms rise. She keeps seeing herself from the outside, in the imagined eyes of the others. And she does look good, doesn't she? Not bad for her age anyway.

These moves...

Then these moves...

Not bad.

Closer to them – but not too close.

A stool rears up, and she tries to catch herself, to make it look like a swivelling dance move not a stumble. Worries, briefly, that they all saw.

But Femi's eyes are shut, his hands raised, and Ben and Mikey are busy bellowing along to The Streets' track that's just started.

Only Si is still sitting down. Maybe he thinks he's too good for this music, too.

Or maybe he's just shy. Just needs a bit of encouragement.

Manda sidles over to him, sticks out her hand.

'Come on Siiii,' she stretches out his name with a sigh, and an enticing smile. 'Dancing.'

Her eyes feel heavy, alluring. Her chest, too, she's taken off a layer, just a vest top underneath, pulled down so that the cleavage is on display. (Keeps pulling down at the bottom as well so her tummy rolls don't get an airing too.)

She thinks Si is about to take her hand in his, when he twists his wrist away awkwardly instead, bending it in towards his ribcage.

He pauses, then mutters, 'I should get going actually, like.'

'Why? Why, Si? Wi-si!'

She faintly registers that she's babbling rubbish.

'Uh, got homework an' that.'

Manda stops, her head tilting down, eyeballing him fiercely. She puts her hands firmly on his bony shoulders.

'Absolutely not, Si. No way. Homework? Fucking... *lame* excuse. You're young, you've got to ... *enjoy* your life. Only get one.

'Now dance.'

'I...'

Manda shakes her hair authoritatively. He can't leave, he mustn't—

'Si. You're not allowed to go. Come on — you owe me this.'

She pushes away the thought that maybe it isn't right to guilt-trip him like that, as she takes his hand and twirls him into dancing with her. The other lads cheer them, and she feels herself buoyed by it, her hips rolling in towards Si, her hand lifting her hair up, stretching back her throat, briefly sure of her sex appeal.

There's a moment when she twirls, and catches Si's eyes looking at her — her body — and when they flick up to meet her gaze she could swear his pupils are dilating.

At the end of the song, she clambers and grasps more shots over the bar — only dimly registering somewhere at the back of her that she is absolutely *pushing her luck here* with how much booze she's snaffling, will have to put a load down as breakage — and Si downs one obediently, with a swift, cheeky smile, and then they're dancing again, him with more energy, as if committing to the situation, in a way that cheers her.

'Flowers' comes on, and she takes his hands and starts winding them, winding into him, trying to meet his eyes, to hold his shy eye contact, that slips and slides away.

Suddenly, Si has dropped the hold. Turned. Moving towards the loo.

Manda follows. Her heart is going double-time.

This is it.

She pushes the door, and as he turns, startled, she places one hand on that thin, hollow-feeling chest, the other sliding briefly into his front jeans pocket, together manoeuvring him back against a wall with a firm assurance that feels hot, sexy.

A confident woman. A woman who knows what she wants.

Manda turns and flicks the lock, then looks back at Si. She can feel her eyes shining, that glitter. It's a bit the coke, but it's also from knowing someone wants you, from knowing you are about to have them.

But as she advances towards him again, Si is muttering something.

'It's OK. Don't worry about it. I'm not your boss right now – you won't get in any trouble.'

His face looks suddenly small as it turns up to her, in the flickering greenish light of the humming neon strip over the sink. A pale and sickly colour.

'Manda, I really don't think this is a good—'

'Do you like me, Si?'

There's a pause that stretches till there's an awkward, desperate laugh rolling up inside her that she can't trust not to emerge as a sob. And those insides begin to harden, crusted with the unfairness, as she prepares to pull away, mustering what dignity she can in the face of this rejection, *another bloody rejection*—

But then – Si is replying, the words tumbling out of him, all in a hot rush.

'Yeah, *course*. Course I like you. Manda. I do. You're ...' She's gratified to notice that he doesn't quite know where to look.

Bless him, she thinks. He's just shy! Just *nervous*. Of a confident, experienced older woman ...

'You're a good boss,' Si continues, struggling with the words a little. 'And you were good to ... to me. I just, it's just that, like, I actually have—'

'I *have* been good to you Si.' Manda leans forward and breathes the words into his soft hair, which she wants to rub her cheek against, run her hands through. 'I've looked out for you. I've put myself out for you. Because I *like* you.'

As she breathes on his neck, she feels his body respond quickly. She lets her lips brush the tender flesh there, which buds instantly into tiny goosebumps.

'I know, and I, uh, I do really appreciate that ...' Manda is close enough she can feel Si swallow as he continues to speak very fast. 'And I love working here – I love working with *you*, honestly—'

She leans backwards, hands lifting her curls up again, displaying her neck, her shoulders, her breasts. 'What is it then Si – do you not find me attractive?' Her throatiest voice, only one answer invited, only one answer even really possible.

He blinks and winces and nods. 'Yeah *course* I do ... I mean—' And there's a small, adorably desperate hand gesture towards her, a *how-could-I-not* admission of desire ...

He looks up at her, and their eyes lock together for a moment, and Manda feels again the flash she'd thought she'd sensed between them earlier in the evening.

And it is enough for Manda, and she embraces Si again with renewed certainty, seeing what she wants to see, sure now that *he definitely wants it*. And her hips press him against the wall, and her lips are hot on his – or maybe it is his that are hot and hungry, for her?

The thought turns her on further, and Manda whispers 'I knew we got each other, Szymon' into his ear, as she begins to wrinkle a hand down to his groin, unzipping, and then her knees descending towards a floor that has a layer of grime she doesn't want to think about.

Well that didn't take long, she tells herself as Si instantly hardens in her mouth. And she stands up again, and undoes her own jeans, manoeuvring him round and down onto the lowered toilet seat. And he gasps as she descends on him, her wetness encasing him, her back arching. It feels like she is drawing him up inside her, as he obeys the string of whispered invitations to *fuck me fuck me Szymon fuck me harder—*

She wonders if he can see her – see them – over her shoulder, their mutual reflection in the little rust-spotted mirror. If he can see both her front and back at the same time as she moves, if he is watching her whole self riding him, seeing her whole body—

He must find her attractive, to come like that.

He must want her.

But when Manda looks down, she sees that Si's eyes are now shut tight.

Chapter 3

Si

Si pokes his head out of the top of the duvet. His mama is standing in the doorway of his bedroom, arms folded over her pink T-shirt, looking unimpressed. She rarely comes into his room these days. Si cleans it himself, allegedly.

And since Jasmine, it does get cleaned more.

'It's time to get up! Are you going to go to school today? What is wrong with you? Are you sick?' His mama's hair is pulled back in a scrunchie, and her face betrays a little actual worry beneath the somewhat comically performed exasperation.

Si mumbles that he's fine, and rolls over, taking the ancient floral-patterned duvet cover with him. It is so old, it's worn incredibly soft, but Si tries not to think what dead person might have owned it before his mama bought it from the charity shop when they arrived in the UK.

He can feel her eyeballing him for a moment, before eventually she makes a jokey, raspberryish sound, and says 'Fine, be late for school, I have to go – see you later,' and he mutters that he *is* up, he is *going*, and he won't be home till after tea anyway. 'Going to Jasmine's.'

Jasmine.

Si doesn't want to get out of bed. Si has been late for school on Monday, and on Tuesday, and on Wednesday, because he

66

didn't want to get out of bed. Because when he is sleeping, he doesn't feel sick and his heart doesn't feel like he's just sprinted, uphill, for a bus.

He was meant to go round to Jasmine's on Sunday night, classic movie night with her parents; they were working their way through the cinematic greats – *Vertigo, Citizen Kane, The Swallowed Woman, Do the Right Thing*. But Si had cried off with a hangover so bad he wasn't able to leave his bed, an excuse which had the benefit of being at least rooted in truth. He'd smoked a spliff out on the stairs to their block of flats, until his thoughts didn't hold their shape anymore. Then he melted some of his mama's cheese on hash browns, alternating bites with pickles straight from the jar, and watched cooking TikToks until he felt thick with fat and fell asleep.

He can't eat any breakfast this morning, just manages half a cup of scalding instant coffee before walking to school. Not that this is that unusual for Si; he's adept at replacing meals with caffeine. So this is just normal. Everything is normal. Everything is fine.

It is still hot – less sticky, but pervasive, a dry heat in the air and in the dusty ground of the park, littered with empty food cartons, and on his skin, which feels itchy. His eczema is often better in the summer, but there are scaly patches on the insides of his elbows and the backs of his knees that Si can't stop scratching, unsatisfyingly, with his bitten nails.

Gross habit. *Habits.* Both of them. The lack of control. He disgusts himself, this desiccated morning, and kicks at a gnawed-clean grey chicken bone that someone's casually dropped on the street. Like it's not a body part.

Like he didn't eat cheese on Sunday.

Si has been vegan since getting together with Jasmine – something her parents are 'supportive' of and keen to discuss over long (vegan) mealtimes, whether it's a 'morally based' decision or an 'environmental imperative', and interrogating what this means as a rejection of the 'cuisine of their heritage' (the assumed sausages of Poland, the salt fish and patties of Jasmine's 'ancestors'). Si's mama just shrugged and said, OK, you cook for yourself, whatever, until she saw the cost of almond milk. Now Si quite likes black coffee, actually.

His eyes itch too. Si is also tired. He'd been working Monday and Tuesday nights, after school – the bar didn't stay open so late on week nights, but he still felt wired when he got home, and then sleep was fitful. Must be the eczema, or the heat. His tiny room – a glorified cupboard – is windowless within what is really a one-bed flat with pretensions.

But it is also that the rest of the staff won't stop fucking talking about the one thing Si wants to never think about again, and every time it is mentioned Si feels like he is cracking, like more of some brittle skin is breaking or shrinking, threatening to expose something soft and sore beneath.

He'd thought maybe it would be OK. Manda had sent him a couple of text messages, Sunday lunchtime:

> *Last night was inappropriate.*
>
> *You're not in trouble. But don't get any ideas lol!!!*
> *Can't happen again.*

And Si felt mostly an uneasy sort of relief, even if he didn't know how to respond. Several hours later he just replied OK with a thumbs up emoji.

Yet seeing her, in the flesh, on his Monday night shift seemed to put an electric volt through his body, as if reanimating some jangling mix of sense-memory and regret and social anxiety.

And Si's body had betrayed him, again. Never mind not

knowing where to look – he felt like he didn't even know how to *be*. What the hell did he normally do with his mouth when listening to Manda brief them at the start of the shift? Where did his hands normally go? Even his feet felt too big, like he might be wearing clown shoes instead of the good fake Nikes from the market.

Ben had been in on Monday too – and of course he clocked the strained vibe between Manda and Si. How awkward they were both being around each other. As soon as Manda went out of the room to get some more pound coins for the till, Ben had rounded on Si.

'Oh my God, I knew it. I knew it! What the fuck happened between you two on Saturday night?' Then, for the benefit of the chef and the pot washer, Ben pointed both fingers at Si and announced, 'This one was last seen sloping off to the toilet with Manda, she came back out and then a minute later he ran off without saying goodbye.'

Si's face burned beneath his fringe, as the guys all clamoured for details, not put off by his shut ups, whatevers, it was nothings . . . Denial wasn't really an option, but even not telling them much only seemed to burnish their interest.

'What a legend!'

'Manda's toyboy, bruv!'

'Nice one, Minty.'

It was a chorus that followed him, echoed on Tuesday night too, the knowledge spreading incredulously through the whole staff. Si's non-existent arse got flicked by tea towels and blow job faces were made behind Manda whenever any of them could reasonably expect to get away with it. All in recognition of Si having somehow, perplexingly, *achieved* something.

Si didn't know how to respond to all this. How to say that he hadn't really done anything. He hadn't expected it, or engineered it, or even really invited it. It had just kind of... *happened.*

And he still doesn't quite understand how. Keeps going over his blurry memories, picking through them, cringing and wincing. He tells himself that he had just been swept along: at first startled by his boss's advances, by the strength of Manda's flattering enthusiasm, which he really didn't know how to defuse without seeming ungrateful. And then his awkward attempts to extricate himself – to say *no*, because he has a girlfriend, and she's the best person in the entire universe – that somehow just weren't loud or clear enough. And then all the booze and the coke clouding up his judgment, his responses...

How his body betrayed him. Wanting what it wanted.

How instead of speaking up, and stopping it, he had just... *let it happen.*

Which was pathetic. A pathetic, passive excuse for cheating on the best person in the entire universe – with his *boss*—

No no no no he can't bear it—

Nnnnnnnnnn-----

Si bends his head as he walks, trying to let the hum resonate inside his skull, letting it drown out the thoughts nonono don'tthinkaboutit no—! His toes curl up in his shoes even as he walks and he tries not to see Manda tries not to think about hurting Jasmine tries to just blank the mind humming humming.

NNNNNNNNNNNNNNNN-----

But trying to stop thinking about it doesn't mean he can stop thinking about it. There, in his mind's eye, there she is again. Manda. The image of the edges of her face, thrown back, her throat bare towards him... at the moment—

The moment when he had come inside her.

And that's the other thing he can't stop replaying – the proof, the external evidence he wants to ignore but can't. The shame. His guilt.

Because after all, he had—

He had got hard in her mouth, and he *had* come actually inside her. Which means he must've wanted it, must've enjoyed it—

Si feels like he wants to throw up. He can taste his own spit at the back of his mouth, faintly metallic.

Because it means he's just a shitty man like all the rest of them, just a normal shitty horny man who'll just fuck anyone given the chance, *any old hole*—

NNNNNNNNNNNNNNN-----

The humming is not loud enough.

Si rams in headphones and puts on a playlist Jasmine made for him, but Bob Dylan's voice sounds like he's both reprimanding Si and also like he knows exactly where Si is coming from, like he's a Gruff Real Man who has cheated on plenty of women, regrettably, a little wearily, but that's just his potent, manly way—

Jasmine.

Si feels like he is leaving dirty fingerprints all over her most-beloved music by even listening to it at the same time as having these thoughts, and presses pause.

He changes to Run the Jewels, and turns the volume up as high as his crappy headphones can go without hissing into distortion, and gets himself to school.

He sits straight down in the sixth-form common room, checking his email as if by looking busy he will actually feel busy, and distracted.

Then his whole body shudders into goosebumps, before he's even really registered the hand on the back of his neck, and he jumps.

'All right Si! Only me.'

It is her, bending over him with her big grin, coming in for a kiss. The face he now knows better than anyone else's, from the hours they have spent in his bed, so close to each other. He has memorised every part of her lovely face, from the pores around her nose to the exact length and direction of her lower lashes (the rebellious ones in the corner that spike and criss-cross) to the whites of her eyes (curves so solid and opaque and smoothly round beneath the bone, they remind him of a boiled egg).

As she comes closer, Si tries very hard to remain soft – not to clench up. But it's all wrong, to strain for ease. He wonders if she will feel his guilt in his body's stiffness. Like a cold suit of armour.

Luckily, Jasmine only gives him a quick public kiss on the cheek; they've never much gone in for PDAs, which Si is fine with. He couldn't bear to be the subject of the jeering get-a-rooms of classmates, the eye-rolls of teachers, like Zee and Amina who snog so wetly you can hear it if you pass too close.

Si likes that his and Jasmine's love is a private thing. It feels too delicate to be exposed to the world.

Love—

'You OK?'

'Yeah, sound yeah. Just, I dunno, tired. Slept bad again.'

Jasmine makes a smoochy sympathetic face (it is an expression he mostly sees her doing at her cats, absurd spoiled fluffy things named Sergeant Pepper and Colonel Mustard), but is there a shard of real concern behind her glasses? Jasmine wears huge, goofy, objectively ugly frames, that work on her because she's so cool and beautiful, but that remind him of the glasses his mum used to wear in a very non-ironic way not all that long ago.

'Come on. Let's get to art. Andi will let you have a coffee.'

'Call-me-Andi' is their art teacher, a woman who appears to paint her own image in hot pink and orange wax-print dresses and headscarves, and 'upcycles' her own chunky jewellery from single-use plastics. In the grand tradition of art teachers, Andi is cool and different, and all her pupils speak in awe of how she treats them like adults. (Si wishes for a moment that adulthood really was merely a matter of being allowed hot drinks and crisps next to you while you work.)

Her art room, Si thinks as they all sling down rucksacks and scuffle over painting aprons and Jasmine goes to put the kettle straight on, is like an archaeological dig of past students: every inch of the tables and floor are encrusted with generations of stains and splatters, while the high walls form strata of favoured work stuck up with Blu Tack and pins, almost overlapping each other, like sedimentary layers of rock.

Art is Si's favourite subject, but the nauseous feeling returns as he flips through his sketchbook (as many as he can get through are provided, without a murmur of explanation, by Andi). His project is portraiture, in pencil, charcoal and oils – unusual among his class, who have mostly opted for photography or film, or are trying their luck with 'conceptual' projects, deconstructing memes or subverting adverts. But Andi praises the purity of his skills, promises that there are good marks to be got on technical accomplishment in figurative work. Si still feels a bit unimaginative.

His subject, really, is Jasmine. The hours he has spent looking at her are reflected, right there, in the pages of the sketchbook. They are good, on one level: they are a literal likeness. And yet his drawings are also never quite right, he feels. He can get all the angles and shapes and shadings, but Jasmine is never really *in* there. His portraits may be praised for their fidelity, but he knows they are just of bodies – not of people.

Today, he ought to be working on finishing a study of her, her head raised and tilted back, eyes just shutting and lips slightly

73

parted and one hand to her throat (he regretted that from the start; hands are hard), wearing a simple, gently exposing top. It is a picture that he wants to feel a little sexy (Jasmine had hidden her face in her arms when he showed the start of it to her, groaning and laughing at the same time in that endearing way she did when embarrassed), but he also wants it to look very private. Intimate. *Honest.*

Only now when he looks at the page he sees...

He keeps seeing...

He keeps seeing *Manda*, doesn't he, her arching back, her breasts pressing forward in her own tight vest. The gasping pleasure—

Si shuts his eyes tight, like he had done at the moment they had finished, trying to squeeze her out of his mind's eye.

'Si – are we planning on doing any work today? Or just having a nap?' Andi's voice intrudes, brusque, but not unfriendly.

'Sorry.'

'Er, interior contemplation is like a very important part of art miss—'

Andi's eyebrows raise.

'Sorry! *Andi.*' Jasmine grins at their teacher. 'He's trying to catch my *essence*, you see. Always on about essence, he gets very unsatisfied otherwise. He's a perfectionist, is our Si.'

'Well, that's fine, but the end of term fast approaches and I don't need to remind you all of the need for nice, plump portfolios. Si, do you know what your final piece might be yet? It's really getting very close to the wire, now.'

Another flash of Manda. No, not of the real Manda, but rather an image of her image. Si briefly sees a whole, huge painting in his head, of Manda with her head thrown back, her mouth open like a tear or a rip – convincing and fleshy, but its colours turned up too bright; not like the polite, empty pencil portrait in front of him, but visceral and messy in tacky slugs of oil paint. And he feels certain, in a moment, that he really could paint it. That it would work, that it would have the energy his work somehow always lacks.

Nothing like the soft lines of Jasmine. The velvet at her most private patches of skin. Maybe that's why he can't draw her, not really. He doesn't want to reveal her tenderness, to bare what she's shared with him to the rest of the world.

Whereas Manda . . . if he could get that image down, get it down and out of him – big rough strokes onto a canvas, angry colours – perhaps he could purge the image from his mind. Not have to see her anymore. Not have to face his own guilt anymore, the memory of what he did.

He slurps at his coffee; it's too hot, and his tongue singes, vibrating fizzily before settling to numbness.

Si looks back down at the drawing of Jasmine, and feels furious with himself. The picture is also numb. It is shit! It is actually shit, it could be anyone, not her, has *nothing* of her specialness . . .

And how can it be possible to feel so differently towards two people, and not be able to get that feeling into what you've drawn? Because the love he has for Jasmine is so enormous it's like when you think about the fact that the universe is expanding and you think *well what into* . . . his feeling for her is as wide and uncontainable and brain-bending as whatever the universe is *expanding into*—

Yet for Manda he felt nothing for her at all except a little gratitude for work stuff, and a little basic, obvious lust, and now this rising tide of sickness . . . And how fucking shit of him, not to be able to reflect his *love* and his *knowledge* of Jasmine in the pictures of her, for pictures of her to look like they could

75

simply be *Manda* (a shudder, all around the back of his own neck), could be anyone, anyone female—

And before Si can stop it, the other thought is circling back, again. *How* could he feel so differently about two different people, and yet *do the same thing* with them both.

How the body betrays the feeling.

He flips the sketchbook shut abruptly.

'Andi, can I talk to you about my written reflections instead today? I'm not feeling drawing.'

Andi looks at him steadily for a moment.

'OK, Si. Sure. Come to my desk.'

Going through the arguments and grammar of the written parts of his portfolio is more effectively distracting. Dry intellectual problems he has to fix, rather than all this dredging of images. Si knows his writing isn't that good. He's seen the frown lines that pucker Jasmine's forehead when she reads it, and how when he reads hers she scrolls, nervously, through her phone, obviously knowing that he'll see how much cleverer and more articulate she is. Her sentences are smooth flowing things, while his seem to yank about or come to abrupt stops in a way he can't help.

But he finds it a bit touching that she worries about revealing to him how much smarter she is, when Si has obviously always known it.

It's one of the reasons why he'd never properly talked to her in school, for years. He had noticed her: had noticed that Jasmine was never embarrassed to put an arm up very straight in the air, and give long, thoughtful answers – she had this incredible confidence to work things out as she spoke, ideas running away with her, then taking luxurious little pauses and tilting her head till she found the right word or argument and continuing. Si always felt like his face was going to burst into

76

flames if he had to say anything in class, wanted to die if his mind went blank for even a split second (which it often did, the English word sliding away when he tried to find it, like those weird see-through shapes that sometimes float, then jerk, across his vision).

But Jasmine was also kind of cool. Not friends with the lads Si had mostly hung around with before, but part of a loud, arty set, who were unabashed to mention choir or drama club, and who set up the student branch of Friends of the Earth and an anti-racist reading club. Their clothes all came second-hand from Depop on moral grounds; they'd scorn girls who shopped at Boohoo or PrettyLittleThing. Yet they wore different kinds of second-hand clothes than Si had always done. Or maybe it was just *how* they wore them.

They were posh, obviously, with their long words and their long vowels. Their school is a very 'good' state school, Si has come to understand since dating Jasmine. And he's learned to understand that that means that rich people proudly send their kids there too.

It was in Andi's art class – which had shrunk massively from dossy GCSEs to more serious A levels – that Jasmine and Si had first really come into each other's orbit. More than half their class was made up of her mates and they chattered relentlessly, fervently, demanding Andi let them play Nina Simone or SAULT while they worked. Si mostly kept his head down. But Jasmine included him in tea rounds, and when she delivered his black coffees, would often praise his drawings fulsomely, with just a hint of – had he been imagining it? – condescension. Like a relative trying to talk to a child they only see twice a year.

Outside of art class, Si didn't ever think about Jasmine.

Then, at the start of spring, Andi had paired them up for a project. Art walks: pupils were to go out together in twos, to find and document 'moments of beauty within the urban environment', and bring them back, magpie-like, to the class. She wanted them to look with fresh eyes at their city, their neighbourhood, to 'see the extraordinary in the ordinary'.

Their first walk had been a lopsided thing. Si didn't say much, and Jasmine's words flooded into the space, as if trying to fill up any gap in conversation, or in experience. She'd been madly enthused about a play she'd seen at the Royal Exchange, a place that Si had never even been to. She'd gone on about how unseasonably hot it was (and was that the first time Si had really noticed her body, as a body? The curve of bum and calf, clad in tight grey leggings beneath a baggy geometric print shirt). Si wondered if it was genuine climate anxiety, or if maybe *she* was also nervous of *him*. For some reason.

And she'd talked about her art project – Jasmine was 'recasting' a series of famous Dutch still lifes, staging them with food that 'reflected her culture': breadfruit and soursop and plantain in place of grapes and gourds and lemons, bottles of rum and Ting instead of decanters of wine (not that Si has ever seen such things in Jasmine's house; her parents disapprove of 'fizzy drinks', but certainly seem to approve of red wine). Andi had adored the idea, murmuring approvingly that Jasmine was taking her back to her days living above Brixton market, while pretending to pocket a custard apple.

'Plus, it'll be really easy to do my critical/contextual stuff,' Jasmine had explained. 'That's what they want to hear: identity as a "theme" or "issue" and all that.' She'd made half-hearted quotation marks in the air, but Si had also been able to feel how genuinely proud she was of it as an idea.

When Jasmine asked what he was going to do his extended collection on, Si had muttered something about starting some pictures of his mum.

'What does she do?'

'Cleaner.'

'Oh my God, wow – will you do a series on, like, key workers? Like hospital porters and carers and stuff? There's *loads* you could write about that—'

'I mean, she just works in, like, rich people's houses.'

Jasmine had stopped talking briefly then. Si noticed the way her walk, her feet, seemed to go a bit funny for a second, and wondered if she also had that thing where your toes literally curl up inside your shoes at awkwardness. But on another, later walk, it was she who suggested he sketch his mum in her work clothes but inside the grand houses where she cleaned. And Jasmine got so excited by the way Si posed the photographs that he worked from that it made him feel like he'd done something really clever: his mama holding up her hands in marigolds next to the fancy matte black taps of a penthouse apartment or standing with her mop like a spear, in the marble hallway of some mock-Tudor mansion.

He managed to capture something in her stance, and something in her expression, that he knew well – a certain knowing glint. A degree of defiance, in the face of a job that people made so many assumptions about; some sense of her laughing spirit of resistance. And then Jasmine helped him use all the right buzzwords in his portfolio's 'reflections' section too – *class* and *status signifiers, juxtaposition* and *framing* – and Andi had written that she was very, *very* impressed (red pen, underlined twice).

But the thing that Si really liked best about his art walks with Jasmine was how whole-heartedly she committed to the task Andi has set them: watching her hunting out all the things that could be considered art, her 'everyday beauties'. How genuinely excited she got when she found a silhouette of a long-gone leaf, caught in the painting of a double yellow line. How she bounced around an ancient, forgotten billboard on the corner of a road, declaring its peeling layers 'almost like a Lee Krasner!'

She generously insisted that Si was better at setting up the photos they took, so he'd get credit in class for his 'composition' while she effused away, insisting that a shopping trolley with a tennis ball floating near it in the Bridgewater canal was definitely art. 'Because I – I mean, *we* – have named this photograph *Game Set and Match*: it's a Surrealist version of a tennis court, right, the grid of the trolley is the net, and the green of the water where the light hits it is like the court! And isn't that partly what art is, translating one image into another image by changing its title and therefore changing its meaning?'

'Yeah but is it beautiful?' asked Flo, one of Jasmine's friends.

'Si? What do you think?' Andi had interrupted.

'I think . . . I think if Jasmine thinks it's beautiful, that makes it beautiful.'

Andi had laughed. 'A very conceptual art response there Si!'

But what had really been beautiful had been Jasmine's face. How Si absolutely knew that big smile was beaming out for him alone.

Over the Easter holiday, they'd started doing art walks nearly every day. What else was there to do, Jasmine said, shrugging her shoulders and not quite looking at him in a way that made a small spark strike somewhere inside Si. And she agreed so vehemently when Si tentatively suggested things, insisting that she could see them too, that he got more confident at spotting stuff: like the buddleia growing out of a chimney so it looked like a plume of smoke (*'yes* Si, oh my God it's *perfect!'*).

Jasmine still found a lot more 'art' than he did. But the best one they maybe ever found was Si's: he noticed how a mirror, discarded on a wall outside the front of a house, reflected a cloud in the sky that – from the right angle – was *exactly the same width* as the brick it was next to. So they looked like two different halves of the same object. A cloud brick.

'A literal. Fucking. *Bricolage!*' Jasmine had said in thrilled awe and Si had looked the word up later on his phone and then WhatsApped her

still thinking about the bricolage

BRICK-O-LAGE

It was a BRILLIANT spot!!!!!

She liked the photo so much, she'd had a print made and stuck on her wall, next to her bed. Later, when Si had lain down under it, and she caught him looking at it, Jasmine had hidden her head in the pillow and said into its feathers 'That was when I knew, I think.'

Now, for the first time ever, Si is not looking forward to being in that bed.

Her bed. Looked down on by her photographs of Virginia Woolf and Francesca Woodman and Audre Lorde and Janelle Monáe dressed as a vagina ('a *vulva*,' he hears Jasmine correcting him) and a picture she took of Sergeant Pepper and Colonel Mustard looking fluffy and furious in paper party hats. A high double bed, with its thick midnight-blue duvet and pointless extra tasselly cushions that they mostly just chuck on the floor. Jasmine likes to watch *Grand Designs* and flip through the interiors pages of her mum's Sunday supplements and glossy magazines. She has a whole 'dream house' planned out in her head. She has opinions on what material floors should be made of, what colours front doors should be painted.

Jasmine has a lot of future in her mind, Si thinks. He does

not. Jasmine went on at him to apply for university or art foundation, when it was early enough between them for the question not to seem too loaded. But Si didn't know what to study, or how to pay for it. He'd decided just to work for a bit, to 'figure it out'.

Now, as he waits for her by the school gates after their last lesson, the thought of *work* brings that coppery flavour, right in the back of the mouth, gathering again.

'Heya. Ready to go?'

'Yeah. Course. That's why I'm here.' *Why does he sound so defensive?*

Jasmine gives him a look. 'Well OK then.'

'Someone needs a nap,' she adds with an indulgent smile, and takes his hand.

It's not that far back to her house. She swings his hand as they walk, a chaste demonstration of the affection that Jasmine has always been so confident in. It still sends a warm feeling up Si's arm, running into his body. But now that heat hits the metallic coldness in his chest and the combination isn't good. It's like different weather fronts meeting, Si thinks, an image of lines moving and clashing on a map (his mum is cheerfully obsessed with watching the weather after the evening news every night on her crappy old telly).

Jasmine chatters away about exam preparation for History, her study group's approach to last-minute revising. Flo is considered to be taking it insufficiently seriously, while Zee is maybe taking it too seriously – 'their anxiety is *super* spiking, we had to like *prise* them away from colour-coding Post-its'. Her fast-paced monologue also includes brief detour to report on a new flavour of crisp she tried, and to express her strong desire to wrap a sad-looking greyhound being walked on the other side of the road up in a duvet. Si murmurs along, and just hopes he sounds normal. He chews at the stump of a nail on the hand she's not holding, as if that offers another excuse for not contributing much.

For a long time, he worried about not having enough to say to Jasmine. She seemed to have a million thoughts a second, and a desire to share as many of them as physically possible. Her eyes would endlessly brighten and bulge with new pieces of information she wanted to offer him, her hands constantly grabbing and squeezing his or being flung at her own heart, as if some emotion there simply couldn't be contained.

Si wasn't like that. Everything stayed inside him.

He'd wondered if she thought he was just boring. Empty. He would walk or lie beside Jasmine, agonised, trying to pluck something from his brain and give it an interesting, external shape. But he didn't know how to turn his thoughts – amorphous, edgeless, cloudy things – into words fast enough to get them out.

Sometimes, Si tries to imagine who he might have been if he and his mama had stayed in Łódź, if he'd been able to grow up seamlessly. Wonders who he might have fallen in love with, if he'd been able to fall in love in his own language.

Eventually, though, he'd accepted that his quietness was OK – with Jasmine at least. More than OK.

'You're just different – I *like* that,' Jasmine said once, on a lazy afternoon curled up on the small sofa at Si's, and she'd covered his face in kisses. Then she'd drawn back, frowned her frown and spiralled at ninety miles an hour into her own worries: *But then, do I talk too much – but there's so much to say! Oh but is it really fucking annoying? Am I, like, vacuous? Maybe you don't want to know every single one of my stupid daydreams!* Until Si grabbed both her flapping, clutching hands, and squeezed them tight, and looked properly into her dark pupils so she stilled.

83

And he had managed to articulate the only words that mattered, really, hadn't he: 'I want to hear all of your thoughts, Jas. I like hearing *everything* you have to say.' Jasmine had mock swooned, and then earnestly cuddled into him and Si felt her heart beating and his own syncing up to it, maybe. And they'd just breathed together for a silent stretch, that involuntary bodily process that seemed newly charged and deliberate and full of matching, mutual love.

Now, Si thinks his general reticence – and his claiming (honestly) that he just feels tired, worn out, this week – is covering for him. Covering up his jumpiness, the way he feels all wrong in his own skin suddenly. He worries if he says much to Jasmine, it'll give him away.

There'll be tea with her parents to get through – but that's OK, they're used to him being shy. Although Si is sure they wish Jasmine was going out with someone more articulate, like the rest of her friends, who are mostly weirdly good at talking to adults. Si has watched her dad light up when Olivia, Jasmine's only really serious ex who had been in the year above them at school, came round as part of a small gang to sit in the garden recently, and they almost immediately started talking in impressive detail about a dodgy policing bill that Jasmine had also made Si go on protests about. He'd noticed Jasmine and Olivia still both had their Suffragette-purple 'Fuck the Tories' badges they'd made together when going out pinned to their respective rucksacks – which exactly matched Olivia's brushily short, violet-coloured hair.

Not that Si worries about such things, actually, or gets jealous. Because he knows exactly how much Jasmine likes him. He is still sometimes – often – taken aback by it, by the force of feeling that just seems to come at him from her open face.

It's almost tangible, like when you open a door out of an air-conditioned shop on a really, properly hot day, and the heat hits you.

Mostly, though, he thinks of their love – a word he definitely can't say yet, but definitely knows is what he feels – as something they are carrying between them. Something delicate but huge, that he is terrified of dropping or breaking.

And Si wants – he *ought* – to tell her what he's done, but he is worried that that might make her step away, let go, and then all their love would fall and smash or just liquify and run through his fingers, right out of his grasp.

He can't bear the thought of it. And so it must stay inside him.

'Si? Everything all right?'

It is Bernie – Bernadette – Mrs Paterson – Jasmine's mum. She looks concerned, although whether she's worried for him or thinks he's being rude is unclear.

Si realises he's been staring into space ever since they got into Jasmine's kitchen, while distantly aware of Jasmine talking to her mum and smooshing Colonel Mustard's big ugly ginger face and putting the kettle on and rummaging in the fridge. Although Bernie has transformed a spare bedroom into her home office (she does something in television that Si has never quite understood, only knows that it's a big deal even though they all talk about it breezily as if it's not), Bernie appears to prefer to work in their massive kitchen. And it is amazing, with huge glassy doors that look out onto a garden, full of untamed greenery, but also a fire pit and a pizza oven and an outdoor sofa three times the size of Si's indoor one.

Bernie still complains loudly: that she's 'ruining' her back using a laptop on the long breakfast bar and constantly being 'distracted' when Jasmine comes in from school or her husband comes down to get his rooibos teas and KitKats. But really, Bernie is clearly down there because she loves the distraction. It has always been obvious where Jasmine gets her chattiness from.

'Yeah, sound. I mean, I'm fine. Yeah.'

Bernie gives him her slightly amused look (her forehead lines pucker in the same way as Jasmine's, just much deeper). Jasmine always teasingly reassures Si that it's OK, her two older brothers became awkwardly monosyllabic when they were teenagers, her mum *gets it*. But Si has seen the pictures ascending up the staircase, of one brother winning debating contests, the other holding up a copy of the student newspaper he edits, and Si doesn't think they look like men who have ever failed to find words. How could they be, as the sons of Bernie and Desmond, who's so articulate he's often on *Newsnight* and Radio 4. (Si has been trying to read Desmond's book, *The Myth of Empire*, but when Si's not with Jasmine or doing homework he's mostly at work so he hasn't got too far with it even though it is really interesting).

'Lost in thought? Or in that picture?'

It's true that Si's gaze has been hovering vaguely in the direction of a painting they have on the wall. The Patersons have a lot of paintings on the walls, and big photographs of the family that Jasmine loathes, and a series of blobby, voluptuous sculptures from a female artist Bernie recently discovered through Instagram and became obsessed with. Si kind of thinks they look like rude Jelly Babies. But he likes a lot of the paintings. Likes them *a lot*.

He had probably his best conversation ever with Bernie when he asked about some pictures he thought were particularly great – amazing bright drippy things, sluices of colour charging down their surface – and she'd told him about Frank Bowling who was also an immigrant, and how he made those poured paintings, and then it turned into basically a tour of all the art they had on all their walls. And Si had loads of questions to ask then, because it was much more obvious what there was to say when it came to art. Or what to ask, at least. Because it was all there, in front of you, to look at and think about and talk about.

The painting he has been looking at – if not quite really seeing – while ignoring Jasmine and Bernie comes into focus now. It is not one that Si likes, actually. He's always thought it's a weird choice for a kitchen. He remembers it's by a woman artist but he can't remember her name.

But now, now his eyes look at it properly, snapping in, and it's like he's seeing it anew.

Or again? Because he wonders if this painting has got inside him somehow.

Because it looks like how he was imagining painting Manda.

Manda— Ma—... Man—... Mar—... *isn't the painter's name something like that too?*

The picture shows a woman's face, blobby and close-up and melting. Mouth open like a wound, in pain, or no – maybe in pleasure? Eyes scrunched closed, but wet-looking, like weeping sores. The paint thick. Although it's only a print, you'd think you could reach out and feel its surface. It is painted in sludgy night-time blues and blacks, not the fevered colours Si was thinking of painting Manda in. But it is still ... well, what is it? What is it that he sees in both?

A howl. *(A hole.)*

'It's, um ... it's a *strong* painting, innit.' Si manages.

'Hope you don't paint *me* like that, Si!' Jasmine says, spearing a bit of carrot into some houmous. 'He's doing a drawing of me with my eyes closed at the minute too, Mum. But I better not look that clapped when you're done.'

'Do you like it Si?' asks Bernie, beadily. 'I'm sure I've got the catalogue somewhere, it was from that big Dumas show at the Tate a while ago – I can find it if you want? For your coursework?'

'Uh, yeah that'd be great actually. Thanks. Thanks very much.'

Si doesn't really want to see anything else from this woman's imagination, this way of seeing that has maybe somehow already got inside his own body, behind his own eyes, without him even realising it. Without him even wanting it. Infecting.

But he does want to be polite to Jasmine's mum, and he doesn't know what else to say.

Jasmine rolls her eyes and mouths *gross*.

'Portraits aren't there to flatter you Jasmine,' says her mother in a hectoring tone, as she fiddles with a bunch of yellow roses, just beginning to open up from tight buds, trying to plump the arrangement in a too-large vase. 'True art shows the ugliness of the human body as well as—'

'Mum. Whatever. I don't want Si thinking of me like that!'

I don't, thinks Si, and scratches at the inside of his elbow, where his eczema has flared up. The flaking pink-red-white skin feels raw.

'Anyway, his pictures aren't like that – they're way more *realistic.*'

Maybe that's their problem, Si wonders. Maybe being less realistic would be more real.

The scratching is going from pleasurable to painful.

He tries to stop, and picks up a carrot. Crunching it makes a satisfyingly loud sound inside his skull. Then he worries that he should have washed his hands before taking one. Maybe Jasmine and Bernie would think the rest of the cut-up carrot sticks were seasoned with bits of his disgusting skin now. Like the fancy flaky salt they use.

'Si. Shall we go upstairs?' Jasmine is looking at him with an intensity that makes him wonder if this isn't the first time she's asked.

'Door open, please!' exclaims Bernie, in her usual stern cheerful voice.

Jasmine rolls her eyes extravagantly, and tilts her chin to the ceiling in a display of weary compliance. 'Yes, Mum, *ob*viously. You don't need to *say* every single *time*.' But she gives a little smile to Si as they turn to go upstairs.

Bernie and Desmond were – as Jasmine had rattled off to Si before she brought him round for 'supper' for the first time – the 'self-appointed most liberal leftie arty, right-on, emotionally-literate, smugly middle-class second-gen parents in the whole of greater Manchester, if not the country'. Nonetheless, they draw the line at Jasmine having a boy in her room while she lives under their roof. Si does not stay over. Si is not welcome when Bernie and Desmond are out (though Jasmine does occasionally sneak him round). And presumably – as Jasmine has taken to sighing ironically – her parents are simply in happy denial about what they get up to when she goes over to his flat...

Even so, they spend about equal time in each of their homes – they may have more freedom at Si's (his mama just greets them with a knowing twinkle as they shyly shuffle in or out of his bedroom), but Jasmine's house is undeniably much nicer. And Si is surprised to find he feels soothed, exactly as he usually does, by being in her bedroom. It is a dim, luxurious space, with dark blue walls and a thick fluffy rug in a deep inky colour. She puts on several lamps and lights the candle that smells of sage (or so Jasmine once told him) and – even with the door wedged open – the room glows gently, their own little cave.

'A bit of revision, and then we can maybe fit in a *Drag Race* episode before supper?' Jasmine says.

Si chucks most of the tasselly cushions on the floor as usual and sits down on her bed with their books – he's rereading *A Streetcar Named Desire*, she's on *The Love of A Nightingale* – and weirdly everything just feels the same. As if everything is normal. Jasmine has no idea. The room has no idea. Everything just ... carries on.

It'll be fine. Just don't say anything. If he keeps it inside, without any light, maybe the guilt will just shrivel.

Jasmine checks her phone.

'Ooh! Flo has just persuaded her dad to buy her a festival ticket!'

Si feels his heart sink further. Not this, not now.

'Do you know when you might get yours yet ... ?' Jasmine's voice is a little hesitant.

It was her, Amina and Zee who concocted the plan to go to Moorlands Sounds that summer: a gang of them from school – without any parents – for one big weekend after their A levels. Jasmine's family had 'glamped' at Latitude and Wilderness, seemed to think festivals were culturally edifying, and so were weirdly happy to buy her a ticket (Si isn't sure how this fits with their bedroom rules, to be honest).

Of course he wants to go too – the line-up is great, and camping sounds fun. But even a student ticket costs £180.

Jasmine initially kept badgering him to buy one, and he kept making excuses. And then, with a casualness that he could tell was actually studied, she started suggesting oh-so-lightly that she could buy it for him, or her parents could buy it for him, or she could loan him the money – she just didn't want it to sell out was all ...

They never really talked about money. Never really acknowledged the gulf, between what effortlessly sloshed around Jasmine, and what had to be tightly counted and cared for by

Si and his mama day-by-day, week-by-week. Even when his mama had been sick, he had – for some reason he didn't quite understand – not let on to Jasmine and her parents how much they struggled that month, Si having to secretly call up about the utilities and council tax to discuss extensions and payment plans. He had found it easier, almost, to explain the situation to Manda – a thought Si now remembers with squirming distaste.

It was silly, really, because he knew that Jasmine always wanted to be generous – because she liked him, and liked having a nice frivolous time together, and because that was simply her big-hearted nature. And also because why wouldn't she? It didn't cost her anything. She'd never known a lack.

But that also meant that she didn't know the hot crackle of shame he felt, scratchy and burning, when she just paid for things *yet again*, and pretended she hadn't. Something about the quick way that she tapped her phone for both their cinema tickets or ice creams, then acted like it was an accident, as if she thought she was just paying for hers, whoops. As if he might pay her back later. The whole charade made Si feel smaller and grubbier than if she'd just asked outright, do you need me to pay for you?

'Yeah. I will get a ticket. I just...' He trails off.

Because to be able to afford a Moorlands Sounds ticket he would need to do more shifts, and he doesn't want to do more shifts. Not anymore. The thought of going back to the bar makes his inside feel cold again.

But if he doesn't, how will he be able to afford to... to do *anything*, with Jasmine, this summer.

And the image of her going off to the festival and having loads of fun without him morphs into the image of her going off to Cambridge and having loads of fun without him, a thought he's been trying really hard not to have, and then there's just a blank, a white empty page stretching out ahead of him—

'Si! What is *up* with you today?'

Fuck.

Jasmine is looking at him expectantly and he realises he's been staring into the middle distance, not saying anything, again.

'Sorry, I'm just...'

She looks so concerned. He thinks he might cry.

Don't cry. Crying, over the fact that you got to fuck a hot older woman, crying over your own selfish cheating dickhead mistake. Stupid stupid stupid stupid—

He doesn't even deserve to cry.

Si shuts his eyes tight.

'Are you stressed about exams? And work?'

Si nods, and then Jasmine is cuddling him, her arms wrapping and squeezing, and her braids rubbing against the slight stubble of his cheek.

'It's OK. You're going to do fine, I know it. You did so well in that English mock! And art is going to be just great, and now Andi has said we can go in any time and work in the school's studios, I think that will make all the difference. Maybe you could take on a few less shifts, just while we're doing exams? I can help you out if, you know, um, if you need to borrow—'

There it is again. Although Jasmine is speaking so low and reassuringly, although he *knows* she's only trying to help, he just wants to stop the words, to stop the thoughts, about work and money and Man—

'It's fine. I can manage it.'

Jasmine looks at him with an expression that confirms how unconvincing he sounds, and for a moment Si has the urge to blurt everything out, to beg forgiveness.

But then the fear zips through him. Surely, if he told her,

she'd finally see through him – see how completely unworthy he is of being with her at all.

'Shall we just try to get on with some reading?' he says.

Jasmine pauses, then nods. He picks up the Tennessee Williams.

They've been reading for a while – or at least, Jasmine has been turning pages, and Si has been allowing his eyes to gloss and glaze and slide down the same one over and over – when Bernie shouts up the stairs.

'Culinary emergency. Your father forgot to buy more paprika, and I can't very well finish this brown stew without it. I will be TEN MINUTES driving to Waitrose.'

'OK!' shouts back Jasmine, giving an eyebrow raise to Si. They both know Bernie never makes it out of Waitrose in under half an hour, and usually with a family-sized cherry pie or tiramisu in her basket.

As they hear the front door shut, Jasmine immediately puts down her books and takes off her glasses, and turns decisively to Si with her sweet, eager smile.

He kisses her, and his whole body lights up, as usual, like something's been plugged in. The warm feeling he gets when she holds his hand, but running everywhere, into all his extremities.

God, it feels good. She feels good. She gives a little tiny breathy sigh and their bodies move into each other – not the awkward stacking of limbs that Si has experienced with the couple of other girls he'd kissed at house parties, but an easy, correct, fluid conjoining, as if both their bodies were simply better when laid next to and wrapped up in the other's.

That *right* feeling – that Si always felt – and now is so grateful for. Something he doesn't have to articulate. Is just known, by both of them.

And it's still there. It's not broken.

After a while kissing, Jasmine makes him take off his T-shirt.

When he lies back down, she moves her lips to his neck. Si shudders. It always sends mad little shocks up and down his body, reliably wakes it up (if it isn't already awake, which it very much is after the kissing). And he lets his hand, which has been mostly round the perfect crease of her waist, move down to her perfect bum and she's wriggling out of her cycling shorts so he can feel the smoothness of her perfect thighs too.

Jasmine pulls back gently, looks at him with those big eyes. He needs to do a picture of her with her eyes open, thinks Si, imagining using what – charcoal? Too smudgey maybe. Something that can get the pearl and the gleam, as well as the solidity.

He lets his gaze float down her body, to where his hand plays at her hip. The shape of it. His fingers mould the curve of the large bone, in from her bum, the smooth crested ridge and then the dip, towards belly, towards . . .

He never knows what to call it, even in his mind. *Vulva* doesn't sound . . . right. Too hard-edged. The word ought to be something rounder, smoother, more inviting. *Pussy* is ruined by porn. The words he barely knew at home, just knew were *bad words,* don't seem right either. *Pizda, cipka.* Also too hard, somehow.

She sighs as his hand traverses the same slopes, over and over, and then smiles down at him. 'I missed you this week. You've been . . . I dunno. Absent. Gone off somewhere.'

Si's hand stops moving. He pretends to need to itch the patch of eczema behind his knee, then makes a show of stopping himself, sitting on his own hand.

Jasmine bends her head to bite, ever so gently, his small pink nipple.

Si worries it will feel cold to the touch. Ice.

She doesn't seem to notice.

He shuts his eyes and focuses on the sensation. *It's Jasmine. It's good.*

Her hand reaches down, and begins to feel him through his trackie bottoms. She pulls at them, and his boxers, and this bit is always ungainly, even with them. There is no sexy way to take off socks, Si once muttered and Jasmine had done a foot striptease for him that ended in very loud giggling, but had actually derailed the sex.

But now, she's wriggling out of her own knickers, and sitting half up to pull her crop top off, and Si feels the usual rush of lust at seeing her breasts being released. Which sometimes he feels bad about afterwards — *bloody male gaze* — but in the moment it's like a mist has fogged up his brain and all he can see is her and all he can feel is very certain want for her.

And she's tugging him harder now, and his fingers are on her too, and she's quietly moaning at his touch, an urgent get-on-with-it moan indicating she wants sex quickly, not the more-of-this moan for when she wants him to take his time. Which suits Si fine, because there is something looming up behind him or inside him that he doesn't want to look at and he just wants to stay inside this sensation and not think about anything else at all . . .

Si moves his body up, and presses himself inside her. And it's all OK.

Jasmine feels incredible, moving herself beneath him, rocking into him.

Then she gives a deep groan, some spot hit. 'Yes,' whispers Jasmine. 'Oh God, yes. *Fuck me, Szymon—*'

But those words — that exact, unfortunate phrasing — bring it all back again, a huge wave: all of the feeling, the sick pleasure, that he felt inside Manda. That he hadn't wanted but did want, that felt good and disgusting and wrong and yet still *so fucking good,* as she told him to fuck her, and he did—

Nnnnnnnnnn-----

Yellow and pink pour down behind Si's eyes, covering and obliterating. He shuts his eyes, tight.

He tries to keep going, to end it, to finish; they need to be quick anyway, it won't seem suspicious. But while he feels very close to coming, he also feels like he might never get there, might be kept suspended in this state of sick pleasure forever.

And he wonders if Jasmine can tell something's wrong, something's changed.

He wonders if he's ruined it between them.

The something that has been swelling up inside Si reveals itself to be a blank red fury – at Manda, or just at himself, for messing this up – and it's a feeling that needs to be forced and funnelled, out of his body and out of his mind . . .

Si pumps harder and faster, wanting it all to be over—

And then – just as he thinks he is surely nearly done – there arrives maybe the worst thought Si has ever had:

They didn't use a condom.

Him and Manda.

Manda had just got on top of him, and he'd just let her. One of many things he hadn't said no to, hadn't stopped.

What if . . .

Fuck.

What if Manda gave him something, and what if he's now, at this moment, in the process of giving it to Jasmine. Who is on the pill, but otherwise unprotected. What if his rotten poisonous penis is infecting her sweet body *right now—*

A flash of the painting he wants to make of Manda, in sickly, diseased, dripping colours. Vomit yellow and mould blue-green and the red raw inflamed pink of exposed skin, of broken skin, scratched and torn and bitten.

Si stops, dead still. His whole body feels inflamed, with the terror. And then he recoils, pulling out of Jasmine and away, disgusted at himself, his own body. His hands retract, and when he looks down at them they appear to him like some horrible scaly claws, unfamiliar, as if they belong to someone or something else.

He scrunches his eyes shut again.

NNNNNNNNNNNNNNN-----

'Si...? What's – are you OK?' Jasmine's voice is confused, concerned.

It is a kindness he doesn't deserve. She just doesn't realise it yet, thinks Si – I'm *poison*.

And he wants to cry out, in guilt and sorrow and disgust, to confess, I fucked someone else, I did this – *this*! *our own special thing*! – with someone else – and I wasn't even *careful*—

'What's going on...?'

Si can't move, or make the words form. It feels too hard to explain what happened with Manda when he still doesn't quite understand it himself, and when it seems such a horribly long rocky distance to have to travel before he could get to the really important words, the words *sorry, I'm so sorry, please forgive me, I'll never – I promise – I love you*—

I love you.

He can feel his stupid mouth gaping like a fish for a moment, a stupid pale pink naked skinny speechless human fish-creature, gasping for breath out of water.

But the longer he fails to say anything – to explain, or reassure, or comfort – the more Jasmine's face changes. The worry replaced by wariness; the fondness by fear.

Si just shakes his head. And she starts to retreat too, gathering

97

the duvet towards her and reaching to put her glasses back on, and he can see that she is trying very hard not to cry, which is awful, because Jasmine cries freely, all the time. She actually loves to cry. She cries at videos of cats with three legs and she cries at Pixar movies and she cries after he makes her come really hard.

It is broken. He *has* broken it. Their love, smashed into a thousand glittering shards. Before they'd even named it, even spoken it aloud to each other.

'Jasmine – I just – I can't—'

Suddenly, it is like the universe has decided to contract inwards at the speed of light instead of expanding, and Si knows with panicked certainty that he can't stay where he is. This bed, this former place of safety and sweetness, seems now to repel him. His heart is beating fast inside his chest – unsustainably fast – like it knows it might be about to break too.

He has to leave. He has to get out.

Si starts scrambling for his clothes. He can't look at Jasmine, is only dimly aware now of her protestations and questions, asking what the hell is happening what is wrong where is he going, all of which sound murky, as if coming from far away, from deep under an ocean perhaps. He pulls on his trackies in a furtive movement that reminds him, with grim inevitability, of Saturday night, and the thought flares that this is maybe what the aftermath of sex will always be like now, daubed with grubby shame. He grabs the playtext and his phone and his rucksack and is out of the bedroom and the steps and the front door.

Nothing feels real as he moves through the streets. It's like being inside a film, or a painting. Everything is off. The colours turned up too bright, the sound turned down. Surely these people – smiling, or distracted by their phones, or wrangling over-tired children – are mere extras, blank actors. How is it possible for them to be so blissfully unaware that everything has changed. How dare they be so untroubled, Si thinks, in a swell of disbelief at what life has done to him.

What he has done to his life.

It is only when he is at the school gates that Si realises where he's been walking. He signs in at reception with a trembly hand and then takes the key and lets himself into the art room. He begins pulling out the paints, with a strangely methodical calmness, as if he knows exactly – *exactly* – what he needs to do now. Which is strange given that inside him is all storm, great billows of nauseous regret.

The hard outline of her body is put down, large and swift and obvious, and then he can start, start working the paint. And there is a new kind of *right* feeling, a satisfaction, a click, when he mixes the colours that he can see in his mind's eye. The greenish yellow, a repulsive phlegm colour. The raw sausage pale pink, the darker red-pink of gums and soft palate and open throat, the brown-purple of a slab of raw liver. And a slice of pure crimson, like the trickle of blood that rises from his skin where he can't stop – simply cannot stop – scratching.

The brush slashes at the canvas, not the tentative careful strokes he usually makes, but certain, vigorous lines and thick, squelching blobs of paint. Pure movement, leading to colour and shape.

He wants her out of him. He wants her off him.

He wants her gone.

Chapter 4

Jasmine

'Let's dance.' Flo looks at Jasmine very intently, her blue eyes beginning to bloom. She spreads her fingers in irresistible invite too, reaching sparkly lime-green nails that she had painted earlier that evening, in the hours they spent getting ready for the party.

Jasmine nods, and swallows the weak vodka lemonade that Flo's sister mixed for them in red paper cups. She takes one of Flo's hands, and allows herself to be led through the bodies in the kitchen, and along a hallway, to the larger front room where decks have been set up. There's a spinning disco light in one of those familiar tulip-shaped Ikea lamps, throwing red-green-blue lights all around the ceiling, and there are many bodies, pressing and moving.

Flo continues to lead her right inside the swell of them, and it's not as solid as it looks. Quite a lot of people are having stupid dance floor conversations, bellowing in each other's ears rather than really dancing. But here is a corner for them, by some overstuffed bookshelves already studded with empty cans used as ashtrays, paper cups that have lost their owners. It is a good corner: where they can be definitely *in the thick of it* and *having a good time* at a *real party* but also just be a bit like detached observers. Because Flo and Jasmine don't actually know anyone here, they can't shriek at new arrivals like everyone else does, can't have a dance floor conversation with anyone except each other, really.

Flo twirls Jasmine, repeatedly, as if she doesn't want to stop holding her hand. Then she pulls some slightly self-conscious moves, little snippets of routines they mess about doing in the common room in free periods. Maybe she is also nervous, thinks Jasmine, about hanging out with her sister's mates.

Then Jasmine worries that maybe this effortfulness is because *she* is bringing bad vibes. Low energy. Maybe she looks like she needs coaxing out of herself – needs twirling, needs leading. And she feels grateful, once more, to Flo and to her other friends, who have rallied round her so fiercely.

A party, it was decreed – especially a proper-proper house party – might do her good. And Jasmine finds she's oddly happy to be told what to do at the moment. In the aftermath of . . . *whatever it was* that happened with Si, there has been something soothing in simply being looked after.

Her friends revise with her, then tuck her up in bed next to them, even though she often fails to fall asleep for hours, instead watching endless Gibi or Sindy ASMR videos with her headphones in. They bathe her new helix cartilage piercing, which Jasmine had wondered about getting for ages and one afternoon found herself no longer scared, but instead welcoming the external pain. They make her go to the park with them after school, even though she mostly just lies back on the dry, spiky grass and looks at the clouds, and tries not to see any beauty in anything anymore.

She just needs to get through her last few exams, get through the summer, and then she'll be leaving anyway. A new start.

She hasn't cried since it happened.

Her! Usually such a drama queen, all the emotions, just sploshing out. Cries at anything. But instead, Jasmine feels numb.

Maybe it's because none of it makes any sense. Her friends have been understanding, invested even, on that front too – dissecting the situation, raking over it and over it. Jasmine's circle have previously proved fully capable of spending weeks examining just one or two WhatsApp messages or TikTok comments, mining them for subtext and symbolic significance – so the sudden treachery of Si's dramatic vanishing act offers seemingly endless content to analyse, yet also a painful lack of concrete clues.

Jasmine closes her eyes while she dances, and scolds herself for even thinking about Si. But, as ever, the questions froth and foam, like waves continually breaking on a rocky beach.

Did she do something wrong? Did he just not fancy her anymore? Was it something she said? Was she crap in bed? Had he slept with someone else? Had he fallen *in love* with someone else? Had he just fallen *out* of love with her? Had he *never* loved her? Was she an idiot for thinking it was special? Or... maybe he was scared or jealous or angry that she was going to uni without him? Maybe something awful had happened, that he couldn't talk about? Maybe he had a terminal illness—

Maybe he was just a thoughtless wasteman. Too cowardly to break up with her properly.

But none of the theories quite feel right, to Jasmine. She's always known Si isn't especially *articulate* – the word everyone always uses about her – but even so. None of it fits with what she thought she knew about Si.

Jasmine opens her eyes suddenly, feeling even more annoyed with herself. The house party was meant to be a fun distraction. The bottle of wine she'd stolen from her parents that they had drunk on the journey over, and the tiny little dab of MDMA Flo's sister Elly had reluctantly allowed them, were both meant to obliterate thoughts. Instead, it's like her thoughts are marching up and down, very insistently, in the front bit of Jasmine's brain.

They had talked to a few people in the kitchen while Elly made them drinks and half-heartedly offered some introductions, but Jasmine found she didn't quite know what to say. She had suddenly felt weirdly young. Elly has already finished uni and moved back to Manchester to get a job, and her boyfriend Shaka – whose house the party is at – is even older than her and actually works as a real DJ and has a lot of very cool friends.

But it felt strange that, as someone usually so good at talking to impressive adults without any problem at all, Jasmine suddenly came over all awkward (her toes had actually curled up inside her trainers).

And then she experienced a horrible gut-clench of fear: what if *this* was what uni was like? Jasmine had always assumed university would be her pinnacle, her peak, her natural environment; everyone said, it was where you really found yourself. Now, for the first time, Jasmine wonders if she would, instead, feel lost. Not know what to say, how to be.

Her piercing throbs slightly, seemingly in time with the music. A whompwhompwhomp, in the hard crunchy bit of her ear. She fiddles with it, although that makes it hurt more, and then wonders why she has done this to herself.

Jasmine tries to dance harder. She wishes all the other people here were dancing harder too. She wants to escape inside the beat, to become pure movement. Colour and shape. To get out of her head.

She's always thought that pressing the self-destruct button in this way was a rather *basic* approach to dealing with problems. Jasmine's style has usually been more the grand dramatic pronouncement: when things ended with Olivia when she went off to uni in Sheffield, Jasmine had flounced around, claiming she was unable to eat a thing, although she actually grazed directly from the fridge once the rest of her family were asleep. That all just seems like play, or performance, now. This time, it's really real. Heartbreak, which always sounded such a cutesy term, turns out to be painfully accurate.

And so it is deliberate, and planned, this rushing towards distraction. A couple of nights at home recently, she has stolen her dad's sleeping pills. Or her mum's wine. And now she has taken Flo's sister's drugs, in a concerted effort to just *have a good time*.

Flo is clearly having a lovely time. Her thin arms go all loopy when she drinks, and her pupils are giant and liquid. She keeps smiling at everyone, and they smile back even though they have no idea who she is. Jasmine feels a rush of affection for her friend: Flo is just a very lovable person. She's reliably interested in everyone she meets, and has a facility for winkling out what is interesting about *them*; she always ends up chattering to old ladies on the bus, or befriending shy new recruits at drama club. And lately Flo has been so thoughtful with Jasmine, always trying to push a chocolate bar on her just before an exam, knowing she might not have eaten enough, and sending her different viral videos of cute otters first thing each and every morning.

Elly waves and weaves over to dance with them, despite moaning about the music her DJ mate Ben is playing ('it's too early for stuff this hard, I wish he'd stop showing off and play something actually fun'). But Jasmine quite likes it. The techno appears to be drilling down into her hands and feet, powering them up and down with increasing urgency, as if it's very very important that she hits every beat with at least one limb. When she closes her eyes, she sees turning grey and black and white shapes, multiplying in time with the music, ominous things with hard cuboid edges.

A man sidles up to Elly. He makes a self-conscious gesture,

moving away his slightly limp hair – he must be sweating underneath it. It is very hot in the house, all the windows open but little breeze making it in.

'Who's this then?' he asks Elly, eying both Jasmine and Flo (although more Flo, Jasmine thinks, feeling this with some certainty in an instant).

'This is my sister, Flo,' shouts Elly in his ear. 'And her mate Jasmine.'

'Y'all right,' the man says, supposedly at both of them, but really at Flo. 'I'm Leon.'

Flo does a ditsy wave of her hand, as if recognising someone on the opposite side of the room, not saying hello to someone right in front of her. She looks about fourteen when she does that, Jasmine thinks.

'So, which of you is the older sister?' asks Leon to Elly and Flo with a stupid grin, and Flo looks like she's just won a prize. She flicks her very long golden-brown hair, but Elly just rolls her eyes. With her scores of tiny, geometric tattoos and her shaggy wolf cut and general air of cool detachment, there's no way that she could possibly be younger than the skinny, baby-faced Flo.

Why did her friends always want to be thought of as older than they were, Jasmine wondered. Why did they always want to be liked by older men, older women. She couldn't judge Flo too hard, really, because she knew the exact feeling. A sense of growing taller, of being seen.

It's just it is so obvious that this Leon knows that feeling too, and is capitalising on the fact that an eighteen-year-old would like to be treated as older. Would be flattered. Flo keeps flopping her head from side to side so her long hair falls about as she talks to him.

Their friends call her Arianne, condescendingly, when they

feel she's overdoing the flicking or the ponytail playing. The amount of vain showing-off that is accepted before brutal piss-taking must begin is extremely finely calibrated, and no matter how adorable she is, Flo still often manages to go too far.

Jasmine shuts her eyes again, and dances for a bit by herself, watching the shapes in her mind rippling and pulsing with the beat. Opens them, and instantly feels weirdly bereft, seeing Flo and Leon now basically just talking up against the bookshelf.

'I'm going to get a drink, want something?' she yells at them, gesturing towards the kitchen.

Leon waves a can and shakes his head, but Flo says 'Yes please,' and then widens her eyes and squeezes Jasmine's hand, as if to ask *are you OK, is this OK*, but it could also be *sorry but let me, I fancy him*. It's too dark to quite tell. And maybe Flo has done her bit really: her generosity in taking Jasmine, hardly the coolest girl in their crowd of mates, to a proper party; helping her with her make-up and lending her a clingy mesh top (now so sweaty under Jasmine's armpits). Maybe Jasmine has to make it work for herself now.

She squeezes Flo's hand back – a benediction; a *go-for-it*, a *you-got-this* squeeze, but also a silent reassurance that she'll be *just fine* without a chaperone – and winds her way out of the front room.

There's a queue for the loo (already disgusting) and then Jasmine wriggles through the kitchen, where a couple are snogging practically on the counter and some guys are having a heated debate over how best to counter online conspiracy theorists. She makes her way towards the booze table. Smiles at a few people. Thinks she ought to try to say something to someone. But the words – the chit-chat which Jasmine is usually fine at, trained by her mum and dad and brothers to talk like an assured adult – simply won't come.

Her tongue feels thick in her mouth, like meat. Like a slab of raw liver.

Jasmine tries instead to just look really busy making two drinks, as if it's super urgent for her to get back to her friend. But once she moves away from the sticky table, its ranks of half-emptied bottles and a few bowls of now disintegrated crisps and crusty-edged, discolouring dips, Jasmine feels no real urge to deliver the rum and cokes back to Flo.

She dithers in the hallway, looking at a big poster map of Bristol – where Elly went to university – hand-drawn in squiggly lines with pictures of local landmarks. Jasmine stares at it, as if cutesy little illustrations labelled 'Cabot Tower', 'Sweet Mart' or 'The Bearpit' mean anything at all to her.

Jasmine had considered putting Bristol as her first choice, and her dad kept saying he thought 'the university experience' might be more 'fun' for her there. What a lot of potential meanings that little word had to convey, had to secretly carry. *Fun*. It had been so strange to hear her dad, who didn't usually mince his words, treading so carefully around the subject.

But Jasmine decided the Cambridge place was too good to turn down, really. And it is obvious it is what her mum wants, although she suspects that is largely because her mum wants to be vindicated in the decision to 'stick to their principles' and send her to a state school (an Ofsted-*outstanding, Sunday Times*-approved one they moved to Altrincham to be in the catchment for, a financial cheat probably almost as expensive as private school – as Jasmine's brother loves to point out).

She sips at one of the cokes. It's too warm, tastes sweet and falsely chemical.

Jasmine hopes someone might see her looking at the map, stop next to her, start a conversation. Of course, they don't. They just push past, in both directions, the party's continual traffic from dancing to kitchen chatting, kitchen chatting to dancing, back and forth back and forth. Only Jasmine is stuck, it seems.

She heads towards the music, winding through a denser crowd now to Flo, handing her the drink. Flo is still with Leon, dancing now, their bodies occasionally bumping into each other as if by accident although obviously not by accident. Ben's techno has been replaced – someone new is on the decks, a man with tiger-striped orange and black shaggy hair wearing a neon green harness over his quite flabby pale chest, and everyone seems to like the lighter, livelier music he's playing more. There are whoops.

Jasmine still doesn't know any of it, but the shift is appreciated. It's like a change in weather in the room; a dark cloud passing over, sun coming out. As she tunes in, yellow and orange orbs and triangles bounce across her mind's eye in time with a particularly springy synth part. Her shoulders feel a bit freer.

Then a sudden stab of pain. Her left ear. Her piercing. A thud of heat, and spreading redness.

Jasmine can't help the yelp that comes out of her mouth as she turns, part of a stumbling collision, as the body that crashed into her fails to regain its footing.

'Fuck! Sorry sorry sorry – sorry!'

Jasmine's hand flicks up to stop her glasses falling off, and then moves to cradle her ear. It feels like an alarm is going off all round her piercing, a pulsation – and she can't wipe the aggrieved look from her face, even in the smiling-sorry face of the culprit. A woman, quite a lot older than Jasmine – maybe late twenties? – with a lot of piercings of her own (septum, nose, a full chainmail of them on the outside of each ear, even a metal dot nestled in the dimple of her round cheek).

'Oh God, what is it? Did I stand on your – God, sorry!' A

hint of a Midlands accent, the descending dip in the second half of each 'sorry'.

'No, it's just, um, my ear. I just got it pierced?' Jasmine winces. 'Cartilage.'

'Oh *shit*. I am so sorry! Ugh! Where is it pierced?' The stranger's nose crinkles in concern, but her dark eyes are sparkling. There's a thick soft line of some kind of subtly glittery eyeliner, looping over the curve of each eyelid. Jasmine finds she can't quite look away.

She gingerly takes her hand from her ear, a slow reveal of the inflamed skin around a delicate gold stud.

The woman peers in towards it.

'Ooh. That does look sore. God I really am so sorry – did I land right on it?' Her mouth pulls back, pained, causing her cheeks and large eyes to scrunch up and those funny, distinct wrinkles in her nose again: V-shapes, chevroning down a broad bridge.

'Um, yeah.'

The woman's peering head pulls away, but she keeps her body quite close to Jasmine's. Locks back into eye contact with her. There's a look in her eyes that Jasmine is sure she knows. A hunger.

She's just not used to seeing it in the eyes of someone she just met that exact minute.

A millisecond of silence, that feels quite loud. A hesitancy or weighing-up. And then . . .

Softly

'Let me lick it better.'

And Jasmine is too taken aback by the boldness of this offer to really say anything, and finds herself just smiling, which the woman takes as a yes and moves towards her and then there's a very gentle cool wet flick on the tenderest, most alert patch of her body.

And suddenly it is no longer the most tender or alert patch of her body.

Jasmine can't breathe. She knows the lights are still turning round them and the music is still playing but for a second, it is like the world has paused.

Then the woman steps back and laughs, releasing the pressure, and all the sound and heat and light rushes back in. But it is a nice laugh – one that doesn't diminish or undo the odd intensity of her putting her mouth on Jasmine's sore flesh.

'I'm Prisha,' she says with a smile that makes the silver dots disappear inside her dimples.

'I'm Jasmine.'

'Nice name. So, who do you know here? We've not met before, have we?'

Jasmine shakes her head, and somewhere in the back of it notices her own hypocrisy for being instantly delighted that this older woman might think she is part of the same scene as her in Manchester.

'Friend of a friend of Shaka,' Jasmine replies, she hopes enigmatically. She doesn't want the words 'little sister' to get uttered. 'How about you?'

'Yeah, I'm mates with the other housemate, Nia, known each other forever. And God, isn't it good to be at a proper house party! It's been ages. For me, anyway.' Prisha laughs, a warm fluffy cloud of a sound, and her eyes, Jasmine thinks, are just fucking gorgeous actually. They are *radiant*. Full of sun, even in the dark.

'I know!' enthuses Jasmine, clutching her hands up together at her chest, ardently, even though she has never actually been to a house party like this before: theirs are always just round someone's vacated parents' house, with YouTube not decks.

'Aaaahhh and it's so fun to meet new people as well!'

Jasmine nods and grins and squashes the thought that really the only significant interaction she's had with anyone new in the last year is probably Si...

But now this person. A new person. *New*-new. Shiny and new and just *glittering* with possibility.

'Like you! Jasmine! So fucking good to meet you!' Prisha gives a sort of delighted squiggle as she extends her arms, her eyes and nose scrunching in eagerness now, and OK she's obviously not totally sober either, but it's more than that, Jasmine thinks. It's also just a very primal, basic kind of joy, at gathering together to dance on a summer's night.

Jasmine throws out her arms and is rewarded with a big hug from Prisha, whose bare arms are incredibly soft, and very warm but not at all sweaty. She hopes Prisha can't feel the disgusting damp nylon of her pits.

It's just a happy, good-to-meet-you hug, but when Prisha pulls away, their eyes connect again – and Jasmine's heart rate has suddenly really got going and this feels like an actual good distraction, *this* feels like an oblivion she could really charge towards. Towards the sun in her eyes.

Holding her gaze, Prisha begins to dance: dancing that is very definitely dancing *with* Jasmine, a dance of intent. A private thing, that is just between them. Something curling up inside it: a promise, of more to come.

Jasmine's limbs feel tingly as she moves, trying to match Prisha, to silently signal her enthusiasm. Her chest is light and full of oxygen, despite how close and stuffy the room is with all the body heat and cigarette smoke and the competing scents of different vapes.

Occasionally Prisha gives a little cheer or blissed-out head roll when a song she recognises starts, or raises her hand to the ceiling, eyes scrunching shut, in appreciation of a well-handled drop. Sometimes she grabs at other people squeezing past, a few words excitably exchanged, but it's very clear, Jasmine thinks, that really Prisha is dancing with *her*.

And slowly, their bodies move in towards each other.

There's no rush; it's like they have all the time in the world, because they both know it's going to happen. Prisha seems to be luxuriating in it, in the anticipation; whenever she moves in, then moves away, she gives a sly private smile to herself, as if saying *not yet, not yet*. Prolonging the pleasure.

Jasmine feels more anxious – what if someone interrupts? What if Flo (who has disappeared, presumably with Leon) comes back and ruins it? What if one of Prisha's friends notices how young Jasmine really is and stages an intervention?

This is not hurtling. This is teasing deliciousness, and oh God it's good, but Jasmine also wants some certainty. Wants to wipe out the memory of Si—

Stop it.

She wants to stop thinking about Si. She wants him gone.

But she also just wants Prisha. All this gorgeous, enchanting newness. This nowness.

Mostly Jasmine has been letting Prisha take the lead – allow-ing herself to be danced towards, allowing her body to be brushed tantalisingly. But with sudden conviction, Jasmine grabs at Prisha's hand and twirls herself under it.

And while she's twirling under it, her body and face close to Prisha's, Prisha's other hand comes firmly at her waist and stops the movement. And they breathe together, in this ridiculous held dancer-like pose, clasped hands raised above their heads, for another moment that seems to pause the universe, before the kiss begins.

It's a very, very good kiss, thinks Jasmine, in what feels like a final conscious thought before such clarity and structure is rushed away. Everything shrinking to just their mouths, their lips, their tongues, the whole world existing just in that small circle of touch, and then everything expanding, a rush that whooshes through her heart and belly and between her legs, where it beats insistently.

And she wants something done about it.

Jasmine tries to nibble Prisha's ear but the scores of tiny piercings clack against her teeth like Tic-Tacs. She presses into Prisha's thigh and groans into her ear, and Prisha laughs softly at her obvious, delicious distress.

'Shall we go upstairs?' she murmurs into Jasmine's neck, and Jasmine nods very hard. Prisha's soft, delighted laugh again, very low this time.

She leads her by the hand, up two flights of stairs, in and out of people standing and sitting and chatting. Jasmine feels light and weightless. She can't quite believe this is happening, but it is good – the prospect of an active, immediate *present* filling her up. Like when you meditate and try to be only in the moment, no other thoughts at all, no Si—

Fuck's sake!

Although they are already halfway up the second, steep set of steps Jasmine yanks on Prisha's arm and pulls her back for another hot, thought-eliminating kiss.

Prisha looks almost unable to believe her luck. 'You are keen, aren't you,' she murmurs. 'Come on – let's make it to the bed, at least.'

Bed is overstating it really – it's a saggy pull-out sofa that's been half-heartedly prepared for some party-goer to crash on later, with a fitted sheet that doesn't actually fit and an ancient floral-patterned duvet. It creaks embarrassingly the minute they both sit on it. Prisha turns on a desk lamp; the attic room is revealed as, presumably, Shaka's studio: egg boxes on the walls and slanted ceilings, another set of decks, lots of cables coiling across the floor. A couple of posters advertising Warehouse Project club nights, poorly tacked up. People's bags and coats have been shoved up here out of the way, and Prisha pushes a few of them against the door, so they won't be interrupted.

Then Prisha is pulling her in close, and the room vanishes as Jasmine is taken back into that wonderful, urgent blur. She's dropping her glasses down the side of the bed and they are lying down, kissing and stroking and taking off clothing piece by piece. Prisha's body feels quite different to most of the bodies that Jasmine has known – more substantial, the firmness of her thighs, the lovely rounded swell of tummy. Something to be held by, and to hold on to, so unlike Si's scrawny arms and—

Don't.

But now it is easy to dismiss him, because Prisha seems to know very much what she is doing, and every part of Jasmine's body feels awake and receptive to every touch, impatient for more. Alive with want.

Jasmine wriggles in her loose baggy jeans, pressing and lifting her hips, until Prisha smiles indulgently down at her. She raises herself to sit astride Jasmine and unbutton, unzip, draw slowly down ... Their eyes click into each other as she does so, giddy smiles matching.

Then finally Prisha fully cups her, and keeps her hand in place, as if holding all of Jasmine, who makes an incoherent noise, her eyes flicking shut. A moment more of pained anticipation, and then there's a rush and flurry: pants off and final crop tops pulled over heads and Prisha scooting her body down, and the electric connection of her tongue touching. And Jasmine's mind flies back to the first touch on her ear, but then all thoughts stop again, replaced by pure sensation. In her mind's eye, a rippling abstracted pink, like opening petals, endlessly multiplying as they peel back to reveal still more, opening and opening.

Jasmine is vaguely aware of her own voice panting out her joy and her need, almost in time with the awful metallic creak of the bed. And finally Prisha obliges and pushes a finger deep inside her, finding the right place quickly, and turning the sweetness that's blooming all through Jasmine into something stronger and more intense. She pushes and presses and grinds against Prisha's mouth and hand – and then there it is—

The muscles in her abdomen all clench up ...

The small of her back juts upwards, uncontrollable ...

A total bright, burning, phosphorescent light, everywhere.

A moment of perfection.

But then Prisha suddenly withdraws, scooching back up the bed, and Jasmine almost cries out at the loss of her, the removal of that warm mouth, that hand inside her, while she is still so in the throes. Her body keeps twitching, and she is still making strange involuntary noises – little whimpers, as delicious shocks keep passing through her body – and there's Prisha's face next to her. Delighted, beaming like a ball of sun, radiating her obvious pleasure at Jasmine's pleasure.

Jasmine reaches out her hand and grabs Prisha's and almost crushes it. Prisha laughs softly, her face creasing.

'You all right?' she asks in an affectionate, lightly incredulous tone.

Jasmine tries to nod and begins to mutter some fairly in-coherent gratitude about how incredible Prisha is, when another shudder takes her whole body, and then they are both laughing, at the ridiculousness and the wonder of it. And Jasmine's laughter turns into an explosion of hot tears.

They are post-orgasmic-huge-release tears, that she wants to stop because it's embarrassing but cannot stop because, as ever, they are simply unstoppable. She flaps a hand in front of her face, and grins again, beneath the crying.

'It's just – don't worry – it was just really, *really* good! Really like . . . *intense.* Sorry – I just – I might just need a minute—'

'Hey, do not apologise. I'm thrilled, frankly.' Prisha pulls her in, wrapping her arms round her in a big cosy hug. 'What a result!'

And Jasmine can't tell whether the laughter that's shaking both their torsos starts with her or with Prisha. She waits for it all to subside, so they can carry on . . .

. . .

. . .

. . .

But it isn't stopping.

Jasmine is still laughing a little and crying a little and twitching a little, and she can't seem to stop any of it. It all feels out of her control. And she feels Prisha starting to stiffen next to her.

Jasmine sits up, as if that might stem it, keeping her head dipped over her bent knees. These sorts of tears are usually just a short burst, a release of a release. But if anything, she seems to be crying harder now, like some blockage has been cleared and a whole river is bursting through.

Jasmine squeezes her eyes shut – *get a fucking grip on yourself* – as, next to her, she's dimly aware of Prisha putting her pants and her little green T-shirt back on. *Ah, good, another one fleeing the bedroom. Driven away. Brilliant . . .*

But instead of running off, Prisha reaches out a tentative hand.

'Hey...Are you...are you sure you're OK? Is this...is this still a...sex thing?'

Jasmine shakes her head.

'I'm – I'm sorry...' she manages between hot, increasingly snotty streams that she furiously tries to wipe away with both hands. In attempting to hold in a sob, Jasmine ends up making the sort of lowing sound you might expect more of a farm animal.

It is absolutely excruciating. Her toes clench painfully, still under the duvet.

But when Jasmine shoots a watery sideways glance at Prisha, her face – rather than looking judgey or freaked out – is carefully held still with a watchful neutrality.

'You do not need to apologise. OK?' Prisha grabs Jasmine's shoulder and gives it a gentle squeeze, and then reaches behind her for a packet of tissues in a bag down the side of the bed and passes them. 'Let it all out, girl. You obviously need a good cry. So go on – just...*go for it.*'

And there's an understanding little smile, and it is this that really gets Jasmine...

She does let go. Her shoulders shake. The torrents continue. Her eyes and the rim of her nose hurt from the salt, and the back of her throat aches with it. And she lets out a full-blown howl on an exhalation, a sound that Jasmine thinks she hasn't made since she was a tiny kid, after falling and scraping all the skin off both knees, or when she lost her beloved soft blue teddy in the park.

She dispatches every tissue in the pack, trying to mop herself up. And Prisha just sits silently with her.

'There you go,' Prisha says, when the tears dry up, quite suddenly, and Jasmine finally feels as if she's coming back to herself. She notices the close, dusty, cardboard smell of the attic; a faint hint of some sweeter, woody scent coming from Prisha.

Jasmine looks up at her then, and clearly her agony of embarrassment must be painted over every feature, because Prisha immediately holds up a mockingly admonishing finger.

'Uh-uh-uh – none of that please. You're OK. Nothing to be embarrassed about, we all need a good bawl now and then.'

Jasmine nods obediently, and fumbles to find her glasses, and the room seems to pulls back into shape too. She heaves the duvet up around her a bit more.

'Do you need anything else?' Prisha asks. 'A glass of water? I think I have a bottle in the backpack I dumped up here earlier actually . . .' She rootles around down the side of the bed again and proffers a zebra-print aluminium bottle to Jasmine, who drinks obediently.

There's a pause, as Jasmine turns the bottle in her hands. She can feel Prisha watching her. Probably desperate to leave, but feeling like she ought to make sure she's not suicidal or something.

'That's never happened before – I swear,' Jasmine offers. She puts the water bottle down on the bed.

'Do you . . .' Prisha pauses. 'I mean – do you want to talk about it?' Her voice is impeccably neutral. And Jasmine wonders for a second why this woman has learned to speak like that: so evenly, so non-judgementally.

Jasmine takes a wobbly breath in, then out. She feels exhausted, as if someone had just shaken her very hard. But also like she's unloosened something.

'I mean, like, I really *do* cry after sex sometimes – because it is good, and I mean, it was *so good* – so I think that, um, set me off – but it's . . . it's like it let out something else, too?'

Then Jasmine's thoughts are suddenly sprinting ahead of

themselves again, as usual, worrying over every possible angle of interpretation of a situation – what if this lovely Prisha thinks it is in some way to do with her? What if she feels guilty, or bad? *Oh God . . .*

'It's not – it's not your fault – I mean, *obviously* it's not your fault, but I mean it's not anything to do with you or what you did . . .'

Jasmine's hands flutter till she runs out of breath, and she peeks up at Prisha. There's just a tiny hint of amusement in the corners of her mouth, her metallic dimples.

'OK, remember to breathe please!' she says, and lays hands on Jasmine's shoulders. 'And . . . rel*aaax*.'

Prisha rearranges herself on the groaning bed, sitting crossed legged. There's a large but intricate mandala tattoo at the top of her right thigh, and another tiny, delicate one on her left inner thigh: a single drifting seed from a dandelion clock. It's lovely – the sort of tattoo Jasmine would quite like to get herself.

'Look, you don't have to explain yourself to me. I'm all good. I had a nice time.' Prisha smiles, more generously than Jasmine thinks she really deserves. 'We can just go back downstairs, or I can book you an Uber, or you can rest up here for a bit. Whatever. But just – if you *do* want to talk through . . . whatever it is that's upsetting you – then go for it.'

Jasmine nods, and then shuffles so she's cross-legged too, opposite Prisha, swathing the duvet around her shoulders now like a cloak. For a minute she fiddles with a braid, rubbing her finger over and over its tripling surface, as she tries to find the words.

'It was . . . a guy I was seeing. I think I was maybe . . .' Jasmine stops, tilting her head as she reaches for honesty. 'No, not maybe. I definitely *was* in love with him. First time I've been in love.'

She smiles despite herself. 'It really felt like it was, I dunno, just *meant to be.*'

'But then. The other day. We were having sex. And . . .' Jasmine can feel water brimming in her eyes again. 'He was . . . he was not himself, somehow? I don't know quite how to explain it. It was like he was . . . *possessed,* or something.'

She has tried, repeatedly, to describe to friends what exactly it had been like, the words *bad sex* not really conveying how disorientating it had been. Or how it was less about the sex itself, and more about how that delicate, intimate bond between them just seemed to fray and splinter.

As if Si had just stopped seeing her at all.

'So, he was going a bit . . . a bit too hard and fast for a second. But it's not like he hurt me. Really it was more *how* he was? Like, his attitude towards me? It was kind of weirdly . . . blank, and absent? It was like it wasn't Si. Or at least, not *my* Si.'

And a strange guilt washes over Jasmine briefly, at even saying his name out loud in this story, and she starts talking very fast again, her hand balling into a fist and pressing into her breastbone. 'Because he's not like that – he's honestly, oh God, he's just like this quiet, sweet soul, not at all like other guys, he's always so tentative and gentle and respectful and I thought he was different and I thought he – he – I thought he *loved* me—'

The tears are definitely back again, and Prisha leans forward in a wrapping hug, checking quietly *is this OK* as she does it, and Jasmine just nods a lot.

'And then what happened . . .' asks Prisha, so softly it's almost not like a question, just merely a murmur of an invitation to continue, if she wants to.

'It was so weird! He just suddenly . . . stopped. And he – he didn't say anything. He just looked at me – and he had this strange look in his eyes – like this *horror,* this total horror, this *disgust—*'

Jasmine feels herself shaking slightly, and Prisha's arms squeeze tightly round her.

'And he just, like, fucked off. Ran out of the room, and didn't message me or explain or try to talk to me – and I just don't understa-a-a-and...' The final word turns into another sob and Prisha gently rocks her, till it subsides, and Jasmine sniffs and snorts unappealingly, like a little piglet with a cold, she thinks.

It is a shame that someone who, mere moments earlier, clearly thought of her as hot now appears to think she needs to be mothered. But it is also extremely comforting.

'Thank you,' she mutters, thickly.

'That's OK.' Prisha sighs deeply, and pulls back. 'That sounds really confusing. And he hasn't been in touch?'

Jasmine shakes her head. 'Nope. Fully ghosted. I was shook. Like, I just wish I knew what I *did—*'

Prisha's eyebrows shoot upwards. 'Hey. None of that. I know you know this, but this is not your fault, OK? And it sounds like maybe this guy has some stuff of his own going on. And it's really upsetting when someone turns out not to be who you think they are... or even just to be capable of behaving in a way you would never have expected of them...'

Prisha pauses, then resumes, with added certainty. 'But that's not on you, yeah?'

Jasmine nods, and tries to wipe her nose surreptitiously on the edge of the duvet.

'And have you... have *you* tried to talk to him?' asks Prisha.

Jasmine shrugs. She hasn't, something she suddenly feels sheepish about. Like her reaction has been a bit immature. Her friends have encouraged her to message him, or to corner him at school, to grandly demand an explanation – but somehow she just hasn't known quite what to ask.

Her! Usually so articulate, so full of words . . . but she's been left stumped. Speechless. As if his own silence has also washed over her, inertia like a thick white heavy blanket.

'No, not really. I . . .' Flustered, Jasmine feels she ought to offer some kind of explanation, her pitch rising and her words speeding up. 'I guess, I just keep hoping he'll message, or come over at school and—'

Jasmine stops. She can feel a guilty look slowly creeping all over her features. And there's a horrid silent moment, where she thinks she can also see the cogs turning in Prisha's mind.

'*School*. Right.' Another pause. 'And how . . . how old are you exactly, if you don't mind me asking?'

Jasmine dips her head. 'Eighteen.'

She feels Prisha recalibrating the situation more than she really sees it, hears a release of air. Then a laugh, higher than her others.

'OK! I did not . . . I did not realise that, bab.' Her accent seems to flare momentarily.

'Um, yeah. Just finishing, actually. I go to uni in a few months?'

Prisha nods to herself, smiling, private.

'Well, I'm sure . . . I'm sure you'll have a lovely time. And to be honest, better to be free and single when you start a new life there anyway.'

Jasmine feels she's losing her. But she doesn't know what to say.

She isn't sure if Prisha is the sort of person who would be impressed by Cambridge, or think of it as stuffy, establishment. Too straight and white and dull.

Prisha runs a finger around the patterns of the edge of the

duvet, her gaze cast down. Her nose crinkles up, as she asks her next question: 'Was that . . . was that your first time with a woman?'

And now Jasmine can allow her indignation to blaze, righteously.

'*No,*' she says, with a scowling vehemence that makes Prisha look up.

'OK!' She raises her hands, an instinctive backing off.

Jasmine huffs the duvet further round her shoulders as she raises herself up within it, and gazes back at her, a little haughtily. *Fucking millennials.*

'What, you think that I have one bad experience with a man with a dick and go running into the arms of a safe cuddly woman?' Jasmine allows the scorn to drip from her words. 'Did you think this was, like, a *trauma* fuck?'

Prisha seems to pull back into herself, her smile turning defensive.

'Most of the people I've slept with have been women!' Jasmine can hear herself, too shrill, trying to sound more experienced than she is. But she can't help the urge, to puff herself up after everything. To prove she's not some fragile little baby.

'Why would you assume I was just a sad straight girl? I'm pansexual, actually.'

Jasmine thinks she sees just a tiny sliver of a smile, and then Prisha composes her expression.

'OK. I'm sorry. You're right – that was a big assumption. It's just . . .'

Jasmine waits, her gaze direct on Prisha now, spine straight.

'It's just, well, eighteen is quite young to know that! I'd not even shagged anyone at your age, let alone worked out whether I liked women or men—'

'I like *everyone*,' interrupts Jasmine hotly. 'I don't judge on—'

'Gender, yes, believe me, I do know what pan-fucking-sexual means.' A little flicker of impatience briefly darkens the light in Prisha's eyes, and instantly Jasmine wants to appease her again, to always please her. Wants those eyes always to be full of light only.

'Well, anyway. I'm glad it wasn't that. And I'm glad . . .' Prisha pauses, casts a look up to the sloping ceiling, and Jasmine wonders, suddenly, what she was like as a teenager. 'I'm just glad you know yourself so well, already. It's amazing, not to have to go through any . . . *shit* about that, on top of this other stuff with that guy.'

Jasmine tries to imagine a young inexperienced Prisha: shy and uncomfortable and not-having-sex. Or just a good girl, maybe: a swot, well-behaved. And she thinks: how did she get *here* from *there*? Must've been university. That promised 'transformative experience'.

The image of Cambridge seems to loom, briefly, in Jasmine's mind. Yellow carved walls, neat squares of green. Gowns and long tables overlooked by portraits of dead white men. Her father's unspoken concerns about what it might be like there, for her.

But also, all that possibility. All those new people.

There better be people like her there. Better be people like *Prisha*.

'Did you have a hard time working stuff out when you were my age then – with your, like, your family and stuff?' Jasmine asks quickly, wanting to keep the conversation going.

But one of Prisha's eyebrows shoots up contemptuously. Her piercings seem to wink at Jasmine, whose face immediately gets hot.

'*Now* who's making assumptions!' Prisha chides with her low, knowing laugh, grabbing at the water bottle and passing it lightly from hand to hand a few times before removing the cap. She swigs at the water, almost triumphant.

Jasmine groans and apologises and pulls a bit of duvet over her head. Completely mortified. *Again*.

'Ah, it's OK,' says Prisha lightly. 'To be honest, my dad's side of the family would not exactly be delighted – but I don't really see them anyway. But my mum ... well, my mum was practically *pleased* that I prefer women, I think. She found herself, as a proper second-wave feminist, you know the type. Or maybe you're too young? What are you, like, fifth wave? Ninth?'

Jasmine feigns outrage, but wants to press on. 'Are you close with your mum, then?'

'Yeah, very. I mean, she raised me by herself mostly. Only child. So I guess it has been quite an ... intense relationship.'

Prisha pauses, her eyes sliding upwards towards the ceiling again, as she rearranges a piercing on her left ear. Jasmine wants to get close to her, to snuggle up with her while they talk about all these intimate things, but she wonders if that's over now.

'It's cool that she's a proper feminist and, like, chill about stuff though ...' she offers, a vague prompt to get Prisha to keep talking.

'Yeah. Well. Yeah. She's always been keen to get to know my girlfriends – partners ...'

The words stop, and it's like Prisha has disappeared somewhere else, somewhere private, and Jasmine doesn't know if she is allowed to ask, to follow. She wants to. She wants to know everything about Prisha. But she also doesn't quite know *how* to ask.

Prisha absent-mindedly bounces the water bottle up and down on the mattress in time with the muffled music coming up from the floors below. Then seems to deliberately throw the conversational ball back into Jasmine's lap.

'What about you?' Prisha asks. 'Have you – can you – talk to *your* mum about this break up?'

Jasmine rolls her eyes, and shakes her head. Bernie has certainly asked. But Jasmine has been uncharacteristically closed off about it all, irritable and resentful of her mum's intrusions – all her offers of hugs and cups of cocoa and walks in the park. She's seen the hurt in her mum's eyes as she's withdrawn instead of softening under any of these loving suggestions; normally, Jasmine talks to her mum about everything.

Well. Not *everything*. Although her mum has always prided herself on being open-minded, the rules and boundaries have always been very clear too – and Jasmine had broken them. *Dis-res-pect-ful*, she could just hear her mum saying, on an icy inhale. And she doesn't know how to tell her mum what happened without admitting that she and Si had been sleeping together, in her room, while her mum was out at bloody Waitrose.

'No, I haven't talked to her,' Jasmine says. 'I dunno . . .'

She blows a long stream of air out of her lips. She can't exactly tell Prisha that she is scared of getting in trouble for having a boy in her room – it would make her sound like a *child*.

'Maybe . . . maybe it would help?' Prisha's voice is very gentle. Then she smiles, and knocks the bottle gently towards Jasmine. 'You don't wanna keep all this stuff inside, eh, or it'll come out at some *really* inopportune moment, you know . . .'

'Like when I'm with some mysterious sexy stranger?' Jasmine tries to match her in looking all wry and knowing.

'Well, *exactly*,' laughs Prisha. 'Seriously though. You should probably even – sorry, you don't *mind* me giving you the benefit of my aged and decrepit wisdom do you . . . ?'

Jasmine waves, faux loftily, as if permitting her to continue.

'Well, you should probably even try to speak to *him*. This

guy. He might just be really, like, ashamed – and awkward? And not know how to start the conversation. I know it's more emotional labour for you blah blah blah, but you might feel . . . *freer*, afterwards. Able to move on.'

'"Closure",' says Jasmine, doing air quotes and a bad American accent.

'Yeah. Yeah! I mean, whatever is going on, it's better to just *know*, isn't it? Get it out the way, before you head off to university. But also, it might be not that bad? And you know, if it is "meant to be" between the two of you,' – Prisha does her own mocking little air quotes, but her smile is genuine – 'well, then even if he *did* do something wrong – and it might now seem like the worst thing in the world and totally unforgiveable . . .'

Prisha disappears again momentarily, and Jasmine feels the beginnings of a fiery indignation roar up inside her, at the thought that anyone might have ever dared wrong Prisha, ever dared treat her badly.

'I mean, stupid mistakes happen. We fuck up. But we can also mend them.' Prisha's hand is loosely, distractedly tracing over the pattern of the one dandelion clock seed tattoo, as it floats across her thigh. 'And also – sometimes those mistakes don't have to be mistakes – they can be, like . . . *signposts*. Pointing you towards a different kind of relationship, or . . .'

Oh, *great*, thinks Jasmine. Not *this*.

And she fixes her gaze on Prisha firmly.

'Are you trying to suggest that if Si was freaking out because *he* was cheating on *me*, that *I* should forgive him and that *I* should make it OK by *allowing it* – by making the relationship "open" or something?' More air quotes. 'Because: No way. No thanks. I respect myself a bit too much for any of . . . *that shit*.'

Jasmine hopes Prisha isn't about to launch into some wise old diatribe about *when you're older, and have more experience, you'll see things aren't always so black and white...*

Because she is already well aware that, yes, life is long and people in long-term relationships seem to love cheating on each other. And that some of the cleverer ones have found frameworks to explain away this cheating. But as far as she's concerned, 'relationship anarchy' and 'ethical non-monogamy' are all just a big excuse for being selfish. She and her friends have already encountered enough polyamorous feminist fuckbois, shamelessly abusing terminology in order to justify sleeping around, to feel really quite firm on this (Olivia has a particularly well-honed, funny rant about the topic).

And besides, love *does* seem black and white to Jasmine.

'If you love someone, be with them. And if you love them, don't fuck other people. It's pretty straightforward. If you're not even willing to give that up, is it . . . is it *really love*?' Jasmine tilts her head, as if pondering the question, although it is obvious what her answer is.

'Well actually—'

'I just think—'

They both start speaking at the same time, and laugh.

'You go,' says Prisha, almost indulgently.

'I was going to say: I just think it is *sad,* that anyone should have to compromise so much that they let their partner sleep with other people . . .'

Prisha meets her gaze, and her eyes look very bright and glossy. And then there's a strange, held moment between them, where their eye-contact seems to have some kind of charge to it again – a vibrating anticipation, a crackle – and Jasmine isn't sure if Prisha is about to lunge in and kiss her again, or maybe to recoil and shout something at her—

But then Prisha just reaches for her phone from down the

side of the bed, as if it had made a noise – which Jasmine doesn't think it did – and she's quickly looking at the screen and calmly reading something there.

In the void of anti-climax, Jasmine obviously begins to panic about what she'd said. *Was she too vehement – might she have offended lovely Prisha – maybe she was . . .*

'I'm sorry – you don't have to agree – I mean—'

But Prisha airily waves her away, tells her she's fine, and she also begins to get up off the bed to locate the rest of her clothes. And she's smiling a big smile so Jasmine tells herself that it probably *is* all fine, and tries to shake off a sense of doing the wrong thing.

Maybe she had sounded naive. Too young, idealistic.

As Prisha stands up to refasten her trousers, she points at her phone on the bed, vaguely. 'My friends are wondering where I've got to. And . . . look – you seem to be doing OK now? Do you . . . do you feel up for rejoining the party? Getting back out there?'

Jasmine nods her head up and down, very fast, as if to override all that's happened, to prove she's fine, fine, totally fine. Besides, it is time to get back to the party. She wonders how Flo is doing.

And actually, she . . . she *does* feel lighter, somehow. Unburdened, without all those tears sloshing around saltily inside her.

'Course. Um, yeah. Let's go.'

Jasmine excavates bits of clothing from around the bed and floor. She worries that she's cried all her make-up off, but doesn't want to ask Prisha somehow. Too vain.

Then Prisha holds out a hand, and Jasmine takes it, and allows herself to be pulled up and off the bed, so they are standing face to face.

And Prisha keeps hold of her fingers for just a moment,

and gives a squeeze of encouragement. Jasmine wonders if she knows just how brilliant she is. But before she can find a non-cringe way of expressing that, Prisha has let go and is turning to head downstairs.

As they pick their way back through the crowds, Jasmine can't help but notice how Prisha is keeping her head down, almost as if they aren't together. It stings a little.

Well fine then. They're done. Jasmine will make her escape as soon as she sees Flo.

And yes, there – there she is. As they round a corner of the stairs, Jasmine spies her, just inside the front room, skinny little arms raised heavenwards and a massive grin bisecting her face. And Jasmine feels another rush of love for her friend. Flo might bat her eyelashes or deploy coy giggles, but at least she never pretends to be cool; she never hides her enthusiasm or excitement about life. It just shines off her.

She's dancing with Elly – no sign of Leon. *Good*, thinks Jasmine selfishly. Maybe he had also worked out she was eighteen.

But mostly it is good because Jasmine just wants her friend now – wants the two of them to be together.

'FLO!' she yells, hopelessly, over Prisha's head.

And Prisha glances behind her, then follows Jasmine's eyeline, and quickly looks away. Then, she steps aside and waves Jasmine towards the dancing, towards her friend. It is an exaggerated but gracious gesture, although Jasmine thinks she can see a hint of something in the glint of her eyes, her dimples.

But she doesn't worry about any of that now, she just grins and rushes towards her friend, barrelling into her, both arms round Flo's bony ribs, shouting *Flo, I found you, I missed you—*

'Jas!'

And the two are spinning together, and now it's them being unselfconsciously clumsy, knocking into people on the dance floor and laughing.

They twirl into each other, and mirror each other's happy little dance moves, and shout updates into each other's ears that will – they know – be much expanded upon on the way home, and probably for the rest of the summer, tales made taller and grander and more impressive with the retelling. But for now – for now, in this bright present – they just laugh at each other's audaciousness, Flo even more excited that Jasmine had pulled than she is about Leon taking her number.

'GOOD – I THINK IT'S A GOOD THING,' shouts Flo. 'YOU DESERVE SOME FUN! MAYBE IT'S GOOD TO BE SINGLE NOW! I JUST WANT TO SEE YOU HAPPY – I LOVE YOU SO MUCH, YOU DO KNOW THAT DON'T YOU ...'

And so on, in this vein, for some time.

Once they are fully updated on their romantic achievements and fully briefed on how much they really do each mean to one another, and once Flo has located her make-up bag and very carefully and tenderly redone Jasmine's cried-off make-up, they both stop and stand still for a second. And they look into each other's faces in the half-light of the party, and grip and squeeze each other's hands with an earnest seriousness that must say all the things they feel that go beyond the words, and beyond the present – shooting forward into their unknown future, into unknown freedoms.

It is a recognition, that one chapter is coming to an end and another is about to begin. That they are just teetering on the brink of something: of new lives, new selves, new friends, new loves, all the excitement and all the terror of being free to be whoever they want to be. A newness that they are so ready for, and not ready for, at the same time, and that is coming for them anyway. It is a recognition that they have begun that transition, somehow, this shimmering night. A new start. Just shining shining shining...

Chapter 5

Prisha

'Good morning, sleepy head.'

There is a moment – a moment that is long and sticky with sleep, but also just a flashing second – where it is just one more morning like the long chain of all the other mornings, waking up together in their home, their bed. The scent of JB's coffee. The distant burble of Radio 4. The light cracking intrusively through the centre of the blackout curtains that Prisha prefers.

Then the previous night crashes back in. The girl – Jasmine – a flush, full memory of her taste – then a grinding memory – *eighteen* – her tears . . .

Prisha groans internally.

JB bends down to put the tea on the bedside table, and kisses her forehead. Prisha keeps her eyes shut. Groans, externally.

'Oh dear.' JB opens the curtains. *Cruel.* Everything goes red behind Prisha's eyelids. She is vaguely aware of JB getting back into bed beside her, the balance of the shoddy mattress recalibrating with their weight, as they bring their coffee with them, the smell settling over Prisha like an extra duvet.

JB always brings Prisha tea to make up for the fact that they are waking her up when she would invariably rather sleep. But although Prisha often complains, she's always been rather fond of the ritual. A little daily proof that, even as a confirmed morning person, JB is bored without her, would rather she was awake.

Prisha tries opening her eyes. It is far too bright. She scrunches her face, nose crumpling. Then rolls over instead, snuffling her face into JB's side, into the material of the loose shorts they wear in bed.

JB's fingers reach down and scratch her skull.

Prisha has a headache.

She remembers the bottle of wine she grabbed from the kitchen as soon as she'd seen Jasmine cheerfully reunited with her friend (who really did look like a teenager, all nobbling limbs like a baby giraffe; as soon as she saw them together she wondered how she could ever have assumed Jasmine was close to her age). She'd drunk it too fast, hiding in Nia's room, as Nia and Clio tossed out reassurances like handfuls of confetti, designed to make Prisha feel better – whether she deserved to or not.

'Morning.' Prisha manages, into the flesh where JB's hip becomes bum.

'Oh *dear,*' laughs JB, with their scratchy, hoarse laugh that hints at their terrible roll-up habit. 'Good night then?'

Prisha grunts an assent. Pauses. A new pounding of dread.

'Did I wake you up, coming in?'

'Yeah, but only as you got into bed. I just went straight back to sleep.'

'OK. Good.' A pause. 'I didn't want to . . . *chat*, did I?'

JB's laugh again. 'No, thankfully, the discourse was not engaged. You were out like a light. Said the taxi driver had to wake you up when you got home too.'

And *relief.*

'Oh well, that explains why I barely remember getting in then. I was asleep. Too much red wine.'

Prisha feels hot and throws off the covers, then gets a bit of a chill when a breeze breaks through the window, and then feels like she simply must eat soon, and then remembers her tea. She pushes herself up, attempts to smooth down some hair sticking up in various strange peaks, and sinks immediately back down into her pillows, holding her mug. *Tea.*

It is too hot to drink.

'Which pig are you?' she asks JB. Prisha's favourite tea-mug has a selection of cartoon pigs on it, all different breeds, and with an array of fairly deranged expressions. Every morning, she asks JB which one they feel most spiritually aligned to.

They consider the options carefully, as they do every morning, despite having chosen a pig, what – hundreds of times? Thousands?

'I think I am the British Lop,' says JB. 'I'm quite eager for this sunny Sunday, but also it is a bit *hot*, so I'm hiding my little smile and shading my eyes under my big piggy ear.'

Prisha continues to spin the mug slowly in her hands.

'I think I . . . am . . .' She alights on a tubby, doleful, head-hanging black-and-white pig. 'Ohhh yes. I am the Wessex. I simply cannot lift my head. It is too heavy with headache.'

'Ah, but you have lifted it. Look at you, sitting up in bed!' JB pats her hand with mildly patronising affection. 'You're doing *so well*. Now have some of these and stop complaining.'

They rootle in a bedside drawer and proffer paracetamol, and their own glass of water (Prisha's is empty, she must've drunk it all in the night). She puts down her tea, snaps the packet, swallows obediently, and is rewarded with a proper kiss. Her mouth feels cool from the water, and she enjoys the contrast as it meets JB's warm, toasty coffee taste.

It's the only way Prisha likes the taste of coffee, on JB's tongue. The taste of soft mornings; of afternoon interruptions

135

when working from home, or after-dinner overtures, invitations to bed.

Prisha's arm begins to snake across JB's body.

'Mm, maybe a shower for you, first,' they say, not unkindly, but ensuring Prisha seeks comfort only as she snuggles down into them, head resting on JB's pleasingly defined bicep, the result of their work in the bike shop.

'Maybe. May be. May well be! Then all may be well . . .' Prisha often finds herself burbling nonsense when hungover. Occasionally, her wordplay even makes it into JB's poems. Well, it did once, anyway, in one of their Protest series ('Disturb the peace /Disturb the police /Make noise /A noise a noise a noise that /Annoys /Those who prefer polite silence').

Her hand is resting in its usual comfortable place on JB's hip, a groove and grip as natural as around a warm mug. But then, floating upwards, the memory of Jasmine's hips. That more exaggerated curve. Something about Jasmine's hips seemed almost deliberate, like it was decided on by an artist, the sculptural shape of it. Flesh firm as if carved out of some smooth material.

So young, thinks Prisha, in a flare of guilt.

She has to tell JB about Jasmine. She knows that.

Let the tea go down first. A shower. Maybe some food.

She will tell them.

Prisha sits back up, slurps at her pig mug. A bird (she doesn't know what kind) is cheeping insistently on the scraggly tree (she doesn't know what kind that is either) that just about reaches the window of their second-floor bedroom. It ought to be soothing, but she wonders if it is in fact one of those birds she read about in the paper, that have lived in cities too long and started evolving to mimic urban sounds. Car alarms and ambulance sirens and revving motorcycles.

Typical, that their neighbourhood bird would decide it was a *car alarm.*

They've talked – of course they have – about finding somewhere else, somewhere with a garden instead of just the world's tiniest balcony. Maybe they could move out of Hulme, and rent in one of Manchester's greener suburbs or even some sweet village in the Peaks, Hope or Edale or Castleton. JB had dashed off a silly poem about it, titled *My girlfriend wants to live in Hope,* and then reminded Prisha – a lifelong city-dweller – that she finds countryside quietness 'creepy'. That she considers it a human right to be able to buy a bottle of Campo Viejo at 2 a.m., and to be in striking distance of shops that stock ramen and methi and Ben & Jerry's.

'Right. I'm going to make breakfast,' says JB decisively. 'Shakshuka? Or pancakes?'

'Ooh. Both sound good. Do we have enough paprika for shakshuka? I think I used most of it the other night.'

'Did you put it on the list?'

Prisha grimaces guiltily, and JB rolls their eyes before decisively getting out of bed.

'Pancakes it is then. I'm too hungry even to go to the shop.'

'You can check, there might be enough . . .' Prisha lets the words fall away as JB is heading already into the kitchen.

'Get in the bloody shower!' JB shouts back at her. But there is an indulgence in their voice, marshmallowy and springy below their exasperation, and Prisha reflects – as she often does, usually when she's fucked up in some small, mildly irritating way – how lucky she is, having JB. How much she simply likes living with JB. No other relationship she's ever had has been as easy. Between them, the little things stay little. The snipes and gripes that had led to other relationships dying, bleeding out via a thousand paper-cut wounds (*running late again* or *not emptying the bin*), simply never break the skin with her and JB.

The relationship is grown-up, Prisha supposes. But there is also a real sweetness to it, to their ease. Something to be savoured.

She presses her fingers around her pig mug – their pig mug – and for just a shiver of a moment, fears she's gripped too hard. Imagines the thin porcelain cracking into pieces in her hands. What would their mornings be without it, without their little habits and rituals?

Hurriedly, she puts it back down on the bedside table and launches herself towards the bathroom.

The sun is shining fiercely even through the window's frosted glass, illuminating Prisha's massive jar of coconut oil, liquid in the heat. The shower trickles over her, the pressure so feeble it runs off her thick hair until she gets in there with her hands, sudding the stale smoky smell out of it. Washing the previous evening away.

But Prisha doesn't want to think about the previous evening right now, or the conversation she needs to have with JB. Instead, that tempting summer brightness leads her to direct her thoughts instead back to their garden situation – or lack thereof. Because it would be nice, in weather like this, to have somewhere they could go out and sit in, wouldn't it. That had room for more than just a few drying, dying pots.

They really should do something about it. The balcony currently is basically a glorified ashtray; it blooms only with JB's cigarette butts. Even Prisha's attempts to grow herbs out there have been thwarted. Sad, stunted things. She's embarrassed whenever JB's mother, Ally, comes over for a visit; Ally's garden is remarkable, sprawling and tangling over half a low hillside behind a barn conversion near Skipton, tended to by slug-hungry ducks.

And the house itself is a huge, ramshackle place, freezing and often leaking, but also stuffed with the wide array of instruments collected by Peter, JB's father, and with Ally's artworks. She makes blobby, voluptuous sculptures, which had made her no money at all for years but had just recently started selling like wild fire via Instagram. The house is stuffed, too, with waifs and strays – from JB's younger sister Bea and her kid Milo to Anas, a Syrian refugee they'd offered a room to. The back door is always open; both the ducks, and the fat dog, Donovan, waddle in and out of the flagstoned kitchen.

Not long after Prisha and JB had first met – six years ago now, at a drag night hosted by Candy de Thrush in the basement of a dingy Northern Quarter bar – JB had announced that they were 'even more broke than usual' and going back to live with their parents in their farmhouse for a while.

Prisha had initially been surprised. She might be used to hearing from her own mother about various cousins who moved back into the family home after university or when they had their own kids; she was used to swerving the suggestion nestled up in those stories. But JB hadn't seemed the type somehow. Prisha hadn't thought grown-up middle-class white kids ever really wanted to move back in with their parents. And although she could smell her own mum's yearning for a multi-generational household, and although she loves her mum with a fierce, protective love . . . the idea of moving back in with her had never seriously crossed Prisha's mind. She'd be smothered. It was hard to breathe there.

Lavanya calls Prisha on the phone most days, and they still have a habit of finishing each other's sentences or collapsing into mutual peals of laughter in exactly the same way, at exactly the same time. But it is a love that can also burn hot with guilt (at not visiting enough) or exasperation (at the way her mother bombards Prisha with questions quickly followed by judgments) or simply with a kind of aching concern – so wanting her mum to be happy, so wanting not to have to be solely responsible for that!

Not long after JB had moved home, Prisha was invited over for the night. Which she had also been surprised by: it seemed too soon in their relationship to meet the parents, or to see JB's childhood bedroom. But she quickly realised that her presence barely registered as more significant than the neighbours popping in for lunch, or a visiting kora-player dropping round to give Peter a lesson. There was something blissfully egalitarian about their open house: no fussing or special treatment, just the expectation that all guests should get stuck in – contributing to the conversation, helping stir a pot or play with Milo, partaking of endless cups of tea.

And something about JB's understated, attractive self-assurance suddenly made sense, snapping into place like a jigsaw piece for Prisha. The way they were able to find common ground with anyone, but were also able to calmly disagree with anyone. The way they were able to ask for what they wanted, and not feel ashamed about that. No wonder JB was like that, with such a solid foundation: a whole bedrock of people who loved you whoever you decided you were, whatever you did; who would not be thrown by any choices or mistakes you made in life.

Of course, Prisha has also heard about the tougher times – the dulled, uncertain years in JB's teens and twenties, when they hadn't yet figured it all out; when despite not quite knowing themselves, they were still somehow a discernible target for idiots at school, or cruel strangers on the bus. A deliberate defiance towards those who once tried to drag them down is also part of the structure that makes JB so strong. But the knowledge that they are wholly loved and lovable certainly helps.

Prisha lets the towel fall off her onto their unmade bed, and gets dressed in her lightest, loosest pair of dungarees, a cheery turquoise colour, over a mustard-yellow T-shirt. She's halfway to the kitchen when she remembers the towel.

She goes back, retrieves it and hangs it back up in the puddled bathroom. Doesn't want to test JB's seemingly endless patience. Not today.

The smell of warm butter coaxes her into the kitchen, where JB is presiding over the hob with a fish slice. The light is softer in here, diffuse; for a moment, it seems to Prisha it is radiating from the yellow roses she'd got on yellow-sticker discount in Tesco, now opened out and practically glowing in a repurposed jar in the centre of their tiny kitchen table.

'Smells amazing.'

'More tea for you there, little yak,' JB says, as they flip a pancake.

Little yak is JB's nickname for her, has been ever since a bout of teasing when Prisha got petulantly grumpy about the fact that Lucy & Yak dungarees had become a 'bloody uniform' for all the young lesbians in Manchester, insisting that they were *her thing* first. Snorting and stamping. *Grumpy little yak.*

'Thank you for the tea. And the pancakes.' Prisha winds her arms around JB's waist, and gives a small huff into the place where neck meets shoulder. Such a well-defined shoulder, she thinks, the blades sharp compared to her own padded torso. She suddenly has the desire to squish herself against JB, her boobs and belly pressing into their firmer back. A small series of too-rapid kisses, in a neat line around the base of the neck, below their cap of close-cropped fur. A buzz-cut on the longest setting, that still gives Prisha delicious little shivers down her spine whenever she strokes it.

JB cranes over their shoulder, tilting their face down, lips inviting the final kiss to land there. Prisha keeps her eyes shut as she delivers it.

'Feeling better?'

'Masses, actually,' says Prisha, breaking out of the embrace and trying to keep her voice sounding normal. 'I'd forgotten how gross it is when millions of people smoke inside, it's like it bloody *clings* to the sweat and your hair and everything. But now I feel cool, and fresh!'

'Well, I'm sure you'll be sweating again before too long, it is *baking*.'

'I know! I'm in the five-minute temperate-bliss window. Enjoy the lack of complaining while you can.'

Prisha gratefully takes the pig mug – which JB must have fetched while she was in the shower to refill for her – and sits on one of their fold-out wooden chairs. Her head feels clearer too, but a little light; she's suddenly ravenous.

But she also feels the presence of looming pressure, the undeclared knowledge of *what-happened-last-night* swelling like a balloon inside her, pressing with its need to be let out.

Prisha's stomach growls.

She'll tell JB after the food, she bargains with herself.

'Have you got the fucking oven on? Jay-Beeeee, what the hell!'

JB turns round, waves the fish slice admonishingly. 'Complaints, already! That was nowhere near five minutes!' They return to the oven, pull out a plate already stacked. 'It's only on low, just to keep the pancakes warm. I know how long you can take in the shower.'

'Actually, I was very speedy today, *I* think.'

'Well you were. Very dynamic. Considering.'

Prisha fiddles with the radio, turning it to 6 Music instead of Radio 4's loathed *The Archers* omnibus. Cerys introducing an electro folk-pop song sung in Cornish. Perfect.

'Just going to do a few more, and then we can eat,' says JB, delivering maple syrup and coconut yoghurt and a dripping colander of rinsed blueberries to the table.

'So. How was it then? Give me the full party debrief.'

'It was really fun!'

'Course it was,' says JB with a grin. They'd had no interest in going to a messy house party with lots of younger people, but had encouraged Prisha to go, to enjoy herself.

'It was really packed though, at its height – you could barely squeeze into the kitchen sometimes.'

JB grimaces. 'If I never have to shout small talk in a kitchen at a house party again, I will be absolutely fine with that.'

'Ah, you've got so old and *bor-ing,* JB,' Prisha teases, dragging her fingers down her face so her cheeks become jowled in mocking impersonation. Then she feels another scratchy twinge of conscience, and covers it by getting up suddenly, rattling around in the cutlery drawer.

'Old – yes. Boring – no. I just like to be able to hear myself think, is all,' says JB.

'I know I know I know,' breezes Prisha, as she lays the table. 'Meaningful connection, blah blah blah.'

She sits back down on her chair, allows her eyes to trail across the scrubby backyards and roofs they can see out of the window. The sky above them is a pale shade of blue, as if bleached out by the sun, with a haziness that speaks to this height of summer. And she talks, perhaps just a little too fast, about the party, sharing updates from the sort of acquaintances they normally see two or three times a year. Who actually didn't come because they are now pregnant, or have left Manchester. Updates on closer friends' biggest bits of news: Nia's exciting new girlfriend ('a Green Party councillor, *and* hot, in a Kirsten Stewart kind of way') and Clio and Duncan's adorable new puppy ('a floppy-eared darling little idiot called Mr Scruff').

And then Prisha realises that JB realises she is blathering. And not making eye contact.

'And what else, Prish?' JB turns towards her, hands resting behind their back on the edge of the countertop. One leg bent back against the cupboard door too, as if ready to spring.

The angle means Prisha can see the tattoo on their inner thigh: the dandelion clock, full and round, just one gap as if a single seed has blown away. Blown over, on to her own thigh.

She takes a deep breath.

'Yep, OK.' And then quite loud exhale. 'So something . . . something happened. With someone.'

And she watches JB's calmly impassive face, their features that had been held in a carefully neutral expression, begin to change.

Their face breaking open, cracking, wider . . .

A great big grin.

'Oh my God! Really? Tell me *more!*' The word 'more' extended as JB's hands stretch out as they scamper over towards her, and start wrangling her, almost tickling, Prisha squirming and squeaking slightly.

'I can't believe you've been so bloody coy about this! As if I care about some bloody . . . *cocker spaniel*, when you could be telling me about your own adventures!'

JB retreats, still grinning, and flips the last pancakes onto the stack on the plate, and brings it with debonair speed to the table, before sitting down close to Prisha (the width of their kitchen only allows room for the most intimate of dining anyway) and raising their cutlery expectantly. As if they might be about to conduct the story out of Prisha with a fork.

'Come on then: spill,' says JB as they begin to energetically spear pancakes onto her plate for her. 'Who what where when – did you sleep with them? Or just a kiss?'

Prisha feels the old familiar rush, that spreads right into her fingertips like sap through a tree, a relief and an elation at how JB always reacts like this. So bloody *genuine*: honest delight at the thought of Prisha enjoying herself, simply shining off their open face. The hint of salacious interest, the pleasure taken in hearing tales of her pleasure. And she thinks that maybe everything is going to be OK. This is what they do. This is how they work.

And then she wonders if there was a little relief in there on JB's part too? Because being open had been JB's suggestion. Not even a suggestion, really: a *fait accompli*. A condition of the relationship. Simply *how things were*.

JB was polyamorous, and Prisha had known this by the end of the drag night where they first met, had known it before she'd told JB to drop the rollie they were smoking in the alley outside the bar, so that they could kiss without catching fire ('although we did anyway' being their own cute, gross, private myth).

Through a mouthful of pancake, Prisha begins to talk.

'So . . . her name is Jasmine. I actually just bashed into her on the dance floor – did I mention it was really packed?'

'You did. Go on.' JB bends their knee against Prisha's, encouraging.

'I hit a fresh piercing – it looked pretty sore – and had to apologise.'

'What a meet-cute! So. What was she like?'

'Well, very cute, actually. Quite short, curvy.' Prisha can feel the old muscle flexing, the way she had learned how to speak about encounters with other people: with honesty, but not *too* much detail; positive, but not *too* enthusiastic. A studied objectivity, carefully picking the right words. Calm, neutralising.

'So she had this quite sweet, funny mix of seeming very dreamy and lost in dancing and sort of... I dunno? Shy? Distracted? But then also suddenly quite... *proactive*, in making a move and stuff...'

Prisha pauses, and reaches a hand down to JB's tattoo, wanting to trace its shape, as she so often does; it is beautiful, the tattooist JB favours is a proper artist. So delicate, even though its fine lines have inevitably smudged out with the years. As both their thighs have also spread a little, with the years.

'OK, so: did we have sex? Yes we did. But it was somewhat... aborted.'

'Oh shit.'

Prisha retracts her hand, and returns to pancake slicing as she recounts, without going into it too much, how eager Jasmine had been, how fun it had been, and then realising that she was all upset...

'It wasn't exactly... *ideal*, you know.'

'No indeed. Shit. I'm sure you were great though. And was she OK? What was going on?'

'Yeah – I mean, it turned out to be nothing to do with what was happening between us, or with me—'

'Well, no. Obviously.'

Prisha can't help raising an eyebrow at this. Absolutely classic JB: they never assumed they were the problem; rarely saw other people's issues, their hang-ups, as a shared responsibility. This rationality protected JB, but it could read cold, sometimes, Prisha thought.

'Well, I worried, that I'd upset her somehow...'

JB squeezes her knee. 'After what? Knowing her for, like, five minutes?'

Prisha shrugs in acknowledgement. 'Anyway, turns out she had some shit with her boyfriend – or ex-boyfriend – recently exed. Fucking *men*—' Prisha breaks off, shakes her head. No need to go into all that. There's other things need saying first, anyway.

'But it was also that...'

Yet some things still aren't easy to say. Prisha's tongue seems to hover in her mouth briefly, uncertain.

'It was also that she was super young. Like, eighteen. You know I've always been *terrible* at working out ages—'

'Oh my God, all right Operation Yewtree! Tell it to the judge!' JB laughs, and then winces.

'Fuck. *You*. It was an honest mistake!' Prisha starts lightly punching JB on their thigh, bare below their loose shorts, who play-boxes back at her, before capturing both her wrists. They shake their head and widen their eyes in horrified judgement, but there's a definite smirk in the corner of their lips too.

Prisha shuts her eyes, scrunching her nose.

'That's not even the worst bit.'

'Oh my God, what a time you have had. I let you out for *one* night...' JB drops their arms, sits back on the wooden chair, still amused.

Prisha opens her eyes. 'I didn't tell her. About... us.'

This time, JB's face drops into their neutral look, their active-listening, not-passing-judgement look. The one that Prisha knows is not always dispassionate, after all.

Prisha starts to count the little stems in the dandelion clock, revealed once more by JB's spread-kneed stance. Letting her eyes focus there. Letting the admission, that all morning she has known she would have to make — that she has been dreading making — come out.

'Look, I was going to tell her. Obviously. But it was too loud on the dance floor for proper chat and then we went upstairs and . . . well it—

'It . . .

'It . . .

'It just "all happened so fast"?' The words drip from JB's mouth.

'I mean. Yeah. To be honest . . .'

JB exhales, and turns their head, as if now they are mightily interested in the view out of the window, a big tabby cat stalking along a wall. Presumably trying to catch the insistent bloody car-alarm bird that is making a racket this side of the house too.

'There's always time for honesty, Prish. Or, like, you have to *make* the time.'

They raise their hands to their head, rubbing at the short, golden-brown fuzz there.

'I know I know I know, it was just . . .' Prisha swirls a fork through the maple syrup and yoghurt on her plate, making eddying little patterns, and wonders how honest she *is* being, even now. 'I just got all caught up in it and I just didn't think — didn't think it *mattered* that much. In the moment.'

On the radio, a song helpfully — or perhaps unhelpfully — exhorts Prisha to prioritise her own pleasure. It has been so long, though, since she'd pursued her pleasure with anyone other than JB: Prisha has been in a serious dry patch. Jasmine had been the first person in months and months.

'And then afterwards — she was upset,' Prisha continues. 'And I just — I just didn't want to add to that. Any complication, or confusion. For her to feel bad . . .'

JB is still looking out of the window. 'That isn't your call to make though, is it. You can't predict – you can't ever *know* – how someone else is going to feel. Why assume she'd feel bad? She might've felt *better.'*

Prisha feels as if a lump of the pancake batter might be stuck in her throat; there's a thickness there, something making it hard to swallow.

Because, of course, she does know exactly how Jasmine feels about polyamory. Jasmine couldn't have been more clear – wielding all the righteous moral confidence of an eighteen-year-old experiencing her first heartbreak. Prisha can distantly remember seeing the world in such terms: the black and white, the right and wrong, the unforgiving scorn when people acted stupidly or selfishly. When feelings felt absolute and forever, rather than the bendier, twistier, more complicated shapes they torqued into as she aged.

She pictures Jasmine's face, the certainty etched into it as she haughtily declared *I just think it is sad, that anyone should have to compromise so much.* Not yet realising that it was the compromising that made you stronger, not weaker; that it was compromising that made things last, not fall apart.

Although who is she to claim any kind of strength at this juncture, really, thinks Prisha: she'd completely chickened out of actually trying to explain any of that to Jasmine. Just went back to the party and her friends and a bottle of wine. Because she hadn't trusted herself to find the right words to explain it and celebrate it, hadn't trusted herself to present her relationship with JB in a way that wouldn't appal Jasmine . . .

But wasn't it also that she had suddenly just felt *tired*? So very weary, at the thought of having to school someone in what it really meant to be poly; to explain or justify the way she chose to live. To love.

So she just didn't say anything. Just walked away. It had

seemed like the best thing to do at the time. Now, it just seems *cowardly*.

Prisha has always found this the hardest part of being open: explaining it to other people. It's something JB is brilliant at – people they sleep with or date always seem to feel fine about the situation, as if they can't help but mirror JB's ease and clarity, simply letting go of jealousies. Wasn't that exactly what Prisha had found herself doing too, in the early days, when she thought it would be a problem and was surprised to find it wasn't? Just dropping into this new life, amazed at how simple it was after all – that you could just choose to do things differently, could simply choose not to hoard sex, guard affection, or make scenes.

But when Prisha tried to communicate her poly principles and initiate open honest communication with new partners, things often seemed . . . more *volatile*. She'd done her best, copying JB's voice, doing the reading, learning the lingo. But that didn't always help, and if she was honest, she did understand when women shouted at her for 'hiding her feelings behind theory' or 'talking bullshit'.

If she hooked up with anyone in their queer circle in Manchester it was almost always completely straightforward. But Prisha loved the thrill of the random encounter – the unexpected joy, the shock of connection – and one of the best things about being with JB was being allowed, in good conscience, to kindle any spark that ever flew. And it was these romances that had a tendency to end explosively. Like the woman who got so jealous she had thrown some of the books Prisha had lent her across a room, the corner of *The Ethical Slut* catching one of Prisha's piercings and making it bleed. A story that even JB hadn't been able to stop themselves from laughing at.

Prisha tries to gulp some tea, before realising she's already finished it. She feels like her hangover thirst may never be quenched.

And she sighs her reply to JB, wishing she could just lie down on the sofa and digest the pancakes while watching terrible TV in peace. 'Look, obviously I know I shouldn't make assumptions, but Jasmine was really crying and . . .'

'It was easier to just not bother, I understand.' JB's tone, as they turn to meet Prisha's hungry gaze, is not especially understanding.

Prisha can feel the silly joy and excitement she'd felt, at meeting someone new like that – the electrical jump of the first held eye contact with Jasmine, the delicious anticipation, the tilting experience of kissing lips that were nothing like JB's – beginning to drain away. JB is so laid-back, so indulgent in so many ways – yet fails to do poly properly, and there was no slack whatsoever. Prisha understands why: they've seen friends try open relationships and stumble without scrupulous truthfulness and clear boundaries. It had been a shared, foundational principle for them both, in their relationship: they had promised each other they would always be honest.

'OK, not to excuse it, but I also . . . I think I'm just a bit rusty at all of this, too?' says Prisha. 'I dunno. I've got out of the habit of talking about things, managing those expectations. It's tiring having to persuade people that it's really OK! All that – it's like a muscle, isn't it?'

'Yeah, it is. I get that. But if you want to have the good stuff, you also have to make the effort—'

'It's not that I didn't want to make the effort! It was . . . difficult, OK?' Prisha can hear the strain in her voice.

'Well yeah! Honesty is hard sometimes! But that's the deal, Prish – otherwise you have basically lied to her! And you've—'

JB bites their lip. They stand up, and begin to fill a sink with water and clear the table, as if the syrup and the mugs and the plates are the ones that have caused all this tension, as if it could just be tidied away. Pushed back in a cupboard and forgotten.

But it can't be. Because it is JB. And in their relationship, every thought and feeling has to be checked-in on. Prisha knows they're not done yet, and recognises that she probably also ought to admit the unflattering fact that she ducked out of explaining the situation to Jasmine partly because Jasmine herself was so vehement in her belief in fidelity . . .

Then JB turns abruptly back around, and they're still holding the plates with a strange tenderness, as if they are very fragile and might be easily broken simply by being held. And there's something so lost in their expression, so mystified, that it catches Prisha by surprise. It is not a look she is used to seeing there.

'It feels a little bit like you've erased me,' JB says, softly. 'Us. *This*. Our special thing . . .'

Something drops inside Prisha.

'Not mentioning it, just so you don't have to have a slightly awkward conversation . . .'

Prisha finds she is rising to her feet and shaking her head. She very quickly and carefully takes the dishes out of JB's hands and puts them in the sink, and along with them she drops the idea of going any further into things with Jasmine – a girl she'll never see again anyway – or relaying her silly youthful opinions, because the most important thing now is to make it right, with the most important person in her life. With wet hands she turns back and grabs both of JB's and grips them tight and looks straight into their face.

'I'm sorry. You're right! And I'm sorry.'

And JB seems to instantly soften further.

Prisha pumps their hands up and down in hers, pulling her most hopefully endearing face. 'I'm a worm. I'm a piece of poo. I am a very contrite little yak!' And she holds JB's hands up, like little hoofs and does a pantomime of wiping her eyes with them.

It's not clear to Prisha who initiates the hug, but they fold into each other, tenderly.

'All right, all right, enough of that. You are not a *worm,* for God's sake.' JB ruffles their nose in Prisha's hair, nearly dry already, the day is so warm. 'And also: *I'm* sorry too. Sorry for ruining your fun, little yak.'

They hug and sway for a moment. And all Prisha's annoyance at how they have to discuss *everything* is swept away in recognition of how it is actually worth it: because JB forgives as quickly as they condemn. No grudges held.

Prisha keeps her head pressed into JB's sternum, her nose filling with the JB smell, that no one else on earth has, that Prisha would bottle if she could and carry with her.

Resting there, she can feel them take a deep breath.

'Prish.'

'Yeah?' Prisha speaks into the sounding-board of JB's chest.

'One more thing.'

'. . . yeah?'

'You know, you said it was all so *difficult,* talking to that woman about it . . . about us?' The husky edge of JB's voice sounds unusually tentative as they speak down into the fleshy part of Prisha's shoulder. 'It's not— it's not that you're . . .'

There is a long pause. The sort of pause where, if you were in a theatre, you'd start to worry the actor had forgotten their lines.

Actually, Prisha thinks she probably knows how to finish the sentence for JB. But she also finds she wants to hear them say it for some reason.

'You're not . . . having second thoughts about being poly?

About the ... *effort*, of that? Because, if it is that, you know we can talk about it.'

And it is oddly satisfying for Prisha to hear JB say this. To acknowledge it might be up for negotiation. (The word *compromise* once more floats around Prisha's head.) Because it is something that, for the first time since the very early days of their relationship, Prisha *has* been wondering about herself, in some dark, private corner of her brain.

It had been a long cold winter. And one of retreat, for Prisha.

There had been a woman called Milly, who she volunteered with at a food bank. She'd thought she was on to a good thing there, but Milly hadn't been honest with Prisha about having a husband, and hadn't been honest with her husband about Prisha either. A sticky, protracted mess ensued, leaving Prisha exhausted, lightly scarred, and with not much appetite for anyone beyond JB.

As the months of not seeing anyone else stacked up, JB had dutifully checked in, regularly, that she was still happy with their arrangement. But Prisha sometimes felt like it was only really JB doing their due diligence. Because she has never been able to imagine a world, really, where JB isn't poly.

JB is someone who needs – and wants – more than one partner. Who firmly believes you simply cannot healthily get everything you need from a single other person ('Even one as wonderful as you, little yak.') They very effectively maintain multiple relationships, of varying intensity and frequency, with an ease that belies how challenging even scheduling all those dates on Google Calendar can be.

Thankfully, JB mostly goes round to other people's homes: their flat is so small, Prisha has to take herself out, or wear noise-cancelling headphones, if JB does have anyone over. And there had been moments during the dry spell – striding round

Alexandra Park in the freezing cold, or listening to Run the Jewels with the volume turned right up, in order to give JB their private time with other partners – when some doubt had slunk in. When Prisha had wondered, with a thought she barely allowed herself to articulate: *would* she rather it was just the two of them?

So there is something gratifying in JB's quiet acknowledgement that this could even be the case. Gratifying – and immediately reassuring.

And rather than wanting to push for the possibility of monogamy, Prisha finds herself knowing in total, almost shocking certainty that she doesn't need it. Doesn't want it.

She squeezes JB as tightly as she can and feels absolutely flooded with love for them, and for who they are – for *all* of it, including their quiet certainty about their need for multiple partners. But also for who *she* gets to be, when she's with JB. For their shared, mutual freedom.

'No. No second thoughts. Only . . . happy thoughts.' Prisha pulls back her head and smiles with deliberate goofiness up at JB.

'OK, that's good.' The relief in JB's body is palpable, almost a bounce in their joints, a letting go of tension.

'Yeah. It is. And last night . . . it was actually kind of reaffirming? Despite the mess. That this *is* what I want. That it is how we work best.' It's a reassurance for JB – but Prisha also feels the truth of it, confirmed in her own body, as she articulates it.

Because it had been a truly delightful surprise – just how easy it had felt to slip back into her old way of living. How hungry Prisha had found herself: not specifically for Jasmine, but more generally for that sense of openness and possibility, again. The sense that you could go out, and you could meet anyone. Walking over to the house party in Rusholme in just a T-shirt, swigging a tinny along the street, it had felt like the dusky evening and the warm city were opening up to her like a flower: petals, endlessly multiplying as they peeled back, full of promise.

That was the thing she'd loved about being poly, the thing that she had let herself forget over a chilly spring.

'It was genuinely just really great to have all that sense of... potential, again?' Prisha smiles. 'I mean in an ideal world she wouldn't have been so bloody young! But it also felt just... *exciting*.'

Prisha peeks up at JB, hoping to share one of the conspiratorial, glinting looks that so often pass between them, reaffirming the deliciousness of their decision to be allowed to sleep with whoever they like.

'That's *great*.'

'Yeah. It is. It still works.'

'Thank fuck for that!' JB laughs.

They bend to kiss one dimple piercing, and then the other.

'I mean, in an ideal world the encounter wouldn't have been cut so short, either...' Prisha pulls an innocently expectant look, and JB gives a satisfied little laugh, with the distinctive rasp to it that Prisha always finds husky, sexy. She presses JB back towards a counter, and they shuffle sideways so their head isn't catching the corner of a cupboard.

And Prisha feels something else catch inside her: all the thwarted, aborted lust of last night reignited. There had been such a strange dissonance at having to deal with Jasmine's anguish when she felt like something was on bloody fire between her legs... She pushes herself in against JB, her kisses wetly travelling down their neck, down their chest—

'Mmm, someone didn't get the satisfaction they needed,

hey . . .' says JB, mischievously, knowingly, before Prisha nips, hard, at a nipple through their T-shirt, making them gasp.

JB firmly takes her face in both their hands. 'Come on, you. To the bedroom. So I can see to this properly.'

Prisha follows as obediently and needily as a puppy dog. They both drop their clothes with easy, practised movements – the days of slow undressing or tearing at each other's trousers long gone – but when they tangle together in the bronzed square of sun coming through the window, Prisha finds herself as turned on as she was the evening before.

It's often been this way though – when they have sex in the aftermath of hearing about each other's encounters with other people, there's a new, fresh little edge to it. That reminder of your attractiveness, or your partner's attractiveness; external proof of irresistibility. It's a thing Prisha hasn't realised she's missed till now.

She makes a mental note to ask JB if they feel the same way afterwards, and then succumbs to the steady, if familiar, pressure JB's fingers are providing, sinking into what her body has been screaming for. But one thought does make its way up – *this needs to be mutual* – and Prisha reaches across JB's arms to provide her own soft stroking, and then less soft, a steadily increasing intensity, as both of their bodies' responses advance, rolling together . . .

What follows is a predictable sequence of events: fine-tuned and efficient, but wrapped and cocooned in the promise and the proof of love – something else that always feels renewed whenever they sleep together for the first time after a new partner. A reaffirming of their ability to satisfy each other; the reminder of how seamlessly they fit together.

As her orgasm subsides, Prisha flops down next to JB, her limbs limp as the relief and release course through her body.

But then—

Oh God

A churning feeling.

A cold sweat swooping over goose-bumping limbs.

Prisha shuts her eyes tight, hoping to ride out the swelling seasick feeling, the slosh in her belly.

A rise of nausea. A rise of... something semi-liquid, up her throat.

Prisha sits bolt upright, a hand to her mouth, eyes wide. JB recoils slightly.

She swallows down the start of a heave, breathes deeply, and reaches across the bed for JB's water glass.

'Oh God. Sorry.'

'You OK...?'

'Yep. Yes. Yep. Fine. No problem. I just...'

JB's smile is increasingly incredulous, amused.

'I *did* just think I was going to hurl those pancakes back up all over the bed. For a second.'

'Wow. Extremely sexy.'

Prisha lies back down, wiping the blooming moustache of sweat from her upper lip. She can feel sweat slicking, too, beneath her breasts. Waves of heat, waves of chill. What is hangover, and what is orgasm, is briefly unclear.

'Oh God. Sorry, my love.'

JB wriggles down, next to Prisha, and eyes her benevolently. 'Dear oh dear oh dear.' They move the hair off Prisha's damp forehead. 'Too vigorous, was it?'

'Yes, it was simply far too hot. So sexy, my stomach couldn't take it.'

'First time I think I've ever come close to fucking someone's breakfast out of them...'

'What about that time, with the girl at the wedding reception in Norwich? You certainly fucked quite a few canapés out of—'

'Prish, please. We do not speak of that event.'

'Sorry!' Prisha smiles up at JB, who shudders performatively.

Prisha shuts her eyes. The swaying feeling, among the contents of her stomach, appears to be passing. But it is very important to be still, and silent, for a time.

Then...

'JB.'

'Yes?'

'Can you hold me please?'

'Sure you can handle it?'

Prisha just grunts, and flaps a hand mock needily at JB, demanding a hug.

JB murmurs comforting nonsense in Prisha's ear as they wrap her fully with their body, stroking her hair very gently, very slowly.

'I love you, little yak.'

'I love you too.'

And any remaining hangover unease passes over as light as a cloud, and they lie together, warm, and full, and sated.

She's just drifting into the fuzzy blackness of a nap, when JB tugs gently on her earlobe.

'You know, it is a gorgeous day – we should probably try to do something with it, hey?'

Prisha groans. 'Just a few more minutes in bed. I'm a little... tender, still.'

JB pats her lightly, but Prisha can feel that they're reaching for their phone with their other hand. Thumb-tapping.

Sleep has, however, been fatally scared off. After a while, Prisha gives up and opens her eyes. The sunlight has moved further down the bed. She asks JB what news there is from the outside world.

'Broadly, the headlines are: the planet is still on fire, and we're still collectively pretending it isn't.'

'Oh good. Is that a literal fire, or a metaphorical one, on this occasion?'

'Both. Those actual wildfires are still raging – getting worse, it looks like, with the weather as it is – but at the same time our idiot government is sneakily giving tax breaks to fossil fuel companies, apparently. Spectacularly dumb.'

'Oh, brilliant.'

'Yeah. However, in more cheerful news, I've just had a confirmation that I do get a plus one for you for that Moorlands Sounds festival?'

'Ooh, nice. Backstage passes, baby!'

'I mean, those backstage passes will get us access to a slightly posher set of festival lavs, and that's about it . . .'

'Don't look a gift horse in the mouth! A gift bog? A present Portaloo . . . ?' Prisha realises she is spouting nonsense again. 'What day are you performing, anyway?'

'Friday. Nice early evening slot on a little stage in the woods.'

'Mmm. Very good.'

'Annnnd . . .' JB takes a small, sharp breath in. 'My other news: looks like I've got a date on Friday. That Briony woman off Feeld finally got back to me just now . . .'

And there it is – the little lick, the flicker of fear inside Prisha's chest: *what if this is the one, the person who's better than me, the person who takes them away—*

And then, as usual, it burns itself out almost instantly.

Because this flame has never been stoked; JB never does add fuel to it. JB is Prisha's bedrock, her own solid foundation. And Prisha has no reason to think they're going anywhere.

'Hey! That's exciting.' She pulls back to sit up and smile at JB, taking the chance to prove she really did mean what she said earlier. 'Are you going to that food hall place they were talking about?'

'That's the plan.'

Prisha reaches over to give JB a good long, tonguey kiss, before murmuring towards their ear, *look at us, aren't we doing well, both so popular . . .*

JB laughs. 'Enough of all that. Come on. We're wasting the day – and the other message I've had—'

'God you're so busy! So in demand!'

'. . . is from Clio and Duncan, who want to know if we fancy the pub? They're in the taphouse, that one with the cute beer garden – plenty of room apparently.'

'Mm. Interesting.'

'Clio has brought the puppy.'

'Mmmm . . . *very* interesting.'

'Shall we get you a nice full-fat coke? Might that help with the hangover?'

'Can there be lots of ice?'

'I think there can.'

'OK. I think I can make it, then. But I shall need . . . sunglasses.'

It takes Prisha a long time to get ready: getting re-dressed and putting on just enough make-up that she doesn't look deceased and finding said sunglasses which are certainly not, she thinks, where she left them (*how* did they get on top of the fridge?). While she faffs, JB sprawls on the sofa, scrolling on their phone and occasionally reading out other dismal headlines, and fiddling with the roll-up that is waiting between their fingers.

'Hurry up,' they say eventually, as Prisha stomps to the bedroom and back out again, repeatedly, forgetting first wallet then sun cream then the Maggie Nelson book she needs to give back to Clio.

'OK. I am ready.' But just as Prisha swings her cotton rucksack over her shoulder, her phone goes.

Prisha fishes for it in her dungaree pockets.

It is her mother. Of course.

She pulls a face – half frustrated, half apologetic – at JB, who simply looks stony.

JB has never understood how much contact Prisha and Lavanya have to have; although JB has their own closeness with their mum, the two of them able to talk about anything and everything, it is a long time since they have been in each other's lives in the same way as Prisha and Lavanya. *Co-dependent*, JB sometimes mutters.

And it's true that they don't need each other in the same way, thinks Prisha: Ally also has Peter and Bea and umpteen friends and neighbours and weird distant relatives and artists who come to stay at the barn for months at a time. And JB has their poet friends and bike friends and activist friends and poly friends and lovers, a complicatedly overlapping set of circles – social networks drawn by Spirograph.

Whereas Prisha's mum . . . she does have people, Prisha tries to remind herself. A small, and now rather dispersed group of proud old-school feminists, the women who Lavanya met through a consciousness-raising group back in the day, and who changed her life. There's the selection of aunties and cousins who didn't shun her after the divorce (who Prisha feels eternally grateful to). But Prisha is Lavanya's only child; her only *immediate* family. And JB has never quite got that, what that means to her mum.

How important just one person can be to just one other person.

She should answer the phone. But Prisha feels like she has been testing JB's tolerance today. And talking to her mum, with this hangover, while making JB late to meet their friends . . . it will not help.

She hates it when she has to choose between making her mum happy, and making JB happy. Because she really does want them both to be as happy as they possibly, humanly can be.

But sometimes, you have to choose.

'You answer it,' says Prisha. 'Say I'm . . . out? Or something. Forgot my phone. Will call later.'

She throws the phone at JB, who catches it neatly.

And she *will* call back later. Will call once they're home again, and she can settle down with a nice cup of tea and a Hobnob and have a proper natter.

'Hi Lavanya . . .'

'. . .'

'Yeah, sorry, she's actually not here at the moment—'

'. . .'

'No she went out but she must've forgotten her phone . . . I just found it, um, ringing under, uh—'

JB is an absolutely terrible liar. They don't sound convincing at all.

'. . .'

'Yeah. I'm sure she'll be back soon.'

'. . .'

'Yeah, of course. I'll tell her you called.'

'. . .'

'OK then. All right, well you—'

'. . .'

'Yep, you too.'

'. . .'

'Bye then. Bye.'

'...'

'Yep – bye.'

JB hangs up and throws the phone back.

'Well, that wasn't too bad. Thought she might keep you chatting on the phone – a substitute me...'

JB merely rolls their eyes, and Prisha feels instantly bad.

It was a disingenuous comment: her mum doesn't have that much to say to JB these days. In fact, communication between her mother and JB seems to be steadily deteriorating.

It had been fine when they first met, her mum putting on an epic spread of food and hugging JB tight and asking a million questions an hour, and JB so polite, so attentive in their answers, even if Lavanya was often on to the next question before JB had finished the last. Her mum had always been enthusiastic about meeting Prisha's partners – partly because she was nosy, wanting to understand every part of Prisha's life (wanting to insert herself into every part of it, Prisha sometimes thought, in ungenerous moments). But it was also almost a *display*: a generous performance intended to prove how open-minded Lavanya was, how completely *fine* she was with her daughter loving women, how understanding she was – in contrast to some of her relatives! – about love taking whatever form it needed to.

But it turned out there were limits on that, after all.

If 'lesbian' was a term Lavanya had been able to whole-heartedly embrace – her old firebrand friends had impressed on her the validity of women loving women some time in the 1980s – JB's pronouns proved trickier. Lavanya obliges in carefully, almost pointedly using the correct language. But she also has an increasing tendency, whenever JB isn't around, to ask irritating questions about whether Prisha is still even a lesbian given she's with someone 'non-binary' (and you could almost hear the quotation marks), no matter how many times Prisha insisted that she and JB actually just prefer the term *queer*.

But the real problem had been her discovery that they saw other people. It wasn't exactly something they'd ever planned to tell Prisha's mum. JB's parents knew, and were predictably blithely unconcerned, tending to use any conversation about it as an excuse to recount their own youthful stories of threesomes or partner-swapping (which even JB would cover their ears at). When it came to Lavanya, however, she'd only discovered they were poly when JB was outed in the most unfortunate, public way.

JB had made a solo show called *Give a Fuck*, a performed cycle of poems about gender and relationships, many of which explored the joy of having multiple partners. It toured a few tiny venues, was programmed as part of a few niche literary festivals; it was not the sort of thing that they would ever have expected to receive national press coverage.

But then the *Daily Mail* ran one of its periodic *taxpayer's-money-funding-filth* investigations, combing through information about Arts Council projects for things to attack: a black drag queen who performed in schools, a trans woman whose show celebrated fatness, an anti-Tory cabaret featuring Margaret Thatcher with a strap-on . . . JB was another perfect target: the article described them as a 'a non-binary polyamorous poet who BOASTS about "f★★king gender, and whoever I want" live on stage'.

The piece caused a predictable social media storm – so much so that many other outlets reported on the furore. Lavanya read about it on the BBC, rang Prisha in tears, and no conversations about how being poly really did work for them both had ever managed to totally convince her.

In fact, Lavanya's sniffy little comments often sounded

remarkably similar to Jasmine's judginess the previous evening. That Prisha should have more respect for herself. That one person should be enough. That it was greedy, or really must take up too much of her time!

Whenever Lavanya used the word 'pol-y-am-o-rous', she'd wrinkle up her nose as if each of the syllables smelled bad.

And so every time it comes up, Prisha finds herself having to judge if it is worth ruining a visit to argue with her mum, or not. Knowing she'll feel ashamed, whichever option she goes with: for betraying JB, and their community, if she didn't challenge her mum; for upsetting her mum by 'spoiling the mood' by 'being so *defensive*' if she did speak up.

No wonder she hadn't really wanted to go into it with Jasmine the previous night.

No wonder she felt *tired*.

Prisha groans, and goes over to JB to wrap her arms around them. 'Thank you for doing that. And sorry for asking you to. But at least now, well, we can go...?'

'About bloody time,' mutters JB, raising an eyebrow.

They take the sunglasses from on top of Prisha's head, and pull them down over her eyes. There's something affectionate in the gesture, understanding.

'Come on then. Let's be off.'

And they head out into the day.

Everything is dimmed to a soft, sepia brown with her sunglasses on, and it's actually nice to be outside – you wouldn't go so far as to call it a refreshing breeze, but there is movement in the warm air. A textbook English summer Sunday. Someone drives by playing Bob Marley very loudly out of their car windows. Lads have their tops off. A faint smell of barbequed sausages. Nowhere to be, and nothing to be done.

Actually, Prisha has plenty to get done, but none of it will

happen today. There's a Dropbox folder full of photos waiting for her to sift through; scores of images from a shoot of
'exotic' fruits, for a feature for a supermarket in-house magazine. Breadfruit and custard apples and plantain stacked up in
elaborate piles. She's meant to send back her selection to the
photographer by 9 a.m. on Monday morning; she'll just have
to get up early tomorrow. Her brain simply can't countenance
it today.

Sometimes, Prisha almost likes having a hangover. The knowledge that all bets are off, that she's absolutely no use whatsoever
– it's about the only time she doesn't feel a bit guilty about
being utterly unproductive.

Things were better when she had in-house art directing jobs,
really – when she was done she was done, and the weekend was
hers to cheerfully destroy. But since going freelance – not her
choice; more and more papers and magazines simply couldn't
afford to have people on staff – she felt always on call. Her time,
her attention, bought by someone else. For not enough money,
really, given that now they were allowed to intrude via midnight
emails, crisis deadlines, the requirement to always always say *yes,
of course, no problem, I'll have it done for you by yesterday!*

And the steady dwindling of budgets had been increasingly
having an impact on freelancers, too: more and more places
simply using stock photos wherever they could. For one painful
stretch of time, the only employment Prisha managed to get
was art-directing shoots actually for a stock photo company –
collaborating in doing her future self out of work, Prisha had
bitterly complained to JB.

JB's work – shifts in the bike shop, and gigs performing their
poetry – hardly raked in much cash, and things had got so tight
at one point in the previous year that they had even talked
seriously about moving together to JB's parents' house for a bit.

Obviously they were welcome there. But the thought of having to vacate their room – going downstairs and chatting to Ally and Peter and whoever else was around – so that JB could have sexy zoom calls with their lovers had not filled Prisha with joy, when she was in her fallow period.

Only the sudden TV banking advert commission had saved them. It was certainly JB's worst-ever poem, a sentimental hymn to 'community' that had little to do with banking and every-thing to do with making a performative nod towards *diversity, optics, inclusion.* JB was filmed speaking the poem to camera while walking through a market, full of same-sex couples and mixed-race children, concluding 'let's grab life with both hands/ let's see how good it can taste' as they caught an apple thrown by a smiling vendor and bit into it with relish, before tapping a contactless card on his machine.

Prisha simply avoided watching Channel 4 for a month or two. Plenty to watch on Netflix instead. It still occasionally catches her though, even now.

JB obviously hated the advert too, but they never cringed, never complained. There'd been a long dark night, deciding whether or not to do it. A despairing google of the bank's ethical credentials. A frank look at their finances. But once they had made the decision, they never agonised over it. Never googled the reaction to the advert either (thank God). Merely paid off the landlord, and got on with life.

It's another admirable quality, Prisha thinks. And JB has genuinely used the money as they promised themselves they would: beyond the debt-clearing and a large donation to a local homelessness charity, they used the cash to build a decent website and to buy time to work on a new performance project collaborating with a very cool percussionist. Not like Prisha, who can't seem to help but fritter money whenever she gets it, on a hot jumpsuit or better wine or a fancy meal out.

Of course, there was JB's rollie habit. That ate up a daft amount of cash. Their one irrational, idiotic vice. Thank fuck, really.

Prisha waits for JB to stub out their ciggie in a bin, then grabs their hand. Their face makes half a turn to hers. A small smile. A small squeeze.

JB swings her hand as they walk on, almost proprietorial. Proud.

And for them to hold hands in public is never without defiance of some potential threat, of course, even in this city — especially when the streets are this busy, so much warm lager consumed by mid-afternoon, the sultriness of heat liable to sizzle over into violence as the sun sets. The confusion over *what exactly* they are seeing still proving perversely enraging to some. To too many.

But here they are. JB and Prisha. Still doing it. Still choosing it.

Hand in hand, holding tight.

Chapter 6

JB

Despite their best efforts, they still have to run for the train. A coffee spurts and spits out of the small hole in its lid, scalding JB's hand, as they try to keep it steady while their backpack bobs heavily against their back. Manchester Piccadilly is busy, seemingly full of teenagers, on their phones, moving as slowly as the occasional bewildered older couples clutching rare paper tickets.

JB pauses momentarily to flash their phone screen at the guard, then slams at the still-illuminated train door button with grim satisfaction.

None of the seat reservations are in use. A missing carriage. Wait – *several* missing carriages? No wonder it's so full. Over the tannoy comes a blaring, barely comprehensible apology, followed by a tinkling pre-recorded safety announcement.

This country is fucked. JB begins composing the grumpy social media post in their mind as the train lurches its departure, and they wind their way down several stuffed carriages, the coffee still precipitous. But nobody wants to read a travel complaint. Just moan to Prisha maybe.

It is, of course, partly Prisha's fault they are late: she'd been determined to rouse herself and to make a nice breakfast before JB's weekend away, and wanted to hear, properly, about how the first date with Briony had gone the previous evening. But there was really no fathoming how it was possible for anyone to chop an onion that slowly. Prisha had started cooking before JB got in the shower; when they got out, she hadn't even started warming the pan.

To be fair to Prisha, breakfast had been delicious, when it came, an improvised spicy hash of potatoes and peppers and eggs and cheese. Prisha never followed recipes, and her cooking usually looked a mess, but tasted great. Perhaps being incapable of rushing helped, too, really.

In carriage M, there is a spare seat, which JB sinks into with relief, even if it is next to a woman having a loud conversation on her phone about gin ('need more of that pink Albion Mill one – yeah, yeah the wild strawberry or whatever it is – selling like crazy in the bar this summer...'). She keeps running her hands through her thick hair as she talks, and one dark curly strand comes to settle on JB's legs, bare below their shorts.

They remove it, with pincer-like fingers, a gesture that's halfway between subtle and pointed. *How British,* thinks JB.

They reach for their phone, and message Prisha.

Made it. Just. Xxx

JB is looking forward to a weekend in Sheffield, but it had been the sort of morning where it is hard to tear yourself away from home: warm cuddles with Prisha, letting her doze with the heavy curtains shut even though it was still hot, the bed slightly smelly from mutual morning breath (JB thinks they can still feel the pickled onions from the bao buns last night in their mouth). Then a breakfast to linger over. And the ghost of the evening before, making them feel extra affectionate.

One of the nice things – one of the most un-sung nice things, JB thinks – about being poly is how low-stakes and win-win dating becomes: meeting someone new who is fantastic is fantastic, but a bad date also just doesn't really matter, because you have someone at home. In fact, it can make you really appreciate what you already have. That *right* feeling; a satisfaction.

Going home to Prisha after meeting Briony, JB felt suffused with a gentle, cosy gratitude for her presence – even if they did get back to find Prisha fast asleep on the sofa, half a bottle of red consumed in front of *Selling Sunset*. But it was also that things felt more even again, since Prisha had got out of her funk. JB had been just beginning to get worried that Prisha might not be a hundred per cent happy with their well-established set-up. But seeing the glitter in her eyes as she smiled when talking about meeting someone new at the party ... well, JB feels fully reassured. That it is still right, for both of them.

But it has also genuinely been so nice to be able to compare notes again – hearing from Prisha how things had gone with the party-girl, and then getting to dissect their own date with her too. There is no one whose perspective JB values more.

'OK, so. It wasn't a *terrible* date, with Briony,' JB had relayed to Prisha that morning while stirring the coffee pot, awaiting breakfast. 'She was just ... a tourist.'

'In a bad way? Like, gawpy rather than genuinely interested?'

'Yeah. I get the impression she'd just gone through something, some kind of mid-life revelation. New in Manchester, new on the scene. She just asked lots of nosy questions, and then looked a bit worried – or a bit excited – and then asked yet more questions ...'

'Which is fine if they're for real, I guess. But it sounds like maybe it wasn't much of a conversation?'

'Yeah. Exactly. I just got the impression I was just a bit ... *exotic* to her.'

'Ugh. Tedious.'

It's been a while since JB has had an encounter like that: people who download apps like Feeld for their own arms-length titillation, rather than to really meet someone. They'd suspected Briony was going to be one of these when they first matched, but then she'd seemed genuinely eager to meet up. Arrived nervous and fidgety, her skinny legs crossing and uncrossing compulsively, fingers fiddling with the shaggy edge of a trendy mullet that JB felt sure was a recent reinvention too. Briony was clearly desperate to just ask a lot of questions about being poly, being NB, about what their girlfriend thinks of it all, if they ever had threesomes... *That's none of your fucking business pal,* JB had snapped, and regretted it.

Because usually, JB doesn't mind talking about this stuff. In fact, they mostly relish it – which is a good job, as they have long found themselves becoming something of an advocate or a spokesperson on all these matters (apart from threesomes; genuinely not their thing). They know they're often interpreted as the ultimate embodiment of a certain hyper-articulate white middle-class queer poly stereotype – but that *is* who they are, and it gives JB distinct satisfaction to broadcast just how *excellent* that life in fact is. To cheerfully discuss – in groups of new partners' friends, or among folks chatting after a poetry night – all of the openness, and the pleasure. Grinning and gleeful as they explain how much they love Prisha, how much they also get from other people. Watching minds whirring. Watching people swiftly turning their own relationships over inside their heads, in this new light (could *they* manage it? Might it even be *better?*).

And yet they still also often meet some defensiveness, when discussing polyamory, and not just among older people where you might expect it really (like Prisha's mum). They also meet a knee-jerk resistance among the most seemingly liberal, politically switched-on members of their own generation – the sorts of people who for the most part, these days, make a polite effort when it comes to gender and pronouns. But for some reason, those same people often seem compelled to tell JB *exactly why* they don't like the sound of non-monogamy, or all the problems they believe it must cause, despite having never tried it.

It doesn't ruffle JB, but it is rude, really. They don't offer damning critiques on the life choices of people they've just met. Don't ask these people how often they've cheated on their partners. How often they've wanted to. Don't ask if their parents are divorced, or parrot divorce statistics, or falling childbirth rates. They just smile. And it is a real smile, because they love their life. And that is the best advert of all for it.

Only, none of that is really what they expect to have to do *on a date*. By the time you're literally dating, hopefully the curiosity is more than just . . . conceptual. But even before they'd been served their bao buns, in the clattering, cool converted market hall, JB had realised that Briony was still in this phase. Interested in JB as a series of embodied theories, or excited by them as a set of new potential identities she might adopt – not as an actual person. She'd seemed surprised, offended even, when JB very politely announced they were going home after eating.

Certainly, the situation hadn't taken too long to dissect this morning – which was good, because suddenly it was the time JB was meant to have left by. At least they have made the train.

They message Soo.

> *On the train. Looks like it will be on time.*
> *Can't wait to see you.*

Cool. I'll meet you at the station!

> *Yep. See you there.*

JB neglects the book in their bag (the new Desmond Paterson one about the British Empire, that everyone keeps saying is 'essential reading') in favour of staying on their phone. They do their usual quick flicking between apps, as outside the world passes in swift fragments – flashing factories, suburbs, stems of buddleia growing upwards like plumes of smoke. They catch up with all the things they've been meaning to read, messages they meant to reply to. Get overly embroiled in hunting down the origin of cryptic posts between two extremely online poets.

The coffee is, of course, terrible.

Then JB googles *Soo Cannon, performance artist*. Because Soo has been quiet on socials lately, and JB realises they have little idea what she's been up to, work-wise. Looking at her website, JB is pretty sure it hasn't been updated since last time they went on it a couple of years ago, trying to find the start time for the performance piece Soo had been doing as part of some arts festival in Salford. The promotional material for that is still the website's front page: a negative photograph in hot pink and white, Soo bent over a giant fuzzy microphone, overlaid with its riffing title, *The Swallowed Woman*, in aggressively italicised, jagged font. The piece projected stock videos of 'women enjoying eating yoghurts' over her and the screen behind her, while she very slowly and softly whispered sexist messages online trolls had sent her into the microphone, like it was ASMR.

This went on for twenty-two and a half minutes. Like most video and performance art, JB found it simultaneously itchily unsettling and crushingly tedious.

But it jogs JB's memory of something else Soo had spoken about, after that event. Given she had all that professional ASMR equipment – funded by an Arts Council grant – Soo had decided to start a real YouTube channel. She explained that she'd started watching videos online merely as research, but then had actually got quite into it. That it was *relaxing* and *weirdly comforting.*

JB had watched the start of a couple of Soo's own ASMR videos back then, but they really did *not* get it. Could not see the appeal of the gently babbling way Soo spoke at the camera, as if babying the imagined, anonymous viewer, while she stroked hairbrushes or tapped her nails against glass perfume bottles – sounds that supposedly produced pleasant, relaxing 'tingles' in the viewer. Well, not for JB.

Obviously, it was all less . . . *intrusive* than the other way Soo made a living. But still.

JB realises they have no idea if these videos are something Soo is still doing. What was it she called herself, or her channel? Ah yes: Sindy ASMR. (Like the doll. *Hm.*) When they click on her page, there are now loads of videos, and the most popular have had hundreds of thousands of views. JB is taken aback. Might this be an actual earner then? A poem that JB had filmed, about being non-binary, had once gone mildly viral yet made them almost no money (if plenty of 'exposure'). But this – this is a whole different level. It is ongoing, sustained.

How had they become so out of touch with Soo this year that they didn't know about this . . . ? JB has always prided themselves on keeping up with people, but somehow that's felt harder recently. Is it just ageing, they wonder – or being so busy, travelling around the country for poetry gigs, while also trying to keep various partners feeling like they're getting enough meaningful time together? Or maybe it was just the fact that it had felt like such a long winter.

But now it is the summer, and they're on a train, and they're off to see a friend. Look out, look up, JB instructs themselves. See the day. The sun.

Actually the day is close and hazy, and the sun a muffled yellow splodge behind thick cloud. Their view of it blinks, obscured and revealed by rushing-past buildings, a flick-book of pale light and mauve shadow. It has been hot for weeks now, but maybe it is finally about to break. The earth begs for rain.

Maybe Soo just assumed they were a subscriber.

Maybe Soo assumed JB was contemptuous of it.

Maybe Soo was embarrassed by it herself.

JB presses play on the top video – 'ASMR two hours of sleepy tingles to put YOU to sleep' – and there is Soo, whispering and bending over the big microphone, bobbing her head gently from one side of it to the other as she speaks, so her voice seems to move around JB's head.

'Hi. Welcome back. Thanks for being with me.'

Her face looks very made-up. Perfect even skin, lips painted in a cherry bow, their natural shape surely exaggerated.

'Tonight, I have two hours of sleepy tingles to help you to sleep . . . sleep . . . sleep . . .'

Actually, she isn't *that* made up: it's only because JB knows Soo in real life, knows she doesn't really look like this. But it's also the smiling. Soo's resting face is usually quite serious. Unimpressed, even. People are often – needlessly! – intimidated by her, at gallery openings and book launches. In her uniform of black. Whereas this 'Sindy' persona is almost . . . *simpering*. Smiling constantly, giving coy little tilts of their head, as she fusses with a bit of cellophane.

Two hours of this. JB shifts in their seat, and slurps at the last bit of coffee (a mistake; the dregs are matte and muddy on their tongue). They look out of the window again. Fields swipe past now, their green so bright it feels almost accusatory, a blow against JB spending so much of the journey intently swiping at their phone screen.

But they can't resist. JB returns to the menu. Playlists of videos: 'Sounds & triggers', 'Personal attention', 'Mouth sounds and kisses', 'Roleplays'. They click on 'Personal attention' first, angling their phone so that the woman next to them can't see what they're looking at. Scalp massage. Ear cleaning (gross). Lice checking (extremely gross). Then they open the 'Roleplays' playlist.

'Girlfriend comforts you to sleep'

'Magical Princess welcomes you to their castle'

'Big sister does your prom make-up'

Their friend's face, suspended in rectangles, smiling smiling smiling.

JB watches a few seconds of various videos and the instinctive revulsion rises up in them again. Soo's performance to the camera is such a naff parody of the soft, caring, ideal woman – delivered out to unknown masses. Probably masturbating men mostly, JB thinks.

Why would Soo voluntarily do this? As if this eroticised idea of pretty, passive women isn't what her art has so often addressed and critiqued. For a second they wonder if the whole thing is an elaborate, clever art prank. A durational work. Something Soo will later brutally deconstruct.

Then JB looks at the number of followers and feels a small judder they want to attribute to the bad coffee or the train, and they simply exit the YouTube app and yank out their headphones.

It is Soo's life, and being friends with Soo means not judging Soo. Always has done. So why does this rankle, weirdly perhaps even more so than—

Stop it. Don't think about it.

And they manage not to think about it for the rest of the journey, or when they see Soo walking briskly down the slope to the station, her arms outstretched, hands reaching like starbursts. Her petite body is reflected and stretched in the long, curving steel sculpture that is that first thing that greets visitors to Sheffield. There is a real smile on her face, below giant sunglasses, and she's wearing one of her standard black, oddly-structured sack dresses, that always prompt Prisha to say Soo ought to be sponsored by COS.

'Jay-Beeeeee!' Soo stops, her arms still held up and out in an arched, awkward-comic awaiting pose, as JB closes the gap.

JB is fierce in their hold. The strangely light yet stiff material of Soo's dress seems to flap and fold like a sail.

Then they both pull back, look at each other properly.

'*Hi.*' The emphasis in one little word carrying so much. Soo grins. 'It's been a while.'

'It's been far too long,' says JB, and means it. It hadn't been either of their faults, really – just work and partners and family and kids and more work and diaries that fill up far too far in advance.

'Yup. It really has. Anyway – welcome to Sheffield! What do you want to do – we can drop your stuff at mine' – JB shrugs; they travel light, always do, just one rucksack – 'or straight to the pub, or do you need lunch? Or there's a cute place just up the road that does excellent cinnamon buns and proper coffee—'

Soo breaks off, smiling at JB, knowing *coffee, of course.*

'I just had one of those giant watery tubs of station coffee this morning. Absolute arse gravy.'

'Right.' Soo grimaces. 'Well, this will sort you out.'

The café is predictably hip: brick walls, salvaged furniture. A colourful, tropical mural, featuring a parrot, and houseplants galore. They sit outside, so JB can have the rollie they've been thinking about since leaving Manchester, and fiddling with since the train stopped in Grindleford.

A stressed-looking young woman with chunky streaks of pink and turquoise in her hair – practically co-ordinating with the mural, JB thinks – takes their order. The coffee takes a reassuringly long time to be made, and is excellent when it does finally arrive, with slightly too intense an apology from the colourful-haired server.

'So, how's Anya?' JB asks, trying to waft their smoke away from Soo.

'Good! I think. Her dad is taking her to swimming this morning, which she used to hate with a raging passion and then, like, a month ago became obsessed with?'

'And how is Liam?'

Soo blows air out of her mouth. 'Liam is ... OK. It's not been great, like I said last time we spoke.'

Anya had been the unplanned child of a relationship that had completely broken up not that long after she arrived. And not that long after that, Liam was in a fairly hideous bike accident, and left with constant, debilitating pain in his lower back and legs. Managing it involved endlessly trying more different kinds of therapies and cocktails of drugs – and their often almost-as-bad side effects – than JB could really keep up with the news of. What they had certainly grasped from Soo was how hard it was to raise a whole new human on stingy child support and Liam's almost viciously punitive disability benefit payments. Not to mention the fact that parenting Anya had gone from being an (allegedly) equitably shared endeavour to effectively a solo project.

JB notices the effort Soo puts in, as she tries to focus on the bright side. 'But physio is going quite well, which is great, and he's on some new kind of painkillers that mean he can do a bit more, and get out a bit more? His mum is with them today, but his even feeling able to take Anya for a whole weekend again is a big step forward.'

'And it must be a relief for you. That he can look after her again, I mean.'

Soo does a sort of nodding shrugging gesture, with a pulling down at the side of her narrow (lipstick-free) mouth. 'Well, yeah. It is.'

JB feels the usual surge, the yearning for a magic wand that would simply make life easier for Soo. It seemed like circumstances simply perpetually thwarted her.

Looking at her now – the chic bob, the bug shades that weren't really needed on this muggy, clouded day – JB thinks that Soo doesn't appear very different to when they first met, when they were both studying at Goldsmiths. (This is a strange thought, given how markedly changed JB's own appearance is since then).

Soo had had such total self-possession, and such a clear idea of her art, that JB had assumed for ages that she was – like JB, like so many of their friends really – supported by understanding arty middle-class parents. It wasn't till third year that JB understood how very much that was not the case. They'd been sitting on the steps of the flat Soo shared with their mutual friend Teodora in Brockley, JB fretting over their final project, and how much they could push the boundaries of the Fine Art degree – having realised that they were much more interested in words and meanings than images and meanings. Could they get away with performance poetry? Or maybe an illustrated collection?

When JB had asked what Soo was working on, she'd sighed, and ground the butt of her cigarette into the steps' concrete, round and round and round, as if extinguishing something far more significant.

'Nothing.' She'd looked up, her dark eyes levelling with JB's. There'd been an intake of breath – a moment's decision – and then a quick, rushing confession. 'I need to defer. I just— I already owe a couple of month's rent and it's not fair on Teodora, and my credit card is maxed . . . That restaurant where I've been working at weekends, they've said I can go up to full time, thank God. But I literally don't think I *can* finish my final project in time if I'm working that much . . .'

Soo had stopped, and then decisively thrown her butt out into the street.

'Can't you, like, go home for a bit? Save on rent?' JB had known that Soo had lived with her parents for the first two years of the course.

Soo snorted. 'Nope.' Another of those weighing-up, deciding breaths.

'My parents have thrown me out. They thought studying art was stupid anyway – I actually applied to Goldsmiths secretly, and they were just . . . horrible about it all the time. So, I tried to keep as much work as possible at uni, but one time my mother was told by a busybody neighbour that someone saw me – God knows where – holding hands with another *woman*, who had *tattoos*, and *long green hair.*' (Must be Amelia from the English course, JB noted.) 'And my mother went through all my stuff while I was out, and found a bunch of essays and supporting material for that project I did – do you remember – it was a bit silly, *The Pursing of the Pussy?*'

Of course JB knew it. Soo had blown up and printed out life-size fine art classics, showing the evolution of the reclined nude from Titian's *Venus of Urbino* to Goya's cheeky-smiled *La Maja desnuda* to Manet's almost accusative *Olympia* to one of

Egon Schiele's masturbating woman. In each, she cut a slit at their labia – or at the side of a coyly concealing hand – and behind that put a small purse, which the viewer was encouraged to reach into, encountering a different lining inside each (soft velvet, a collection of coins, sandpaper, a cold pouch of lube). As their hands reached in, Soo – moving around behind the paintings – would shriek with outrage and shame, or pleasure and delight.

But Soo's parents discovering that their daughter had faked an orgasm while her professors rummaged in a vag-shaped purse of lube had not gone down at all well, she recounted. Nor had the discovery of a whole sack of home-made badges, reading +++SEX POSITIVE+++ and EQUAL OPPORTUNITIES SLUT and MY BODY MY JOY, which Soo made a point of handing out at any performance they ever did, 'for the avoidance of doubt'. JB had taken one of each despite, at that stage, feeling far too estranged from their own body to actually live by such slogans. It would be years till they felt able to articulate their own desires with such force, such clarity.

The upshot was, Soo's parents packed her stuff into suitcases, telling her they wouldn't fund such filth, and that she was not to come home till she'd 'sorted herself out'.

In the end, JB had helped Soo apply for hardship funding so that, with an extension, she could still graduate. But she missed out on the big end-of-year showcase, and while peers whose parents magically provided flats in Peckham or studios in Dalston made buzzy head-starts on careers, Soo spent most of her time working, and struggling to afford materials. No wonder she'd eventually settled on performance art, JB thought: women's bodies being a free source of endless fascination.

It was in one of her better poorly-paid employment stints – uploading gallery listings information at *Time Out* – that

Soo had hit on an idea that JB had recognised instantly would go down well in the art world. Soo was always caustically mocking the 'fucking word salad' of exhibition press releases, which made no literal sense and had to be largely rewritten. She decided to take the obscure, pretentious copy from a press release, and attempt to make the artwork it was describing, without seeing the original. Then she'd include a photograph of the real original alongside her faked end result. It was JB who, over a pint of Taddy Lager, came up with the title for it: *An Artist's Impression.*

A practice that explores digital formalism and computational aesthetics, deploying Information Age technologies to examine our networked, media-rich world.

Soo displayed: Teetering stacks of tessellating computers, each screen showing streams of data about what news articles were most shared on social media that day. (Nothing at all like the fractal, patterned digital images the artist really produced.)

The artist conveys the intense gravitational tension – the embodied and politicised drive that exists between potential energy and physical action.

Soo filmed: herself jumping off ladders onto a series of mattresses, that she'd painted with political slogans: 'No justice, no peace', 'We are the 99 per cent', 'Nothing about us without us'. (Not much like the series of photographs of dancers that the description actually applied to.)

An Artist's Impression gathered a cult following on Tumblr, then on Instagram – and soon became a staple on lists of art accounts to follow. A real-life show followed at a gallery in

Shoreditch, and for a while JB watched as their friend's star seemed steadily to rise, with Soo's more personal performance work – prodding at the links between sex, gendered stereotypes, and performativity – also proving extremely zeitgeisty. JB considered themselves open-minded, but even they baulked a little at the opening in a Hackney Wick warehouse, where Soo masturbated while reading out the most icky lines from reviews of her work written by men.

At events like these, JB – who by this time had got so sick of London prices and being utterly broke they'd moved back north – would sometimes feel a small prickle of doubt about her friend's work. Where was the line between critiquing the commodification of women's bodies, and being complicit in that? Soo certainly got a lot of attention, but it was clearly partly because she did put her own (young, attractive, female) body on display. It was – wasn't it? – a literal selling of *her self.*

But JB could also understand it. Women inevitably got shit all their life simply for having female bodies, and this was Soo's attempt to control that narrative, and to capitalise on it. To work with what she had.

And maybe JB's discomfort with their own body at that time had had something to do with how they reacted to Soo's use of hers.

It had been shocking when Soo announced she was pregnant, and keeping the baby – *how could someone so in-tune with their body be three months pregnant without even realising? And how could you let your partner's enthusiasm persuade you that it could, indeed, be the right time?* Anya was a blessing – of course she was, a true joy – but Liam's enthusiasm for having a child, it turned out, didn't really extend to making many sacrifices himself. They'd moved to Sheffield to be nearer his parents, but Liam's mother offered less help than Soo had been led to expect, which meant it was harder to make work, and to tour work. But if she left Sheffield, she'd have no help at all, still being estranged from her own family . . .

Unsurprisingly, Soo's art had to go on the back burner. And then Liam had his accident, and she became a full-time mum, and the creative flame practically snuffed it completely, she'd explained to JB.

'It is a tough time in general for performance art – but especially up here, to be honest with you. There's not *so* much of a scene in the north really,' Soo says, dabbing regretfully at the last crumbs of the pastry, when JB brings the conversation round to her work.

'What happened to that proposed tour – what was it called – the emerging thing?'

JB dimly remembered that Soo had been working on a performance piece, where she'd attempt to push out of a giant box made of various materials – sheets of newspaper, white gallery stud walls, a literal glass ceiling – using only her body.

'*Always Emerging?* Yeah, I did a mini tour, here at Theatre Deli, a festival in Leeds, Warwick Arts Centre . . . but I had to cancel a string of dates in the south. Just . . . too long being away from home. It didn't make financial sense really, either. It's expensive, destroying your materials every show!'

'That's awful. I'm sorry.'

'Ach. You know. There are more important things in life.'

JB looks briefly blank.

'Anya!' Soo laughs, and prods JB in the ribs, teasingly. 'Being the best mum I can be! I love my work – *fuck* I miss the thrill of performing – but I tell you what, I miss Anya an awful lot more when I do go away. It hurts, in here. Like, a physical *tug.'* Soo prods now at her own ribcage, at the soft flesh in the triangle at her midriff where the bones part way.

JB nods repeatedly, a display of understanding they know they will never quite have. They have no interest in having their own kids, and zero angst about it either: their life is full and rich enough, and not lacking in small people. But while they adore their nephew Milo, have a deep affection for one long-term, older partner's teenaged kid Zee, and love spending time with Anya . . . JB also knows that what they feel is not on the same level as what Soo has always clearly felt.

The first time JB had met Anya, Soo had tried to describe how altered, how inside-out she had been turned by her arrival. 'It's like I don't matter anymore, and weirdly I don't even care? I just . . . it's like my purpose on this planet is to love her, now,' Soo had said, as she gazed down at the pink tangle of little limbs in her arms, the silken black hair like a cup cradling the perfect nut of her tiny head.

'Anyway, I think *Always Emerging* is, ironically, dead in the water,' continues Soo, sipping at her coffee. 'Unless I can raise the cash to film it and distribute that. But would that lose its power? Doesn't it need to be, like, live and messy?'

'Maybe.' says JB. 'But it's only getting harder for artists to emerge – it's not like the piece had lost, you know, its relevance?'

'Yeah.' Soo sighs. 'It's just hard, when you've been so excited about something and it's been completely scotched by stupid things, like *childcare*, to get back into that . . . well, you know what I'm talking about – that juicy, crunchy, creative bit?'

JB does know. They think it is probably the most exciting part of their own writing – when an idea seems to shimmer somewhere in the back of your mind or your peripheral vision, and you don't want to look at it too closely too soon. And then, eventually, when the time is right, pulling it into focus, pulling it into the light, playing with *what words* in *what order* best make the idea come glittering to life, right inside someone *else's* mind . . .

Of course, performing their poetry is also exciting – especially since they've started working with Jamie, a sensational percussionist who layers and loops all sorts of weird stuff below and around their words. The propulsive beats only add to the sensation JB often experiences, that the words are bubbling up out of them like a fountain, powered by some mysterious, internal force. And the magic feeling, when an audience *gets* it too, when they start to go with you, to click in. When something bigger than the sum of its parts is made, together and collectively, that fills the room and your lungs and your . . . *'soul'* feels like the wrong word – too religious – but JB doesn't know what else to call it. And this sensation is something they know Soo gets, too, when performing. The higher state she goes into, onstage. Just vibrating with it.

And the wave of love comes all over JB again, the yearn, the yen, to help. To allow Soo to make the work that matters to her. It is a source of eternal frustration to JB, that you cannot simply *love* good luck into someone else's life. All JB can ever offer, really, is platitudes or advice.

And Soo has never wanted advice.

'Yeah, fair enough. I get it.' JB says instead, simply.

Perhaps this shitty cancellation of the tour is the blow that has really done it for ever-resilient Soo. JB watches their friend, as she begins to rummage in a chic tote bag from some obscure gallery, eventually bringing out a high SPF lip balm and busying herself applying it.

God, JB hates the word 'resilient'.

Why should anyone have to be resilient? Why should that quality be so feted? It's less a laudable attribute, than a sign we've simply been failed by circumstances beyond our control. The curling idea for a poem begins to sprout in JB's mind, and they reach for their phone, tap in a quick note: *resist resilience – reliance – their reliance on our resilience—*

And they feel it – that first shimmer . . .

When they look up, Soo is smiling. A smile of recognition. Apart from Prisha, Soo is probably the only person who always seems to recognise immediately where JB has gone in those moments. It's not so much the 'flash of inspiration', thinks JB, as a retreating into the cave: the dark cool internal place where ideas begin to stretch, to take root.

But then. *Oh God.* Then there's something about Soo's smile – the slightest tilt of the head, as she fiddles with her lip balm stick – that makes them think of those fucking videos again—

Stop it. We all just do what we have to do to get by.

'I think you *should* do it, actually. Film it – *Always Emerging.*' JB is surprised by the force in their voice, the unsolicited advice they know they oughtn't to be giving. They start rolling another cigarette, needing something to do with their itching fingers. 'Prioritise it, Soo. Your work. Your *art.* Not above Anya, obviously, but above—'

They break off. Make a bit of a meal about fiddling with a stray bit of baccy, as if they're not a total pro at rolling one-handed if needed.

'Well, yeah. Sure. "Prioritise art". But that's easier said than done. It's about *time.* Isn't it?'

JB thought it was about money. But maybe it isn't, not anymore. Maybe being a demure little doll on the internet pays the bills. JB wonders how many hours a week Soo wastes, whispering into the void.

Or if it is her other work that pays the bills.

As JB lights the cigarette, they feel a corresponding flare of rage, a feeling they try never to let themselves feel – how hard they try, to always be accepting and neutral – at how Soo must continually sell herself in order to survive. But also (*there it is, the lick of horrid judgement*) that she *chooses* to sell herself. Her image. Her body. An object, of desire.

Objectified.

JB has always known that they must be non-judgemental – they must *not object* – to Soo's sex work if they want to remain Soo's friend, and if they want Soo to feel like she can ever talk about it. Not that she does, really. But JB still is careful to watch their words, to watch their language, around Soo – to do the right reading. When it comes to this ASMR shit, though . . . well, JB doesn't even know if they *do* know the right terminology. And so instead of broaching any of it, the words that come out are:

'Right, are we going to the pub then or what?'

It's a knee-jerk response, they recognise immediately. And an old one, really: JB isn't a big drinker these days – has been very careful with it ever since becoming poly, preferring to be really present, trying to make conscious choices. The less they drank the more clear-minded they felt.

But setting things to rights over the cheapest pints available was how Soo and JB's friendship had been founded: sneaking away from the shows of former coursemates to merrily pull them apart over a cider and crisps in a beer garden or meeting inside cosy pubs, away from freezing flatshares, rubbish housemates, or creepy bosses, and feeling just so damn *glad* of each other. There had been a growing, fuzzy satisfaction in the way their lives seemed to Velcro together in their years in London – the thousand tiny hooks that bound them to each other, the pleasure of finding someone who understood you, who instantly cackled at the same time you cackled when you witnessed some idiocy occurring. JB and Soo had been in cahoots. Them against the world, for years.

And there is pleasure at sinking into that feeling again – although thankfully they no longer merely seek out the cheapest pints, sitting indoors with alcoholics in nicotine-stained pubs that were so uncool they became kind of cool. Instead, Soo takes them to a pub on a hill in Heeley, nearer to where she lives, with nice beer and a nice beer garden and a nice view. And the things they moan about are different now, too: how hard it is to get a mortgage when you're both freelancers; the appalling focus on testing and 'attainment' in schools these days. Although some things will never change – there'll always be Tories to loathe, the Arts Council application portal to complain about, and each other's talent to affectionately hype.

It does not take long for JB to start to feel quite drunk off the nice local beer. They are matching Soo's drinking speed, and Soo seems demob happy. And as they lose track of the number of drinks they have had, they also lose track of the time – the hours seeming to roll into each other much faster than they usually do.

The pub has got steadily busier and busier. They keep having to share their table with new strangers, who usually say hello, and sometimes do a double-take at JB – the usual figuring-it-out stealth glances, or full-on stares. One young set of parents are quietly absorbed in their own pints, but their two young kids with Milky Bar blonde hair do screeching laps of the beer garden and then embark on a series of impersonations of all the animals they'd seen in the nearby city farm. Soo joins in, eventually getting up to do a surprisingly hilarious full-body impression of a goat, and making both children collapse in delighted giggles.

'A natural performer,' JB comments when Soo is finally allowed to sit back down, and Soo points out that they are, in fact, *a professional*, and laughs with a lightness that lifts JB's heart.

Soo suggests another round, but JB winces. 'I might need a lie down if I have another. Possibly under this table.'

'Oh come on JB! This is the first weekend I've had all to myself in *so long*! Let's get some more pints, and some pizza. To mop it up. You can get this really good, whatsitcalled – the thing – oh you know, the trendy bread—'

'. . .'

'It takes ages. You know. All the bread bros! Oh my *God* you know what I mean—'

'Sourdough?'

'Yes! But sourdough pizza. Here! It comes to us. Takeaway. We just need to get the app . . . thingy.'

This proves remarkably difficult. JB's fingers feel like thumbs, and their thumbs feel like sausages. They do not understand, or like, the app.

Soo orders more pints, while they wait for the pizza.

JB is not totally sure what they were just talking about, but they are sure that neither the YouTube videos nor the other way Soo makes money have come up, and that they really ought to be able to talk about such things.

'So, Soo. Come on. Talk to me about this . . . this ASMR stuff.'

Soo, who is drunk enough that she has stolen a fag and keeps making disgusted faces as she smokes it, raises its glowing tip in line with her rising eyebrows, rather haughtily.

'Well. What do you want to know?'

'Just...' What *does* JB want to know? Do they actually want to know anything or do they just want Soo to know they know? 'Just I went on your YouTube. And it's ... it's a lot isn't it?'

'Yeah. Well. I mean. It's not *art* is it—'

'It's not?'

Soo looks at JB blankly, and JB feels like they did once wonder if the YouTube videos were – something else – something arty – but the thought doesn't cohere – they can't—

'Never mind.'

'I mean, I know it's ... trash, I just – it's quite fun, OK?'

She sounds defensive, which is unfair JB thinks, because they haven't even said anything negative about it yet! And their face is definitely carefully neutral. Very careful.

'Yeah, no, cool, sure.'

'It's an easy way to make a little bit of money and ... I – I don't have to think about it? I just look at what's trending and I just do it, record for a couple of hours at night once Anya is in bed, and then I just – get on with my life ... OK?'

There's a thought, that's struggling to take shape in JB's mind: that maybe Soo *should* think about it more. That it is – what's the word – problematic. *Objectionable.*

That would sound a bit too critical. Too damning.

'Yeah no I get that. And it seems harmless ...'

JB's thoughts seem to have been chopped up in little pieces and it's hard to keep them in the right order.

They're briefly distracted, by an older man and a younger woman asking if they can share their table; the family have gone home. The woman looks dimly familiar to JB, though they can't think why – something about the curly dark hair. But that won't come into focus either.

JB and Soo just nod, make some small welcoming gestures, then JB continues.

'But is it? Is it really?'

'Is what really what?'

'Are these videos really so . . . *harmless*?'

Soo stubs out the cigarette in the large plastic ashtray, although she isn't even close to the end of it. Not saying anything.

It feels to JB like a defensive move.

'I just think . . . look, it's always *young women* isn't it?'

'Oh come on, don't go there. It's such a tedious argument.' Round and round Soo presses the half-smoked cigarette. Grinding it down. '*No*, ASMR isn't sexual, it's a totally different kind of feeling. But even if it was – what exactly is wrong with—'

'Uh, that's not what I was saying! Don't put words in my mouth!'

Soo's own mouth snaps shut, she seems to pull back in her seat which is impressive given she's sitting on a picnic table.

JB shoots a glance at their taciturn table-sharers, who don't seem to be saying much to each other. Fortunately, they don't seem to have any interest in Soo and JB's incoherent spat, either.

'I was saying . . .'

What were they saying?

The arguments that felt very urgent five seconds ago have shattered into ungraspable tiny particles in JB's mind.

'Um, right. Yeah. What I was *saying* was . . . It's – it's not really just about them being sexually attractive, it's . . . like, it being all women, *serving*. Offering pleasure and comfort and—'

'Is that not what women *do* do, though? Everywhere?'

Then JB feels full of frustration, foaming up inside their chest. Frustration at the world, and at how it has shaped Soo's life. Frustration at their own, sudden, fat-tongued inarticulacy. It's an unfamiliar feeling, and they don't like it.

They're usually really *good* at chatting about things.

'But those AM— AM – ASMR videos, right, they're not, like, a *comment* on those expectations, like your art is! It's – oh what's the fucking word – it's *complicit*.'

'Oh for God's sake, Ja—'

Soo interrupts angrily, then instantly breaks off, bites their lip. And there's a new, large, solid silence between them.

The shape of JB's deadname.

JB feels like they can almost see it in the air. Imagines it, in big bubble writing, hovering, bobbing. Like ominous Clipart.

'Sorry. It just—'

'Don't worry.' JB manages to sound breezy, but it's such a long time since this has happened to them, it feels strange. A rip, a rupture, in the fabric of the evening.

Then the pizzas arrive.

They both fall on them, grateful for the displacement activity, for the excuse not to have to talk for a few moments.

'Now then, Manda, I've got summat to tell you, actually.'

It is the man sitting next to JB. They've been vaguely, increasingly aware of his smell, even outdoors, his blue-and-white football shirt looking like it could use a good wash. JB had shuffled as far over on the picnic table seat as possible, but somehow this utterance really carries, cutting through their heavy, pizza-munching silence; there's a volume-raising note of pride to it, perhaps, and it piques JB's drunk interest.

'Oh yeah.'

JB glances swiftly at the younger woman. She doesn't look too optimistic about whatever it is the man has to tell her.

'I'm going out with that group, tomorrow. You know. One you always go on at me about. Bill's walking group, in't it. Kinder Scout way.'

And there is definitely something hopeful, in his voice, his delivery.

'Paid me dues for the minibus in advance. He'll be round ha'past nine, so you'll have to shuffle off home then, love. That all right?'

The woman's pint glass is raised halfway to her mouth, and hovers there, as her expression changes. The effect is like someone wiping a mirror clean: you can suddenly see a whole new face. Lit up, by a bright, real grin.

'Dad! That's ... oh, that's great. I think – I think it'll be really, really good for you.'

She dips her head, and holds out her glass, to cheers him. And as she does so, she says something, in a lower voice, her face hidden a little below her hair, and it's like she addresses whatever it is down to the table – all of which means it's hard for JB (who's become weirdly invested in their awkward, tender interaction) to hear what she says.

But what they *think* they hear her say, is:

'I'm right proud of you, Dad.'

And the dad clonks his glass a little too energetically against his daughter's, and then both of them drain a goodly portion of what is left in each, and then they start discussing exactly which train after nine-thirty she'll be able to catch back to Manchester and if it'll be the fast or the slow one and...

And JB flicks their attention back to Soo, wanting to catch her eyes and do a shared silent acknowledgement of this incredibly British display of father-daughter bonding. But Soo doesn't seem to have noticed it at all, and JB wonders if she is just absorbed in the pizza, or if she had been busy internally scrabbling for a safe topic for the two of them, because Soo suddenly starts holding forth about the imminent wedding of a mutual friend to her terrible boyfriend. And soon they are once more finishing each other's thoughts, on how reading bridal magazines for a year has turned said friend into a hetero-normative bore, and how dismal wedding bands usually turn out to be...

JB and Soo are cheerfully shouting at each other about this, when the darkness comes.

It feels too quick for nightfall, and Soo points upwards behind JB, at a fat, solid bank of clouds the blue-grey colour of slate that are rapidly rolling almost over them.

'Oh, shit.'

The thunder rumbles a warning, and then the rain comes down with almost comic timing, just as everyone in the beer garden has turned their heads to the sky.

And then it is chaos. The rain is both a distant roar and a present xylophonic tinkle where it hits scores of pint glasses. Everyone is struggling to get up, to disentangle badly-behaving limbs from the picnic benches. The cool of the rain is welcome for only the briefest moment and then surprisingly cold on JB's neck. Their body shudders into goosebumps.

JB and Soo abandon the ends of their pints and run out onto the street, worried about slipping as they run but giddy too, the daftness of rain, the release of moving moving moving, together...

Soo has taken JB's hand, to steer them down the correct road. A group of teenagers pull hoods over their heads as they do a scooching sprint; a couple are bound under a brolly, and a small dog trots like it's personally affronted by the wet. But Soo and JB keep alternating between a crouching, protective run, and then bursting into laughter at the downpour, raising their faces, letting the rain streak down and into their mouths.

JB is incredibly thirsty. They could simply drink the sky.

Soo's hands are so wet they can barely get the key in the door, something which seems extremely funny to JB. Then a great crack of lightning briefly illuminates the flat as they step inside, and they both reel dramatically at it.

A long glass of water in the kitchen, a tiny offshoot from a small sitting room studded with Peppa Pig paraphernalia. JB keeps the lights off, hoping for more lightning – that blue-silver flash of electricity.

Soo comes back in with towels, but JB just shakes their head like a dog. 'Practically dry already!'

'Well your hair is. But you're soaking.'

It's true, JB's T-shirt clings to them.

They strip it off, and their shorts, why not, and gesture for Soo to throw a towel.

Instead, she comes toward them. Opening the towel. Passing it around JB. Its slightly scratchy surface feels abrasive at first as she rubs down JB's nearly-naked body. Then it begins to feel softer, warmer. Wrapping. Cocooning.

Soo has her own towel tied round her, toga-style. Her hair has separated into thick, damp strands.

They are dripping.

Something about the rubbing action – although it is gentle now, caring – causes Soo's towel to come loose. It drops to the kitchen floor, puddling around her feet, and she is fully naked below it.

JB is very used to seeing Soo's naked body – on screen, in galleries, on holidays. But it's been a long time since they had sex – *when would it have even last been,* they wonder – their sense of time feels muddy and indistinct – *years ago – certainly before Prisha – before they had decided on 'JB' – before Soo started sex work—*

Soo opens the towel she's drying JB with so that she can step

198

in closer, and now JB takes hold of its edges, and is wrapping it around Soo so they are both swaddled within it, and for a moment they wonder if this will be all it is, simply a hug. A binding of the two of them together.

But then Soo raises her head, and there is a kiss. The second towel soon drops, too.

Something rises up inside JB, but their brain feels a little disconnected from what is happening in their body.

Do they actually want this?

It is happening, anyway.

It is familiar, and it is not familiar.

The next thing JB feels aware of is a sweet pressure, Soo wrapping herself round them, almost leaning off them, in order to rub and press.

Then Soo is whispering about being at the end of their period, how there *might still be some . . .* and JB mutters about not caring (impossible to be poly and not embrace period sex, scheduling nightmare).

Then they are somehow in Soo's bed—

But the experience refuses to cohere. It's like JB can only see or feel one thing at a time. Like they're distracted, fragmented. Pixelated. Their eyes travel over Soo's body, somehow not able to piece it all together—

The sight of Soo's nipples, so much larger than Prisha's, rolling between finger and thumb.

A flash of pleasure from Soo's tongue, licking between their legs.

The sight of Soo's head, bobbing, her damp dark hair slick as it snakes on JB's belly and thighs.

A flash of discomfort from Soo's not-lubed-enough finger shoved up their arsehole.

The sight of Soo's mouth, close up, open like a wound, a wet red hole in the darkness.

Anatomised.

No, that's not the right word.

Atomised.

As if they can only ever see part of the picture, even now, as their bodies come together...

Then JB realises that Soo is looking very intently at them, as if she's been watching them watching her, and now is trying to find something in their face. But JB finds they can't quite hold their gaze either. Everything is too slippery.

Soo has been making all the right noises, but JB wonders if it feels a bit off to them too?

And JB wants to stop – to laugh, and hug her, and say 'whoops, this was a silly mistake'. But they still feel drunk and sloppy, and their thoughts still aren't cohering, and calling a halt to things seems more effort than simply . . . carrying on. And it's not like it's awful, they've had much worse sex with people they massively fancy. Maybe it's just that—

That they don't really see Soo that way.

Or maybe it's that Soo doesn't really see them that way, anymore.

A lightning-flash memory of Soo calling them the wrong name; the way it just burst out of her.

Probably nearly done now anyway, JB tells themselves. They might be near to coming.

. . .

. . .

. . .

Oh God, it is actually taking ages.

. . .

. . .

. . .

Finally. But it feels empty, hard-won. They should have just acknowledged that it wasn't working. JB feels a heavy sense of disappointment in themselves beginning to drag through their body.

And maybe Soo feels the same, because she makes no attempt to snuggle or kiss. Just rolls over to grab a tissue, wipes herself, throws it in the bin. *An almost professional demeanour,* thinks JB – and then hates themselves for it.

Soo passes the tissues to JB.

They dry themselves, and rub a little rusty residue from their nail beds, then toss the tissues in the bin.

Almost immediately the weight of sleep – of heavy, sodden, irresistible sleep – pulls over them like a thick, heavy, downy blanket, and they sink into the oblivion.

JB wakes to incredible dryness. Brief disorientation, until the room reassembles itself – not their room, not Prisha, but Sheffield . . . Soo . . . Soo's bed.

JB reaches around on the floor next to the bed – a dim memory of bringing a water glass – *please God* – and yes, it's there, and half full. The water tastes almost sweet, such is the relief.

They start a little, when they see Soo is sitting by the window. At her desk. Looking out of one corner not quite covered by a pair of thick curtains, as if pointedly not looking at JB.

The tangerine haze from the street lights outside gently illuminates her face. She is sitting, hands folded in her lap. Her face unreadable – is it the dimness? Is it the distance?

There's a funny, held stillness to the moment, as if Soo is a statue, frozen in space and time.

JB registers what's on the desk, next to her. The oversized microphone, so comically large it looks tumescent, somehow. Boxes and organisers full of make-up and brushes and bottles and different bits of crap they've seen in the videos. The bobbles of a sheet of bubble wrap catching a little of the light; weird textured sponges piled up like cumulus clouds. A neat little camera on a stand. Lights: angled, poised, ready to work.

When their eyes flick back to Soo's face, she is looking directly at JB.

'Hey,' she says, softly. Almost whispering.

'Hey.'

'Go back to sleep.'

'You OK...?'

'Yeah. Fine. Just thinking.'

'Do you want...' JB doesn't know what Soo might want, what to offer. 'Do you want me to sleep next door? I can go on the sofa...'

'No. It's fine.'

But something doesn't feel fine.

'Go back to sleep.'

JB is about to get up, to locate their 'let's talk this through' voice. But they feel so very tired. A digital clock says it is 3.13 a.m. Maybe, just this once, they can leave it.

Till morning, anyway. Everything will no doubt seem lighter, brighter then. It will be easier to talk, properly.

And they will; they must.

Just be honest about what just happened. About the fact that maybe it shouldn't have happened at all. Because what matters is their friendship. The sex is just a side product of all the... *love*, that they feel for Soo. Unimportant, in the grand scheme of things.

And, on this occasion, maybe just a silly little mistake.

JB lies back down, and pretends to sleep. Hoping that making their breath sound slow and heavy and asleep will actually help them fall asleep. But when Soo comes back to bed they are still awake, as stiff and posed as some reclined nude.

Chapter 7

Soo

On the train. Great to see you.

Soo is typing

. . .

Soo is typing

Are we going to talk about this?

What bit of 'this' exactly?

Soo is typing

I don't know. Things just feel . . . weird.

Yeah.

JB is typing

I mean, I did try to talk to you about it this morning.

But you seemed determined that we just went out and met your friends.

JB is typing

. . .

THE START OF SOMETHING

JB is typing

I didn't feel like I could talk to you. Like you were willing to talk.

Have I upset you?

> *No!*

> Soo is typing

> *. . .*

> Soo is typing

> *I just feel weird about what happened.*

You mean having sex . . . ?

> *Yeah. I don't know, I just felt strange afterwards.*

I know what you mean.

Should have said something . . .

> *Well you could have said something too!*

That's what I meant.

*I should have said something.

Well we both should have?

> Soo is typing

Silly

> *. . .*

> *Right*

> *Sorry*

. . .

No need to apologise, I don't think.

Soo is typing

. . .

Soo is typing

I dunno, it didn't feel great. Between friends.

I mean I think we can just be friends who don't have sex?

*I don't care about having bad sex I care
that you can't talk to me about it!*

*That seems a bit unfair, I did tried to talk to you but you
didn't want to.*

*Try

. . .

Soo is typing

I just wanted you to make it OK and you just went to sleep!

When I tried to you told me to go to sleep?

And I was drunk.

And really tired.

So

. . .

Soo is typing

. . .

*Soo you must see you are being unfair here. What is this
really about?*

I think it's really OK if we just don't fancy each other.

Or have once had slightly regrettable sex.

But why have things changed?

But this feels like something else?

Soo puts her phone back in the capacious pocket of her dress. *Enough.* Stop it.

But it doesn't feel enough.

She doesn't even really know why she feels this urge to keep prodding JB, but she does. She knows she is being unfair. But she finds she wants to needle them. To poke them, provoke them into a reaction. Despite having spent all day avoiding talking to them about it, rushing around Sheffield being sociable, pretending nothing was wrong.

The early evening is still bright, the sky a crystalline blue that makes Soo think of cut, clear gemstones. She is waiting for a bus. It's already late. Luckily Soo has left plenty of time. Always does; being late puts you on the back foot and she likes to remain on frontest bit of her front foot. Always.

Why *had* things changed? It's not like Soo has particularly treasured memories of the few times she and JB had hooked up before, in those hectic years rattling around South London after graduating. If it had been amazing – if they'd had real sexual chemistry – they might've got together properly.

But it *did* use to be fun. What Soo remembers most is laughter. Just rolling around together. That feeling of liking that person more than anyone else, so why bother spending your time with anyone else. And then being horny and also being in bed with your best mate, so why not. No big deal.

But Saturday night . . . Saturday night had felt more like being on a job.

207

Soo burns with shame to think of it like that – *not with JB, not with a friend, not her and JB* – and ducks her head down even as they step forward to flag down the bus, finally lumbering down the road.

Because it had been such a good day, up until that point. It had been so good to see JB again – truly nourishing, to spend that time with someone you care about that much. Someone who, no matter how long the gap between seeing each other, it feels instantly easy with. And someone who knows all the different sides to her: the pre-Anya self, and the artist self, and the mother self, and the struggling-to-get-by self, and the silly, laughing, weightless self.

It was quite unlike spending time with the group of young mums Soo has got to know via nursery and the school gates. They are great for gossip over a slice of cake or complaining about the tyranny of a six-year-old's dietary requirements with a cheeky glass of 'savvy b', and Soo is just ridiculously grateful for their support (the emergency pick-ups; the sharing of babysitters). It is a practical imperative that she keeps them on her side; she's been honest about the situation with Liam, which elicited a lot of useful sympathy, but has remained deliberately vague about work ('digital comms and content – webby stuff!').

But they have absolutely no idea who she really is.

Sometimes Soo wonders what they'd be more shocked by: her sex work, or her artwork.

It is JB who Soo has always thought of as the one person in the world who really sees her whole self. The one person she can be this whole self with – unfiltered, to use the modern parlance.

And this is why the end of the night felt so jarring. The kissing had begun sweetly, but the minute they were in her bed, it was like they had both slipped out of gear and just couldn't get back in. Something that had felt easy and natural and right suddenly felt . . . off. It wasn't really that it became transactional, or that she needed to disassociate, like she sometimes did with clients – she'd just felt the need to get through it. There'd been none of the old laughter, their shared lightness.

And while Soo really isn't sure what went wrong, or how, she *is* pretty sure it came from JB. Something about the way they looked at her—

Come on now, you *were* both just quite drunk, Soo's sensible internal voice intrudes, trying to damp down this strange rise of petulance she feels, this spoiling for a fight. (It's the internal version of the voice she uses when she talks to Anya, she realises, when her daughter has a rare tantrum.) And yes, OK, normally when she and JB get drunk they get closer . . . but maybe this is just another thing that has changed lately. Drinking isn't part of Soo's life in that way, not since Anya. Saturday afternoon had been a strange aberration; an explosion of freedom. Or just a lazily nostalgic harking back, to how she and JB used to interact with each other. Putting on old habits, like a saggy, comfortable coat.

Outside of the bus's window, the city looks washed clean by the storm. The air is fresher this evening than it has been in weeks.

Soo's sensible voice tells her to 'centre'. Tells her to ignore her phone and to stop going over and over things, niggling over why she feels so shit, and to simply watch life from the window. To be in the active, immediate present. Deep breath in; deep breath out.

Witness the municipal plants in the large concrete buckets, that seem to have picked up a little from drinking all that rain, their leaves lifting.

Witness the fuchsia bush covered in dangling pink flowers. They look like tiny ballerinas, dancing on the air.

Witness a woman making a face into a buggy. It reminds her of when Anya was small and how she would kick her chubby little legs constantly while in the pram, and Soo thinks well *no wonder* she likes swimming and bike riding and the trampoline at her friend's house. Just a little froggy.

Then she sees a lost soft pale blue teddy, propped up on a wall near a bus stop they wait at for ages while some teenagers try to get away with not paying. It looks so forlorn—

Soo gets her phone out again.

Messages from JB.

She puts on her headphones instead. Maybe a podcast.

But after about ten minutes of two women nattering away, she realises she has barely heard a word of their discussion.

Because really, all that she can hear – playing as loud and clear as if recorded on a professional microphone – is the thought that's been trying to push its way into her consciousness all day: *Maybe JB is disgusted by you.*

Disgusted.

Soo sees JB's face, and that expression – that flash – that they have seen often, micronanomilliseconds of it, revealing a thought that is tiny and suppressed, but is *there* whenever they talk about her sex work. Sometimes, it's also there when JB looks at her art; the ruder stuff, the sexier stuff, the more explicit stuff. And now, it is there around any mention of the ASMR videos – barely disguised, rippling over their evenly-spaced, usually carefully held-still features: the thick, straight eyebrows, the clear direct gaze, a smooth brow below the neat symmetrical framing device of their buzzcut hairline. All briefly, unusually, animated, revealing true feelings. An inner horror at what Soo does.

At who Soo is.

Oh, they'd never say anything. They are too good a friend for that.

No, actually, they are simply too *progressive* for that, thinks Soo, allowing her indignation to rustle through her again, like dry agitating leaves. JB has always read all the right books, says all the right things. Follows the correct kind of theoretical feminist orthodoxy. Soo knows that after telling them about the sex work, they went away and read half a library of the most radical literature about it. JB has, on at least two occasions, proved themselves more cognisant of the arguments in favour of legalising brothel-keeping than she is – elegantly trouncing ignorant or reactionary opinions spouted by acquaintances who have no idea how Soo actually earns a living.

But sometimes, Soo wishes JB would just unleash their gut feelings. Because this neutral non-judgement feels too polite, too restrained, for their true friendship. She remembers seeing the flash the very first time she had told JB, years ago, over a pint in a pub in Manchester, that the only reason she could afford the ticket there was because she'd started sex work. And she thought – didn't she – that she saw the flash in bed last night, as they had sex, as JB's eyes darted around her body.

Somehow, Soo felt that her old friend wasn't looking at her like a person, but *as a body*.

A body for sale. Probably wondering who else saw it, touched it, used it.

Music. Soo puts on a Planningtorock album she's been listening to a lot. She almost instantly pauses it. Not the right vibe.

She should try to cheer herself up, pull herself out of this mood she's sinking into. But the day had been spent being too bright, almost ignoring JB (who she found she couldn't quite look straight at) in favour of chatting garrulously with a couple of other friends she'd insisted they met for brunch before going to the new Stephen Schad exhibition, installed around the outside of the Kelham Island Museum. A quick drink on the terrace outside Social Works, and then it was time for JB's train without them having had a moment alone together.

The whole day had been a silly rushing towards distraction. As if the weirdness between them would just evaporate if she ignored it.

Obviously, it's only made things worse.

And now she is wasting her precious last few hours of her precious weekend off from *being-a-mum* going all the way to Broomhill for a client. She'd seen the request when she got home, and agreed to it before she had time to let herself think about why she was feeling so weird.

Further distraction. *Paid* distraction.

Soo wouldn't usually go to a client's house, but she wanted to get out of her own. And couldn't face the thought of changing the sheets, twice.

She returns to Spotify. Puts on Bob Dylan, which for her is the musical equivalent of wading into the middle of a cold pond. Wallowing.

She tells herself to look out again, but all she can see is the blank public-transport look on her face, blurred in the window's reflection so it appears like a plain yellow–white mask. As if her face is a canvas about to be painted on.

Tonight, it will be the character of the willing innocent young girl, ready to be corrupted. There is a pleated mini skirt and sailor blouse and long socks in her bag.

This 'character' is always the most popular – much more so than when Soo used to try to be glamorous or sexy in her profile. She doesn't really care. She won't do a baby voice, or actively pretend to be underage or anything like that. But she simply is small, and she can easily look young, and that pays. It is not her fault this is what society prizes. It is not even really the men's fault this is what they have been trained to find attractive – in art and adverts and films and *everything*.

Even so, Soo doesn't want to think about that or look at herself in the window anymore at this precise moment. She reaches for her phone, looks at JB's messages.

I don't know why things have changed.

Maybe you should tell me.

Then there was an eleven-minute gap.

I didn't think it mattered to be honest.

But maybe it does.

Maybe we have both 'changed'.

Fuck you JB, thinks Soo.

She is nearly there. The tree-lined streets are broader in this part of town, the houses large Victorian things, set back from the roads.

When she gets off the bus, she still has a few minutes to spare before she's meant to arrive. Soo checks the navigation on her phone, then goes back to WhatsApp. The urge to say something back to JB is rising up in her chest, crunchy and rattling.

She slides the microphone symbol up, to leave a voice note.

'*Hey. Thanks for your messages. I was just on a bus. Sorry for not replying, like, right away. It seems like you are pissed off and I'm not sure why?*'

Untrue, Soo knows exactly why, it is because *she* has acted pissed off: sending a series of icy messages and then stopping replying. But she feels shit and it is as if the urge to also make JB feel shit too is overwhelming everything else. The dark waters of the pond, an irresistible downwards drag.

'Why don't you just come out and say whatever it is you are really thinking JB? Why are you always so ... I dunno, so fucking careful with your speech? Like ... like, what do you mean, about 'changing'? Of course I have changed, I've known you for literally years and it would be weird if I hadn't ...'

Soo pauses, wondering what more she has to say – wondering how far she dare go in accusing JB – and then gives up and presses send.

She doesn't really feel better for having left the message, which is annoying. She feels, if anything, more worked up. Because she hadn't really said anything. She's not good with words. That's JB's thing. Or it's meant to be, anyway.

But here is a gate and a short flagstone path to a large, dark-green front door, its surface glossy as a boiled sweet. Double-fronted, a tangle of wisteria up one side, a sprawling lavender bush on the other that is in need of a prune. Soo flicks her phone to silent.

The door is opened very quickly after she rings the bell.

'Come in.'

Classically furtive. No doubt worried that little Tabitha across the road might see something and tell mummy, or that someone will dob him in on the Nextdoor app.

Soo applies her own glazed, unfocused expression as she steps into a large hallway. A way of seeing, without looking like you are really looking.

A quick assessment: it is fine. It is safe.

The hall is stuffed with, well, the stuff of family life. Teenagers, by the looks of things. Multiple unmatched pairs of scruffy trainers and sandals, looking like they've been paused in the

moment of kicking each other, scuffling on the wooden floorboards. Politer boots in rows behind. Coats and jackets fighting
for hook space, the whole system looking like it might be
about to collapse. Sagging, empty totes and backpacks looped
over the banister.

The man – Anthony or Antony? – Soo can't remember and it
doesn't matter does it – is tall, but not too heavily built. Narrow
of hip and shoulder, in a shirt of some fine, pale material, open
at a lightly stubbled neck. Pale brown hair curls back off an
only slightly receding hairline, in soft waves. A little awkward
in posture – a hangover from a lifetime of feeling like he's
towering over people? Or a reaction to this particular situation?
Maybe the latter: he is blinking, nervously.

'Hi. Hi. It's Cindy, isn't it?'

Soo nods. 'Yes, that's right.'

'Do you want a – a drink, or anything?' He gestures his
long body towards what is presumably a kitchen, then flicks an
eye upstairs, rests a hand on the crowded bottom post of the
banister. 'Or we can go . . .'

Soo notices that one of the totes is from the South London
Gallery. It's one of her favourites, and she wonders if perhaps
they might—

Nope. Tonight, it needs to be businesslike. No finding a connection.

Usually, she spends a good deal of her time putting clients
at ease, chatting about their day or hers, trying to help them to
relax, and communicate what it is they really want. She is adept
at pretending to be *interested*. Always has questions. Has a knack
for making people feel seen, and heard. Feel *special*.

But actually, this one had been clear and respectful and
straightforward about exactly what he was after in his email.
And more to the point, Soo is just not in the mood. She cannot

be arsed. If that means he reviews her badly – *didn't smile;*
unfriendly; not engaged – so be it.

'Actually a glass of water would be good.'

'Sure. Right. Coming up. Or, well, um, why don't you come
through . . .'

He turns and leads her into a big kitchen extension – elegant,
beneath and around the mess. Gorgeous pendant lights in thick,
almost dripping, heavy glass over a kitchen island. A beautifully
glazed, deep indigo fruit bowl filled with bananas and lemons.
Large vintage posters for shows of Gauguin, Picasso, Matisse,
in very nice pale wooden frames. But also on the island: a
single, half-empty takeaway carton of rice he'd clearly forgotten
to throw out (someone else enjoying a weekend away from
children, Soo guesses); mountains of paper and newspapers
and books (a copy of *Ways of Seeing* that looks like it's about
to fall apart; a shiny hardback of that book JB was talking
about, *The Myth of Empire*). One whole stretch of wall is a
giant blackboard, with reminders – *ring optician!; Daniel's concert
NOW STARTS AT 7PM* – and a shopping list: *ramen, fenugreek,
Ben & Jerry's.*

Large French doors reflect the scene back at them, the light
seeming too bright and yellow in the glass. There's presumably
a nice garden outside, but the glare is impossible to see beyond.
Soo can only see herself.

Anthony fills a glass for her hastily, looks at a wine bottle,
blinks rapidly, looks away, and then looks again.

'I might . . .?' he gestures to the bottle. Soo indicates with a
tiny shrug of her shoulder, her mouth, that it's fine.

'Right!' he announces cheerily, as he replaces the rubbery
stopper in the opened bottle of Cabernet Sauvignon and lifts
his glass (smaller than he would usually pour, somehow she can
just tell).

He leads the way back down the hall, and upstairs, turning lights on and off as they go. More nice prints and posters. A couple of Manets, and an unusual Egon Schiele; a Lucian Freud nude placed in dialogue next to a Suzanne Valadon one. They go up a floor, and then another. Here, there are quite a few of what she considers the less-tasteful Gauguins. Those exoticised women from – where was it – Tahiti. With their tits out.

Underaged, weren't they. Famously. Liked them young.

Makes sense.

Soo observes all this – she is always vigilant, watchful, taking in all the information she can – but it's also a fairly neutral observation. Because as long as she's safe, she doesn't care about the lives of these men. None of her business.

And because, really, her mind is on the rectangular object in her pocket. Wondering if its screen is lit up with a message from JB. Wondering what words are lurking, now, on both her phone and JB's.

'So, ah, this is the bedroom . . .'

This is definitely not his bedroom. Guest bedroom; tucked out of the way at the top of the house. An attractive but quite ancient floral-patterned duvet cover. An ever-so-slightly musty smell, in the thick, risen heat of the attic room, even though the skylight is open. A large chest of drawers in heavier wood than would suit the pale elegance of the rest of the house.

And, weirdly, a series of photographs on the wall. Sexy, contemporary. Helmut Newton. Guy Bourdin. Off-the-peg, self-conscious eroticism for people who think they like art more than they think they like porn, judges Soo.

Weird choice for a guest room.

He fusses around, lighting a scented candle, turning on the bedside lamps and then killing the overhead one.

Ah. So this is not this room's first use specifically for sex, thinks Soo. Good. The more straightforward, the better.

'There's a little bathroom next door, if you want to, ah, to—'

'To change. Sure.'

Soo can't help but look at her phone as she slips off her dark charcoal grey dress, and folds it neatly on top of her bag, awaiting her later return to her self.

A message from Lyds, who they'd been hanging out with that day. Which can wait.

An eBay alert: Soo has been unsuccessful in bidding on a scooter, which she'd wanted to get for Anya.

A notification: a headline about Tory infighting. *Plus ça change.*

And messages from JB.

You know what change I'm talking about.

Maybe it didn't work last night because you just didn't fancy me anymore. Because I have changed. Obviously.

And if it is, I get that. That's actually really ok.

Then there are two voice notes. With – intriguingly – a gap of fully seven minutes between them. Frustrating, because there's no way she can really listen to them while this guy is waiting next door.

Soo looks again at the messages, and feels a brief flare of irritation that JB always uses such proper punctuation and spelling but never ever softens anything with exclamation marks.

!

Then her parent voice scolds her for being so petty. And she thinks it's probably just another distraction from what she's *really* annoyed about: how *absurd* it is that JB would think that any of this is about them being non-binary, for heaven's sake.

She takes off her pants, slides a little lube inside her, and then pulls on clean, tiny, lacy white knickers and a push-up white cotton bra.

She pulls on the little pleated navy skirt and the almost see-through white blouse.

She pulls on the socks, which stick momentarily to the bottom of her feet, slightly tacky from going barefoot in her little white plimsole trainers on the journey over.

She hopes they don't smell. Well, the socks will cover it if they do. She stuffs her feet back into the plimsoles.

And while she does it all she thinks: *Fucking JB.* And wonders what else is in the voice notes.

Soo fluffs her hair in the small bathroom mirror, reapplying the tinted lip balm that gives her lips a youthful sheen, an interior pinkness, and returns to the bedroom.

His Adam's apple visibly moves up and down as he swallows heavily when she moves towards him.

She does a bit of coy business (finger in mouth; kneeling up on the bed; slowly lifting her skirt), but it's all on autopilot. And when it's this straightforward and unalarming (his eyes are heavy with lust, but he's slow in his movements, careful, as if figuring out what he's allowed to do), it becomes an easy, mindless performance. A part of Soo's brain always remains on high alert – her phone in reach on the bedside table; her bag near the door should she need to grab and run – but most of her thoughts are occupied not with how his hands feel, but how JB's did.

With what they might've been thinking.

Did JB really think that she cared what fucking gender they identified as? As if the attraction between them had *ever* been about bodies or identities, instead of ideas and jokes and joy and laughter and safety ...

Did they really think that was the sort of thing that she was bothered by, turned on or off by? JB, who had known her even in the days she wore fucking badges declaring that she was an Equal Opportunities Slut? Who'd seen her performance work 'Still Life with Men and Women'? (Soo had staged two beautifully lit, Caravaggio-worthy still lifes – one full of suggestively displayed figs and pomegranates and peaches, one full of proudly erect bananas and cucumbers – and then got on her knees and enthusiastically lapped at both.)

!

He gives a very loud groan on sliding a finger inside her, and she can't help think that he might be trying to convince himself of how turned on he is. He's not especially hard yet.

Shame. Soo had hoped this would be quick.

She ups the volume on her own performative moans, and then grasps his penis (unexpectedly short and thick) and pumps it efficiently.

What a silly thing for JB to worry about. And so unlike them! They were usually so secure in their identity, their sense of self and what they wanted and how to ask for it. Or at least, they had been for years now – Soo has to remind herself sometimes of how far JB has actually come, of how uneasy in their own skin they'd once been. How much effort they'd put into working themselves out into finding that strong, authentic self.

Perhaps even JB needs a little reassurance now and then. Like after a bad shag, for example.

A thought seizes Soo: how grim it is, that maybe she and JB had both had basically unwanted sex, given how good both of them are supposed to be at talking about this shit. How they are both supposed to be really properly *skilled* at navigating such things. By now.

Maybe it's harder, though, with old friends, wonders Soo as

she reaches for one of the condoms she brought with her. Easier to fall into old habits.

She attempts to unwrap it and put it on as seductively as she can. This action – which never really *is* that seductive, she thinks, no matter her efforts – is one she's often thought about using as the starting point for an art piece, too. Something about the attempted sexy performance of what is essentially a health and safety measure. But she's never got much further than that, the seed of the idea never quite getting to stretch, to take root.

Health and Safety would be a good title actually. Could you have a series of unexpected things in the condom wrapper, she ponders, as he presses his penis inside her—

'Fuuuuck!' he practically stutters. 'Oh, you're a good girl... God you're a good girl...'

She tilts her hips and rolls her head a bit, whining in faux pleasure, an excuse to keep her eyes tight shut.

But what would fit, snugly, inside the wrapper? A coin? Bit on the nose. Reminds her of her old project, with the pussy purses.

He's muttering on, and making the right noises, but there's something in the increasingly furious pace he's now forcing himself to go at that makes Soo think he, too, is just keen to finish rather than really getting all that much out of the situation.

She wonders briefly what his wife is – or was – like. She's not noticed any photographs on display. Hey, that's a thought: you could have a little round photograph of someone horrible inside the condom wrapper – a comic reveal. Sling them into the audience like tiny frisbees. Someone like Trump, she thinks. Maybe Freud? Or Mary Whitehouse. Probably no one would get that these days.

Well, this guy would – must be about the right age.

A pain in her upper arm abruptly yanks Soo back into the present. He is gripping her bicep, hard.

'Hey – stop it.' Her voice immediately snaps to professional, commanding, no hint of the pliant gasping girlishness she'd put on till then.

But as she speaks he jolts inside her and lets go of the only fleetingly tight grasp he had. He looks like he's choking, and then his torso deflates over her.

For all that she does genuinely consider herself equal opportunities in bed, there is something about the spluttering arrival of a man ejaculating that often makes Soo want to laugh.

And that would be very unprofessional.

He pulls out and sits on the bed, his long back hunching away from her as he deals with the full condom. His spine is knobbly, like the ridge of a mountain range. Some small amount of loose skin ripples in folds around his chest, his middle.

'Uh, thank you . . . um, thank you Cindy. There's . . . there's a towel next door if you want to, you know, shower.'

'Great.'

She gets straight up, and into the water.

Payment is all sorted through the website, but as she is going to leave he thrusts an extra twenty at her, *for the taxi,* unable to meet her eye. Soo attempts to look at him directly – this is, after all, what their interaction is: a *transaction,* nothing more or less – as she says *thank you* in her most politely professional voice, but he won't meet her gaze. He keeps blinking, too fast.

The cab is a relief though; she can't be arsed with public transport, would've got a taxi anyway, but she would rather his needless guilt pay for it.

On her way out, Soo notices another still life in the hall, above a little table busy with keys and water bottles and the

Wi-Fi router. It is one of those old classic gloomy Dutch ones – Jan or van-something. Piles of grapes and gourds and lemons, and a flood of memory. Being made to copy it, and then to do her own version with fruit brought in from home, by her art teacher at school. Oh God, what was her name?

Call me . . .

?

Call me Andi.

And she remembers Andi's big grin when Soo brought in textured, blobby custard apples and neon-hued dragon fruits, rather than the bananas and oranges everyone else in the class chose. How she always wanted to stand out, even as a teenager.

Soo had been praised by teachers for her drawing all through school. But it was Andi who repeatedly said words like 'talent', 'aptitude', even 'calling'. And it was Andi who introduced her to a world of art beyond just drawing-what-you-see. It was Andi who took the class, squawking on the Tube, to see Eliasson's vast glowing sun and Schad's giant steel sink holes in the Turbine Hall, and who marched Soo upstairs to get lost inside the deep deep red of the Rothkos and to argue over whether or not Michael Craig-Martin had, in fact, turned a glass of water into an oak tree.

During A levels, Andi had introduced her to Carolee Schneemann and Cindy Sherman and Yoko Ono, and Soo's rebellious restlessness found a focus. An outlet. Soo planned to perform *Cut Piece*, following Ono's performance instructions – inviting the audience to come on stage and cut off a piece of the artist's clothing – while wearing her school uniform, as a protest against 'enforced institutional conformity'. Andi liked the provocation. Their head teacher flipped out. The performance was banned, and Soo was grounded for two whole months by her horrified parents. But not before she found herself at the centre of endless meetings and arguments and performed *concern* among all the adults, as well as whispers and admiration and – yes – some disgust, from other pupils at the thought of what she *might have done*. The mere idea, of her letting a male pupil snip off her bra strap!

It was a good feeling. Both being the centre of all that attention, and the realisation that the threat of using her own simple human body could provoke such high feelings, such high drama.

Soo had no disgust. Soo had just found her own power.

The green blobs of JB's un-listened-to voice notes seem to accuse Soo, as the cab putters its way back through the evening. But this isn't the place. The driver isn't chatty (which she is glad of, just now) but nor does he even have the radio on. The silence feels thick.

She replies to Lyds instead:

> *Such a fun day! So good to see you. Remind me to*
> *bring that book for you next time!*

She sends Liam a message:

> *Hope you had a good weekend. Anya behaving?*
> *Anything I should know about?*
>
> *Let me know when you're on your way over!*

She browses various websites, reads an article about melting glaciers, then distracts herself with a vacuous piece announcing that the summer of love we've all been waiting for is here ('hot, hot, HOT!'), then reads a review of a terrible-sounding new Rowland Booth movie she has no real interest in seeing, and then an interview with its gushing star who she hasn't heard of – igniting a familiar fear, that's smouldered since she had

Anya, that she just can't keep up with culture anymore. *Losing her edge.*

'Here y'are, love.'

'Thanks.'

She rounds up the fare. Passing it on in the gig economy.

!

Inside her flat, Soo opens all the windows as she waits for the kettle to boil. She makes herself a green tea, and gets a bar of dark chocolate, and sits on the sofa. A sharp pain is revealed to be caused by a Daddy Pig toy, hiding beneath one of a series of tasselly cushions that she has embroidered colourful shapes onto, in an attempt to brighten up the drab greige furnishings the tiny flat came with. Soo might only wear monochrome clothing, but icy minimalism is simply not an option with a six-year-old or a ready-furnished flat, and so she's leaned into enlivening their rental instead: painting watercolour swirls onto ricepaper lampshades, seeking out clashing-coloured vintage throws and rugs. Covering the walls in proper prints and framed doodles she'd been given by artist pals. And to counteract all the horrible, gaudy plastic toys, last Christmas she'd hand-made Anya a doll's house – well, a doll's flat – matching the décor exactly to their own, sewing miniature rugs and recreating tiny hand-drawn versions of the pictures on the wall.

She tosses Daddy Pig into Anya's toybox, then sits back and looks at her phone. Turns it off silent mode.

There's a message from Liam – all is fine. He'll bring her home in about an hour. And she feels the tug, that pulling *heaving* feeling, straight from her heart, her ribs. For her daughter.

A weekend away from Anya's constant demands for attention has been amazing, but it's also been awful. Insane that she can miss her this much, when it's only been two days, and when it'll only be another sixty minutes. Last night, when she couldn't sleep – JB lightly snoring beside her, while insomnia's uneasiness crawled round Soo's brain and body like a slow spider – she had tried to soothe herself by scrolling through pictures of Anya on her phone. She makes up ninety per cent of the photo reel: standing proud in her school uniform (showing no sign of rebelling against 'institutional conformity' yet), holding some certificate on the last day of term. Poking her adorable disgusting pink tongue through a gap in her teeth. Looking super-cool in Soo's giant shades while sunbathing in Meersbrook Park.

Liam doesn't exactly help matters, when he does take her: always sparing on detail in text messages, refusing to give Soo the reassurances she craves. But he has never been very good at relaying what he and Anya get up to, or how he is coping. It's bravado, Soo suspects. The need to prove he can manage.

Which is understandable. But it might also just be that he is lazy. Liam was always shit at texting, actually. It had made Soo – usually cool in relationships – mad with hunger, for his replies, in the early whirlwind phase. Before the true extent of his selfishness became a turn-off, rather than a withheld, dangled carrot of potential.

Soo flicks back to the chat with JB. She really ought to deal with it now, before Anya gets home. She presses play on the first voice note.

JB's disembodied voice, sounding very controlled. Wary, and distant.

'OK. Soo. I'm not sure where this . . . irritation has come from. And I . . . I don't know what exactly went wrong last night. Maybe I've been barking up the wrong tree, worrying you weren't, um, attracted to me.

'Maybe . . . maybe it just wasn't a great idea – and we both realised that a bit late . . . And we both should have just said something? But we didn't.

'I think that is maybe all it is?

'And I think that is OK.'

There's a pause, and then JB's voice rushes back, unusually ardent.

'Look, I love you – as a friend – and I respect you – as a person. And I admire you, as a mum, and as an artist, and – and I just don't want some bad sex to . . . to, um, affect that.'

Soo feels some grudging relief. *Fine.* Maybe she's just being paranoid. Overthinking it.

Maybe they *were* just drunk and tired and sloppy. If JB doesn't want to talk about it – JB, a person who always wants to go into everything! – then she will just take them at their word.

A square of the chocolate, almost matte and muddy, begins to slowly dissolve on her tongue. And Soo feels herself melt a little too.

Then Soo remembers there's another voice note. Left seven minutes later.

She presses play.

'Hey. So. You said I should "say what I'm really thinking", and actually there is something else. It's . . . well, it's what I was trying to say just before the pizza arrived yesterday. About those bloody ASMR videos.

'I just find them really, like, uncomfortable. The stereotyping, the permissiveness. Wait, no – the submissiveness. The cliché of the servile, docile woman . . .'

The sound of JB breathing, steadying themselves.

'I know that does sound judgey. But your whole art career has been about busting stupid gendered assumptions and this stuff just upholds them? That's what I meant by complicit. *I guess I feel like it is selling out, Soo! So if there was a weird atmosphere, well, perhaps it*

227

was a little bit because that was rattling round in my head, as well as the worries that you weren't into me anymore and . . . yeah. I guess.'

How bloody dare they.

Suddenly Soo's mouth feels dry, and she reaches for the tea, slurps it; it's too hot for such a big gulp, and her tongue singes.

She knew it.

She *knew* it.

She knew JB – fucking perfect poised JB, so high-minded – was judging her. She just didn't realise it was over *this*.

Kind of funny, really, that they would be more bothered by this – her selling *an idea* – than by her selling her *actual body*.

Although actually, that might be JB all over. Ideas over actions. Any action allowed as long as it's been thoroughly discussed, ethically worked through. *Rationalised.*

'Uncomfortable'.

Fuck off.

Maybe JB should try experiencing some real discomfort in their life! Should try having insomnia. Anxiety. Racing thoughts. PTSD. All the things that people below the line praise Soo's videos for helping them with. With their big supportive family and multiple supportive understanding partners, JB has probably never struggled to fall asleep in their whole life, Soo thinks ungenerously, before the memories of JB as an anxious student butt in, disputing her theory.

And granted, when Soo herself first watched ASMR for research for her video piece, *The Swallowed Woman*, it had been with the assumption that this was just some crazy bit of the internet that she could usefully appropriate in her work. A topical digital trend that seemed perfectly mouldable for exploring the experience of being a woman online.

But then. Watching ASMR channels had proved to be . . . *weirdly comforting*. And oddly familiar. They produced a feeling she had first experienced at school when teachers looked at her work: something about the close-up, individual attention, the soft murmurs of praise ... it provoked a flush of feeling, warm and tingling, spreading over her like a soft, new outline. A feeling Soo would not have known how to articulate, had never even realised other people had. A feeling that as an adult she occasionally also got when someone cut her hair.

As she watched more and more ASMR videos, any sneers subsided. And then she tried watching them in bed.

And she fell asleep. Easily. Sweetly. For the first time in *years*.

Soo often cannot sleep. Her thoughts chase her round: a gnawing sense of failure in her career, as a parent, as a partner, as a woman. As a daughter. And it is at night-time that her endless to-do lists really spiral. These lists seem to promise to provide the solution to all her failings – only to then oppress her with their impossibility.

Because there simply aren't enough hours in the day to raise a child and make money and find love and clean the house and come up with a brilliant new idea for a touring exhibition and finish that Arts Council application and meet with the heads of all the galleries in the North and update your website and update your Insta and keep coherent records of expenses and actually do try to find an ethical alternative to Amazon for buying craft materials and bulk boxes of condoms and check the privacy settings on your phone and take the bins out and get Anya's special toothpaste from Boots and wash Anya's uniform and hand-wash your stockings and talk to Anya again about the girl that was upsetting her in singing and for God's sake cook something anything other than fish fingers for tea and do a Yoga with Adriene and finish that prize-winning novel Lyds lent you months ago and go to the sexual health clinic because it has definitely been more than a month and answer that email and answer that text and answer that DM and put that nasty drain unblocker down the sink because it works best overnight and go to bed earlier and write down three things you're grateful for each evening before you go to sleep . . .

Sleep.

!

ASMR actually helps. It is like wrapping cotton-wool around her mind at the end of the day. And starting to record her own videos felt, at first, like almost a way of giving back. As well as then, surprisingly quickly, a small but welcome earner.

The videos offer a fantasy, of course: fake intimacy. The pretence that someone cares for you. Pays attention to you. Wants to soothe *you*. And who are we to police fantasies, thinks Soo. Who is JB to police what strangers on the internet find kills their anxiety, eases their loneliness?

But she doesn't know how to summarise all that.

Soo sips her tea more carefully as she goes to the comments section underneath her own video. 'Tingle Princess does your make-up.' She screenshots it, and sends it to JB with no comment:

MimiTheWitch

I had really big problems to get sleep, but since I listen to her videos, I sleep really well. Such a wonderful person. ❤

Tubsy

Bullies: your worthless. We hate you.

Me: OK but are you friends with a real princess who treats you so good? No. Exactly.

JasmineP

I have exams today and tomorrow, and my heart is broken, and my anxiety is super high . . . but your videos helped me relax and I just wanted to say thank you so much!!!

JB replies almost immediately.

OK. What's your point?

People like garbage. That doesn't mean you should give them garbage.

Wow, thanks. Thanks a lot.

I'm garbage now am I.

Obviously not.

Sorry that was too harshly phrased. I meant this stuff is garbage, obviously not that you are – you are brilliant. I just don't know why you'd do it?

Soo's heart is racing, as adrenaline continues to charge round her body. She finds herself propelled up and off the sofa, abandoning her tea and heading towards the bathroom. She has a sudden urge to take off the day, to try to put a line under it, before Anya gets back.

But as the sink fills with water, she still messages JB furiously, the words now tumbling out, her thumb racing across the screen.

That's why I sent you those comments.
People actually find it HELPFUL!

It just really isn't that deep!

231

OK.

*I get that the intention is good. But I just think that the
result is that you are supporting something that is harmful in
the world.*

'Harmful'. For God's sake. Such an *overreaction*. And surely
masking something else – or revealing something else: JB's true
squashed-down feelings, about how Soo lives.

How Soo *makes a living.*

The disgust.

She puts the phone into her pocket, then squishes out both
her contact lenses, and flicks them into a bin. Scoops two fingers
of balm cleanser and massages it vigorously into her face, before
scrubbing it off with a flannel. The fine skin around her eyes
feels tender, where she's been too rough with it, trying to
dissolve away the waterproof mascara she always wears when
seeing a client (never wants it to run; always wants to keep
control of her image).

Soo pulls the plug out, and as the opaque, pearly water drains
away, she listens to the voice note again. JB's voice is annoyingly
steady.

'I guess I feel like it is selling out . . .'

JB thinks *she* is selling out—

Unbelievable!

*And I can't believe you have the CHEEK to
lecture ME about 'selling out'.*

Soo sends the reply before she really has time to think what
she is doing.

She puts the phone back in her pocket and starts brushing
her teeth.

The image of JB, speaking their tritest-ever poem to camera while walking through a market, full of same-sex couples and mixed-race children. Catching an apple and smiling like some obliging enby Eve, and spouting some crap about seizing the day.

JB, of all people, embracing – shamelessly capitalising on – *identity as a 'theme'*. That JB claims to be so ideologically pure, yet there they are, profiting from making a financial institution that invests in non-renewables and probably sells fucking arms or whatever, appear woke. Soo hates that word, emptied so fast of meaning in recent years. But she bets – she just bets – that some stupid suited white man in an ad agency schmoozed some stupid white man in the bank with the word and with the concept of detoxifying their brand. And who should you source to help you look *woke* – oh, a Northern genderqueer spoken-word poet! *Perfect.*

Soo hated JB's advert but didn't say anything at the time. She understands the need to make money. Of course she bloody does. But to then be scolded for selling out by JB Wylie-Wallace – the face of non-binary banking! – was just too much.

She has been brushing her teeth too hard, for too long. Her spit is a raw sausage pale pink, blood mixed into the toothpaste.

She looks at her phone again.

What do you mean?

Well just that all this high and mighty stuff is a bit much

Coming from someone

Who did a banking advert

Want to talk about selling out!

Selling your self to a ducking BANK.

Your words your poetry, your art. Your IDENTITY.
Knowing they only want you because you are nb.

Hows that for supporting something harmful
in the world. Helping a bank pinkwash
themselves fucking capitalist bullshit!

Soo is still standing at the sink, stuck, somehow. She stares at her own face in the mirror. It is speckled with toothpaste stains. And oh bloody hell, she still hasn't bought Anya's preferred, non-minty toothpaste. The squeezed dry, old tube seems to sneer at her, curled up contemptuously on the sink.

She picks it up and chucks it in the bin.

She looks down at her phone. Glowing, alive with their words.

Wow.

I won't apologise for making that advert. I did it for the
money – I needed the money and I used it well. It enabled
me to go on writing and performing my poetry – giving me a
platform for my activism, and for making a living as an artist.

WHAT DO YOU THINK I AM TRYING TO DO?

Soo pats some moisturiser into her face, rather too aggressively, and retreats to her bedroom.

And I have a BLOODY CHILD to look after BY
MYSELF do you know how hard that is?

She slams the door shut, as if JB might hear its reverberation across the Pennines. Relishing the chance to behave like a child herself for once, without Anya around to hear.

Yeah, of course.

I really don't know that you do.

JB is typing

. . .

Soo is typing

. . .

Soo puts down the phone and takes a deep, trembly breath. She undresses and gets into her pyjamas and swaddles herself in a big fluffy grey dressing gown, that Anya loves to snuggle in. She'll be exhausted when she gets back, ready to be swept straight into bed, and Soo wants to be bed-ready too.

But as she sits on the sofa, waiting, she doesn't feel like she's winding down. Various annoyingly competing feelings continue to race around inside her chest.

She knows JB has a point, that the girlish, covertly sexy stereotyping that she leans into – that is a trend across ASMR videos – is not *ideal*. That it is . . . icky. But God, those videos are popular. And they are *easy* for Soo to rack up the views on.

She has experienced shit all her life for being who she couldn't help but be, hasn't she. For the simple fact of having a female body. The boys at school who decided she was 'a slut' because her breasts grew early; the blokes who yell what they'd like to do to her across the street; the tutor who came up way too close behind her, shortly after hearing she was struggling financially; the bosses who underestimated and underpaid her compared to male counterparts; the lovers who thought that just because she was upfront about wanting sex it was also fine to choke her during it; the critics whose reviews of her

235

work fixated on her naked body but refused to take it seriously because it featured her naked body...

!

Soo has long since determined that if she was going to be sexualised by men anyway, she could at least be in control of that. Could monetise that (in her sex work). Could weaponise that (in her art).

And the YouTube videos are more in the former camp, only without the bother of actually having to interact with anyone in real life. Without having to actually be touched. She follows the market, goes where the money is, uses the assets she has, and she won't feel bad about that.

But also... it's not *her* that she's selling online; it isn't real. It's just a performance.

It's *all* just performance.

> Look I know the videos are not great.

> But this is such an overreaction. It's just taking it all far too seriously!

> They aren't REAL!

The whole thing is very and knowingly *not real*. The awareness of its fakery is built in to ASMR; everyone watching knows it. Suspension of disbelief. The doting girlfriend role-plays are no weirder or more implausible – and no more authentic or accurate – than miming an eyebrow-plucking appointment or pretending to be a whispering witch.

> But what message about women does it put out into the world? And is **the message** itself not real?

> I might have capitalised on my identity in that ad – but at least that poem **in itself** was tilting towards what an ideal

world looks like, not a regressive one. They might have
wanted me for the wrong reason – but the words still put
out the right message.

Ooooh sorry, is my feminism not good enough for you?

It never was though was it

Not really

Just listen to yourself JB!

You say you're fine about me literally selling my body
for sex – because 'sex work is real work' amiright
– but you object to a few silly roleplay videos?

HOW DOES THAT MAKE SENSE

JB is typing

. . .

JB is typing

. . .

Soo stretches out on the sofa, watching JB fail to respond. Because there it is – they've got to the heart of the matter now, finally.

She opens her mouth and lets out a frustrated groan, directed at the opposite wall, where a watery face of a woman in a Marlene Dumas print stares back at her dispassionately, like she's seen it all before. She looks as knackered as Soo feels. It's as if she's weary inside her actual bones, tired inside her skull. A whole weekend without Anya was relaxing in one way, but a whole weekend socialising is exhausting in another – eating and drinking and chatting through the hangover today when she would have rather seen no one, stayed under her lovely duvet. And then having to perform and be perky for that man. Strange choice, that.

Money in the account though. Which reminds her. Soo opens the eBay app. Scrolls through the second-hand scooter listings, then bids on another one.

She wastes time for a while, browsing other toys for Anya, then getting sucked into searching through vintage homewares, till she's somehow down a rabbit hole of collectible Memphis glassware that costs five thousand dollars and imagining what kind of breakage-free life such things could possibly fit into . . .

Then, ripping through the darkness (when had it got so dark?), the phone starts vibrating and trilling.

It is JB.

Soo sits up and holds the phone, and for a second she thinks she understands how JB had felt the previous evening. Almost too tired to actually deal with it. To have the conversation.

But she will; she must.

She slides the bar to accept the call, and reaches over to flick on a lamp too.

'Hey.'

'Hey.'

. . .

'I'm sorry.' JB's voice is husky, as if their vocal cords have fibrous little tears all through their fabric.

'Yeah . . . me too.'

'I . . . I've just been sitting here, trying to compose the right response, and I realised I just needed to speak to you. And to actually, like, be honest about some things.'

'Go on.' Soo's own throat feels tight, and sore, holding all the tension of their exchange.

'I guess ... I guess you're right: my standpoint doesn't make that much sense. I just – I really have worked hard, Soo, to overcome my instant, like, gut reaction to – to your work. To the idea of random men, just *buying* ... my friend's body.'

'I – yeah. I wanted to be a good friend,' continues JB. 'To support you, and be non-judgemental. And of course I understood *why* you'd do it. I know Anya is more important than anything. And I know what it's like to try to make art when there's no fucking money for it, anywhere, ever. And I also get that working shitty uncreative exhausting minimum wage jobs, ten hours a day, leaving you no time to spend with your child or with your creative self doesn't make any sense either. I do get all that.'

'But ...? I'm sensing a "but".'

'Yeah – the but. *But* ... I guess I just wish everything could be different? That your life – that Liam or your parents – that the world, the systems, that fucking *capitalism* could be different! I don't judge *you*, OK? But I do, fundamentally, still just wish that you didn't have to sell yourself. And that men couldn't simply *purchase* women's bodies, for their shitty selfish pleasure ...'

Soo can hear the crackle of a cigarette, the sound of JB pulling greedily on it, now they'd got out their words. What they needed to say. And she takes a big breath in of her own.

'The thing is JB, I wish that too! Genuinely! I need you to support me because it's what I need to do – but that doesn't mean that I *like* it. I don't powerfully hate it, either. It is simply the best means to an end available to me, right now. It's ... *fine*. And that's also why I carried on doing the videos – yeah they're silly. But they're also less ... draining. No interaction – pure broadcast. Not much money in it, but *easier* money.'

'Yeah. I do get that.'

'OK. Great. But when you react like they're ... *disgusting*, it's hard not to feel like actually you're disgusted ... *with me*. And the way you looked at me last night – I dunno, it was like I could see that disgust – for my work, for my ... body. And that— that really hurts, you know?'

JB doesn't say anything for a few seconds, and then exhales, hard.

'Ah fuck. I'm sorry, Soo. I really am. That's – yeah, that's just incredibly shitty. I'm sorry.'

Soo pauses herself.

'It's OK.' Then she decides to offer what perspective she can. 'The thing is – and I'm not sure you'll be able to see this yet, but maybe it'll help – the way I see it, I don't actually sell *myself*, in either context: I sell the *idea* of myself. My clients touch my body, but they can't buy the real me. They don't even know my real name.

'You wanna know who gets to see the real me? *You do*, JB. So I need you to ... to be real too. No more hiding how you feel, behind how you think you *ought* to feel, and then it all finally coming out in some weird snobby kneejerk reaction to stupid YouTube videos!'

'Yeah. Point taken.' And then there's a smile in JB's voice, that Soo can hear, that she recognises of old. 'So what you're saying is, it's still OK for me to point out that they *are* kind of stupid, right?'

'Well yeah, I mean they are. But so are rainbow-coloured banking adverts.'

'Touché.'

Another hiss of the roll-up, burning.

'And I'm sorry about being mean about that, by the way. I do totally understand why you did it. Obviously.'

'That's OK. It is cringe, I am well aware.'

A comfortable silence descends down the line, but Soo knows there is something else they need to make clear.

'JB?'

'Yeah?'

'One more thing about last night. I guess we both had some . . . stuff. But I want you to know it was absolutely nothing to do with you being non-binary.'

JB doesn't say anything.

'I promise you.'

'OK.'

'You are beautiful, to me. You always have been. Always bloody will be, even when we're both old and wrinkly in rocking chairs.'

'Thanks Soo. And same, darling. Your body could never disgust me. I can't wait to see your wrinkly old tits!'

'Anytime darling.'

'All right then. I better go.'

'Yeah, me too. Anya will be back in a minute, anyway.'

'Don't forget to give her that hug from me.'

'Yeah, of course. And hugs to Prish.'

'Night night then. Love you.'

'Love you too.'

And all the adrenaline and anger has subsided, has dissolved and run out of Soo, puddling in regret and love and weariness around her on the sofa.

She puts down the phone. All she wants is her daughter.

And as if the world is – for once – actually listening to what she wants, the doorbell goes immediately.

Anya stands there, rubbing her eyes.

'Hello Mummy. I'm sleepy.'

Soo resists the temptation to make a dig at Liam, for insisting that he have the whole weekend – making some stupid point by not bringing her back till this late – and instead she just reaches out to grab Anya's koala-bear shaped rucksack from him.

'I know, pumpkin. We'll get you to bed now.' With her other hand, she takes Anya's, and leads her inside.

'Say bye-bye.'

Anya mutters bye-bye, and Soo feels guiltily gratified that she doesn't run in for a hug or grab Liam's leg or any of the things she, at one time, would often do.

'Everything OK?' she murmurs, in an adult voice, to Liam. He looks worn out too.

But as he nods, he gives a small, almost private smile, and she follows his gaze which, of course, is resting on Anya, who is making a big show of pulling off her sandals and jacket as if she's too weary to bear it. And it warms something in Soo's low belly, to see that travelling adoration in his eyes, too.

'Yeah. It was great, actually.'

'Good. Great! Do you want to take her again sometime soon? If you can manage, I mean – no pressure—'

'No, definitely. Definitely want to. Yeah. For sure.'

'OK. *Great.*' Soo pauses.

Go on, she tells herself, say the nice thing. Be the grown-up. Be a better parent. 'I know she'd like that. Really.'

And the weak smile and half nod and half-sigh that seem to sink down over Liam's face contain hints of all the things she knows he won't ever talk to her about. She has to accept that maybe she'll never know the exact percentages of how much he does or does not want to parent Anya, or how much he can or cannot parent her; how much is guilt and how much is frustration and how much is pain and how much is selfishness.

'Yeah, cool. Well. I'll be in touch. Soon, yeah?'

Soo just does her own slightly sighing nod, and shuts the door. Turns her attention to the one that really matters.

'Come here, you.' And she scoops Anya up in an enormous hug, and it is sheer bliss to feel her daughter put her tiny arms around her and rub her little head into the soft dressing gown and then just give in completely. Anya flops into Soo's body with the confidence of one certain it will always be there to soften any fall, any blow.

For probably the millionth time, Soo wonders how her own mother let her petty blinkered little worries about *respectability* get in the way of this kind of roaring, primal love. How spiteful did that prudish outrage have to be, to make her whisk away Soo's safety net, leaving her to freefall through this awful world alone?

Soo realises she is squishing Anya just a fraction too tightly. She turns the grip instead into a lift, and puts away thoughts of her own parents. With some effort, Soo carries Anya to her bed, and helps her out of her clothes and into her favourite dinosaur pyjamas. Anya is often spiritedly determined to do such things all by herself now, but this tiredness makes her seem so young and tender. And Soo can't help but savour her neediness, just a little.

'Do you want a story? Or are you too sleepy?'

Anya shakes her head, but then still extends her arms out of her duvet, and Soo is relieved that she wants a hug, that she is allowed to scoot into Anya's bed with her, to hold her skinny limbs tight and safe in the circle of her arms, and stroke her fine hair while she drifts off to sleep.

She inhales a deep breath of that particular, sweetish Anya-smell that comes off her head.

Sometimes, Soo thinks her heart might expand to fill her entire body, she loves her daughter so much. And it is a beating reminder of a fact that she knows in her bones: that she will do whatever she needs to do to give Anya the best possible life.

Chapter 8

Anthony

'Yes – I'm ready...'

She looks up at him and nods decisively, as he straddles her. Her face looks very small below him, her mouth open, inviting.

Anthony pushes his penis into her mouth, and starts to talk.

'Do you like that, you dirty girl, you disgusting girl, you little whore...'

He keeps thrusting, even as she struggles beneath him, her eyes beginning to water. Enough; he pulls out and she gasps for air as he moves himself back down her reclined body, her slender legs pressed tight together.

With a swift certain movement he spreads them apart as she starts up a pitiful pleading *no please no don't please...* Anthony raises himself up over her, and slaps her left cheek.

'Shut up.'

She whimpers, as her cheek blooms red, but stops talking and lies very still. He pushes himself inside.

He tries not to allow himself to think about anything other than how good it feels.

'That's right, feel my... feel my cock inside you, right inside you, you love it don't you – you dirty whore...

'You love it, don't you? Say you love it.'

'No, stop – please...' Her voice is barely a whisper.

He raises himself up once more and his left hand grips around her neck. He puts his right hand over her mouth, presses down.

'Shut the fuck up, whore.'

His right hand releases her mouth, so he can slap her again. She chokes for air.

'Say you love it, you bad girl—'

'I love it I love it I love it—'

Then she can't hold out anymore, can't help herself, her body twisting and thrusting up at his, a hand grabbing desperately at the sheet, the mattress, her eyes widening, rolling around.

'Oh God—'

And the feeling of Rachel coming, her body clenching around him, is enough to tip him over the edge too and for a moment it does absolutely feel worth it. A satisfaction, in the way that her desire, so focused and intent, finds its resolution. The pleasure of bringing that to someone. To his wife.

Or is it mere *relief*—

Anthony sometimes worries he's doing it wrong.

'Oh my God.' Rachel is rubbing her eyes, catching her breath. She rolls over onto her side towards him and gives him her private, pleased smile, the one which always makes him feel like the most special person in the room. On the planet. In her life.

He remembers when they first met – sitting next to each other at a dull dinner at a conference – how she turned on that smile, just for him, a conspiratorial look. The glint in the eye and the turned-up corners of her lips conveying how boring she thought everyone else, but that, somehow, miraculously, she considered him an exception. And then the whispered invitation: 'How about a drink somewhere else?'

He wonders, now, if she does that smile for the others.

Anthony rolls over too, and kisses her cheek. It is pink where he hit her, carefully, with his palm widened so it made a flat surface against the softest part of her angular face.

'I wasn't too hard, was I?'

'No! No. No no no. It was fantastic. Just right. Really. And I loved all the – all the *chat*. It was really good. Exactly what I want. Honestly. Thank you.'

'OK. Great.'

Rachel is always generous in her thanks and praise after he's indulged her submissive fantasies, and this is good – the whole point is to give her what she wants, for her to have the very best time. But Anthony also can't shake a slight uneasiness at being *thanked* for such an act. Thinks he can detect a whiff of some article or book on 'how to encourage your reluctant partner to play in the bedroom'.

'And did you ... was it OK for you? Are you starting to ... you know, get more into it?' she asks, not quite looking at him, her head resting against the thick cotton of the creamy pillowcases.

'Mm, yeah.'

In truth, Anthony is not getting any more into it. Apart from the actual moment of orgasm, an oblivion which he manages to thrust towards, he never succeeds in losing himself inside the experience of having sex this way. It is a performance, and he feels like a bad actor, worried he might forget his lines, or stand in the wrong place.

Of course he's worried: he is hitting and slapping and choking his wife. How could anyone possibly relax into that? A part of Anthony's brain always remains on high alert. Terrified of actually hurting her.

But also: terrified of not hurting her enough. Failing to give her what she wants. Failing to be the big strong overwhelming man that she, for some reason, wants to whip her and smack her and humiliate her in bed.

He knows this stuff is all terribly normal, practically vanilla, these days; he's seen the cuffs and chains in gaudy high street knicker shops, seen the middle-aged receptionists at work titter over *Fifty Shades of Grey*. But fundamentally, Anthony does not understand why anyone gets turned on by hurting women.

But isn't using a prostitute violence against women . . .

A shock of shame fires through him, at the intruding thought.

He blinks it away, and reaches for a glass of water, not wanting to be looking into Rachel's face when even thinking such things. Anyway, he reassures himself, with the worn theoretical arguments he's been repeating to himself, that is actually a very old-fashioned patronising sentiment, they were empowered *sex workers* making a choice to make money using what assets they have. And anyway, he would never hurt one.

'One'.

Would never hurt *anyone*.

Anyone except his wife who asked him to.

Anthony rolls back over, and looks again at Rachel. Her hair – glossy brown strands that usually frame her face, her lovely long neck – is now all mussed and chaotic. He reaches out to smooth it, and she nuzzles up into his hand, and then scooches in towards him, resting her head in the triangle where his shoulder becomes chest. This is her space; her head fits perfectly, as if made for it.

Anthony continues to gently stroke her hair and lightly scratch her scalp – something he loves doing, something she loves having done to her. And he wishes this moment – just the two of them; so soft, and so close – could stretch on forever.

But life is always chasing them, always at their heels.

'How long have we got?' asks Rachel.

Anthony reaches for his watch, an old wind-up one that had

been his father's – about the only thing he'd inherited from him when he died.

'We're fine. Almost half an hour.'

'OK. Well, I'll need a quick shower. And then we can get the dinner on. Thought we could have that nice eggplant bulgur thing?'

'The one with the . . . what is it? Star anise?'

'Allspice.'

'Ah yes. Lovely.'

'Come on then.' Rachel is rousing herself, pulling away from him, and he tries to hold on to her, but what is meant to be a seductive murmur – *just a few minutes more, darling* – ends up sounding like a needy wheedle.

'Bubby – the kids'll be back soon. Come on.'

But he notices she's reaching for her phone, rather than actually getting up. And then the anxiety all rushes back in, a cold gust in the space in his chest that she so recently rested upon. And the barriers between them all seem to come sliding down again in a series of silent whooshes. Anthony increasingly has the sensation that there are these planes of glass separating them, invisible walls that he hopes Rachel can't see, simply looks straight through. The planes are made of:

- His pretence, that he enjoys these domineering performances.
- His pretence, that he's relaxed about her having sex with other people.
- His pretence, about who else he is having sex with.

They had originally opened up their marriage because neither was getting enough sex within it. But ironically, since doing so, they have actually had a lot more sex with each other. Enough, really, to make Anthony feel like they don't need to be open anymore. Then again, Anthony suspects that Rachel doesn't realise that it has lately become – on his part – mostly panic sex. Desperate attempts to make her happy and fulfilled.

He would have always been willing to try the role plays, but he suspects he would never have agreed to doing them quite so regularly (every other Wednesday evening, before Emily and Daniel get home from chess club and youth orchestra respectively) had it not been for the underlying terror of failing to keep Rachel satisfied. The dread, that she might find those things with another man and . . .

He has told Rachel that he has started dating someone new, called Cindy ('spelt with a C – like the artist'). Rachel was bright and enthusiastic; of course she was, she wants to carry on fucking Scott and going on all her fun nights out with him and his hip mates, and for that to be OK both of them need to carry on being keen on being in an open relationship.

Anthony has not mentioned the fact that he paid Cindy to sleep with him.

How *pathetic* that is.

Anthony feels suddenly exhausted, immobile. Rachel is tapping away at her phone with her index finger in the way their kids mock her for, like a bird stab-stabbing with its rapid little beak. But he just stares at the wall across from their bed.

He's stared back at by some of the Francesca Woodman prints that Rachel put up a few years ago, above the attractive period fireplace that they had painstakingly restored when they bought the house – what was it, fifteen years ago now? Before Daniel, anyway. The black-and-white of the pictures goes with the subtle taupe and plum colours of the room, and the elegant cream palette of their own wedding-day photos too. A soothing cocooning space of thick linens and heavy curtains, that Rachel has created for them to retreat to. Alone, always alone; no one else comes in here. That was part of the deal.

Anthony does not much like the Woodman prints, really. Formally, they are atmospheric, granted; they carry the biographical charge of her suicide, of course (although that's a bit grim for a bedroom, to his mind). But really it is that he finds the sad-naked-girl thing, the Tormented Female Artist™, to be . . . *tiresome*. It reminds him of his students – year group after year group will always reliably feature some intense-eyed young woman who desperately wants to write about Woodman.

Her dark eyes seem to look down with unspoken accusation at him, from a photograph where she bends backwards towards her camera, breasts and shoulder bones peaking in perfect symmetry. Her face thrown back, her throat bare towards him.

Rachel thinks these pictures are sexy, while also being 'authentic'. And Anthony at least prefers them to the soft-core photographs that she also started getting really into, around the time they opened up their marriage and her sex drive went into overdrive. He had made a clever play for those to live in the attic room instead, where guests were allowed; to 'inspire' them both, in their extramarital adventuring.

Lena had liked those pictures. She called it the 'Bourdin boudoir'. But then Lena was one of those middle-aged women who really did go in for the classic high heels and red lipstick version of glamour, and presumably enjoyed seeing that vision of sexiness reflected on the walls the few times she'd come over. Usually, they'd slept together in hotel rooms, the cheap anonymity of the Premiere Inn, or at Airbnbs they'd scorn for their bad Argos artworks (the Eiffel Tower on the wall of a flat in Birmingham, a hideous multi-coloured picture of a stag in Lancaster).

Anthony would see Lena every couple of months or so, at

work events around the country, or when he could get away to visit her; she lectured in modernist and avant-garde art at York, and had brought a sense of Scandi-chic to a small, low-beamed apartment absurdly near the Minster. The casual arrangement suited her very nicely too, that was obvious. There was a grown-up, clear-eyed lack of romance to the situation: they fancied each other but would never fall in love with each other, a state of affectionate equanimity that Anthony saw reflected in her eyes. Lena was always happy to see him, but also quite happy to say goodbye the following morning, to retreat inside her flat by herself. None of the long-distance lovers' tortured train station farewells between them.

Still, he feels mournful for a moment, remembering that flat, now rented out to some stranger; Lena had gone back to Denmark, something she'd been dithering over doing for some time. Not that he would be arrogant enough to think that he had been any part of what was keeping her in the UK – their relationship had been effortless and easy, but that also meant it had felt rather inconsequential.

Yet when she left, he had felt surprisingly bereft. For a weightless relationship, her mere presence in his life had certainly helped balance the scales, against whoever Rachel was seeing. And without her, Anthony felt like his open marriage had become woefully uneven. Now, when Rachel goes out with Scott or is away for work – which she has to be so often that they rent a minuscule studio flat in London – all Anthony has is the infinite scroll of online indifference.

It had really worked in the first few years. It really had. They didn't tell many people – Anthony somehow couldn't shake the fear that people would see them as *swingers*. But between the two of them, it had been remarkably simple. Civilised. Life was long, and so was a marriage. A little newness, a little variety, seemed only to strengthen it – something they discussed a lot, smug and pleased with themselves.

But of course, there was more of a thrill to things in the early days, that sense of *openness* and *possibility* which overwhelmed any nagging doubts or insecurities. And Anthony wonders, looking back now, if beginning things with Lena within just a few months of the arrangement had also been the key: solid proof that he was getting something from the situation. Besides, Rachel had had far fewer lovers than he might've expected, given how gorgeous and clever she is, with that smile he still thinks of as *American*: regular and effortlessly white.

But now . . .

Now things were so bloody arid, he'd resorted to *paying* someone to fuck him, just to try to even things out.

Anthony doesn't want to think about it. He turns to paw at Rachel, hoping for the soft reassurance of another hug, some little innocent kisses.

But Rachel just pecks his forehead, and gets up with a sudden, certain movement, as is her way, wrapping herself in a silk kimono.

'Come on. Showers.'

Anthony makes a noncommittal noise.

By the time he gets downstairs, Rachel is already in the kitchen, briskly chopping onions.

'Can you halve the eggplant?'

'Righty-o.'

The enormous fridge – another of the notably American things about Rachel, her insistence they buy this silver double-doored behemoth – is stuffed with food, and it takes several attempts to find the aubergines (back of the salad drawer, beneath a box of complicated-looking mushrooms and frothing green bags of rocket and coriander). Somehow, this abundance

– along with the cost of the weekly shop – never ceases to surprise Anthony, as if he still expects to open those doors to see merely his parents' frugal culinary habits: wafer-thin ham slices in a damp plastic packet and a few eggs, lonely on a shelf all by themselves. Condiments not stretching beyond sour cream and Colman's mustard.

At last count, in this fridge, they had seven types of mustard alone.

Ah well, this is family life. Two hungry teenagers to feed. A wife who does actually get round to making the recipes she rips out of supplements. Their Alison Roman and Claudia Roden and Ottolenghi tomes actually spattered, folded, scrawled on.

The aubergines are plump and taut, pendulant in their squeaky skins. One rolls off the chopping board he can't quite fit on the countertop. How is it that they have this enormous kitchen (Anthony gets another flash of the one he grew up in, Formica and cramped and gloomy), and yet still there never seems to be anywhere to *put* things?

He moves a jute bag of empty jars that need to be taken to the refill shop from the countertop onto the island. From the island, he takes a stack of Emily's GCSE textbooks and puts them on her place at the dining table. From the dining table, he lifts a green jug of crisping yellow roses, empties them into the compost and puts the jug in the sink to be washed. But there's no room on the draining board so he puts the dried pans away and then reassembles the food processor and . . . puts it back on the countertop, an action which causes the particularly buoyant aubergine to, once more, roll to the floor.

By this time, Rachel seems to have done most of the rest of the cooking, in her usual efficient manner. And he's just bumbling around with aubergines – the most comical vegetable, Anthony thinks, to fumble. Thanks to his hopeless attempts at finding a new, willing partner on dating apps, he has become more aware of the uses of the aubergine emoji than most men his age, he suspects.

Rachel pours herself a glass of fizzy water, and turns to him. 'So, how was your day?'

Such is the tightness of their schedules – and to help maintain whatever scenario is agreed on in advance – they usually go straight into the sex when they both get home on these alternate Wednesdays, without chit chat.

Anthony shrugs, not a very clear action given he is holding a tray of halved aubergines. Rachel opens the oven door for him, their dance of domesticity slick and in-tune.

'It was fine. Wanted to look properly at that paper I was saying about, but I was continually interrupted.'

'Who by? Surely summer holidays are quiet, at least.'

Summertime *is* usually better than termtime; a chance to get on with research, although this year, he feels like he's barely making any progress. Anthony is aware that whenever Rachel asks about his day, he mostly answers with complaints, something he tries to stop himself doing. But there's always so much to complain about. Usually, his top gripes are:

- The volume of marking.
- Being interrupted by admin tasks, and students.
- The entitlement of said students.

This last one is only getting worse, Anthony reflects as he returns to the sink to properly wash up the flower jug. Actually, all of the things he hates about his job seem to be getting worse, but it is the increasing air of entitlement – to his time, his support, or more crassly, simply to a good grade – that truly rankles.

Ever since tuition fees went stratospheric, there has been a steady shift of students into *consumers*. Not gatherers, seeking knowledge, but customers who have bought credentials. He understands their frustration, when they pay so much and get so few contact hours. But it just doesn't make sense to him that they would moan about that and then also show up to seminars ill-prepared. As if they deserve a degree on a plate, just for paying for it, without actually doing the work.

Of course, some students go in the other direction. Decide that if they are paying so much money, they better get every last drop of value out of it. They approach it like a job, a ladder to climb – as if they won't have the next sixty years of that! Academia should be about space and time – to learn, to think, to discuss. *To wonder.*

He's sure the vice chancellor would laugh at such idealism. So would Iona Blythe, probably.

'Well, first there was a student – altogether too dedicated by half – wanting to talk about her dissertation. I managed to put her off till tomorrow morning – my official office hours. But actually the *main* thing, that I quite wanted to talk—' Anthony is about to launch into his real problem when Rachel interrupts.

'Which student was it?'

Rachel always has more questions. It's one of the things he adores about her: how interested she still is, in everything, after all these years. Then Anthony thinks: well that's probably why she's good at dating. She's *interested*, as well as interesting. Always has questions. Has a knack for making people feel seen, and heard. *That smile . . .*

The faint smell of rotting foliage lingers in the sink, and Anthony rootles in the cupboard (also over-stuffed chaos; no wonder the cleaner brings her own supplies) for some kitchen spray.

'Oh it was just that MA one I was telling you about – the

intense one. Staying near the library all summer. Wants to go over, *in depth*, some things that she almost certainly won't actually have room for in her dissertation.'

You certainly couldn't accuse Iona Blythe of laziness, Anthony reflects. She'd hurried in that afternoon, lopsided with books, a zeal in her big eyes that made him think she might not have seen a lot of sleep or daylight recently. In the grip of a mental health crisis, no doubt, as they all seemed to be these days. Still, he wished she would respect his Summer Office Hours, which he both emailed and has pinned up, very clearly, on his door (Thursday morning, by appointment only).

He is also aware she has a crush on him – something which almost feels novel, these days. In recent years – well, the last decade really – the number of students who develop crushes on Anthony has been steadily diminishing. And the age of the online tutorial has certainly not been kind, making it impossible for him to ignore the evidence that his neck is becoming turkey-like and his previously lustrous hair is getting thinner and lesser and paler. You can also blame the changing times, though, he thinks: the fact that so much of his research has been into Gauguin and his underaged lovers – no, *subjects* was the more better, more neutral term – at one time used to give the students ideas. These days, it seems to actively put them off. And fair enough, thinks Anthony.

Not Iona Blythe though. Her interest is painfully obvious, from the way she self-consciously flicks her hair – dyed in big ridiculous stripes of pink and turquoise – to the way the colour flushes up and down her face like a stereo's equaliser whenever she discusses the depiction of the naked female form.

'What's her dissertation on?' Rachel asks, measuring out the bulgur with one hand and reaching to flip on the kettle with another. 'Was it an interesting chat, at least?'

It has started to rain again, the sky a sulky purple-grey. Classic British summertime. Anthony watches, as the droplets hit the glass of the French doors and stretch like needles.

'Oh, well, yes, I suppose it is quite interesting. She's writing about "the awkward nude", a load on Suzanne Valadon, which I suppose is why I've ended up supervising her. A lot of writing about *thighs*,' he laughs.

'Ah, she's *that* one. The one with the crush?'

'Yes. Eyes as mad as the pictures she's talking about – you know, that Valadon glare? Faintly terrifying.'

'Don't say "mad" about a female student, bubby.' Rachel's voice is non-confrontational, but she gives the bulgur a notably vigorous stir as she adds it to the pan. Its sweet-spicy scent begins to fill the kitchen.

Anthony grimaces into the cupboard as he reaches for the pan lid to pass her.

'Yes, *dear*.'

She turns it down to a simmer, puts on the lid, and gets out a bowl for mixing the yoghurt dressing.

'Can you grab the preserved lemons?'

And that is the extent of Rachel's concern about the student-with-a-crush. But then, Anthony has never given her any reason for concern. It had been a ground rule when they opened up their marriage: no sleeping with students.

But the rule had been quite unnecessary, even then. Anthony has never slept with any of them.

The notion is so unprofessional and immoral, that he simply cannot think of them like that. His job is to *teach* them. Even the most objectively attractive students are appealing to him only in an abstract way; like Hollywood movie stars, or pornstars. Or the models in an old oil painting, for that matter. Untouchable, and unreal. And so *young*.

He opens the fridge.

In real life, Anthony has always been drawn to womanly women. Confident women. Like Lena. Like his first love Ally, older than him and strident and sure of herself in a way that shockingly few women were back then, even at art school. Like the busty woman who was briefly friendly and then ignored him on Hinge (you weren't meant to say 'busty' anymore; were meant to say 'ghosted'). Granted, Rachel was a decade younger than Anthony, but he had actually thought she was older than she was when they first met – something about her way of holding herself. Such total self-possession. Anthony has always favoured the grown-up over the watery, nervy, unformed things that have meltdowns in his office.

What is he looking for? He stares at the full shelves, lost in thought, lost in the jungle of jars and Tupperware. The multiplicity of mustards. (Did they really need French and English and American and German – it was like the bloody UN in there).

The idea of sexy young girls was pure aesthetic fantasy, not reality. He might choose to watch that in porn (the alleged babysitters and, yes, students), but that wasn't *real*. It was fiction – silly, unconvincing fiction, at that. Their ages as fake as their shrieking, instant orgasms.

Except wasn't that exactly what he tried to do when he booked Cindy. To make the unreal, real. To bring the fantasy to life. Browsing online profiles like they were porn preview images, the experience just a click away, somehow not reckoning with how *really-real* it was until she actually turned up. A living body in his hallway, his spare bed.

Anthony slams the fridge door shut.

It had been a mistake. A really bad mistake.

For a start, Anthony had been less attracted to Cindy than

he'd expected. The girlishness was completely unsatisfying in person; there was something unnerving about her poor performance of it once it was actually taking place, fleshily, in front of him, rather than cropped rectangularly and safely behind a screen. Then there was her obvious lack of interest, her tediously faked pleasure. Sleeping with someone who had no true desire to sleep with you left Anthony feeling as grubby as if he *had* abused his power and fucked a fresher.

The rain is coming down the glass doors in spooling, braiding streams now. Anthony's reflection among them is only a ghostly half-thing, smeared and indistinct.

'Lemons?'

Lemons. That was it.

Rachel's voice is appropriately tart.

He goes to the fridge again and locates and passes the jar of squashed little preserved lemons, a dull ochre colour, to Rachel. Then he turns, giving her a small, obedient peck on her cheek, back to a normal colour now, which is good, as there's the front door. Anthony and Rachel turn, in well-choreographed anticipation.

I'm hungry, signs Emily as she comes into the kitchen, her mousey hair (she had the misfortune to inherit his colouring rather than Rachel's more coppery tones) darkened by the rain.

'Dinner's on its way – twenty minutes?' Rachel says as Daniel trails behind Emily, before hastily signing it too.

Emily rolls her eyes, a move she has always been adept at communicating volumes through. There's the scornful roll, the indulgent roll. The you'll-never-understand-me roll, the you're-so-shit-at-BSL roll, the that's-so-unreasonable roll.

How was chess? Rachel signs.

Fine, Emily signs. Then adds that she beat someone whose

260

sign name seems to be *'nut'* – tapping the heel of her hand to her chin – two times in a row.

Emily notices Anthony's micro frown and finger spells out *A.D.A.M. N.U.T.T.* Then adds: *I beat him three times last week too.*

And a slow smile spreads across her face. This smile – something so self-satisfied about it – is an echo of her mother's, and Anthony wonders momentarily if Emily's pleasure is in *repeatedly beating* this boy, or in repeatedly beating *this boy.*

Chess was Rachel's thing – she learned from her father, a difficult and exacting man for Rachel to live up to. And also for Anthony to live up to. Robert Schechter is about as close to an oracle as the art world gets, a formidable critic, and while Anthony has long been relieved that at least he can engage with Robert in his relentlessly highbrow dinner-table discussion – he at least has the correct expertise – the masculine, competitive edge that creeps in during every conversation is exhausting. As is Robert's exclusionary performance of Jewishness when Anthony is around, the peppering of conversation with Yiddish words or phrases, despite – as Rachel often notes drily – the fact that her father is barely observant. The deliberate acting-out of this identity for Anthony's benefit can only, he thinks, be intended as a cold reminder that he will never *truly* understand his wife, or where she's come from.

Rachel's father is one of the reasons they live in Sheffield rather than New York, an ocean being a useful thing to have between them. That and Anthony's job, of course.

Anthony's own father had also taught him to play chess, on long beige Sunday afternoons. He's passable at it, but the first time Rachel played him it was obvious that she was so far ahead it was faintly embarrassing. Emily has also been able to wipe the floor with him since she was twelve, always coolly switching off her hearing aids and entering into a state of astonishing focus.

This is not embarrassing; it makes him proud of her. As does her own complete lack of embarrassment at being into such a middle-aged activity. (Rachel always tries to tell him, board games are cool these days, but Anthony cannot quite believe it).

But then, Emily doesn't seem to get embarrassed by much. Like her mum in that regard too. And she's always so clear about what she wants for someone so young – although occasionally he wonders if this is a side effect, or an aspect, of her language. BSL still seems so condensed in its intent, to him; it doesn't muck about. Has it made Emily more direct too, he wonders?

But is that an ableist thing to think? Anthony lives in a continual fear of saying the wrong thing. Of using the wrong word.

He so desperately wants to get everything *right*. For everyone.

Whatever has caused it, the fact that Emily seems so able to ask for what she wants gives him hope; at her age, Anthony was barely able to answer the question 'milk and sugar?' without going into a spiral of uncertainty. Certainly, he couldn't have played chess against a girl without having a complete meltdown.

Of course, there had been one time Emily looked embarrassed: when he and Rachel had called a 'family meeting' and explained about their new open arrangement. Both Emily and Daniel seem generally unbothered, then and since, but at the sign for 'sex' Emily had recoiled (understandably) in horror.

Anthony and Rachel have been careful never to inflict this cringe again, careful to make sure their children never meet their lovers – although, Anthony wonders how long Scott will be in their lives before it gets to the point where he really *ought* to meet the kids. Four years, five? Ten?

He suspects Rachel actively enjoys keeping things separate. It allows her to be a different person. *An escape,* he thinks bitterly.

Emily dumps her rucksack on the floor and heads out of the kitchen before Anthony can sign *take that with you.* Daniel, who has been roaming the room with his dripping mac still on and a viola case in hand, finally locates what he is looking for (a tattered set-text copy of *A Streetcar Named Desire*) and drops the case at the end of the island with a thump. Anthony winces. He imagines several hundreds of pounds of instrument shattering inside its blue velvet.

'Daniel!'

'What.' Daniel is almost out of the door, his damp, wavy hair falling into his eyes.

'Are you going to leave that there?'

A generalised huff, and he returns to pick the case up. On the way out, Daniel gets distracted by one of Emily's magazines, with a shrieking pink-and-red cover, that shouldn't be on the island, and while sneeringly flipping through it, he removes his soggy coat and plonks it on a stool. He leaves the kitchen with the folder and his case – and leaves the mac to drip, steadily, onto the floorboards.

Anthony opens his mouth to bellow after his son, and then shuts it again.

He turns, to ask Rachel about *her* day, but she's on her phone again, head bent, tap tap tap.

There . . .

A little smile.

It is like the curling edges of it are knives pressing into his stomach.

Anthony moves the magazine from the island to Emily's pile on the dining table, then turns back to the stove but there is no more cooking to be done. The bulgur is gently bubbling, beneath its glass lid. He goes around and fiddles with the lights instead. Bright lights off above the island and the stove; lamps and low lights on around the dining table. A nice family meal.

He should just talk to her. Shouldn't he? Let her know how he's feeling.

But how he's feeling is . . . *pathetic.*

Unattractive and left behind. Needy and whiny and self-pitying. The very opposite of the rough tough brute that Rachel wants. *Silly,* Anthony tells himself, as he lays the table, *she only wants that in bed. And even then, only sometimes!* But it's as if that pretence has infected things between them, who and how he is able to be.

Anthony fears that if he is honest about his humiliation – the desperate failure of being unable to attract any other women anymore; the shame of *paying* a woman to fuck him in a misguided attempt to keep up; the bone-deep regret at actually having gone through with it – he will invite Rachel to see him in this tragic, fading light too. Will put her off, just at a moment when she has plenty of other options, ready and waiting.

Well, one other option, at the very least. Anthony has met Scott on a single occasion. A bottle of cab sav, served in those ridiculous balloon-sized glasses, in an elegant wine bar in Nether Edge. Neutral territory. Gave the best performance of nonchalance he could manage, but still felt himself blinking too much when trying to answer Scott's breezy questions, and accidentally inhaled some wine, prompting a coughing fit.

Scott seemed almost suspiciously good at projecting an air of *relaxation.* Pleased with himself, like a lion that's just had a good meal. And he was rather leonine: one of those rare British people whose tan goes darker than their hair, their golden eyebrows, the curls of yellow chest hair springing from a shirt louchely unbuttoned just a bit too low. It was easy to imagine him prowling, successfully, around an orgy, picking off the most attractive mates.

Although when Scott had called him 'mate', Anthony had been relieved to notice Rachel try not to wince.

They go away sailing, some weekends. Anthony imagines Scott in hideous boat shoes, hand-feeding Rachel oysters at some 'little place' he knows. Scott micro-doses LSD for 'creativity at work' and he and Rachel take baby amounts of MDMA when they sleep together sometimes, something she's suggested they also try 'because it just makes things so open'. Anthony refuses because for God's sake he's fifty-eight and also the idea came from Scott.

Maybe Rachel knows that something is wrong, he wonders, watching her fiddling with a bit of hair that won't stay tucked behind her ear, her face bent over the small screen. Maybe that suggestion is her chemical attempt to help him feel able to share what's wrong.

But he doesn't think so.

In fact, Anthony thinks Rachel is probably blithely oblivious rather than worried. This summer, she's spent more and more time on activities with Scott and his group of exhaustingly *active* middle-aged mates: cocktail bars, concerts, weekends in the Cotswolds (with a fancy dress *theme*, as if they were *students* for God's sake). She's off to a festival next weekend. Rachel didn't go to festivals even when they first met.

She was ambitious then, more focused on getting ahead in her work than partying. Had just got the job at Christie's, a big deal for someone still in their twenties, and every weekend began with dutiful Friday night dinner at the suburban home of some distant relations, not the pub. In fact, that was another way she was visibly American: Rachel never quite looked right holding a pint. She knew about wine, and wore chic, well-cut shift dresses; you wouldn't have caught her dead in *glitter.*

Anthony checks the time. Another ten minutes for the food.

Taking Daniel's soggy coat through to hang up in the hallway, he can hear the TV going in the front room, and pops his head in. Emily appears to be virtually ignoring the TV, eyes glued to her phone, but looks up when he stamps his foot on the wooden floorboards, and gives him a big grin.

What do you want? she signs.

Nothing, he signs. *Just saying hello to my best daughter.*

She rolls her eyes, but there's also a massive smile beneath them.

He and Emily have always had a close relationship; Rachel works away so much, her job demanding so much of her, that he's usually been the one doing the school runs, making dinner, helping with homework. And while they'd both been completely committed to learning the language Emily could be most comfortable communicating in, Anthony had made much quicker progress with BSL than Rachel, initially – able to take a sabbatical when Emily was just a toddler, to really immerse himself in intensive lessons. Which had meant that, from the time when she was very small, Emily would turn to him first when she needed something, or needed to understand something.

He hopes she will always feel like she can do that, no matter how grown-up and independent she becomes.

Anthony starts to ask her about her day, but she waves towards the TV and the episode of *Friends* she was barely really watching anyway, as far as he can tell. Emily's enthusiasm for the out-of-date show perplexes him. She even dresses like them: all those little strappy dresses and tight white T-shirts. (There are worse ways for a teenage girl to dress, he reflects, thinking of the students who seem to wear bras as tops now, paired, inexplicably, with exercise gear: slack jogging bottoms or tight cycling shorts.) But then, Anthony never really saw the appeal of *Friends* the first time around – although he remembers being amused when Rachel explained to him that she did, in fact, have 'the Rachel' haircut when they first met. It had suited her.

When he told Emily about this, she had informed him The Rachel was actually back but now it was The Octopus. Anthony had feared communication breakdown – wondering if he'd misunderstood the sign – until she showed him a TikTok of a wavy choppy hairdo that, he supposed, did look faintly tentacled.

Back in the kitchen, his Rachel is still on her phone.

He sits at the kitchen table and, resigned, looks at his own.

Some very dull global emails from work. A newsletter he signs up to from a cutting-edge American art journalist, which he simply never reads. An email from Uber Eats, who seem determined that he should start doing his grocery shopping via courier bike (they should see the size of the fridge; it'd take a fleet).

Dating apps: a desert. No new replies, still.

Anthony doesn't do social media. Doesn't really see the appeal, although Rachel has got very into Instagram since she started seeing Scott. The account is private, so the kids can't see, but as Anthony doesn't have Instagram this also means he can't look at it which makes him nervous. She insists she mostly follows artists and gallerists and collectors, and that it's long been necessary 'for work'. But he has seen her posting pictures of her and Scott holding stupidly elaborate cocktails on the terrace of some overly trendy Kelham bar, a nice pink sunset in the background.

The only app Anthony does have is TikTok. And that's only because he tried to find the video about himself on it once – unsuccessfully, probably thankfully – and has yet to bother deleting it.

He had become aware of the video when sitting in the actually good coffee shop near the university (the coffee in the ones run by the university is, of course, terrible). It was full of students, gathering to gossip over oat-milk lattes. They weren't his, or they'd have recognised him; there is nowhere to hide in this particular coffee shop, one of those airy (draughty) places that seems to be made of plywood and scaffolding poles and houseplants.

Anthony has become skilled at blocking out student chatter and, increasingly, the sound that comes from the phones they always hunch over. But that day, among the conversation and the blare and the continually shuffling snippets of pop music, he heard his very own name.

Oh my God . . .
Professor Roe
On TikTok, yeah
His reading list . . .
His own book
OUT OF PRINT
So embarrassing—

He'd stared very concertedly down at the book he was no longer reading and gripped his coffee mug hard. So hard, he briefly imagined the porcelain cracking into pieces in his hands.

Shattering.

The students replayed the video (or whatever you were meant to call them – the post? The Tok?) but what it said and what they said have since muddled in Anthony's head.

She does his course
She's really funny . . .
Not even on eBay—
Not even
Something about Gauguin
I know I'm dead
There's ONE copy in the library and we're all sharing it because no one wants to tell the old white man that his book—

OUT OF PRINT

Anthony puts his phone face down on the dining table and gets hurriedly to his feet. Must be time. A cloud of fragrant steam envelopes him as he lifts the lid. The heat of the steam obscures the heat of his cheeks, burning at the memory.

The grains stick to the bottom of the pan a bit as he stirs. Shit.

'Think this is definitely ready.' He can't help the small bit of reproach in his voice, as if Rachel ought to have been watching it, as if they weren't both on their phones. 'Can you go grab Em?'

'Sure,' says Rachel.

As he reaches into the oven for the aubergines, sagged and soft in their skins now, Anthony returns – as ever – to the three thoughts which he uses to brick up his defence against this persistent, cringing memory:

- It doesn't matter, because he is actually well liked, his lectures comparatively well attended and his evaluation forms always broadly positive (and none of these are a given these days).
- It doesn't matter, because probably no one even remembers the video now.
- It doesn't matter, because probably no one except a few undergrads saw it anyway.

But tonight, the thought that maybe in fact the entire student body *had* been mocking him will not let Anthony go. Even his toes curl up inside his slippers, grey felt things which he wears all year round, sagging and flat now. They look rather like the floppy roasted aubergine halves, in fact.

Did his MA students know about it? The PhDs – do they

have TikTok? What about other members of staff? No one said anything. But for weeks, Anthony had moved around campus like a spotlight was trailing him; he felt sure a laughter track followed wherever he went too. The paranoia, that people were sniggering at him, for being so old and white and male and irrelevant that he hadn't realised *no one wanted to read his book* to the extent that it had gone *out of print*. And that making a video about this was funny! Entertaining! Worth *sharing*.

People wanted that. Wanted his public humiliation.

At his next seminar, he'd handed out photocopies of the relevant chapter from his book but also of the other book he was making them read that week as if that might not be available too (although he knew it definitely was) and someone made a snarky comment about dead trees and the environment.

He couldn't win.

Rachel returns, and takes a seat with a sigh, as Anthony delivers four plates and then the bowl of saucey yoghurt to the table.

'They're coming. Allegedly.'

The way the kids moan about having to wait for food and then drag their feet when it's time to actually come and eat also makes no sense to Anthony.

'Anyway, sorry – what was it you really wanted to talk about?' asks Rachel, and it's like he can see her return to the room. (To their marriage.) 'Or should it wait till after?'

'Oh it's just this thing – the open letter – rumbling on. Had the head of department in to see me—'

'What's for dinner,' asks Daniel as he slumps towards the table.

Strange how younger generations seemed to have done away with punctuation in the way they speak as well as the way they type.

'Aubergine in tomato and allspice, with bulgur and lemony yog.'

A grunt. 'Again.'

'Yes, *again.*'

Daniel bends over and starts shovelling.

'Can you wait please?'

His son has a fairly good line in eye-rolls too. He slumps, somehow, even further over the food, chin pressing forward and head tilting back at the unfairness of this minutely brief delay.

Initially, Anthony had been disbelieving at how every cliché he'd ever heard about teenage boys had come true overnight. It had been almost to the day of Daniel turning thirteen, it seemed, that his curious, bouncing boy had turned into a sullen, monosyllabic sack of a human. The only time you saw any vestige of his old self was when he played the viola – suddenly the spine straightened, the shoulders lifted; there was a frown of concentration rather than generic moodiness.

Daniel had shown a distinct talent for music since he was tiny – picking out tunes on the piano, singing sweetly, and when they rented him a little baby viola in primary school, he actually practised it, almost obsessively, like it was something to be solved. In fact, he would get the exact same expression on his face that Emily had when playing chess, and that Rachel had when studying a drawing or painting for signs of expert forgery. Genetic concentration.

Anthony wondered, sometimes, if it was right to encourage Daniel in the one art form that Emily was so excluded from – but then, he also wondered if that was, on some level, why it so strongly appealed to Daniel in the first place. Emily got so much attention as a child; of course she did. But music could be Daniel's thing, his special thing. His own language. Anthony and Rachel had had long conversations about it, and decided together – presenting a united front, as they always did as parents – that it was to be encouraged.

Emily comes in, and moves the pile of her textbooks and magazines from her place at the table back onto the island. Anthony is about to remonstrate with her, before deciding he simply can't be bothered. He is hungry, and he just wants to *eat* together, a *nice family meal*.

How was school? Rachel signs at both kids.

Daniel just shrugs.

Pointless, Emily signs, vehemently. *End of term. Barely doing anything. Can I stay at home?*

No. You should go in, signs Rachel.

It has been a battle persuading Emily to keep going to school, after finishing her exams, and Anthony had thought that she deserved an extended break, really. But Rachel prefers not having the kids at home in the daytime. Her work – authenticating artworks for a mix of institutions and extremely wealthy private clients – needs concentration, even the bits she can do remotely, from home. And although Emily and Daniel are old enough to shut the study doors on, somehow their presence in the house can always be heard and felt. Toasters popping, phones chirruping, viola practice.

Besides, it's good for Emily to have the company, Anthony and Rachel both agree. She'd used the run-up to GCSEs as an excuse not to go into school as much – revising at home, alone, or in targeted remote sessions. But her concentration fatigue seems even worse than usual after all the online lessons and revision and exams, even if she hasn't wanted to admit it. She is strong and stubborn and – what's that awful word Rachel uses about her all the time – ah yes, *resilient*.

To his mind, Emily's constantly proving her *resilience* is less a laudable attribute, more a sign that she has simply been failed by society. Anthony frequently burns with a quiet inner fury at how badly the world is set up for *difference*. The problem is not Emily. The problem is *never* Emily. She just requires slightly different, slightly more, provision. Signs, captions, interpreters, extra time. Simple things, really.

It is called 'reasonable adjustment'. So why are they so often made to feel *un*reasonable?

Rachel is wonderful at advocating for access; with her bright American forthrightness, she actually gets things done. No, he is being too hard on himself: it is not just Rachel. They have learned, *together*, how to advocate effectively for Emily; have become something of a crack team. They have had to help each other find their own ways of being resilient too, over the years.

Recently, they have stealthily been contacting chess summer schools, but have yet to find any who can 'accommodate her needs'. Anthony had chucked his stupid phone across the room when the last of those emails came in, a rare instance of his inner frustration actually boiling over. How dare they not want his talented, brilliant daughter, just because—

'Daniel!'

His son has spilled yoghurt all over the crotch of his school uniform trousers.

'You're meant to change before dinner,' says Rachel, in exasperation. 'Your other set of trousers are still in the wash.'

Another set had to be thrown away the week before after Daniel tore the crotch while allegedly 'practising parkour' in a multi-storey car park. Daniel makes only a generalised groaning, grumbling sound.

'I'm sorry, what was that?' asks Anthony.

'I *said:* it doesn't *matter!*'

'Well, you can't wear those now—'

'God, I *know*. I'll just wear my black jeans.'

'You can't wear *jeans*—'

'It's the last, like, two days of term—'

'That's not the point. You can't just wear whatever you like—'

'For God's sake, why do you ever care about it? I *hate* wearing a uniform, it's bullshit – *just enforced institutional conformity*—'

'Daniel. *Enough.*' Rachel holds up a hand. They have all encountered this rant before; it's so familiar, Daniel doesn't even bother signing to include Emily on this occasion. Even his teachers have been subjected to this rant, after Daniel and his mates produced a petition against the wearing of ties ('a literally pointless item of clothing'.)

In private, Rachel and Anthony actually agree with most of Daniel's complaints. But if Daniel gets expelled from the private school that Rachel's father pays for – via significant personal sacrifice that he pretends not to be making, the fees being more than he can really afford since he stopped writing regularly – they will never hear the end of it.

'I will wash the trousers tonight. It's warm enough that they'll probably be dry by the morning, OK? And please can you change your whole uniform when you get in from now on, not just the shirt and tie?'

'Fine, whatever.'

Rachel breathes out concertedly, and then turns her head, with moving-things-on intention, to Anthony.

'So, what were you saying before dinner, about that meeting?'

'Ah yes. Well . . .' Anthony takes a deep breath. 'Yes, Matthew came to see me about the bloody Gauguin business. Again.'

There had been an open letter, sent at the end of summer term, to the student newspaper, criticising the course he was due to run for second-years in autumn term, on Impressionism and post-Impressionism – objecting to the inclusion of Gauguin. Written by a student, Olivia, who argued that Gauguin should be removed from the syllabus entirely, because of his 'morally reprehensible actions as a coloniser, and as a man'. They were a bright, quick first year with a Mancunian accent and an androgynous, bright purple crew cut, who he'd taught in 'An Introduction to Painting'. Anthony still couldn't fathom why they hadn't just come to talk to him about it first.

'The university haven't changed their mind?' asks Rachel, fork aloft.

The university has so far stood by him – his head of department, Matthew, knew how he taught, and agreed it was ridiculous that he should be painted as some defender of a paedophile. And anyway, it was just one student complaining at this stage. They'd nip it in the bud. There'd been a statement online, and in the student newspaper.

'No no. It's just about the exact wording, on the website, and syllabus materials. They want me to release that as a second 'statement' to the newspaper for the start of term too. Lots of nice clear trigger warnings, assurance that we do indeed *deal* with it . . . all. The problematic stuff.'

Rachel nods, with apparently weary understanding. She has heard him complain about this, plenty, since it all kicked off.

But Anthony had just been so outraged!

'Hello?' says Emily, loudly, while waving – frustrated at them leaving her out. *You're speaking too fast – what are you saying?* she signs, angrily.

And Anthony feels bad, as he always does when he just allows the words to splurge from his mouth rather than including her properly. He lays down his cutlery, contritely signs *sorry*, his closed hand circling his chest, and then summarises the latest developments as swiftly as he can in BSL.

Sounds fair, she says. *Give people the choice. A warning in advance.*

Yes, replies Anthony. He sighs.

Anthony does not have a problem with Olivia having a

problem with Gauguin. Olivia certainly *should* have a problem with him. He was indeed – to use the parlance they preferred – *problematic.*

Objectionable, had been the word Anthony himself had used.

Because when Anthony had started his career, *he* had been the one launching the attacks on Gauguin. For his repeated use of passive, willing woman stereotypes, the exoticised and eroticised underaged Polynesian women; the fantasy of those sexualised figures, with their placid, glazed expressions. He had been one of the academics who fought to bring the artist's grim biography further into the light! Called on museums and galleries to properly contextualise his work. Was even attacked by other academics for being 'too destructive' in his criticisms.

If Olivia had signed up for his class, they would have discovered that, in fact, Anthony dealt very thoroughly with the issue of *the persistently objectifying, colonising male gaze* in Gauguin's work (as the statement read). His ethical failings, and his disturbing sexual proclivities.

But in Anthony's opinion, this simply made Gauguin *more* interesting to study. So thorny, to hate the man – yet love the work! The lushness, the heated ripeness of his paintings. Convincing and fleshy, their colours turned up too bright. Acknowledging the artist's failing was a moral imperative – the era of bland hagiography was dead, thank God – but that didn't mean you couldn't appreciate shape and form and stroke and pigment. The strange heady sensuality of his work.

I am happy to do content warnings, Anthony signs. *But I don't think that this student will be satisfied by that – they want him off the syllabus. Cancelled—*

Dad. Emily's face seems to be dripping with scorn, as she signs. *Please don't talk about cancel culture.*

'I know, I know,' says Anthony, signing his agreement at the same time.

And he really does agree with his daughter on this; cancel culture *is* a tedious topic, one that a few of his colleagues seem to relish but most find faintly embarrassing. Just a Tory pet peeve. A political distraction, and a shamefully obvious one at that.

But in this case, complete removal of the artist is what the student wants, he continues.

Why?

They feel that studying his work is the same as endorsing him as a person.

Isn't it? asks Emily.

'No of course it bloody isn't!'

Emily scowls. Whether at his outburst, or the fact that the words came out faster than the thought to sign them, is unclear.

And Anthony knows that, really, he is raising his voice at his inbox.

The image of it comes to him: a ghoulish greenish-white. Olivia's emails, lurking, on his computer. And on his phone.

Tomorrow. He must reply to Olivia tomorrow. Professional, polite. Simply updating them of the actions agreed with the head of department, about warnings and opt-outs.

He pours himself a glass of sparkling water.

Actually, Olivia's emails don't lurk. They *assert.* Each missive a hard line, almost impossible to argue against. So inflexible.

Re: Re: Re: Re: Gauguin
Continuing to venerate Gauguin's work upholds the idea that art is more important than action. Given so many of Gauguin's paintings feature his victims of sexual assault, to appreciate them is the equivalent of participating in their abuse.

For God's sake, they're all dead!!! Anthony had wanted to reply. How much more harm can we do these poor women? What we're talking about are just pictures, not people; they're not *real*.

He can understand not wanting to pay to watch, say, the films of Roman Polanski – to put money in the pocket of someone still living and making work, something he has in fact argued with colleagues about many a time, for he is far more on Olivia's side here than much of his department... But Gauguin isn't profiting from a new exhibition at the Royal Academy. More indigenous women are not getting hurt by students writing undergraduate essays on him. All we'll be doing is denying ourselves great art, he had tried to explain, ever so carefully, in yet another email reply.

Anthony had also suggested that Olivia put their *undoubtedly strong and well-articulated feelings* into an essay, intimating that they would be sure to get a good mark.

Olivia had replied that he clearly didn't understand the *violence of that suggestion*.

That continuing to look at these pictures was to continue to promote the view that women are objects to be looked at and used for men's pleasure.

Anthony has not yet replied to this.

The accusation *of violence* lies curled in his inbox. Lies curled up in his chest too, like some horrible worm, or parasite, eating away at him.

Involuntarily, the image of Cindy. Lying prone and passive, beneath him. A placid, glazed expression, with only an occasional half-arsed imitation of pleasure, put on for him. *Not real.*

A slideshow image of the porn he watches, the young women dressed to look younger, always the glazed gaze. Just a fantasy. The awareness of its fakery is built in; everyone watching knows it. It's not real.

A performance—

The feeling of hitting his wife in the face. Pretending to want to hurt her while also literally hurting her . . .

But it's not real—

Anthony blinks rapidly, and takes a gulp of his water. The fizz goes up his nostrils and he starts coughing, makes a show of getting up and getting still water from the tap instead.

'Jesus, Dad,' he faintly hears Daniel muttering. Embarrassed.

The rain is beating harder now against the doors and windows, the light falling with it. His own face is revealed, fully at last, in the yellow reflection above the sink. The rivulets on the glass's surface adding extra wrinkles on his *old, white, male, out of print* face.

Embarrassing.

And for the briefest of moments, Anthony has the urge to raise the water glass high in the air and then bring it down hard, to smash it repeatedly against the edge of the sink, till it disintegrates.

Instead, he drinks from it very deeply and swallows. Puts the glass down and stares into his own eyes, which look like dark voids in the uneven reflection.

He has been avoiding his own face; avoiding looking at himself, in mirrors, since it happened with Cindy. Since he *bought* Cindy. Her body. Her time, at least. By the hour.

And he knows, really, what he needs to do, if he wants to be able to face himself again. If he wants to be able to look Rachel in the face again. To meet the expectations of his kids. His students. His colleagues.

He needs to start with Rachel. He needs to talk to her, properly. Not just to ask about her day or what's for dinner or to fret about the kids or to feel cosily proud of the kids or to

279

offload about work. But to have that painful conversation, about the sex and the dating, and his crushing sense of inadequacy . . .

About what he has done.

'Anthony?' Her voice is like a bell, and he turns automatically back round to her. She looks expectant.

Or is it just impatient.

Maybe he doesn't have to tell her absolutely everything.

Anthony walks over and kisses her on the cheek, and then sits back down to finish his nice family dinner.

Chapter 9

Rachel

Rachel pauses a moment on the doorstep. She wants to breathe in a great lungful of this air – so cool and fresh, it seems to almost sparkle as it hits her lungs, although the heat is already coming through from the acidic sunshine. It is going to be a scorching day.

But she is taking in something else, too. A sense of possibility.

This freshness, of being her, on this bright new day: Rachel Roe, mother of two wonderful children, top-tier authenticator at Limburn & Double, daughter of noted art critic Robert Schechter, wife of art historian Anthony Roe. And then firmly shutting her own front door on all that.

She is going to camp in a field, with her lover, and his friends, and none of their children. She does not have to look after anyone (not even herself, if she chooses not to). There will be no emails, no ironing, no Zoom; no driving of kids, no credit card bills, no one-time authentication passwords. No explaining to angry people why her daughter has apparently been ignoring them or their instructions. No doing her aged colleague's work for him because he doesn't possess the most basic IT skills. No making sure Anthony feels OK after she comes home late.

No responsibility.

This is the bliss of having this casual thing with Scott, Rachel thinks – all of the fun, none of the reality. How long that will last (for it surely can't last forever) is a matter for another day; today, this glorious sunny Friday, she's not thinking about the future. Or the past. She's simply choosing *not to worry* about things, mentally scrunching up her to-do list and tossing it in an imaginary trash can.

She will be only in the moment, no other thoughts. Seize the day.

And the day is so gorgeous, it does feel almost graspable. The scent of lavender fluffs up out of their overgrown bush (really need to prune that back actu— *No. Not today. Not this weekend.*)

The cab pulls up, and the act of lifting her backpack into the trunk brings a slight apprehension slinking back in. It is incredibly heavy. Rachel repacked it twice, the first selection of clothes and toiletries and snacks simply failing to remotely fit. A sleeping bag and a tin cup still dangle off the sides.

They are almost at the station when her phone starts ringing.

'Sweetness – it's me. I've got some terrible news.'

Her heart stops. He sounds dreadful.

'I've started throwing up and . . . er, well, let's just say, the last half an hour has not been pretty.'

'Oh shit. Scott! No . . .'

'Yup. Hideous timing. Are you on your way already?'

'Yeah – in the cab.'

'Oh, God, I'm so sorry sweets. Well, look, why don't you just go? I'm hoping it might be mere food poisoning and I can join you later, or tomorrow. Although my colleague did just come down with some pretty hideous bug, so it's possible he's given it to the entire office . . . But no sense in us both missing out.'

Rachel's brain whirrs with what this might mean.

'Bella and Lyds are obviously already at the site, and Beadle – you know, from the cottage – is heading down today too.

Then there's Bella's Manchester lot, who you've mostly not met, but they're fun, I promise. You'll have a lovely time. I'm actually very jealous.'

'Oh, well ... sure. I guess.' All Rachel's excitement has rapidly gone flat. 'Are you feeling OK? You don't want me to come over?'

'No! No, I promise you, you don't want to witness this. And I'm absolutely fuming about missing the festival, but not so ill I need looking after.' In fact, apart from a croak in his throat, Scott sounds as laid back as he ever does. Certainly doesn't seem to have considered that she might not want to go, or might feel weird about it, and Rachel finds herself (as she often does) simply accepting his relaxed take on a situation.

She gets on the train, and by the time she gets off she's clearly surrounded by other festival-goers. A friendly anticipation ripples off them all, as they wait for a shuttle bus to the Moorlands Sounds site, banked by rucksacks, tents and Bags for Life full of cooking equipment and food.

There's no need to be apprehensive, Rachel tells herself as the bus winds through increasingly narrow country lanes at an alarming clip. But the promise of an easy weekend away has already dampened into a rather more tricky prospect. There is a little squirming, wormy feeling in her low belly, one she hasn't felt for some time.

Fundamentally, Rachel is fine in any situation so long as she knows the rules. She can play the game: it is usually perfectly obvious to her, in any moment, exactly what move you need to make next in order to get what you want. She is adept at putting on a coolly confident professional demeanour for clients: after all, if art forgery itself is partly a confidence trick, being the one to see through that requires an even steelier gaze. She knows how to play the part in other segments of her life too, whether that's asking convincingly interested-sounding questions of Anthony's ancient colleagues at Christmas drinks, or open-ended, encouraging questions of men on first dates, or being non-threateningly assertive of Emily's legal rights on the many, many occasions where access requirements are woefully unmet.

But what she's about to plunge into feels... *lawless*. Free from the ordinary rules; *a weekend of freedom*, as Scott promised.

And the resulting squirm that she feels is distantly familiar, Rachel realises, with a lurch: it reminds her of the feeling she had on arriving in London, in 1996. Alone and friendless, apart from her mother's cousin and her husband – who let her stay in the spare room of their house in Bushey, while she studied at the Courtauld.

Moving from New York to London, and studying at a British art school, had been like playing chess on a snakes and ladders board: there were all sorts of unspoken rules and assumptions and meanings that kept slipping out of her grasp. It was an exciting time for British art, and London was the epicentre – where artists made headlines, a host of new sexy galleries were opening, and the YBAs were making serious money for often profoundly unserious work. Yet it felt as if all the interesting things that were happening in the city were constantly slithering away from her, or proving a disappointment.

The supposedly hip gallery openings she did find out about in East London actually seemed quite dull, the work tawdry and ill-thought through, the parties tame; did she not know the right people, or did she just leave too early? The cooler of her fellow students seemed obsessed with affecting to be working class even if they clearly weren't, constantly going to terrible 'caffs' serving cheap greasy breakfasts that made Rachel feel nervous about hygiene standards, or to shabby brown pubs serving horrible warm beer. And she felt sick, at the way the sneering response to any hesitation by her was always couched in unfair insinuations that she was *rich* or *spoilt* (read: Jewish), rather than simply having a preference for ice-cold beverages.

It took some months of feeling lost and shaky from trying to be someone she wasn't before Rachel felt able to admit to herself that whatever this 'scene' was, it was not for her. She put away the poorly-fitting new uniform she'd attempted to adopt, of torn jeans and slobby bucket hats, and got out her simple well-cut dresses and the delicate silver *Chai* necklace her mother had given her as a leaving present. She stopped pretending to like smoking, or house music, or having unbrushed hair. Admitted that that was all just... *fake*.

Instead, Rachel dedicated herself to her Masters, and funnelled her youthful energy into absorbing all the *proper* culture and history that London – and indeed the Continent – had to offer. Who wanted a warehouse party when you could have a weekend in Paris or a trip to Rome? And she ambitiously pursued the sort of internships that weren't deemed edgy enough for her more anti-establishment coursemates. Auction houses. Conservation departments. The most traditional of art dealers. Then a PhD, on why female artists of the Dutch Golden Age so focused on the still life. A good job at Dulwich Picture Gallery, another at Christie's, and then head-hunted for a move into art authentication.

With the result that she ended up right back in the world she had thought she wanted to escape when leaving New York. Respectable, and intellectual. Her father's world.

Rachel's moving to London in the first place had really been as much about avoiding her father's reputation as for any particular passion for the YBAs. She had recognised that it was a grotesque privilege, being parachuted into summer jobs in

Manhattan via her father's connections while still at college: compiling the art listings for *Time Out*, stuffing envelopes for the Met's press office. But it consistently left her feeling icky. People might scorn her father's outsized influence, but the art world was also afraid of him and the effect a bad review from this dominant voice could still have. And so no one treated her normally; in each new role, Rachel felt like a spotlight was trailing her along the corridors, whispers following. People offered *her* coffees rather than shouting their orders for her to fetch.

She felt sure that moving to London would dim that, and it did. Rachel's fellow students rarely joined the dots, and although her tutors certainly did, they seemed to want to pretend they had not. *So British*, thought Rachel, telling herself she was pleased. Relieved.

She also told herself it hardly mattered, because she had been busily making herself into an attractive proposition to employers anyway: a conscientious, hard-working, charming American, with stellar credentials and glowing references. By not seeking to play the rip-it-up, conceptual games of her grungier peers, Rachel found herself warmly accepted into the establishment, as a bright young expert in that suddenly most old-fashioned of things: *the painting.*

If there might have been a whisper that followed her – *Robert Schecter's daughter, doing well for herself actually, one to watch –* Rachel found she no longer minded so much. At least she was on her own path. Climbing her own ladder.

The climbing stopped fairly abruptly at thirty-one, when she got pregnant. If it was not *quite* a snake taking her back to square one, maternity leave certainly slowed her progress. Ah well. It had, of course, been worth it; she'd always wanted a family, and Anthony wasn't getting any younger, after all.

When she first met him, Anthony had felt like a startlingly

rare find: a supremely intelligent man who wore that lightly, who actually listened to what you said, and whose obvious attraction towards her was tempered with a kind of awkward respectfulness. Rachel had been used to rich art world types crassly wanting to impress her, or more established academics and experts wanting to undermine her – as if *that* would drive her into their arms! Anthony's lack of presumption made him seductive – that, and the fact that the stoopingly tall, wavy-haired, shy Englishman was literally the American-in-Notting-Hill dream in the early 2000s. Even her mother had readily accepted him, to Rachel's shock.

And Anthony has always supported her career, her ambitions; he's always been front-footed with the children, taking time out of work where he could. But what is odd, is that now the kids are of an age where Rachel can really double-down at work again, pushing and climbing, embracing international travel and so on . . . she finds she has far less inclination to. The concept of 'achieving success' has become oddly fuzzy and remote to her recently.

Maybe it is Scott's fault. Because Rachel has lately found herself gripped by a compulsion to do all those things she hadn't done in her twenties – to dance and drink and stay up late; to be silly, and spontaneous, and feckless. To sleep with new people, and to sleep with people in new ways. To be free.

Still, it is funny, she reflects while queuing for a wristband, that despite rejecting the youth culture of her youth *in* her youth, she is now at a festival that appears to be practically a recreation of it. Half the people in the queue with her are about her age, and look like they are very concertedly trying to relive the nineties, while the other half are *half* her age and look like they are cos-playing the fashions that Rachel remembers being bemused by herself back then. The fanny packs, the neon mesh, the clingy nylon flares. The goddamn bucket hats.

Finally, she is given her wristband and begins a trudging slog along a wide, dusty path towards Red Camping. Scott had put her in a WhatsApp group with his friends while she was on the train and she had been assured that she would be 'unable to miss' Bella and Lyds's camping spot – demarcated by a large rainbow unicorn flag.

When she finally finds it – after a detour to refill her zebra-print water bottle at a spluttering standing tap – Rachel can't help but notice that the unicorn flag is the sort of image Emily used to have on all her fluffy notebooks and pencil cases. And has now scornfully grown out of.

'Rach-eeellllll!' Bella comes bounding towards her, arms outstretched, her breasts barely contained in a rust-coloured halter-neck dress that suits her colouring perfectly. 'You found us!'

Rachel does not want the hug, she's so sweaty from lugging her stuff that she feels repulsive. She needs a shower and a change already – two things that, she knows, won't be happening till tomorrow morning, at the earliest ('no one really showers, sweetness, you just stew in your own delicious juices,' Scott had told her, with lascivious glee).

'Absolute dis-*aaa*-ster about Scott! I can't belie*eeeve* it! But so glad you're heeeeere!' Bella's vowels stretch like chewing gum when she feels something strongly, which is almost all the time. She must be near Rachel's age, but seems much younger; like Scott, that's down to the lack of kids, Rachel supposes. Bella teaches yoga and Pilates and works as a 'healer', although the amount of cider Rachel has watched her put away would suggest she isn't especially concerned about her body being a temple.

As if on cue, Bella reaches into a cool box and proffers a can. 'Cider, babe? It's thirsty work.'

'Thank you,' says Rachel, and goes to take it, even though it is barely lunchtime. Then she stops herself. 'Don't suppose you have a beer in there, do you?' She has never acquired the taste for alcoholic apple juice.

'Sure babe! Oi, Lyds, chuck Rachel a Hazy.'

Lyds pops her head out of a tent, waves, and passes out a can from a different cool box in her tent's porch.

The Hazy Jane is remarkably, thankfully cold still, and Bella immediately shows Rachel where to add the cans she brought with her, in yet another cool bag in the porch of what is to be her home for the weekend. Bella and Lyds are bunking up, and letting Rachel have Lyds's tent, something she is profoundly grateful for. Rachel hasn't attempted to put up a tent since an ill-advised family camping trip in the Lake District when it rained so much even stoical, staycation-loving Anthony agreed to give up and go home.

Inside the stuffy heat of the tent – which smells faintly of hair grease and dandruff, the floor freckled with previous-years' glitter and dirt – Rachel unrolls her bedding, inflates her mat, plumps her mini pillow, and wonders what to do next.

No signal on her phone; exactly as Scott had warned her. Something she had, in fact, been looking forward to. But now it means she can't message Scott, to see if he's coming. Or Anthony. Or the kids.

Rachel lies down, feeling suddenly tired at the prospect of spending a whole weekend with people she doesn't really know. The effort of it. *Perhaps this was a terrible mistake.*

But lying down reminds her that the back of her T-shirt has a backpack-sized continent of sweat on it. She decides it can't be helped, she will simply have to use up one of her changes of clothes. *And then get back out there*, she tells herself.

Rachel rolls on more deodorant, then slips into a striped T-shirt that she knows suits her, with an almost off-the-shoulder Bardot neckline, and a pair of shorts. They're shorter than she would usually deign to wear anywhere but on a beach holiday, but she's had a good enough wax and spray tan in advance to feel confident getting her legs out. Scott loves her legs; so does Anthony, actually, but Scott is far more vocal in his appreciation.

It's one of the things she likes about him: there's an incredible cheesiness to his wolfish grins, the raised eyebrows and licked lips, but there is also something so pleasingly *clear* in the way he articulates what he likes, what he wants. Scott has taught her to ask for more, and to ask more directly. And he is usually keen to provide whatever she asks for.

But it's also been a revelation, seeing how enthusiastic and open Anthony has become too, after years where a satisfying sex life had slowly settled into little more than faintly dutiful missionary.

Opening up their marriage has been good for them both.

She finds her biggest sunglasses. A floppy brimmed sunhat. A slick of tomato-red lipstick. A squirt of her summeriest Jo Malone (English pear and freesia). She is as ready as she will ever be.

They hang about at the tents for a while, Bella snacking on warm Babybels (*gross,* judges Rachel) and waiting for Beadle to join them. An old friend of Scott's, Jake Beadle arrives with arms spread and a fantastically large number of bags containing communal breakfast supplies. A beer-gut threatens to burst out of his too-tight shirt, and his toes spill over the ends of already disgusting flip-flops. But he has a freakishly good memory, and as he sits down next to her, asks a lot of very detailed questions about how Emily is getting on with exams, and what progress Rachel had made dating a Flemish oil painting that she'd just sent a microscopic sample of to the lab last time he saw her. It is a concerted attempt, she can tell, to make her feel included, and it is welcome.

Then Beadle puts up his tent very slowly, and after Lyds has packed and repacked her tote bag repeatedly, and framed her pointed, pixie-face with curves of emerald glitter (it is too early and too sweaty for such things, in Rachel's opinion), they eventually all head into the main site. Lyds is determined not to miss a band Rachel doesn't catch the name of, and yet is also the one who keeps delaying their progress, stopping at the Portaloos.

Festival bathrooms were something else Scott had been blasé about, and which Rachel had nerves at the mere thought of, but there is paper and a real seat and hand sanitiser and even a mirror, albeit slightly warped.

'Oh yeah, Moorlands is pretty classy. Well set up,' insists Bella wisely, before launching into tales of Glastonbury in the nineties, jumping over the fence only to land in human shit. Rachel shudders.

There are lengthy queues at the beer tent, plastic glasses of craft ale, a plate of mezze featuring succulent vine leaves and dried, chewy falafel ('like a mummified ballsack' is Bella's review). It is too hot to stand up, and they beach themselves on a bank next to the main stage, along with most of the rest of the festival it seems. Rachel doesn't say too much, simply drifting in and out of the music and the conversation. But Scott's friends make for easy company because they will always reliably fill in any gaps, ceaselessly shouting and laughing and jerking around.

Still, it is clear that she has little in common with them except Scott. Rachel hadn't quite realised what strong glue he was.

All Rachel really wants to do is find some shade from the sun, beating down from a remorselessly cloud-free, lapis-blue sky. But it's been decreed they can't move until Bella's friends from Manchester finally find them. There have been several painful, bellowed attempts by Bella over barely-existent phone signal to convey first where their tents are and then which stage they are sitting at. And when they do eventually arrive, Rachel feels unable to deal with the straggling group of more new people, and so she simply lies back on the dry, itchy grass and lets the unexpected combination of kora and synths coming from the stage wash over her for a time. Someone offers her a joint, and even one light puff almost sends her to sleep.

It is still far too hot. From behind her eyelids, everything is bright red, even with sunglasses perched over her face.

'Am I burning? I feel like I'm burning,' she says to Beadle, lying next to her, while keeping her eyes shut. 'I can't believe I left my hat at the tent, the number of times we went back for things.'

A shadow passes over her face.

'Can I be of service?' A voice, pleasingly sonorous and definitely not Beadle's.

Rachel opens her eyes. A man, framed only by sky, is looking at her. A small smile moves around the edges of his mouth. He holds one of those silly straw trilbys, although there is something chicly offhand in its angle, the way he is waving it gently towards her, over her.

She pushes herself up on her elbows, a move that raises her bare shoulders and clavicles up out of her T-shirt, in a way that she dimly hopes is attractive. Then she registers the flamboyant pink and green jungle pattern of his shirt, a well-groomed barely-there beard, Tom Ford sunglasses. Something about the way he holds himself. *Well, never mind.*

Rachel smiles, not quite certain what exactly he is offering. 'Would you like my hat?'

'Are you sure? I'm Rachel.' It sounds like a weird non-sequitur.

'I'm sure Rachel.' He puts it, lightly, on her head, then lifts his sunglasses as if inspecting her. His eyes are an unusual hazel colour, a pale-flecked brown shading to an almost lichen-green. Holding his gaze for a moment makes Rachel feel like she's just downed a shot of iced coffee. A shock of connection, amid the hot, hazed afternoon's indulgence.

'Suits you,' he says with – was it? Is it? – a quick tiny wink. 'And I'm Elijah. What good biblical names we both have.'

He smiles, wider, which causes creases in his face, attractive lines like brackets around his mouth, and then drops his sunglasses back down.

'How do you know Bella?' she asks.

It is a banal question, but she wants to keep Elijah's attention. It's been a while since she's had this sensation – the instant hunch, that you will get on with someone.

Rachel is good at reading people. Taking them in, in a quick, judgemental set of tiny glances. Assessing some ineffable quality that defines them. She correctly guessed, for instance, within seconds of meeting Scott that he would be excellent in bed, and that she would never truly fall in love with him.

Whereas on meeting Anthony, she just knew that she could. Just *knew*.

It is a little like what happens with a painting. Rachel doesn't go on about this because it sounds boasty and also deeply unscientific, but her gut instinct on that first, long look – the work freshly exposed under strong bright white light – is actually correct a freakish amount of the time. Of course, her 'gut instinct' – her own way of seeing – is informed by decades of art historical study, and also always backed up by masses of further examination: analysing the painting under raking light, ultraviolet light, infrared light, intense magnification ...

And, of course, sometimes her gut instinct is wrong.

Sometimes she can't see what is right in front of her face.

'I don't know Bella well, actually. She's old pals with that lot ...' Elijah proceeds to give Rachel a speedy, rather gossipy run-down on who knows who and how from the Manchester gang, which is entertaining even though Rachel knows she hasn't a chance of retaining a quarter of it.

The band finish with a final, ecstatic flourish of kora, which rather unexpectedly turns out to have been played by an old white hippie, and Rachel politely applauds. Elijah looks at her, slightly amused. *Probably look like I'm in a concert hall, rather than a festival*, thinks Rachel.

'How about you?' asks Elijah.

'I know Scott? Who knows Bella. He was meant to be here but he's ... unwell. Some quite dramatic vomiting, apparently. And I was already on my way ...'

'Oh God! What a shitter. Poor Scott.'

Rachel thinks she sees Elijah's eyes dash fleetingly to her ring finger, as she raises her water bottle, and is about to try to explain it all when something stops her. It momentarily just seems too complicated to bother with.

'Well, don't worry, I'm sure we can all look after you *very well* in his absence.'

Rachel can't help but smile. It is such a pleasure, to be flirted with by gay men. So performative, so simple, and so safe.

'*Would* you? Honestly, I've never been to a music festival before – embarrassing, I know . . .'

Rachel offers up this show of shame-facedness, but doesn't actually feel it, so it is a surprise that Elijah does genuinely look shocked. Faintly appalled even.

It's also slightly comforting: she obviously *looks* like she might be a real festival-goer. Pulls off the part.

'Well fuck me backwards. Where have you been all this time? Do they not have festivals in the States?'

'I'm sure they do, but I've lived here since the nineties so not sure I can blame it on that. I don't know. Not been my . . . thing. I don't really do camping. Mud. You know.'

'Well, you've lucked out. Best weekend of the summer so far. I think it's going to be *glorious* all through.' He smiles again, slightly sly, as he takes in her mostly-drunk pint, and her water bottle, and the several cans that have gathered around their group like a fairy ring. 'I was going to school you in how important it is to stay hydrated, but I see you are really working on that already.'

'Lads!' It is Bella, addressing the whole group, her arms spread. 'We are going over to the other stage to see Planningtorock. FOLLOW!'

Elijah looks at Rachel, expectantly, and she merely shrugs. His smile breaks in those creases again as he stands and offers a hand. He has sparkly lime-green nail polish on; it seems to twinkle in the light.

A nice firm grip pulls her up, and then as they stand, face to face, he doesn't let go. And there is a moment, when Rachel isn't sure how to read him. At all.

Then he firmly pumps her hand.

'Very nice to meet you, Rachel . . . ?'

'Rachel Roe.'

'Rachel Roe. Excellent. We do approve of alliteration.'

'And what's your—'

But he has turned and is gone, slinging a loose arm over a friend's shoulder, and then Lyds takes Rachel's arm (she wishes she wouldn't, she can feel the sweat patches under the armpits of Lyds's jumpsuit) and they process, in a straggling formation, to the other stage.

Someone leads a snaking, jostling train just far enough into the crowd where people are dancing to the fizzing music. Despite the big group she's with being possibly the most loud and annoying in the field, shouting at each other over the songs – or shouting along with the lyrics, something about gender being just a game – Rachel finds she feels surprisingly unselfconscious. Because no one seems to really mind how loud or silly they are being. She's been smiled at by more passing strangers than in any other single afternoon of her life.

And Rachel realises she . . . *feels good*. She understands why they all like festivals so much. She genuinely hasn't thought about emails for hours.

She does, however, find herself thinking about Elijah. Or rather, not thinking about him, but just keeping a vague awareness of where he is. She wants to fully befriend him. And at the end of the set, when they stand around making slow plans as the rest of the crowd drift away, she's pleased when Elijah does deliberately include her in his general invitation – or instruction? – to go back to the tent.

'I want to get changed, fully fabulous tonight, darlings. Once I've had a few more of these sherbets, I doubt I'll have it in me. Sackcloth and ashes the rest of the weekend.'

On the way back to the tent, Rachel briefly finds a spot of signal, a small flutter of messages arriving.

From Anthony:

Hope you're having a wonderful time. X

From Scott:

Hope you're having the most DELICIOUS time, sweetness, and that the gang are looking after you. I've a fever, and the vomiting continues apace; no festivaling for me, I fear . . .

DISTRAUGHT to miss out on taking your festivus virginity, but I'm sure you're popping your cherry in style!!!

Rachel pauses, and sends brief replies to both, before hurrying after the others towards their camp. She doesn't want to quite look at the mix of feelings inside her. A disappointment that Scott isn't coming – his arrival would have made it all so much easier – but also a strange little undertow of . . . relief?

Because now, she is really free. Truly at liberty to do whatever she wants, at any given moment. No one else's desire to think of, at all.

At the tents, Lyds issues strict recommendations to Rachel about 'layering up' for the evening, and she dutifully wrinkles herself out of the shorts and into some leggings – leopard print, but subtle, in shades of charcoal and indigo, and finds a large, slouchily soft lambswool jumper to go over them, and stuffs a packaway puffa jacket and a beanie hat in her bag.

She is one of the first ready, apart from Beadle, who says he 'doesn't get cold legs' and so is remaining in shorts. He might have made a better choice; it is still far too warm, really, for her leggings. Rachel deposits Elijah's straw hat in the front of his zipped-up tent, and then sits and nibbles at the supplies she's brought – an artisan sausage roll, an apple, a handful of almonds. She cracks another beer, and feels listless.

The urge, she realises, is to be once more on her phone. The itch, to put the picture she took, of the sun coming through the bushy oak trees in a perfect dapple, onto Instagram. *#goldenhour*

It really is golden though, the light low and beaming and honey-warm. Around them, all the tents look illuminated, like they might be paper lampshades over lit bulbs. Rachel tells herself to just *be in the moment*, even if the moment itself is fairly dull, really: Beadle desultorily doing a *Times* crossword, and everyone else still getting ready.

She keeps trying to capture the sky, the light, on her phone's camera, because it keeps getting better and better, minute by minute, streaking pink and orange like smoked salmon. The moon is a pearlescent promise high in the sky – but proves impossible to capture.

Slowly people emerge, ready-ish, pulling open bags of tangerines or cutting out lines on a shiny hardback copy of the new Ishiguro novel they definitely won't open all weekend. The sun concentrates into a blood-orange orb at the edge of the field, shooting last bold rays towards them.

And then ...

'Well, hellooooo queen!'

Rachel's head turns, following Bella's gaze, and there is Elijah. Finally emerging from his tent. Striking a pose, hips jutting, one hand draped up around his head, with a pouting expression that demands:

Look at me.

His waist is cinched in tight in a hot pink and lime green corset, made of the sort of shiny latex material that looks, Rachel thinks, squeaky to the touch. Hot pants give the top of each thigh, and each buttock, the same treatment – left in pink, right in green, and dear God, a bulge that unites both and that Rachel can't let herself look at (clearly no tucking going on here). Below . . . *all that* stretch a honed, tanned pair of legs, leading to long black boots with heavy-duty buckles and platforms. Elijah's eyes are stretched out in huge, swooping wings of green and a dark pink lip is outlined, exaggerated. But his hair is unadorned, and as he raises his arms, he reveals full tangled bushes of curly armpit hair.

Or should that be *she*? Rachel can't remember which pronouns you use for drag queens when they aren't actually performing, despite Emily making her watch several seasons of *Drag Race*.

Rachel's face feels very hot. She can't stop looking at how Elijah's pecs spill over the corset, like pert tiny breasts, as he catwalks up and down the uneven ground of the campsite. She is startlingly, instantly turned on. At how masculine Elijah is, below and alongside and within this performance of femininity. The suggestive dusting of chest hair at the cleavage, the beard. The strength of those legs, but then the length and shape from the heels. The pinkish light, slipping and gliding off the patent curves.

She shifts on the camping chair she's co-opted from someone and is glad of her sunglasses still. She wants to stare, to look and look and look, to study what *exactly* it is Elijah has done and why it is having this effect on her. To analyse him.

Because *this* is certainly a new one on her.

'Oh my God, fierrrrrrce, slay queen, yass!' says Bella, clicking her fingers, as if on RuPaul autopilot, in a way that Rachel can't help but recoil from. Bella is herself decked out in rainbow hotpants over thick leggings and a ridiculous marabou-fur trimmed purple jacket, and Rachel feels, once more, like she's not quite grasped the rules for the weekend. Scott had told her to 'pack something fabulous, people like to dress up', but clingy leopard-print leggings are about as fabulous as she gets.

'Right then, who wants to drink the profits with me?' Elijah bends over to the porch of a tent with flirty deliberateness, legs spread wide and rear waggling, before standing up holding a large bottle of gin. It has a faint lavender colour, and a pretty label. Paper cups are sent round the group, branded with the words 'Albion Mill – Craft Gin of Manchester'.

Elijah parades around, sloshing a worryingly large measure into the paper cups with one hand and topping them up with tonic from the other.

'For you, madame?'

'Um, sure.' Rachel proffers the cup. 'Amazing outfit. I mean, look?' She feels weirdly shy.

'Why thank you.'

'So what's your, you know, your drag name?'

'Candy de Thrush.'

A barking laugh escapes Rachel. 'Fantastic.'

'You're very sweet to say so.'

'And ... and your pronouns? I mean, are you in performance – should I be saying—'

'Don't fret yourself, he she they, whatever you fancy. I'm off-duty-Candy. And I'd never persuade this shitty lot to actually remember to say "she" anyway ...'

'Oh. Well, I mean, I'm very happy—' Between Anthony's job and Emily's teenage righteousness, Rachel is well aware of how important it is to get such things right.

But Elijah fixes her with another of those looks, eyes dancing behind the huge false eyelashes (and the irises look greener, now, surrounded by that emerald make-up). Like he might be *entertained* by this earnest desire to *get it right*.

'Don't sweat it, honey – "he" is just fine.'

300

'Got it,' says Rachel, more sharply than she quite intended.

Elijah finally pours the tonic, and it fizzes up the side of the cup and threatens to spill over.

'So are you professional – is this your job?' Rachel asks quickly.

'Not quite. Weekend queen. I dabble – don't want it to be my job, to be honest. It's meant to be fun? It's all got a bit... *commercial,* lately, darling. One eye on what is most sellable if you know what I mean, rather than what's... authentic?'

'Mm. That makes sense.'

'I have been doing it for yonks, though – have a monthly night, cornerstone of the Manchester scene if I say so myself...' A flick of an imaginary curtain of hair.

Rachel raises her cup in a cheers, and sips the gin. It is wildly strong – surely almost half and half gin and tonic. It tastes faintly floral. Could use some ice.

'Is this your gin? I mean, do you make it or something?'

'God no, I just market the shite. We'll have ourselves some branded content in a sec for the Insta account: middle-aged folk still dragging their tired arses to a festival is *very* on brand for Albion Mill...' He gives an eye-roll worthy of Emily. 'We've got a stall on site I need to check in on, and that is about the extent of my work for this weekend.'

'Did you get free tickets?'

'But of course!'

'Nice.' Rachel raises her cup again, and he gently clonks at it with the now almost empty gin bottle.

'Actually, saying that, I might force you all to watch some poetry in a minute: there's a Mancunian non-binary spoken word artist we are trying to woo – my boss actually thinks some poems about gin will help us shift units – but apparently they don't really like the stuff. Bringing a crowd to their performance might help my cause though, right?'

'Of course. However I can help,' says Rachel, and worries she sounds too eager. 'Well, at least the gin tastes pretty good!'

Although this is Rachel's honest response to the drink, somehow it sounds deeply fake.

'Well in that case, let's give you a cheeky extra measure . . .'

'Woah, no, I'm good. This is, ah, quite strong enough.'

'Oh, fine then. Anyway, you are sweet to say you like it but you don't need to be polite to me. It is not a great product: Jonty and his little brother Leon, who set up the company, are absolute chancers. They buy the cheapest grain spirit they can and then just slap in one fancy-sounding local ingredient – winberries from the Peaks! Lavender from the roof garden of a former mill! – and call it small batch, artisan, Manchester. Fancy label. Forty-nine pounds a bottle.'

'Yikes.' Rachel sips it again. 'Well, I've definitely had worse . . .'

'Oh, sure. At least I didn't bring the sugary, chemical strawberry version they also sell. Half the gins on the market now are just overpriced ways for people to drink alcopops.'

He looks at her for a second, as if sizing her up, the slyness in the corner of the mouth exaggerated by the lipstick which – up close – she can see is fizzing with a glittery sheen.

'Have I just offended you? Do you and this Scott hit up the pink gin every Friday night?'

Rachel pulls herself upright (no mean feat in the bucketty camping chair) in a show of offence.

'I certainly do *not*. The only time I ever order gin is in a Martini: bone dry, ice cold, if you please.'

She is disappointed to notice that he looks amused again. She suspects he thinks she's simply too try-hard.

'OK well, *fine,* you can stay then.'

Or maybe he is just indulgent? *Fondly* indulgent, even?

'Oi you two, stop bloody flirting, I want my G and T some time before we have to go back in, please,' interrupts one of the Manchester lot very loudly.

'Patience, please, bitch,' says Elijah — or Candy — and is gone, continuing to pour.

The temperature drops in a hurry as the sun finally dips below the edge of the horizon, and seems to galvanise Bella to herd the group back into the main arena. There's a split over who to see — but Rachel hasn't heard of either of the suggested acts, and so when Elijah stands up and makes an impassioned plea for anyone who'd enjoyed their gin to *please* do him a favour and swing by a performance poet on a cool little stage in the woods... well, Rachel is obviously happy to help.

And most of the group also oblige, following Elijah as he leads the way. Festoon lights hang in loose swags over the darkening campsite, and every food stall and drinks tent is similarly bedecked. Green and pink floodlights — matching Elijah, Rachel thinks — illuminate the great big oaks, adding frivolity to their foliage as they stand otherwise solemnly over the festivities.

The crowds have a different energy now, jumpier and excitable, that peculiarly, tangible British *up-for-it*-ness that animates high streets on a Saturday night or beer gardens on the first hot day of summer. A cascade of bubbles ascends over the streams of people re-entering the site, coming from a gaudily-painted stall that seems to sell — of all things — old-fashioned steamboat toys. Some children still gambol and leap in front of the stall, reaching for the bubbles. But many parents are heading in the opposite direction now, carrying sleeping toddlers back to the tents or pulling heavy-duty buggies and fairy-light-strewn trailers.

Then Elijah leads them away from the main path through the site, and instead along a winding trail into a woodland

area, through some giant rhododendron bushes that have their
thickest and twistiest branches all twined with lights. Skeins of
colourful wool are spread taut between taller trees, like some
cheerful Lygia Pape sculpture. And there, in a clearing, is a small
stage that actually makes Rachel let out a tiny gasp: it is almost
entirely made of and surrounded by bowers of bent willow
branches, threaded and bedecked with stems of flowers and
grasses, twists of ivy and gently fanning branches of glossy green
oak leaves. It twinkles, with hundreds of tiny lights; all around
the glade, the waiting crowd look appropriately enchanted,
dusted by its illumination.

And it's actually quite a large crowd, Rachel thinks, for a poet
on a tiny stage who hasn't started yet. Her expectations begin to
rise. Elijah ushers their group to his desired spot – near enough
to the front to definitely be able to be seen by the poet, *JB
something-someone,* but not right at the front either, in case they
want to make an early exit. Rachel briefly wonders if they will
recognise Elijah in drag – presumably not an outfit he wears
when at work. But maybe Manchester's performance scene is
small enough that they know each other already.

'Racheeeell, you need some glitter babe!' It is Bella, her eyes
dilated and dark, coming at her with a series of tiny pots and
a stick of lip balm.

Rachel shrugs. *Why not.* It is certainly time.

'What do you want? There's some electric blue...'

'Er, excuse me. Allow me to curate.' Elijah steps in front of
her, a small frown looking comically serious on his painted,
perfect face. The razor-sharp cheekbones, Rachel can see at
this proximity, merely an illusion – a clever trick of bronzer
and blusher.

He hands his drink to Bella, and takes Rachel's face in his
cool hands, and she tries not to give a little shiver. *Get a hold*

of yourself. He moves her face this way then that, catching the light, examining her. Finding her best angle.

Elijah dabs a little lip balm decisively above the outer arches of her eyebrows and then round, down, till it reaches the top of her cheekbones. He chooses an iridescent glitter, with a finish like oil – slippery, shifting, blue-green-purple.

'Yes.' He says with certainty, tapping away. 'Gorgeous.'

Something about this close-up, individual attention, the soft murmurs of praise, provokes a flush of feeling, warm and tingling.

Elijah pauses to consider Rachel, head cocked, then opens a very fine pearly glitter and his fingers flutter round her face quickly.

'Yes! Perfect.' Elijah steps back slightly, and there is something soft in his gaze. Pride in his work, perhaps, thinks Rachel.

'Yes Rach!' bellows Bella (Rachel hates having her name abbreviated). 'Nice one.' She claps Elijah on the shoulder.

'Well, she makes for an excellent blank canvas.'

The wink, again.

'Now you just need the spangles to go with it . . .' he says, voice dipping. And holding Rachel's eye contact rather than ever looking down at his hands, he carefully slips her a small baggie of MDMA.

Rachel grimaces as she licks her finger, but just as the foul taste hits her mouth the lights change, and the crowd gives a weak cheer. She throws her head back to get at the last of the beer in her can, to drown out the bitterness, and then grins at Elijah. He grins back, and Rachel wonders if she's passed enough tests now. She thinks she feels an understanding there, between her and Elijah, a promise: that they shall be in cahoots for the rest of this evening.

The poet saunters onto the stage, an androgynous figure in

loose dark trousers, and an oversized, multicoloured worker jacket over a tight white vest. Their short hair glints, catching all the lights.

'All right Moorlands Sounds! All right, uh . . . Woodland Stage massive!' They laugh gently at themselves. 'Seriously though, thanks for coming out. I know this is the prettiest stage on the site – maybe at any festival ever, right? – but I also know it's your Friday night and there's some serious sonic competition here.'

There are a few eager whoops, and Rachel notices how many of their fans are notably young, students and twenty-somethings. In fact, the little gang jostling into formation just in front of her are still teenagers, surely.

'So. I'm JB Wylie-Wallace, and tonight I've got a very special guest with me – this is Jamie Ewen on percussion. He's been working with me on a new vibe, and I hope you like it.' A man with a ratty bun waves at the crowd as he installs himself behind a complicated array of drums, shakers and assorted bits of junk, hemmed by pedals and cables. Then JB begins.

Why does spoken word always have this exact rhythm, Rachel wonders. That mannered flow, that is both slickly fluid but also constantly catching itself, staccato in its point-making. That somehow sounds the same in this Yorkshire accent as with London cadences. And the words – something earnest about needing to *claim space* . . . Rachel feels her heart sinking. She is fairly bored of bland platitudes about 'taking up space'. She'd first encountered the phrase in all the YA-friendly feminist books that had flooded the market in recent years, which she and Anthony had embraced, giving them to both Emily and Daniel. But their demands sometimes struck her as tamely inadequate, really – as if empowerment was just a matter of standing with your hands on your hips.

Rachel shoots a look to Elijah, who reaches out and gives her arm a tiny squeeze.

And then the poet pauses, at the top of a sentence, and shoots their own look to the percussionist. A held moment, before they crash together, him into an incredibly rapid, complicated rhythm and their words tumbling, going everywhere and tackling everything. It's like the beats are an urgent shot in the arm, transforming the deathly sincerity into a compellingly fast and furious explosion, as JB draws lightning-speed links between policing bills that smuggle in anti-protest legislation, and limits on citizens' right to roam, and segregated social housing, and the privatisation of public space, and the policing of bodies... and and and—

It gets faster and faster, running on and on, words and rhythms and ideas looping round and back on themselves, and Rachel feels her heart rate responding, the breath becoming light in her own throat. It's unbelievable how they are both sustaining such force, till reaching a final spitting crescendo—

'These are our streets, these are our feet, these are our woods our trees / Not our please and thank you but our *right* / Our right to roam, not your right to own / Our right to grow, and our right to sow—

'To sow seeds' – the beats cut out, and the poet bends over double, their heavy breathing briefly audible in the rapt silence, before they finish on a low sighing breath – 'of change.'

Rachel feels herself shrinking, again, in response to the performed solemnity of this final utterance. But around her people are whooping and applauding, the heartfeltness of it landing rather than prompting sniggers. Even Elijah's friends keep looking round to nod at him, as if to say *okaaaay, not totally my thing, but they've got something to them*... And more people

307

keep arriving, as if drawn through the woods, as if word has got out; clearly, Elijah did not need to bring an audience after all.

As the crowd swells, they all draw closer to the stage, closer to each other. Some of the teenagers in front of them bash into them a bit, but Rachel can't begrudge them their lack of spatial awareness, because their unaffected excitement is really rather adorable.

And the set just gets better and better. The poet looks almost like they've gone into a trance, Rachel thinks, entered some higher state. Just vibrating with it.

'This next one is about enjoying yourself, OK,' they mutter. Then they look out, across the clearing, and grin. 'Fuck it – dunno why I'm being coy. This one is called "Asking For it", and it's about claiming the pleasure of *fucking!*'

A roar from almost everyone around them. Over looped polyrhythms played on a milk bottle, a snare, and child's rainbow xylophone, the poet expounds the importance of knowing your body, your pleasure. 'Learn how to ask for it – ask for it – ask for it . . .' And this refrain builds into a defiant, demanding chant, the whole crowd soon swaying and shouting along, arms raised.

Rachel feels another little shiver, despite the warmth of the bodies gathered around them. And she wonders if Elijah has bent down towards her, because it feels like he is shooting those words almost directly into her right ear.

Ask for it – ask for it – ask for it—

But it also feels as if this JB Wylie-Wallace is speaking straight to her – because isn't this exactly what *she* is doing, has been doing, has *done*, these past several years. Learning how to find her pleasure. Naming it. Asking for it. Without shame, or embarrassment.

That can mean being bold and brave and unabashed – walking around Scott's apartment naked, even though the neighbours could probably see; telling Anthony exactly what she would like him to do in bed. But it is also about accepting that your fantasies don't always have to be... *appropriate*. That the things you've felt embarrassed and guilty about secretly desiring all your life are legitimate: that it's OK to want to be tied up, humiliated; to want to be dominated by a man; to want to feel small and helpless for once, instead of always having to be strong and in control and successful and responsible...

To be free from all that. To play. To pretend.

And as long as everyone is honest, no one will get hurt. (Unless they want to. And she does.)

A blaze of light swivels out and around the audience, as a new poem starts. This one is about escaping *the prison of monogamy* and *prising open the bars of sexual jealousy*, and Rachel feels even more radiantly illuminated by the sense that this is all just addressed to her, very specifically.

And then she wonders if it isn't, perhaps, also the effect of the MDMA.

As the poet continues to extol the pleasure of sleeping with more than one person, the light catches a teenage boy in front of her, and Rachel is struck by his expression. His face is completely lit up with worry. With panic.

Rachel feels sorry for the poor thing. He is slight and pale – can't be much older than Emily, if at all. She follows his gaze, which is nervously directed at the girl next to him. She looks much cooler than he does, thinks Rachel: pink and gold threads woven through her long braids, stick-on gemstones curving round her forehead above chunky glasses, a fresh-looking, delicate flower tattoo spreading over a shoulder bare beneath a little crochet bra-top. She watches as the girl takes the boy's hand and gives it a performatively reassuring squeeze, lifting it very slowly to her lips. There's something weighty and solemn about the moment, amid the skittish excitement all around them.

But then the poem turns into a chant, asserting that to really know yourself you have to be *free, free, free*. And suddenly the girl drops the boy's hand, and turns back to her friend on her other side, a skinny thing with very long straight hair. And they grab at each other, and hug, and throw their young arms into the air, first in fists and then in pure abandon, and they roar the word *free* like it is a password, a promise, a pledge. To each other, as much as to their own selves.

The girl with the long hair keeps accidentally swishing it in Rachel's face, which ought to be annoying, but she finds she can't care too much because really she just wants to squeeze them all as tight as she sometimes still wants to hold Emily. And Rachel is seized with both a gladness that's she's not a young woman in the current world, and with a conviction that young women growing up with such role models are probably going to be just *fine*.

The set finishes in a final endorphin rush, drumsticks thrown into the audience, enormous beams on the sweating faces of both performers. And the crowd is alive, with the sense of having really *been there* for something. But Bella is brisk in galvanising their group once more – on, on, to the big top, where a woman is playing who is one of the few people who even Rachel has circled as must-see on the very expensive programme she'd purchased.

When they get there, the band has already begun, and it is hot and crowded as they squeeze inside the stripy tent. Rachel feels momentarily like a little kid: she remembers being taken to a circus in just such a venue, with actual live animals, when they went to visit her cousins in Maryland. This set is almost as exciting, song after delicious song blending the sort of pop

Rachel would once have dismissed as bubblegum with an energy and a wit and a rage that is particularly female. The crowd is completely whipped up here too, singing along with nearly every number.

And then suddenly, the evening starts speeding up, hurrying by, their group fracturing to different stages. It's all going too fast for Rachel who can't stop smiling, even when it's just a blur of more queuing, the bang bang bang of plastic Portaloo doors, a shudder at the chemical hand sanitiser drying in the night air, the smell of spilled cider and BO in the drinks tent, a portion of fries ruined with vinegar (another sour English culinary tradition Rachel can't stand). And then sitting, and pints, and Bella and Lyds smoking cigarettes (Rachel still loathes them). And through it all, she and Elijah are always next to each other, arm-in-arm or knee-to-knee, chatting and chatting and chatting, the conversation constantly sprinting away from them, so many avenues they need to go down it's hard to stay on topic: the brilliant queasiness of Francis Bacon's paintings, how broadly fucked-up the West is about death, the catharsis of sitting shiva, how weird it is to have a well-known father...

Yes yes yes

You're so right

Yes, *exactly*, that's *exactly* what I think

No one ever *gets* that—

I get it, I know exactly what you mean—

And although Rachel would be happy to just stay sitting, cross-legged on the dry ground opposite Elijah, Lyds and Bella seem done with their own shouted heart-to-heart and are insisting that they should all 'actually watch some fucking music'. And so on, to the main stage, floodlit trees waving and swaying behind it like a chorus, Rachel's thoughts swaying too in her head as she tries to concentrate on the *highly respected* artist in the distance. But the music is lumpen and leaden to her, an abrasive voice drawling and arrogant, feedback squalls and moody echoey atmospherics that just—

'Is it me, or is this a bit shit?' she says, turning suddenly to Elijah.

'It *is*, isn't it? Why are we watching this?'

'Like, it's not the *worst* – maybe I'd listen to it in the car or whatever – but it's not . . . *fun*, is it?'

'It's a fucking fun *vacuum* darling. You're very right. Let's go.'

They tell Bella, who they can see is keen to leave too, but Lyds doesn't want to, and Rachel wonders if she's imagining it but it feels like Elijah is as keen as she is to leave without them too, and they practically run off while Bella and Lyds are still debating it.

Her feet feel too large as they walk back up a dusty slope of seated people watching the main stage, and her eyes feel like they might be being held open for her, pinned back on her head somehow.

'I think. So what I think is. We should find somewhere . . . to, to dance, maybe?' Rachel's voice sounds strangely grave.

'Oh, yeah. Obviously. Abso*lutely*.'

Then Elijah grabs her hand in his, and she registers briefly how shiny his nails feel before her fingers are entwined, gripped tight.

'Where the fuck else did you think I would be taking you?' he says, mischief contained up in the words, and an eyebrow raise that promises . . . what?

Fun. It promises fun, thinks Rachel, who is briefly over-whelmed with gratitude for this, her one and only life. That at *this* stage in its seemingly well-plotted trajectory, she could find such new pleasures, such new people.

Such a new person.

Then she realises Elijah is running his thumb over her wedding ring, a simple thin band.

'So, are you going to tell me about your... your spouse, then? Because I know you're not married to Scott...'

For a second, it's like that cold-coffee shock runs through Rachel's body again. For all that she and Anthony are very good, she thinks, at making all this work, the moment of telling someone you like about your husband almost always feels icy, for her.

Not that it matters, here, of course. With this little crush.

'You don't have to.' Elijah's voice is gentler now, and he gives her hand a squeeze, as they simultaneously navigate an uneven bit of path.

'Oh no, of course. It's fine. I...' Rachel seems to have no words and a surfeit of words all at the same time. *Come on*, she should have this stuff nailed down by now. 'Yes. So. Right. I am married – I live with my husband, Anthony, in Sheffield. Obviously in Sheffield. That's where I live. Although I do travel a lot and I am in London loads for work, like I was saying earlier...

'Sorry. I'm gabbling. Um, yeah, so we've been married seventeen years? Two kids. Emily and Daniel. And... it's a wonderful relationship. But, you know what it's like in a marriage – or any long term thing... so, well, a few years ago, we opened up our relationship. And I met Scott. And so I see him... as, as well now. Yep.'

Why is this suddenly so weird? Here's a chance to be completely gloriously open about her very different feelings for the two men in her life: how much Anthony still and always will mean to her, the depth of their connection and their love, but how much reinvigorating *fun* she is getting to have with

Scott, the new person he is allowing her to be. Yet she feels instinctively oddly guarded.

'Nice. Sounds like a good arrangement?' She can feel Elijah responding to her tone. No pressing. No nosy gleeful questions.

'Yeah! Yeah. It works really well, actually. For all of us. He – I mean Anthony – has maybe found it harder recently, since someone he was seeing moved away. But he's just started seeing someone new now too, so that's great. And – well – you know Scott, and Scott's friends—'

'Not that well. But yes.'

'Oh. OK. Well, he's, you know, he's . . . he's a fun guy. We have fun.'

And then Rachel says 'I wouldn't be here if it wasn't for him!' in a jovial tone that sounds faintly desperate, at exactly the same time as Elijah softly says 'Look we don't have to talk about this', and they find themselves stopping, briefly, under the large spread out branches of one of the big oak trees. In this half light, the flecked colours of Elijah's eyes look gold, Rachel thinks, honestly actually gold.

Which is ridiculous.

'Dancing!' she almost shouts, yanking at his hand and beginning to step backwards, away from him. 'Come on!'

And then Elijah gets a naughty look on his face, his smile lines deepening, and he says 'Right then!' and grabs her whole body and slings her over his shoulder so her head and hair go upside down and she shrieks and kicks her legs and his arm is tight around her as he's stomping over the grass in those boots and the latex of his outfit creaks beneath her torso, and she doesn't quite know what to try to hold on to.

Eventually he puts her down and Rachel feels herself flushed and giggling like a little kid and they scamper on, Elijah leading the way back into the woods, towards a thudding beat.

314

And it is magical. As they wind through narrows paths, they encounter tiny lit-up dolls' houses perched in the trees. In one glade, a film of someone seemingly dancing underwater is projected on a sheet that flutters slightly. And the beat draws them on, till there is a stage playing instantly joy-inducing music that Elijah has promised is 'Italo disco'. A man with orange-and-black striped shaggy hair presides over the decks.

They join the dance floor, and Rachel strips off her sensible puffa jacket. Elijah, of course, is a sensational dancer, and ordinarily she'd feel self-conscious even being near such unabashedly fabulous moves. But because she is *with* Elijah, anointed by him as a dance partner, it seems to liberate something inside her. Rachel dances like she is meant to be there. Like this is her natural home, with its ceiling of stars and branches and its floor of mud and grass and Elijah's arms around her, spinning her, dipping her.

After a while, she strips to her T-shirt, and after another while, more water is needed. Away from the small but committed crowd, she immediately has to put all her layers back on. It seems like a very long time since the fries, and her limbs feel hollow, her stomach jittery. But she knows she couldn't eat a thing.

They finally find the water tap, surrounded by a small quagmire of mud. Looking up while Elijah gallantly fills their bottles, Rachel notices a Ferris wheel, shrieks streaking the night air as people descend and rise, descend and rise.

'Elijah! *Ferris wheel!*'

He turns, and bursts into laughter, presumably at the intense, determined enthusiasm on her face.

'Yeah, go on then. Let's get in the queue.'

But there isn't much of a queue, and they run practically straight into a cart.

'Nice outfit mate,' drawls the man who clamps them into the seat, before sending them off with a rock. Rachel frowns, but Elijah merely blows him a kiss as the wheel lurches to let the next pair on.

'Do you get much shit from people when you're all, you know, in drag?'

Rachel can feel Elijah's mostly bare leg, surprisingly warm next to hers, while the handlebar is cool in her tight grip.

'Oh sure. Depends where you are, obviously. These days, the response is often pretty excitable from women – just straight blokes you have to watch out for. And you know, they really find the beard-and-make-up thing a challenge. Leg hair, and a mini skirt? *Gracious!* All very unsettling.'

Rachel can tell he's putting it on a bit, the blasé insouciance something of a shield against a less-pleasant truth.

'Well, that is what drag ought to be, though, isn't it?' she says. 'Subversive. Not just looking like a glamorous woman . . .'

'Tell that to Instagram.'

They lurch, again, higher into the air. The lights on the wheel are those old-fashioned, pear-shaped fairground ones, reminding Rachel again of her childhood; *I've run away and joined the circus*, she thinks, briefly. They dazzle, so they can barely see beyond their own little carriage, just some inky trees.

There's a pause, while the next passengers are tucked in below, and she thinks she feels Elijah also taking a pause. It's about the first lull in conversation since they left the tent.

'There are also . . . well, occasionally there are the odd queens and gays who aren't so keen on my take on drag . . .'

'Because of the beard?'

'Kind of. Yeah. And well, just in general . . .' His musical tones are low, almost tentative; slightly difficult to hear over the terrible blasting Europop played on the wheel. 'For having that more gender-fuck, masc drag look, and also for being bi...'

The wheel lurches once more, but this time it is different, they are shunted into continual motion, turning, rising and suddenly they are out up over the forest and can see the whole festival site, lit up and sparkling, a dark and glittering toy town. And Rachel is not sure if it is the sudden movement or Elijah's news that has made her catch her breath.

Why hadn't she even thought that might be an option?

And she lets out a shout of pure joy, at the movement, the motion, at being whisked up and around like this, so light and fast and terrifying—

And then Rachel and Elijah look at each other, eyes wide, mouths widening, and then they both simply scream.

And scream

And scream

And they kick their feet

And they raise their hands

And scream and scream and scream

The wheel stops abruptly, with a metallic clunk, with them halfway to the top. They breathe heavily for a second.

'So.' Says Rachel, now not looking at him, but looking upward at the carriages above, swinging wildly. 'You're bisexual, then?'

'I am indeed. Did you not...?'

'No!' Suddenly she turns to him, smiling and embarrassed and biting her lip but no longer caring about the amused expression in his eyes, because now it *does* seem fond. 'No, I just assumed you were definitively, totally, a hundred per cent gay.'

More than fond.

'Why the fuck did you think I was flirting with you then?'

Rachel loses her breath again as the wheel shunts them up a place, and now they are at the very top, and if she doesn't look down it's like it might be just the two of them, up in the sky, alone, all the lights merely winking at them, encouraging them.

'I don't know.' Her voice is hushed.

'Daft bugger.'

And Elijah's eyes gleam green and brown and blue all at once, like a kaleidoscope, and Rachel thinks she could look at them forever but it is also like she can't quite bear it, like the anticipation is actually *hurting* her—

Their heads draw in at the same moment, and there's the beginning of a soft, perfect kiss before—

Clank

The wheel whisks them back down a few metres, and their teeth knock as they descend and they draw back, and laugh. And then look at each other again, a little disbelieving, before having another try.

As they get off, hands all over each other (Rachel isn't totally sure she likes the texture of the latex), they notice the surprised look of the bloke manning the Ferris wheel and Elijah whispers, *see, told you, it confuses people . . .* and wipes some of his make-up off her face.

They make out against a tree trunk, then back on the dance floor, then while queuing for a Portaloo, then against another tree on the way to the tent, unable to wait till they get back before touching each other again. Rachel's neck starts to get tired; Elijah is tall in the boots, although not as tall as Anthony (but it is a long time since she's kissed Anthony for more than a few seconds standing up). She can feel Elijah's false eyelashes, fluttering against her cheek, but his stubble is giving her a slight rash, and their mouths keep getting dry; they get through both bottles of water and have to fill up again. They also both carefully and thoroughly wash their grimy hands, and then have another kiss at the side of the path.

Rachel feels about sixteen.

She wonders what Emily would think of it all.

She hopes Emily has such experiences of her own, some day.

They finally make it back to the camp, whispering and creeping into his tent. For a brief second, Rachel feels ungainly – the tent is dark, and with all his bags, there's not much room. But then Elijah finds and props up a flashlight, shoves his stuff out of the way, unzips the sleeping bag decisively, and grabs a blanket. He unhooks his corset, with a small releasing flourish that reminds her of taking off a tight bra. And he turns back to her with an inviting smile.

They lie down, giggling slightly and shushing each other, and then things turn serious as their hands begin to undress and explore, and they breathe into each other's ears and necks and try not to make any louder sounds, even though that feels almost an impossible ask for Rachel when Elijah reaches between her legs, the rightness he finds there.

But when she is falling asleep next to him, this strange new body, it is not the hushed and furtive sex that she plays over in her mind, but the start of it all – the moments of nearly, of not quite, of about to be. The way that Elijah looked at her; the gold and the promise in his eyes.

Chapter 10

Elijah

The coffee is, of course, terrible. He should have known better than to opt for this bucket of watery liquid from a chain in Piccadilly station, but Elijah is having trouble waking up this morning.

God, ageing is awful. It is a week since he'd been at Moorlands Sounds, and he still feels groggy from it. He settles back into his seat, and considers if he really needs to be wearing his sunnies, as the train pulls out of the station. A child behind him is screaming something about Iggle Piggle, and Elijah prays the parents will just give in and pacify the brat with a screen (Elijah has enough friends with enough kids to be well-versed in children's TV).

Outside, everything is changeable, the clouds moving with a rapidity that seems implausible; some look threatening, a saturated dull grey. He sighs inwardly. *Perhaps this was a mistake.* He could just be on the sofa, watching some nonsense on Netflix. Or still in bed, reading one of his innumerable back copies of the LRB with a full cafetiere. (Or, more likely, simply scrolling the internet.)

Pre-10 a.m. feels terribly early to be out in the world, actively going places, on a Sunday. And with, of all things, the tune of ABBA's 'Take a Chance on Me' chugging ceaselessly through his brain. Where the hell had *that* come from.

He keeps the sunglasses on.

He checks his phone. Nothing.

It had been a relief, initially, when Rachel messaged. After a weekend of caution-to-the-wind hedonism and rapidly accelerated intimacy fuelled by the un-reality of the festival setting, that sense of being in a bubble had rather burst on Monday morning. Driving rain and wind made packing up the tent a nightmare. Dehydrated, smelly, exhausted, and not looking forward to the drive home to Manchester or the work calls that awaited, Elijah knew he had been a little brittle with Rachel, still all moonbeams and fairydust, gushing about what an amazing time she'd had, etc.

He'd wondered if he'd got himself in over his head – she already had two existing partners! And kids! When Rachel had earnestly said 'I will see you soon . . . ?' as she heaved her preposterously large rucksack on her shoulders, he'd been almost rudely breezy in his 'Course, I'll let you know if I'm ever in Sheffield' reply.

But then there'd been the recovery period, alone in his neat little city-centre flat (which had seemed a great idea when he bought it, but had proved to be . . . *isolating,* at times). Elijah wouldn't inflict that foul-tempered, fragile state on anyone, had to just crawl towards normalcy via days of working on autopilot and evenings spent steaming vegetables and watching *Schitt's Creek.*

But the four walls of the apartment seemed to box him in with his glummest thoughts, and Elijah immediately found himself texting everyone, desperate for any distraction, and the urge to hear from Rachel in particular spiked high and sharp. The expected needy messages from her didn't materialise (*she has two existing partners! And kids!*), and it was him, instead, who seemed to seek reassurance.

How's the recovery going???

She simply didn't reply.

Miss being in a field with you

Xxx

And she still didn't bloody reply! The lack of contact made Elijah doubt himself, doubt the authenticity of what he thought they'd had. Temporary, maybe, but still *real*. The total silence made him feel like he was coming down off Rachel, off romance, as well as off everything else.

It was mid-week before she responded.

Sorry for being slow. Things have been a bit crazy since I got home.

My husband decided it was the moment for a Big Honest Discussion about our marriage, and openness, and all that stuff. It was necessary I guess, but it was also . . . a LOT.

Oh shit. Are you ok?

He really knows how to pick his moment, eh?!

Ha. Yeah. I don't know that I was in the clearest mind frame really.

But yeah I'm fine. There's just some stuff I wasn't quite aware of that I am still trying to process.

Of course. Well, let me know if it would be helpful to chat at all – and no worries if not!!

Thanks x

And then: nothing. Elijah felt himself wiped from her list of priorities, easily slipping out of her life. *Ah well*, he thought.

That was that. You always did go in one direction or the other in the aftermath of these whirlwinds: completely romanticised them and knocked your life sideways, or sheepishly pretended it had never really happened. Well, fine. The latter, then.

In fact, now Will is back in touch – and now both of them are finally free, and able to meet in person – it is actually more than fine. It is a surprise, but also a bit of a relief, that Rachel is fading so quickly in life's rearview mirror.

Elijah checks a few of the brands he reps on socials, just in case someone's posted something accidentally offensive, and then likes a poem shared by JB Wylie-Wallace, whose poetry had turned out to be so much better in performance than in that dreadful banking advert or on their Instagram. Before seeing them, he'd dismissed it all as too performatively pious – what you would once have called 'woke' before that word became stripped of meaning – but live, they bristled with a controlled, articulate fury. Their politics (anti-police, anti-Tory, anti-TERF) burned true and gut-felt. Even Elijah's cynicism was washed away on their fast tide of rhythmic righteousness.

Their meeting the following day – just a quick introduction, really, at the Albion Mill stand – had also gone better than he could've hoped: JB had not only spotted him at their set in the woods but in fact recognised him as Candy de Thrush. It turned out they'd been a regular at his drag night at one time, had even met their long-term partner there. This goodwill helped ease over the underlying ick of discussing corporate partnerships, and JB promised they would consider, at least, writing a poem about Manchester for Albion Mill – as long as they were allowed to say whatever they wanted, to be genuine, not a sell-out! *Of course, that's what we want too, authentic content,* Elijah had purred, passing them a complimentary bottle of gin to seal the deal, which JB passed immediately to their grinning partner.

323

As Elijah scrolls JB's Insta, he gets sidetracked by a reposting of an artist in Skipton who sells blobby, voluptuous sculptures. He thinks they would make an excellent birthday present for his mum, until he clicks through to their website and clocks the price.

He puts his phone back in his pocket.

Then he gets it out again, and finds the artist again (aha – Ally *Wylie* – some relation of JB's, then) and leaves the tab open on his phone to remind himself to look through and chose properly later. His mum deserves it. If she loves the sculptures – and he feels quite sure she will – then the price tag will be worth it.

He puts his phone back in his pocket again.

The suburbs have long since given way to green. ABBA has been replaced, too, in his mind by a repeated refrain about a chaise longue, and Elijah briefly wonders what it might be like to live in a quieter brain. The only way to block out his perpetual, shuffling soundtrack is to play something else, but he forgot his headphones. Instead, his thoughts semi-consciously circle the tune and the lyrics, as well as the text messages he has sent, or should have sent, or might have sent.

At least the scenery is nice.

Alight here for—

And then he has arrived. At Hope.

It was Will's suggestion that they should meet in Hope, to the inevitable jokes about his optimistic spirit, etc. But aside from its name, it is a sensible location: a charming village, not too far for either of them to travel, good for walking.

But there is no sign of Will yet, and Elijah strolls out of the station, affecting insouciance. The wind rustles the trees in their full, ruffled summer regalia, and snatches at his tote bag. Elijah can't abide a multi-strap, water-resistant rucksack; doesn't do practical clothing.

Lounging against a low wall of pale yellow stone, watching as walkers stream off the platform, Elijah finds himself remembering the first time he came out into the Peaks from Manchester. He'd been stunned to discover that there was such obscene, swooping beauty, only a short train ride away.

He'd been seeing an older man, who insisted on whisking him away for a night in a country pub. But overall, the trip had not gone well, Elijah yawning ostentatiously in the cosy snug as the bloke (what even was his name? lost to the mists) tried to engage him in a crossword after dinner. Elijah had wet feet the whole trip because the closest thing he owned to walking boots were some banana-patterned Converse. For a long time, he had no interest in being anywhere with less than Manchester's 24-hour pulse; weekends could be spent in Barcelona, Berlin, or Brixton – but certainly not Buxton.

These days, countryside walks feature rather more heavily in Elijah's repertoire – albeit with some residual reluctance. Walks were usually instigated by wholesome friends, often with kids in tow. On holidays, he'd agitate for just dozing by the pool or a leisurely lunch, and instead get dragged up a mountain or along a coastal path.

But he always enjoys it once he's out. So when Will suggested meeting in Hope in the morning, so they had time for a 'proper walk', with a packed lunch, he'd accepted without murmur.

'Hiya.'

Will's voice, coming from behind him, sounds youthful, even though Elijah knows that, at thirty-seven, Will is only four years younger than him. A gap that, at their age, is barely noticeable. But when Elijah turns, Will looks bloody youthful too: skin unnaturally smooth, practically *glowing*, etc. That's what a healthier lifestyle gets you, Elijah supposes, feeling like his own face has probably sagged a few centimetres since he last saw Will, thanks to what he put his poor body through the previous weekend.

And then the sun seems to burst through a very specific gap in the hasty grey clouds, as if to illuminate just Will. How *convenient*.

It's very silly how attractive he looks, in this light. Despite his objectively incredibly ugly hiking gear. His rucksack, it has *many* straps. His T-shirt is made of some unpleasant synthetic taupe material, that no doubt *wicks*.

'Hey,' Elijah smiles. He is glad of his sunglasses, letting him drink Will in. The good, the practical, and the ugly, and none of it remotely mattering. 'How are you?'

'Good.'

There's a beat. Then Will takes a decisive step forward, and kisses him on the cheek quickly. The catch, of lips on stubble. And Elijah can't help but allow an eager arm to briefly encircle Will, as a rush of gladness hits him with a strength he wasn't expecting. It is a feeling exactly like light breaking through a cloud.

Very silly.

He withdraws the arm. They are still in the countryside, after all. Probably Tory Brexit territory, etc.

'Good to see you. How've you been?' His voice betrays, Elijah thinks, nothing of the sudden swell of affection he is feeling, the returning memory of how very good their previous dates have been.

'Yeah, not bad. Actually quite glad to have some time at home ahead of me – I got a bit sick of traipsing round the country with the exhibition.'

'I bet. The sort of thing that seems fun at first, and then becomes tedious ...?'

'Well. I dunno. Not sure it was that much fun anywhere except ...' A micro-pause. A giving in, to the cheesy grin, a moment of *them*-ness. 'Except Manchester, of course.'

'Of course.'

They'd met at an opening at the Whitworth. *The Equation of Time*: an outdoor exhibition of Stephen Schad sculptures, arranged in front of the art gallery. Great hulking metal things, sticking up at odd angles, that looked – to Elijah's untrained eye – rather like horribly mangled farm equipment. They actually functioned as a series of complicated pseudo-sundials, creating clever patterns of shadow on the floor at different times of the day and evening.

Albion Mills was a small local sponsor. But having taken plenty of snaps for socials, and quickly grown tired of talking to the other corporate sponsors he'd been introduced to – absolutely, without doubt, the most boring people in attendance – Elijah had grabbed himself another tooth-achingly sweet 'Sparkling Whit' cocktail (gin, elderflower, Prosecco), and determined to mingle.

Will had been alone, standing at a slightly awkward angle – half towards the party, as if hoping someone might talk to him, and half towards the sculptures, as if pretending to be absorbed in them if no one did. He didn't look very arty – wearing a pair of jeans and a polo shirt, bless – and it was impossible to call from a distance whether he was gay or straight. But Elijah knew he'd be doing the man a favour by saying hello. Plus, he was gorgeous – that much was clear even half a courtyard away.

It soon transpired that Will had actually helped to make the art: working for the fabricators that built the things, and travelling with the exhibition to oversee the installation at five different sites across the country during the summer. Quite an undertaking. Elijah was tickled, privately, at the idea that the least arts-scene person in attendance was in fact the one most intimately involved with the work – bar the artist himself.

And it also explained the muscles.

The conversation had flowed, but Elijah was still trying to figure Will out when he cocked his head to one side, along with an empty glass, and said 'I know this is your gin, so don't take this the wrong way, but shall we go somewhere where we can drink something nicer?' And when Elijah had nodded in assent, and asked where he had in mind – a pub, another cocktail bar, did they want to be inside or outside – it was Will who replied 'what about your place', without so much as a discernible question mark.

It had been a very good evening. And it has been a pleasure, since that night, messaging someone who is so up-front. Who says exactly when he's away, or when he would very much like to see you. If it's been hard to build up much momentum – the summer has been so busy – at least Elijah has always known where he stands.

'You ready to walk?' says Will now, looking him up and down with a faint pucker of eyebrows.

'I certainly am. These are my best walking shoes. My only, in fact.' Elijah knows Will is more likely referring to his smart grey shorts, his cute print shirt, his flapping tote and his straw hat, that is already threatening to fly away.

'Let's go then.'

Will's stride is faster, more concentrated, but Elijah has the longer legs. They make their way along the road and into the village, Elijah snooping in at the little square windows of various chocolate box cottages and then claiming it would be awful to live somewhere so full of tourists.

'Well, it would be all right if they didn't try to peer in at your windows . . .' suggests Will.

'Shouldn't have such damn cute homes,' retorts Elijah. 'Or should invest in net curtains.'

'Would you ever live anywhere like this?' he asks Will, after a moment.

'Maybe. Doubt I'd ever be able to afford this' – Will gestures vaguely to a neat cottage garden and a gleaming parked SUV – 'But the countryside? Yeah. I think so. But not yet.'

They begin to climb, the road winding out of the village and up towards a steep footpath, where there's a minor queue to get through a kissing gate.

'Not while I'm . . . Not alone, I mean,' continues Will. 'It would be too much, I think.'

'Yes, agreed. Singledom rather weds you to cities, doesn't it?'

'Yeah. And even that can be . . .' Will pauses, his eyes flicking to Elijah's. A flare, as they meet, of recognition – and he seems to make a decision. 'Living in a city can be . . . can be really *lonely*.'

Elijah knows Will is probably referencing his own pain, shared on a previous date: he'd been open about how he'd broken up with a girlfriend, been left alone in the flat they'd rented together, while she moved back to London.

But it is uncanny how Will – despite being so different to Elijah, in so many ways – often seems to cut to the heart of something he has also been thinking or feeling recently. And there he goes, bravely naming the very thing that Elijah himself has been trying not to face in recent months.

'It certainly can,' he agrees. And then he forces himself to say it, to say the word. 'Be lonely, I mean.'

It is their turn through the kissing gate. Elijah only learned recently about the tradition – kissing the person coming through behind you – from his friend Milly and her five-year-old, who always wants to be lifted up so she can deliver a sticky smack onto 'Uncle Eli' during walks.

So he turns, looks expectant, tipping his straw trilby into his hand as if readying himself for Will. Sees the micro flash – *is it safe* – as Will's eyes dart to the surroundings – or is it *who might see* – and it's so small an action as to be barely perceptible because they're just on a nice walk, no one's going to kick off about two nice young men—

touching lips

– across the gate, a spoke of iron swinging into Elijah's chest, cool in the gap between shirt buttons, as he registers Will's warmth, his smell. Just a hint of wood shavings. And breath mints.

A good sign.

A good kiss.

But Elijah wonders, as he backs out of the gate to let Will come through, who exactly Will was worried might have seen them.

As he turns back around, he notices a group of older men, in their sixties maybe, up ahead. A few dogs. Grubby trousers and sturdy boots, that speak of odd cash-in-hand jobs or afternoons on the allotment. A couple of them in muddy trainers, their blue and white striped football shirts straining over beer guts.

None of them are looking back, at two men barely kissing over metal. Of course they aren't.

Thank God.

'It got amazing reviews though, didn't it – the sundial-show tour,' says Elijah, suddenly feeling keen to get the conversation back on safer ground, as they continue up a narrow, ascending path. 'I saw one in the *Observer*, positively gushing.'

'Yeah, I think so. Stephen seemed very happy. And I think people coming to see it have really enjoyed it.'

'Well, of course. It's very ... fun? Despite that portentous name. It's, like, family-activity art — art you can picnic around. But still, it must be nice to see your ... your *craft* — being appreciated — in print — and on — like — an aesthetic—' Elijah runs out of breath, abandons all hope of making it to the end of the sentence, and heaves in a new lungful.

A flush of shame washes over him briefly. Will does not seem to be out of breath.

'—an aesthetic level?'

'Yeah. I mean, I guess so. Those reviews don't mention us though. It's all just about Stephen. Obviously.'

'Yeah, but you know you had a hand in it.'

Will just shrugs.

'Does it annoy you?' Elijah asks. 'Not getting credit ...?'

'No. Not really. I couldn't do what he does. Come up with it all.'

'But — he couldn't do — some of what — *you* do ...'

'Well, ideas have always mattered more than labour, haven't they? Been worth more, anyway.'

Elijah tries not to literally pant, as the hill seems to approach a complete vertical slope and his boots skid on loose gravelly bits. His calves are screaming. They're in a cleft in the valley, that provides shelter from the wind. Just at the moment it would be most welcome, thinks Elijah, sweating under his hat.

'I suppose so — although I don't know — for many people — artists, I mean — most probably make less — than manual labourers.'

Will gives a slightly weary murmur of agreement, and Elijah wonders if he's thinking about Teodora, the struggling-artist ex who'd dicked him about in the name of her 'craft'.

'Do you—' – another deep breath in – 'Do you think – of what you do – as "labour" though? Or as craft – as art?'

'It's not *art*. Yeah, it's just... I dunno. It's just what I do. It's work. Yeah, it's just *work*.'

'Ooh, have I touched a nerve...' Elijah tries to tease, but it comes out more accusatory than he's intended.

But Will glances over, and grins. 'Nah. You're all right. It's just... I dunno, other people always seem to want what I do to mean more than I do. Some people want you to be a... "creative". Some people want you to be, like, whatever, a rugged man, banging metal. It's just about *their* shit, really, their – what do you call it—'

'Gender expectations...?'

Will laughs. 'Yeah, I guess that too. But really I meant just their, like, *snobberies*, really.'

Elijah winces internally. *Guilty as charged.*

'My parents, right, hated it when I didn't go to uni, and learned a trade instead,' continues Will, hotly. 'Welding: not something they could brag about to their friends. But then working with fucking – Turner prize-winning – internationally renowned, biennale – whatever – artist Stephen Schad... well, that's great. But then, with Teodora: totally the opposite. When she worked as an artist's assistant, that was developing her artistic language. But when *I* started working with Stephen – it had to be just a job. I was just *muscle*. So I dunno...'

They are almost at the top, but Will still stops, pulls out a water bottle, takes a long series of chugs. Elijah can see his Adam's apple bobbing as he swallows, his head partly thrown back, and longs to simply nuzzle into that neck, to insert himself into the negative space created between broad shoulder and corded throat and raised arm.

He gets out his own bottle to distract himself.

'It just doesn't define me. You know?'

Elijah nods.

'Come on then. Nearly at the top.' Will sets off again.

You were the one who stopped, thinks Elijah. Not that he hadn't been glad of the break.

They push on, getting stuck behind some complaining teenagers with very wiry, fit-looking parents, and then finally cresting the hill. And whoosh – in comes the wind, and Will has the quick reflexes to snatch at Elijah's hat as it sails off his head, and they're both laughing.

And the view... the fields and slopes below them are an almost technicolour patchwork under the here-then-gone light of the sun amid the racing clouds. The electric green of distant bracken, the bruised purple of rock formations in shadow, some fields of wheat the exact, implausible peachy-yellow colour of very good scrambled eggs.

'Bloody hell. Not bad.'

'Yeah. It's one of my favourites, this walk,' smiles Will. 'This view... this landscape... It always makes me feel like things might, one day, be OK.'

'One day?'

Will pauses.

'Maybe today.'

Then, as if to puncture the sudden profundity hanging in the air between them, Will reaches into his pocket, and brings out a scrunched plastic packet. 'Shrimp? Or Banana?'

Elijah melts. He'd done a whole bit on a previous date about the weirdness of foam bananas and shrimps as a combination, as confectionery. It is surprisingly touching to him that Will has remembered, has gone to the – even, admittedly, minor – effort of finding some.

'Well it better be a shrimp. Still better not *taste* like shrimp...'

Will feeds it to him, and Elijah has to fight the urge to overextend his jaw, to clamp his teeth down on Will's flesh.

The sweetness dissolves on his tongue, as he watches Will. He is busying himself, consulting both a book of Peak District walks and an actual OS map. Elijah usually just navigates, poorly, by his phone.

As they strike off on the less obvious path, curving around the windy hillside to the mild interest of a few recently shorn, scrawny-looking sheep, Elijah takes a banana sweet.

'So, how did you even get started in the banging-massive-bits-of-metal-together trade, if your parents wanted you to study – well, what?'

'Ah, just something respectable. Law, medicine, economics, whatever. Not a chance, man – not how my brain works, you know? But my grandfather, on my dad's side, it was him that came over and set up a car mechanic's. Did well for himself. Very well, actually – grew this, like, mini empire of them across South London. Well enough to send his son to a "good school", and then *they* could send *their* kids too, the great upward mobility swing...

'But when I was just not managing school – dyslexia, innit – my grandad was the one who, like, got it. Saw me for who I really am, not who they all wanted me to be. He used to let me help him out at the weekends, and fixing stuff, using my hands, all that... I dunno, it just made sense to me?'

Elijah nods, as if he could understand. He's always been proudly unpractical, can barely put up a shelf. But when Will talks, he finds he just wants to know more.

He wonders how to phrase his next question. The terror of accidentally stumbling into 'but where are you *really* from?' with someone he knows was born and raised in South London.

'So, your grandfather. Where did he... I mean, you said he "came over"...' Elijah feels annoyed at himself for not knowing how to ask a simple question, and sneaks a glance at Will. He doesn't look especially annoyed.

'Oh, right. Yeah, he's from Jamaica. Initially lived in Liverpool, met my grandmother there – she was Irish. White. Redhead, even, though good luck seeing that in me,' Will laughs. 'But they got a lot of shit for, you know, just being together. Both outsiders...'

Elijah just nods.

'My grandad doesn't like to talk about it too much, and she's no longer with us. But what he will say – ah, it's cute, man – is that they "just fell stupidly in love". That's his phrase for explaining it. And he gets this big grin on his face.'

Will pauses, stares out over the countryside.

'That's *very* cute,' Elijah replies.

'Yeah, really. And the way he'd *look* at my nanna – like he still couldn't believe his luck, even when they were proper old. Like, it had obviously been really, *really* hard for them sometimes, they struggled to be able to rent a place together at first, all that shit. But it'd been so worth it, too, you know?'

Elijah sees Will's eyes flick towards him, and then back out to the spread-out hills.

'They must've all been very strong people, to navigate all that stuff.'

'Yeah. I guess they were. Must've taken a lot of... whatsit-called – resilience.'

Elijah reaches out, and squeezes Will's hand briefly.

The things that people had to face, just to live together. To love.

Will looks over at him, and there's something soft, or maybe rueful in his smile.

Is he thinking he has it easy, comparatively? Or is he sad that it *still* isn't totally straightforward – to love who you love, Elijah wonders.

Love.

Well, that is a big word.

Very silly.

The Beatles' 'And I Love Her', with its swooping vocal, comes abruptly into his head.

'Come on.' And Will is off again.

Soon the path begins to tilt downwards, into a wooded area, snaking between gnarled oaks, the banks of bracken giving way to shaded ferns and twists of ivy. Somewhere below them, a stream just about trickles through the undergrowth, through the thick summer air.

It gets hotter as they descend, despite the shade; a certain sultriness enveloping them now they're out of the wind. A damp greenness, encroaching and enclosing. Elijah is sweating again.

Will stops, a little abruptly, and consults the map and then his phone.

'Mm, I think it's here – this little path – if we want to take a detour, someone at work was saying there's apparently a pool that's nice for swimming in, or might just make a nice place to eat lunch? It's not on the official route—'

'Well, I'm not interested then. Officialdom only!' teases Elijah.

Will snaps the map shut. 'Lunch, then?'

'Let's do it.' Elijah is ravenous and his feet hurt.

The even smaller path straggles further down through lush foliage, the progress impeded by a fallen tree in the process of being absorbed back into the earth, a slippery navigation around some boulders where the path had been washed away, and then a tiny, rickety wooden bridge.

'What about you, then?' asks Will.

'What about me?'

'Well, you've told me literally nothing about your family, I notice, whereas you're making me go back generations!'

And this is the cost, isn't it, of knowing more – also having to share more.

Funny, how he'd felt so willing to talk about his father with Rachel, to spill it all out, all weekend. But that had been mutual: the way they both seemed quickly willing to pull their guts out, slop-slop-slop. And besides, she'd gone first, Elijah thinks, on the father chat. Had her own shit, in that direction. So he knew she'd understand.

He kicks a fallen twig out of the path, and the action feels more decisive than he'd intended.

'My grandparents are all dead. Not much of note, there: middle England, one grandfather a rural headteacher, the other a suburban hairdresser. My parents ... well, they're divorced. My mum – also a redhead actually! – was a make-up artist; they met on the set of a film, and she was my dad's third wife. He's now on his fifth.'

'Wow.'

Elijah is glad that the path has narrowed, that now they are in single file, that he doesn't have to say this while Will can see his face. He never manages to compose his expression, to keep it the appropriate blank neutral, when discussing his family. But that's because everyone else's reactions are so often so strong.

'OK. But so. A film set ... What does your dad do, then?'

And here it is, here it comes, the moment Elijah always has to navigate eventually, the switch-flicking, lightbulb-clicking moment that always happens when he speaks his father's name, when everything changes.

'He ... is ... a *film* director. You *may* have heard of him.' The irony back, like a cold suit of armour. 'Rowland Booth.'

337

'God. Wow. Really?'

As reactions go, it is contained. Admiring. But careful.

Will *is* careful, though, thinks Elijah. His words rationed. Well-placed.

'That's crazy. Wow.'

'Yep. There you go! That's my padre.' Even his voice sounds high-strung, too-taut, thinks Elijah, whenever he talks about this. *Not with Rachel though; Rachel did understand—*

'Amazing. I mean . . . his work is amazing, I don't know— I mean, I just loved—'

'Let me guess – *The Swallowed Woman?*'

'Um, yeah. It's a really good movie . . .'

'Well it is. A *classic.*'

It is Elijah's curse, he thinks – like something out of a fucking Greek tragedy – to only ever be sexually attracted to people who, at some point, had gone through a 'phase' of loving Rowland Booth movies, with *The Swallowed* sodding *Woman* very reliably being their favourite. There had been times, on dating apps, when Elijah had deliberately discounted men and women he liked the look of because they included, literally written down in their profiles, how much they loved his dad's films.

He doesn't like to think too closely about what that might mean. A psychoanalyst would have a field day, etc.

'OK, so I'm sensing some . . . something here,' says Will. 'You not close to him? Or is it that other people get weird about it?'

'Oh, a little from column A, a little from column B . . .' Elijah tries to sound breezy, as he pushes under a branch, holding it out of the way for Will too. Sneaking a look at his face, before falling in step behind him.

A pleasingly plain expression actually. People often can't contain their excitement, their nosy idiotic questions.

'Rowland lives in LA, so I hardly see him. Didn't even go to his last wedding – a woman less than half his age, a true cliché. And he won a nasty battle against my mother, years ago, not to have to give her too much money, so if you're thinking I'm stinking rich, I'm not, and also I don't *love* that he put her through that. And he wasn't exactly around much when I was a kid. We are not ... *close*.'

'Right, sure. That sounds tough.'

'I mean, it's fine. Lots of people's parents split up, absent dads are nothing unusual, etcetera etcetera. And my mum is fabulous. Taught me everything I know – not *least* how to contour the perfect cheekbone...' It's an old familiar line, an old familiar deflection.

But something else he said to Rachel now wants to be said, again. Something truthful. And Elijah wonders briefly if this new honesty is brought on by these specific people – Rachel, Will; that both are special somehow – or if it's something new in him. A less guarded approach. And if that change in *him* is why he's having better connections with people, all of a sudden.

'The thing ... the thing that's strange is just that the idea of "Oscar-winning legendary director Rowland Booth" looms so large, in what people suddenly know and think about you. And I get it! It is interesting! But actually, in my life – in my real actual life, my day-to-day experience – he barely figures. It's this ... *gap*, in perception and experience, I suppose, that's weird for me.'

Will is quiet for a moment.

'It doesn't define you. His fame.'

'Right. But it also ... *does*. In other people's eyes. Once they know.'

Will stops, abruptly, again and turns. His face looks serious, carefully held.

He looks like he wants to say something, but doesn't know what.

Then Elijah feels aware of all the features of his own face, the bones and their angles, the shapes he exaggerates or hides when he paints himself as Candy, and he knows how much they are like his father's. And sees how Will is now doing that thing that everyone does, that everyone can't help but do – mapping it – *seeing his father in him*—

Seeing that face, familiar from a thousand interviews and profiles and red carpets, now showing up so clearly in Elijah's brow, his chin, his jaw—

And the reassurance Elijah suspects Will was about to make – *it doesn't make me see you any differently* – becomes impossible. He just has.

'We don't have to talk about this,' Will mumbles instead, and then turns, continues, saying over his shoulder, 'I'm pretty sure we're there, actually.'

And they round a corner, and there it is, and it's perfect: several large, baskable-on rocks, a couple of frayed rope swings, and a still, black pool of water.

No one else around.

'Hey!' says Elijah, brightly. 'Well this is *nice*. Some real *Fern Gully* shit.'

And it is nice – no affectation needed. A slinky electric-blue dragonfly flits by, as if scoping them out and deciding they can stay. They both see it, their eyes raising, following, as it zooms out across the water of the pool and vanishes into an explosion of fern fronds.

Then Elijah and Will look at each other. A moment, of held silence – of understanding, or of promise – and then in mutual silent assent they are stripping off their clothes, with a childish haste and glee. The air is warm and wet around them, although still cool on sweat-coated patches of skin now released to the open. Elijah wonders if Will is in swimming trunks, but no – off everything comes, unabashed . . .

And why would you be abashed, with a body like that. Such smooth skin; such a small, pert bum; strong arms, and just the right, small amount of belly chub so that he looks human, not gym bunny. Before Elijah can take in all that he wants to – slowing in his own undressing, faffing with socks, really just watching – Will has leaped into the water, a reckless, briefly graceless abandonment of limbs.

He bursts up back out of it in a splashing fountain of tinsel. Will has, somehow, found the one square-foot where the sun cuts through the thick canopy of trees and fully hits the water. *Illuminated.* His thinning wet hair and smooth skin look like they've been varnished, lacquered, in this drenching of water and light.

They look at each other, eyes wide, mouths widening, and when Elijah runs – half hobbling, really, over the rocks – and then leaps towards the water too, his arms spread wide and penis swinging in the air, they both simply scream.

And the water takes Elijah in its icy totality, swallowing him whole like a tiny fish, and then his limbs stretch up and up, back towards the light, till he emerges, body tingling in delicious shock. Nose full of water. Spluttering.

And they splash.

And gasp.

And laugh.

And grapple.

Limbs sliding over each other, entangling like young fleshy roots, legs kicking in the water to stay afloat, and the water

– cool but thick-feeling somehow – is no doubt full of sheep piss and dead leaves but it is also like silk around them. It tastes clean and fresh in their mouths as they meet and kiss and lose themselves in each other.

Eventually, Will wordlessly disentangles himself and swims over to an edge, hauling himself up with frankly outrageous ease and grace. Elijah knows he will not be able to manage the same, and it is so; he grazes his right shin trying to clamber out in one movement, lacking the arm strength to simply heave as Will had done.

But Will doesn't seem to have noticed, or doesn't care. He's there, leaning back on a rock, proud. Smiling slightly. And he doesn't need to say anything. Elijah bends, takes a moment to find a position that works for his knees – although not even really registering any creaks at this time, because he doesn't feel old, he feels young and reckless and free, and Will is green and glorious and absurdly god-like in his wet nakedness, as he takes him in his mouth . . .

Elijah doesn't worry about anyone finding them; doesn't worry about rough stone on tender flesh or insects or dirt or anything at all for now.

Hearing Will come and feeling him leap, finally, in his mouth, gives Elijah the greatest satisfaction. And he shuffles awkwardly up the rock, to lie on Will's chest. Then Will's hand reaches down and begins to coax Elijah . . . gentle at first, then sensing how close he is, how close he's been this whole time, the movements become swift and firm and deliberate—

Elijah closes his eyes, as his world shrinks. The da-da-da-*dum* refrain of 'And I Love Her' continues to ripple in his mind. Aware of wetness, everywhere, the smell of wild water, of sweat, and sweet, and salt. A naked inner warmth and external coolness, at the same time. Shivers, and shudders, passing over his body until a quick—

Certain—

Final—

Will laughs at the force and fountain of it. A sloppy mutual kiss. Breath, loud and laboured. But only his. Will's breath is even, as ever. *Does he never lose his breath—?*

For one moment, Elijah's mind is blissfully, beautifully blank.

Then Will makes a decisive movement, stands up, and extends his clean hand.

'Come.'

'I think I just did . . .' Elijah can't help himself, and winces internally at Will's eye-roll at his cheesiness.

'A rinse, please.'

He lets Will pull him up to standing, their bodies close together briefly.

Elijah feels overwhelmed by the straightness and solidity and sheer bodily presence of this man, this naked body, here, amid these tall trees. There is a satisfaction and rightness in standing so close to your match, your mirror. Bodies in parallel. A flush of feeling, warm and tingling, spreading over them both.

A smile plays round Will's face, as if sensing the vertical force of Elijah's desire. Then he turns and slips back into the pool, gasping, sluicing himself clean.

Elijah does likewise, and suddenly really feels the cold. Goosebumps spring all over his body and he hurries to pull himself out (undignified, once again) and to find a different small patch of rock, one with more sunlight hitting it. He flicks his hair, trying to squeeze out what water he can, and then grapples for his tote bag.

Will has laid himself out flat on a wider, shadier rock, but for now Elijah needs what sun he can get.

'An excellent recommendation,' he says, feeling the need to speak and instantly regretting it. Will's arms are stretched over his head, his eyes shut.

There is no need to speak.

Elijah admires the way Will says what he has to, but doesn't feel the need to simply fill gaps, silences.

He drinks some water, and then opens and eats his sad-looking M&S prawn sandwich. But as he reaches for a packet of crisps, his hand also finds his phone and it is too automatic. He is looking at it before he can resist the impulse to.

A photo of his friends' kids face-painted as lions and tigers, sent to a group WhatsApp to many adoring responses. Updates on potential Airbnb bookings for a friend's birthday weekend away that is proving interminable to plan. And messages from Rachel. *Lots* of messages from Rachel.

He opens them. A photo dump. Slow-to-load images, the signal not great in the valley, spinning wheel of death. And then there they are, the two of them, all round the festival site. Heads together during golden hour back at the tent. Illuminated in ice-blue by Caribou's light show. Rachel eating crumpets at a stall in the middle of the night. Him trying on a spangly jacket in the vintage stall. Him in full drag. The whole gang, underneath some flags. A badly-angled selfie of them kissing, covered in glitter.

Sorry for the silence. Just thought you might like to see these. God, what a good weekend!!!

You must find an excuse to come to Sheffield...

Elijah feels a stab of affection for Rachel, and a flicker of intrigue – clearly she and the husband have sorted something out, then. But he can also look at these pictures as if he is looking at someone else. A different person, a different time. It is almost a nostalgic feeling, for a sweet past moment – although it was only a week ago.

He puts his phone away. He will reply, but not today. Because right now, he wants to be nowhere but here.

The thing is, the present is just so full. So swollen. He can't be anywhere but in this active, immediate now.

When he looks up, Will has propped himself up on his arms, and is looking over at him.

Then Will beckons, with a small but unrefusable gesture of his head, and Elijah goes to him as surely as if pulled on a thread. He lies, once more, his head on Will's chest, and Will's hand this time strokes his bare shoulder, his upper arm. His body is surprisingly warm.

'Important messages . . . ?' Will's voice sounds idle; Elijah can't tell if he's simply re-initiating chat, or if he somehow noticed Elijah's expression changing when looking at the pictures.

'Not at all.' His instinct is always to deflect. Even though he and Will have so far found it easy, to be loose and laid back about the fact that they are obviously seeing other people.

He should offer more.

'It was just someone – someone I was with last weekend. At the festival. Sent a load of photos.'

'Nice.'

'Yeah.' He pauses, and somewhere high above them, unsee-able, a bird tweets an insistent refrain that feels like it is almost a McCartney melody. 'They're cute pics. But to be honest, it's *weird* – it kind of feels like it was a lifetime ago? This summer is . . . it's doing strange things with time.'

Will just murmurs in agreement, and then they lie in silence. But perhaps Elijah has tensed, a little, because then Will asks.

'Is it just . . . "someone"?'

345

'No. Not *just* someone ... A woman. Rachel. She was pretty great. *Is* pretty great. But married, you know, open relationship, kids, etcetera etcetera ...'

Elijah can feel Will's head nodding, a small awkward movement while lying on a rock. He shifts too, it feeling hard below him. Newly aware of all his bones on this unforgiving surface.

'Have you – have you had many relationships with women?' asks Will.

'A couple. Nothing too long-lasting. But then ... I've not had that many super long-lasting things with men, either,' reflects Elijah. 'Probably *daddy's* fault – commitment issues,' he adds, waspishly, and instantly regrets this old defensive quip, when the truth is that he has always simply had a swift and skipping enthusiasm for new people, new things. Has been more keen on collecting experiences than continuing them.

A preference that is definitely nothing like his father's getting through multiple wives, because he was barely raised by him, so how could he possibly be *influenced*. By Rowland. And anyway, Elijah's restlessness is the desire to do things differently, to never be tied down or constrained by convention; he would never get married once, let alone five times. Absurd tradition to try to follow. And even more absurd to fail that often at it, and to keep trying.

'What about you?'

'Um, well. I've only really had relationships with women. Three serious ones, each lasting, like, years.'

'Oh really. *Wow.*'

Now Elijah can feel Will tensing a little, beneath him. Is he imagining it, or is his heart beating faster?

His dear sweet heart.

It doesn't seem like Will is going to say anything else. Elijah wonders if he can't find the words.

'And so how long... have you always been openly bi? Or queer, or whatever?' The memory of Will's eyes dashing about before their brief chaste kiss at the kissing gate. And another intruding new thought: how much more willing he was to come to meet Elijah in Manchester than to have him over to stay at his place in Sheffield.

A sinking feeling.

Will's chest rises, a full breath, held. Then it falls, Elijah's head going with it.

'I guess... Not long, really. I mean – I've kind of always known. But it wasn't something you could exactly, like, chat with the guys about, in the shop – you know? Although I have fucked one of them...'

'I mean, that is a story I would *love* to hear more of...' Elijah, again, instantly regrets his tone. He pats Will's chest. 'Sorry. Go on.'

'I did try to tell my first girlfriend about it – and she was, I dunno, it was awful. She was really... disgusted? There were a lot of other things that were wrong with that relationship to be honest. And we were very young, a different time and all that. But, like... it just shut down even thinking that I could be bisexual. For *years.*'

'God that's grim,' says Elijah. 'And also... shades of what happened with that idiot woman you went on a date with recently?' He turns his head and dots a few light kisses on Will's chest. 'Poor straight-presenting lamb, you do know how to pick 'em.'

'Yeah, I know. Although to be fair there was, like, two decades between those two.'

'And yet people say we're making progress...'

Elijah's tone remains carefully light, but he had been actually horrified when Will had messaged him, clearly upset, about his date with some small-minded woman. Horrified by her reaction, and slightly surprised that Will was confiding in him when they hardly knew each other. And then oddly rather pleased that he was... It was the sort of unguarded, unforced, unasked-for display of honesty and intimacy that Elijah was not used to in the men he dated, who too often were all front and sheen. Who too often had a hard, protective surface it was difficult to pierce.

Maybe *that* was the shared difference with both Rachel and Will, he thinks: they both consciously made the effort to be their own, unvarnished selves.

'What about you? I mean, what response do you get from women?' asks Will.

'Well, I've not ever had anything like you've experienced really, because I'm so screamingly queer... no one ever thinks I'm straight, you know.'

'But how do they – I mean, how do women react to that? To you *not* being fully gay...?'

'Oh, usually fine – surprised, sometimes... no one thinks the drag queen is gonna hit on them!' Elijah is alarmed by how tense his laugh sounds, how fake. Will doesn't join in. 'To be honest, there can be some wariness. Or annoyance, even.'

A flash of memory: the perfectly nice woman, a friend-of-a-colleague, who he thought was flirting with him but who had turned furious when he made a move. *Betrayal of trust*. Claimed she never would have been so vulnerable, or been so honest, if she'd thought he just wanted to get in her pants.

Strange reaction. Surely you should be *most* honest with people you wanted to sleep with.

But then, gay men were worse, if anything, in their reactions to him being bi.

'Actually the problem is more men, for me. Not trusting it.

348

Thinking you're just fucking around, having your fun till you are ready to get married and have kids. I mean ... as if.'

But Elijah doesn't want to return to thoughts of weddings, doesn't want to talk about children (*not* interested), definitely doesn't want to have the supposedly theoretical 'but would you ever consider adopting' chat. He knows these are things you should talk about, bring into the open, when dating at their age. But he also profoundly resents the idea that the destination that any relationship – even gay ones! – should inevitably now march towards is marriage and babies.

'So when ... when did you start to be, more, you know, OK about liking men?' Elijah wants to turn the attention back on to Will.

Because he does not feel reassured just yet that Will even *does* feel OK and out in the open about liking men.

Please please please—

Elijah is gripped by a vertiginous feeling, a short shock of realisation of how much he wants this to be the start of something, just as he reaches a precipice that reveals it might be the end.

Because he is not being any man's dirty little gay secret. He's been there, done that. Never again.

He only wants Will if Will will be in the light. With him.

Will shuffles, and Elijah pulls away. Sits up. But Will puts his hands back behind his head, an overly-studied relaxed posture that surely isn't at all relaxing on this fucking stone. It now seems cruelly uncomfortable, to Elijah and his bony arse. Unyielding.

Will's eyes go straight up, and when he speaks it is as if addressing the bird hidden in the canopy of tree branches above. 'It was Teodora, really, when things changed. She was straight, but her group ... artists, innit. They were all sorts. All combos.

349

Very open about it – like, no shame at all. And when I finally told her, that I thought, maybe I was bi...

'Well she was just very cool about it. Helped me think about it, talk about it. Didn't want me to *do* anything about it' – and Will glances over now, and then breaks into a big grin – 'but just her being accepting... I dunno, it changed something. In me. And after we broke up, I started, like, *actively* seeing men too.'

'Well halle-bloody-lujah. I should be doubly thankful for this woman – triply, in fact' – Elijah counts the reasons off his fingers – 'she brought you to the north, she brought you to Stephen Schad's workshop, and she brought you to bisexuality...'

Will just rolls his eyes.

Elijah cocks his head, still looking down at him, holding the gaze.

'And do you think... do you think you could ever *be*... with a man?'

Will releases his arms, pushing himself up on an elbow. His face is serious, turned up now towards Elijah. And Elijah is suddenly startlingly aware of his heart beating inside his chest.

'In a relationship with a man?' Will asks.

Elijah nods.

He doesn't want to say that word out loud.

He doesn't usually like that word very much.

But he knows he wants *Will*.

And so maybe that means saying it. Out loud.

'Yes. A *relationship*.' But Elijah can't help himself, and adds: 'Whatever exactly *that* is.'

Will raises an eyebrow, but his smile is inquisitive, a little mischievous.

'And what exactly *is* that to you, then?'

'Well!' A big old rush of air comes out of Elijah's mouth, and now he's looking everywhere except at Will. 'I don't know, I just ... I don't want to limit or, you know, *assume* anything. Old ideas about how things *should* go cause a lot of trouble, don't they. You know – a relationship can still be a relationship if it is long-distance or if it's living together, open or closed, or shared, or part-time – married with kids and a dog or deliberately kicking the arse of heteronormative expectations, etcetera etcetera etcetera ...'

He has run out of breath again.

He looks back to Will, who is still looking at him: steady, intent. Actually really listening to what he is saying.

'Yeah. I agree. And I think ... I think maybe all that matters is what it *feels* like, from inside, not what it looks like, from the outside,' says Will. 'How you see each other – not how the world sees you.'

And for Elijah, it feels like the forest has closed in all around them; his existence has shrunk to this, their own private green world, as if for a moment nothing else exists, no cities or bars or computers or phones or families or anything, just the booming of this big muscle inside his ribcage.

Just Will's sweet upturned face, and his heart beating. Da-dum, da-dum—

da-da-da-dum ... and I love—

He fights the urge to crack a joke, to break Will's gaze, to say something arch and ironic and distancing.

'Well then?' He can hear the strain in his own voice, an earnest kind of hopefulness he usually guards against. 'Do you think you could – be in a relationship, with a man?'

'I think so, yes,' replies Will. 'Everything has changed. Everything is ... changing. So yes.'

'Yes?'

'Yes. I hope—'

Elijah knows there's still plenty to potentially be apprehensive about – but he can't help the leap he feels, as he rolls himself down over Will again, on one elbow, and he kisses his lips, very, very gently.

And Elijah's heart unfurls, in green. In hope.

Because yes – surely this is...

It is...

The start of something.

Just the start.

Acknowledgements

Many people helped make this book. To everyone at Orion, and especially super editor Charlotte Mursell and brilliant assistant Sanah Ahmed, Dan Jackson for a gorgeous cover, Becca Bryant and Lucy Cameron for publicity and marketing – I appreciate your hard work very much. Thank you.

Thanks are certainly due to everyone at RCW, and especially agent of dreams Tristan Kendrick, whose thoughtfulness and enthusiasm are apparently limitless. I owe you a great deal.

A big thank you goes to Jean St Clair, for consulting on the character of Emily, and also to Rachel Veazey for putting us in touch in the first place. And another huge thank you to Charlie Castelletti, for the most sensitive of sensitivity reads. I am so grateful to you both.

Enormous gratitude goes out to my brilliant and insightful early readers – Kate Smith, Roshni Goyate, Ayo Adesioye, Paddy, Roxanne Green and Ana Fletcher. Your responses helped more than you can imagine, and meant an awful lot. Thanks also to Annie May Fletcher, Marcus Emerton, and Julie Bell for answering my specific location-based questions, and to Rebecca Hammond for loaning me Candy.

All the love to all the South London Lovers, for the support, the listening ears, and the welcome distractions – and I'm especially grateful to Daisy Buchanan, Ana Fletcher (again), and Heloise Wood for the many reassuring book-chats.

Thank you to my family, Lynda, Martin and Lyall, for all the love and understanding. Please skip over the rude bits (all ten of them). Tommo – thank you for listening to me talk endlessly about work I hadn't let you read, and then for reading it, but mostly for holding me, literally and metaphorically, throughout this whole process. I love you.

Finally, thank you to anyone who has indulged my demands to go round on a Ferris wheel in the middle of the night. Which is quite a lot of you. And thanks to Arthur Schnitzler, for the satisfying, stealable narrative structure.

Thanks also to Annie May Fletcher, Marcus Emerton, and Julie Bell for answering my specific location-based questions, and to Rebecca Hammond for loaning me 'Candy'.

Credits

Holly Williams and Orion Fiction would like to thank everyone at Orion who worked on the publication of *The Start of Something* in the UK.

Editorial
Charlotte Mursell
Sanah Ahmed

Copyeditor
Sally Partington

Proofreader
Laetitia Grant

Audio
Paul Stark
Jake Alderson

Contracts
Dan Herron
Ellie Bowker
Alyx Hurst

Publicity
Frankie Banks

Editorial Management
Charlie Panayiotou
Jane Hughes
Bartley Shaw

Finance
Jasdip Nandra
Nick Gibson
Sue Baker

Marketing
Ellie Nightingale

Production
Ruth Sharvell

Sales
Jen Wilson
Esther Waters
Victoria Laws
Toluwalope Ayo-Ajala
Rachael Hum
Ellie Kyrke-Smith
Sinead White
Georgina Cutler

Design
Dan Jackson
Joanna Ridley

Operations
Jo Jacobs
Dan Stevens

*If you enjoyed **The Start of Something** don't miss*
Holly Williams' gorgeous and romantic debut . . .

1947. 1967. 1987.
When Violet and Albert first meet, they are always twenty.

Three decades.
Over the years, Violet and Albert's lives collide again and again:
beneath Oxford's spires, on the rolling hills around Abergavenny,
in stately homes and in feminist squats. And as each decade ends,
a new love story begins . . .

Two people.
Together, they are electric and the world is glittering with
possibility. But against the shifting times of each era, Violet and
Albert must overcome differences in class, gender, privilege and
ambition. Each time their lives entwine, it will change everything.

One moment is all it takes . . .
As their eyes first meet, for a split-second it's as if the clocks have
stopped. Nothing else matters. Yet whichever decade brings them
together, Violet and Albert are soon forced to question: what if
they met the *right* person at the *wrong* time?

AVAILABLE TO BUY NOW